LAD[illegible]

WITCH OF THE GARGAUTHANS

BLOOD MAGUS

MORGYNN

I will walk my own path, even if it is paved in my own blood!

The bittersweet flavor of adrenaline danced ghostlike across her tongue, and her eyes rolled back. She moaned as he staggered backward, dropping his sword. His heartbeat slowed, and, pulse by pulse, she felt drawn into his death.

Gaping oblivion yawned in his mind and tempted her. That second between life and final rest, the twilight of existence where she'd been the past decade called to her, but death would not have her. Buried once in soil that would not keep her, she had risen to a power bound only by her skin.

"Toys and playthings," she whispered. "They barely know they're alive."

Rage replaced her ecstasy as the man fell lifeless.

BUT CAN SHE BE KILLED?

THE WIZARDS

Blackstaff
Steven Schend

Bloodwalk
James P. Davis

Darkvision
Bruce R. Cordell
September 2006

Frostfell
Mark Sehestedt
December 2006

THE WIZARDS

Bloodwalk

james p. davis

The Wizards
BLOODWALK

Published by Wizards of the Coast, Inc. FORGOTTEN REALMS, WIZARDS OF THE COAST, and their respective logos are trademarks of Wizards of the Coast, Inc., in the U.S.A. and other countries.

Printed in the U.S.A.

Cover art by Duane O. Myers
Map by Todd Gamble
First Printing: July 2006
Library of Congress Catalog Card Number: 2005935519
9 8 7 6 5 4 3 2 1

ISBN-10: 0-7869-4018-2
ISBN-13: 978-0-7869-4018-9
620-95546740-001-EN

U.S., CANADA,
ASIA, PACIFIC, & LATIN AMERICA
Wizards of the Coast, Inc.
P.O. Box 707
Renton, WA 98057-0707
+1-800-324-6496

EUROPEAN HEADQUARTERS
Hasbro UK Ltd
Caswell Way
Newport, Gwent NP9 0YH
GREAT BRITAIN
Save this address for your records.

Visit our web site at www.wizards.com

Dedication

For my Megan.

Acknowledgments

I'd like to thank Peter Archer and Phil Athans for getting me started, and Susan Morris, my wonderfully patient editor, for all of her help and hard work along the way.

LAKE OF STEAM
TARGRIS
DERLUSK
LOGFELL
RUINS OF JHAREAT
LITTLEWATER
RIVER STARTH
RED CUP INN
SPLONDAR
TAERMBOLD
BROOKHOLLOW
QURTH
THE BARONY OF GREAT OAK
RIVER SCELPTAR
FOREST
OEBLE
BLOUTAR
OWLHOLD
MAP OF
QURTH
FOREST
0
90
MILES

PROLOGUE

The Year of Lightning Storms (1374 DR)
Early Autumn (Uktar)

Nuressa clung to the low stone wall, facing the sea. She stared at dark ships that approached on reddened waves as chaos erupted in the streets behind her. Shouts, screams, and inhuman roars faded into the background as the tide swelled, carrying its ominous burden closer.

The crimson light of early sunset grew deeper and more inflamed, casting the small town of Logfell in tones of blood as she struggled to pull herself up on weakening legs. Her pale, sickly skin was covered in red welts and painful lesions, signs of the blush, a plague that had sprung to grim life a little over a tenday ago.

Clouds of steam rolled atop the lethargic waves of the Lake of Steam, carrying the handful of strange longboats closer. But Nuressa's eye was drawn by a lone figure clad in tattered red robes walking barefoot upon the sea ahead of the shadowy fleet. It was a woman with flowing dark hair and eyes that were flooded with red. The woman extended her arms outward as she neared, as if gathering the town in a distant embrace.

Warmth flowed across Nuressa's lips and she tasted blood. Her nose dripped, succumbing to the bleeds the blush induced as its grip grew stronger.

A droning chant drifted on the air, emanating from the longboats behind the woman in red. No words could be made out in the menacing litany, but power rippled in the syllables that reached her. The sound of the deep voices rose gooseflesh across Nuressa's body, and the chant drove a chill wind, early for the season. Nuressa shivered.

The steady drip of Nuressa's nose became a bloody stream as the woman in red's voice joined the macabre chorus. The waves around the woman pulsed in a circle as she spoke harsh words in an arcane language. Blood spilled from her eyes and curled across her cheeks in unknown symbols and sigils, runes of power that changed from one to another as she spoke.

The fear and terror Nuressa had been numb to just moments ago returned with a vengeance. She gasped as pain lanced through her chest, arms, and legs, a dull ache that crawled up her neck as the chanting grew louder. The chorus washed across the town and raised screams from the maddened masses behind her. Paralyzed by horror, she could not tear her eyes away from the woman in red, who rose in the air, her toes barely touching the water. Closer now, Nuressa could see strange, scarlike designs and markings on the woman's body, horrific and beautiful, like a poem of fine lines and old pain.

The chant reached a crescendo that throbbed behind Nuressa's eyes, and just as she considered acting on her fear and running away to find shelter or sanctuary, the noise stopped. Silence crashed across Logfell as the woman in red tossed her head and arms backward, arching her back in ecstasy or pain, the focal point of some dark working.

Then the blooded eyes lowered, seeming to meet Nuressa's. Crimson lips smiled and whispered a single syllable, releasing an energy that thundered across the water's surface in an ever-widening wave. The ground shook as the force crashed against the coast, flooding across the town like a choir of swarming locusts.

Nuressa fell from the low wall, trembling as her veins pulsed and became visible beneath her skin. Muscles throbbed and strained against tendons and bone. Her mind was full of the sound of the chant, unable to escape it as she crawled toward the mass of limbs and stampeding terror that filled the street in front of her.

Her friends and neighbors had become like animals, clawing and biting at one another to reach the gates. Nuressa did not look at their faces, pale shadows of the people they'd once been. She focused on going home, finding her daughter, and praying for release from this incursion of chaos, pushing and screaming through the crowd, and trampling across the bodies of the fallen as she passed.

The same scene lay in the streets beyond—people fleeing or fighting one another. All of them were held in the grip of the blush, the plague excited to growth by the chant they could all hear playing in their minds. Nuressa stood and stared at her small home for several moments, searching her memory, unable to imagine what it must have looked like before the blush. Frustrated, she pulled the door open and fell to her hands and knees inside, holding her breath as fresh pain washed through her head, and gulping for air as it passed.

On her stomach, she crawled through the simple kitchen, pushing chairs out of her way in the dark. Down the hallway, darker still, the bedroom door was open, allowing the dying light of the sun to illuminate her path.

Whispers surrounded her and she realized they were her own, a stream of nonsense, spilling out the contents of her mind in a rush so fast she could not cling to one thought before the next was gone. An emptiness hovered in the back of her mind, growing larger as she poured out the myriad details of her life, until the empty thing filled her head.

She imagined it behind her, some creature crawling and mewling in infantile tones as it pawed at her ankles in the dark. It seemed she could hear its claws echoing her own fingernails as they strained to pull her weight. She sobbed in pain and fear as she reached the doorway at the end of the hall. Gripping the frame, she slid her body into the room and kicked the door shut against the imagined demon that hounded her.

She pulled herself to a sitting position and winced as the dim sunlight found her eyes. A growing twilight colored the sky in violets and reds as she muttered uncontrollably, trembling and shaking as pain wracked her body. Her eyes rolled, trying to recognize the room she sat in, seeking some memory to link it to herself. Her whispering slowed and the words became meaningless and distant—a language she could not recognize though she'd spoken it all her life. The last dregs of her mind bled out as silence surrounded her.

The stabs of pain intensified, but she was no longer fully aware of their ebb and flow, nor could she identify where she hurt. Her eyes, now blank and unmoving, stared at the darkening sky, and though her heart still pounded madly, her head slumped forward, limp and lifeless, privy only to the darkness.

Soft scratching came from beneath the bed and small hands appeared at its edge. Young eyes, rimmed in tears, peered over the rumpled blankets at the intruder whose lifeless head now slumped forward. The girl, frightened and alone, stared at the body of the strange woman who'd entered her home. Listening carefully, she could no longer hear the droning chant or the screams and wails outside.

She stood, tiptoed to the door, and eased it open, wincing as it creaked. The door was soon ajar just enough that she could slide her small figure through the crack. She stared down the hall, shaking in fear, the darkness of early evening undisturbed by candle or lantern. Moments passed like decades as she gathered the courage to step out into the ebony terrain.

Slow footsteps thumped by the door to the outside, and the girl froze in place, listening and waiting. She stared into shadows that danced with the shapes of imagined beasts. A low moaning rose on the wind, and she knew this would not be her mother or father coming home.

She turned away, easing herself back into the bedroom, intent upon returning to her hiding place. Halfway through, she glanced at the fallen woman against the bed, and in the soft darkness of early evening, found glossy eyes staring back at her.

CHAPTER ONE

He remembered playing games as a child. Or rather, watching other children play games as he stood alone.

Quinsareth threw himself into a dive, sailing over the rail around the high balcony of the Red Cup Inn. His tattered cloak trailed behind him like a shred of shadow, twisting with his tumbling form as he negotiated the fall. He prepared his outstretched arms for impact with the stone floor below. Flashing knives followed his descent, spinning and whistling past him, narrowly missing. He could almost hear the clicking stones of the Fate Fall, its intricately carved pieces falling to the ground, as the floor rushed up to meet him.

His fingertips touched down and he rolled, somersaulting and catching himself in a low crouch as knives clattered to the ground around him.

The Fate Fall had been the game of choice among those petty children. He had not been allowed to play, but he had watched—and learned.

Those startled few drunks still in the common room stared wide eyed at his cloaked figure, surrounded by several lazily spinning blades on the stone floor. A quick glance beneath the rim of his well-worn hat told them it was time to leave, and the almost inhuman voices cursing from the balcony above punctuated the idea with sobering clarity.

Glancing over his shoulder, he watched the shadows on the ceiling as his foes gave chase. He stood and leaped toward the front door, shoving several stumbling drunkards ahead of him, making sure that all those capable of escape did so. The others, too long in their cups for the evening, snored in blissful ignorance. These he forgot as Vesk, leader of the assassins known as the Fallen Few, reached the balcony's railing, near the ancient altar that gave the Red Cup its name, and stared down with black eyes and readied daggers. His three companions joined him, their horrific appearances made more so in the guttering light of the torches below them.

Quinsareth turned back to face them, breathing calmly. The game had become both his meditation and his mantra—a game he'd never played with stones that he watched resolve in blood and steel.

The striking blue eyes of the pale one were on him. Sniffing the air and spitting, Blue-Eyes's wide mouth scowled as his raspy voice broke the silent stand-off.

"Sweetblood," Blue-Eyes muttered.

The game began by placing the small rectangular stones on end, one at a time, in neat little rows and twirling designs across the ground.

Quinsareth held his head low and walked backward as the assassins descended into the common room, drawing cruel weapons and moving into place. Vesk walked down the stairs behind Blue-Eyes, who in turn followed a hulking brute with scaly gray skin and a jaw and brow lined with little spines. Their fourth crawled along the opposite wall, hidden in a living cloak of shadows.

Each stone in the game each held a different meaning, inscribed in a symbol or rune.

Quinsareth could feel their hate, like an aura reaching for him with clawed fingers, eager to squeeze the life from this "sweetblood," a devil's term for the angel-touched, the aasimar. His feet found the small wooden bridge that separated the entrance from the common room and he continued, stopping about halfway across.

The game the children played was random, unknowing of the rules and nuances of the game.

He could see the brief look of confusion on Vesk's face and he pitied them, his celestial blood stirring at their nearness even across the stone floor of the broad inn. Obviously, they'd thought he would take flight into the darkness of the ruins outside. Vesk's right hand formed a swift and intricate gesture, a sign in the quiet language of rogues and thieves meaning "caution," and his companions halted and spread out, forming a semicircle around the bridge and their quarry.

But Quinsareth knew the game's secret sense, reading the tales and stories in their chaotic patterns.

Beneath his cloak, Quinsareth searched a small interior pocket and withdrew a small sphere, holding it before him in the palm of his right gauntlet. Its surface was glass, but within, it looked rotten, veins of ochre tracing through the dark mass. Vesk raised a knife, prepared to throw but watching for the slightest hint of magic from the sphere. The dark tattoos across his neck and shoulders squirmed and twisted in anticipation.

Quinsareth turned and hurled the sphere at the front door, his left hand already resting on the hilt of the curved bastard sword at his side. Glass shattered on the doorframe, and he drew his blade, turning back as viscous liquid burst forth from the broken globe, the alchemical mixture reacting explosively as it gulped air. The liquid grew thick and tough, and roping tendrils of goo covered half the door in moments, sealing the entrance.

The sword he drew screamed in rage, a piercing shriek that pulled sweat from his skin. He swung the blade in a wide arc, deflecting Vesk's thrown knife and sending it splashing into the dark waters of the reflecting pool beneath the short bridge. The two locked stares for a brief moment, Vesk's black eyes meeting Quinsareth's pearly gaze, then the scaled brute charged, raising a serrated long sword to attack.

Quinsareth reversed his swing, knocking the brute's sword aside, and spun. Crouching low, he brought the blade around to cut into his attacker's hips. The sword wailed as it passed neatly through the tough layer of thick scales and bit the soft flesh beneath. Humming in pleasure, it cleaved all the way through, spilling foul, black blood to the boards of the bridge.

Quinsareth had always watched that first stone, wondering at its simple descent, catching the image in his mind just before it struck the next piece.

The brute's top half fell into the dark water below, splashing into its rippled surface and following Vesk's knife to unknown depths, his legs left behind on the bridge. Quinsareth stood, raising the bloodied edge of the long, curved sword known as Bedlam in a defensive stance, and eyed the faltering resolves of his remaining enemies.

The first stone had fallen, now must they all.

Blue-Eyes hissed, his toothless maw opening wide as he spit forth a cloud of foul-smelling mist. It swelled quickly, turning a yellowish color and smelling of sulfur. Though he couldn't see them through the mist, Quinsareth could hear them retreating to the balcony, taking the higher ground. He sprang through the thick cloud, his lungs burning and eyes watering in the noxious vapor. Once through, he saw Vesk and Blue-Eyes running up the stairs. Blinking the moisture from his blurry eyes, he moved to follow them. He stopped as movement on his left caught his attention.

Barely ducking in time, he avoided a bladed chain that swung over his head. The dark folds of shadow surrounding the third assassin unfolded in midair as it attacked. Quinsareth struck at the shapeless foe, thrusting Bedlam into the center of the shifting mass. The assassin stepped back, avoiding the shrieking blade, but came back quickly, the chain once again lashing toward Quinsareth's legs.

Quinsareth rolled backward as the chain struck the stone floor in a shower of sparks. Standing again, he caught a brief glimpse of a man within the shadows as they shifted, revealing a masked face and thin shoulders. Learning that his opponent was corporeal gave him new confidence. Bedlam struggled in his hand like a wild dog on a leash. The sword's desire for battle was palpable, and Quinsareth allowed himself to be drawn into its raw emotions.

Rolling forward, he caught the end of the chain before it could be pulled back to strike again. He felt a tug on the other end and leaped into the shadows, now blind but fully in the thrall of Bedlam's rage. His weight slammed into the body within the darkness, knocking them both to the floor. They rolled as they struggled against one another. Quinsareth felt his opponent's hands around his throat, cold and clammy.

He reached up and felt the assassin's shoulder, judged the distance, and swung Bedlam's pommel into the dark where his foe's masked face should be. He was rewarded by the sounds of the mask cracking, a grunt of pain, and crunching bone. As the fingers around his throat loosened, he looped the end of the chain, still in his right hand, around the assassin's neck. The cold hands drew back and he heard a muffled cry of alarm from beneath the mask.

Quinsareth freed his leg and planted a boot on the shadowed man's torso, pushing hard while pulling on the looped chain. All resistance quickly went slack as the bladed chain tore through flesh and sinew. The shadows dispersed, exposing the damp, translucent skin of the man beneath. A crack in the white mask offered a glimpse of the disfigured face within.

Quinsareth swiftly abandoned any thought of the horrors that could have inflicted such injury and looked up to the balcony. Vesk stood there waiting, drawing his arm back to throw knives as the darkness disappeared. The assassin's wrist flicked like lightning, loosing three blades in the space of a heartbeat.

Bedlam danced upward to block the first knife as Quinsareth rolled sideways, dodging the second. The third opened a ragged gash across his collarbone. He winced at the pain of the wound, but jumped forward, tumbling as he ran for the stone column at the base of the stairs. The last of Vesk's knives sang against the floor as he moved.

Putting his back to the column, Quinsareth caught his breath. He reached up to the bleeding wound on his collarbone with his right hand, which also bled from many small cuts inflicted by the bladed chain. Bedlam seemed to feel these pains and its handle twitched in Quinsareth's left hand, a sibilant hum emanating along its length.

Quinsareth looked to the front door. It was still covered by the tanglefoot mass, but he knew he didn't have much time left. The exposed liquid could last only so long before it would grow brittle and flake away. He'd tracked the Fallen Few's assassins for too long to allow these last two to escape.

He turned and ran up the stairs, Bedlam raised defensively and prepared to strike. Blue-Eyes awaited him at the top, smiling ominously with purple gums and inhaling a deep breath, mist curling at the edges of his mouth.

As the yellow mist belched from the maw of the assassin, Quinsareth charged through, heedless of the sulfurous smell and disorienting nature of the vapor. He threw his weight and momentum into a punch. The blow landed squarely on the pale man's chest, knocking the breath from his lungs. Quin held his own breath, but his eyes still burned in the yellow mist. He followed the punch with another, slamming Blue-Eyes against the wall. Bedlam immediately followed the strike, thrusting into the heaving chest of the deformed man. Blood and mist flowed freely from the wound once Quinsareth withdrew the blade.

When he turned around, Vesk was gone. Quinsareth cautiously sidestepped along the rail, peering into the shadows near the balcony.

He caught a flash of bright eyes watching him in the darkness, tucked in a corner between a stone column and the wall. Then they disappeared on a sudden breeze, causing the torches nearby to flicker and wave. A strange sensation passed through him, a kindred chill that he both loathed and recognized at the same time. He shook the feeling off quickly as Vesk's silhouette appeared on the balcony near the top of the ancient altar.

Long ago, the stone building had been a temple to a dark deity, a fiendish lord demanding sacrifice and blood. In recent years, the remote location of the temple and the ruins that surrounded it had become a prime location for secret and unscrupulous meetings, catering to those with no wish to be found or heard. Much of the temple's macabre elements had been stolen or carted off as building materials, but the large sacrificial bowl and the twisted statue that supported it remained. Stained by years of spilled blood and now filled with a deep red wine called *erskilye,* or the oathwater, it was a reminder of the nature of the Border Kingdoms, a symbol of false permanence and ruin.

The unlit ground between the two attackers drew them forth. For Vesk, the darkness was a familiar field of killing and revelry, a place to contact the Lower Planes and bargain for the lives of those his masters wished dead. For Quinsareth, the darkness echoed a familiarity with the hunt, conjured a home for the part of him that called Bedlam brother, and played a dirge for the man he might have been.

The men ran to meet in the middle, Vesk's crawling tattoos glowing a faint green to mirror the turquoise glimmer of Quinsareth's shrieking bastard sword. Their blades clashed in a blur of slicing steel and sparks. Though he'd charged to meet the assassin, Quinsareth focused on defending himself, destroying those few moments in which Vesk was most effective. Assassins struck to kill, exploiting immediate weaknesses and imbalance. Quinsareth knew a prolonged fight would wear his opponent down. He could see frustration in Vesk's face already, the assassin's tattoos writhing and twitching.

Bedlam's magic tingled along Quinsareth's arm, infecting his senses with its voice and drawing forth his hidden emotions. He swayed forward as he pressed the attack back to Vesk, swinging his sword faster and more precisely. Vesk cursed as he was pushed back, backpedaling to avoid the shrill voice of Bedlam and its master's well-trained arm.

With two sudden strokes, Quinsareth disarmed the assassin leader. The first knocked his sword to the ground, which slid to rest in a corner. The second opened a deep wound in Vesk's arm as it swung wide without the weight of a blade. Bedlam halted before the middle of Vesk's chest, humming ominously and lying uncharacteristically still in Quinsareth's hand. Slowly he pushed the assassin back the few remaining feet to the wine-filled altar.

Quinsareth was reminded of the nobles in some of the larger cities to the north who trained hunting dogs to sit unmoving while small morsels were placed on top of their muzzles. The dogs would sit still until given permission to eat the tempting treats. He had needed several years to teach Bedlam the same trick, and even longer before that to teach himself.

Vesk took a breath, but found no words waiting to save his life. No bargain, no blackmail, nothing came to mind to sway the intent behind those pale, white eyes that stared at him.

Quin could smell the stink of the Lower Planes on Vesk, that faint aura of the fiendish. He did not begrudge the assassin for making unwholesome choices, but neither would he spare him. No quarter, no surrender, and no mercy would be offered. He imagined Vesk had never considered begging for his own life before that moment.

Bedlam scraped along the edge of the altar's bowl as it pushed through Vesk's chest with lightning speed. Quinsareth watched as the assassin's eyes faded and his head slumped. The strange living tattoos tried to crawl along the now-quieting blade of their master's killer, but they faded and turned black as they dripped to the floor, mingling with Vesk's blood.

Quinsareth pulled Bedlam free, cleaned and sheathed the sword, and let the assassin fall to the ground. He stood, smelling the horrible scent of the dying tattoos with grim satisfaction. They had provided the link between the Fallen Few and their fiendish lords, infesting the body of Vesk and making a once small-time cutthroat into an ambassador to the dark courts. His nature, like that of those who followed him, was a twisted, perverse mockery of the man he had once been.

As the long-held chill in his body faded, Quinsareth felt his stomach turn. Fatigue claimed him, and he collapsed into a chair, breathing heavily and squeezing his eyes shut, his pulse pounding behind them. Sweat beaded on his forehead as the trapped heat of the underground temple-turned-tavern returned in a wave, and he rested, quiet in the knowledge that this long work was over.

He feared opening his eyes again, feared the hush, wind, and swirling darkness that would come soon, calling him elsewhere. The will of Hoar, a poetry of anger and sorrow burning in his heart like a dark prayer, telling him where he had to go, what he had to do, and who he had to kill next.

He stood lazily, stretching and flexing his sore muscles. The wound across his collarbone ached, and the blood was sticky beneath his breastplate. He winced and pressed down on the gash as he walked away from the gruesome altar. Though the remaining inebriated had not awoken and innkeeper was nowhere to be seen, he tossed several coins onto the table.

The tanglefoot on the front door had turned gray, and it crumbled to a flaky dust as he pulled on the door's handle. The temporary seal had been unnecessary. The Fallen Few had been more confident than he'd expected, apparently not having heard of the fate of their brethren in Theymarsh only a tenday earlier, but Quinsareth had been prepared. He'd spent long enough tracking them down and had no wish for them to escape and be aware of what pursued them.

Outside, at the top of the deep stairwell that served as the Red Cup's entrance, Quinsareth inhaled deeply, smelling the fresh night air. He could hear the crashing waves of the Lake of Steam from the abandoned town's north side, the water swaying the wrecks of the formerly swift boats that littered the small harbor. Those rotten hulls, bumping one another in the tide, were the only sounds that disturbed the peace of the ruins.

The town was one of many that dotted the lands of the

Border Kingdoms, overthrown, forgotten, and left to collect dust and fall apart—home only intermittently to those seeking solace between fell deeds. Quinsareth had come to enjoy them since arriving in the region and felt he might miss their emptiness when called away by the will of Hoar.

As if listening to his thoughts, the wind picked up, whistling through the broken windows of hollow buildings and rustling the tall brown grass that grew through cracks in the cobbled streets. He sighed as the eastern horizon caught his eye, distant shadows leaping to life and flickering like black flames. All he could see became wavy and insubstantial as the familiar call, visible only to him, whispered in the wind and shadows.

Something seemed different this time, more substantial, even slightly painful. His head ached as he felt himself almost physically pulled toward the east and the shadow road that awaited him. He spotted a strange red star on the horizon, bright and staining the night sky in a crimson glow. A tingling sensation covered his scalp, like the legs of a hundred spiders crawling and seeking entrance to his mind, to some weak spot in his will.

Gritting his teeth, he resisted, and the strange compulsion slowly disappeared, leaving him confused and curious. The red star remained in the far eastern sky, but it seemed translucent and dimmer than before, unreal and fabricated. He raised an eyebrow, interested in this little break from tradition, and focused on the tendrils of shadow that swirled before him. Recalling a prayer resting within him, he stepped forward, shifting himself into the Shadow Fringe and disappearing on a road of darkness.

CHAPTER TWO

Thin tendrils of jasmine-scented smoke rose lazily to the ceiling above Sameska as she fell to the floor, exhausted. The dark-veined marble floor was cool on her forehead as she clenched her jaw and flexed her long fingers, pressing down as frustration passed like a tremor through her prone form. She did not open her eyes—she wouldn't, afraid of seeing only the simple walls of the temple's sanctuary, unchanged, unmoved, with no sign or vision from her absent god.

She ground her knuckles into the floor, causing her aged joints to ache with the strain of her barely-contained rage.

"It would not do for the high oracle to give in to such emotion," she told herself.

The thought did little to quiet her growing anger. If anything, it reminded her even more of her sacred duty and devotion to the All-Seeing Savras, who remained silent and withheld his prophecies from her.

Keeping his secrets to himself, she thought, then quickly admonished herself for such heresy. Her lip trembled as the horror of it all came crashing down on her. Her eyes widened and rolled as vertigo overtook her senses.

Quickly she whispered an incantation, tracing her finger on the marble in a complex symbol as the spell was completed. All sound in the chamber evaporated. The nearby candles and torches ceased their popping and guttering, and the chimes were silenced, though they still swung in a breeze from the small shuttered windows above. Rising to her knees, Sameska threw herself backward, bending back over her ankles, her arms spread to her sides, and her hands clenched into claws. She screamed in the spell's silence, giving unheard voice to the turmoil within her, venting it into the sky or whatever hellish place it had come from.

Thirty years earlier, the High Oracle of the Hidden Circle had been Sameska's grandmother, an ancestor she held in high esteem. Always, her family had been favored by Savras's visions and sight, allowing them to guide their followers and grow the faith in the communities that gathered around them. The Church of the Hidden Circle had become the foundation of each new town that sprang up near the Qurth Forest. Its leaders had been the oracles of tomorrow, the seers of what was to be, and the high oracle guided them all with confidence into the unknown realm of yet-to-come. The necessity of the Qurth's resources, and the dangers that guarded them, demanded the vigilance of the church.

After a long morning of magical castings and prayers, Sameska found herself lying on her back, staring helplessly at the ceiling and out of breath, without vision or prophecy. She had only silence to comfort her damaged pride. Her heart hammered in her chest and pounded in her ears, but she could not hear it. She could only feel her body succumbing to fatigue and slumber. Lazily, she rolled her head sideways, looking to the large, barred doors on her left.

She could imagine the lesser oracles there, praying and

meditating, waiting for her to appear. She had nothing for them, and inwardly she hated them for it. She loathed the looks on their faces, still young and full of faith and immortality. She could see the disrespect in their eyes, the jealousy in their hearts, and she knew their secret desires, their whispered offenses. They despised her and wished failure upon her at every chance. Yet they smiled and played at kindness in her presence, for each wished to be her favored as they waited for the old bat to wither and die so they might take her place within the Hidden Circle.

None of them carried her blood, the blood of a Setha'Mir. She was the last, the end of a bloodline that had built the six towns of the Qurth Forest as surely as any farmer, woodsman, or carpenter who had settled there. Her true successor had died many years ago, her daughter, Ilyasa, who had been born sickly and weak. She'd barely lived a year before passing away while Sameska could only watch, helpless.

A candle sizzled as it burnt itself out behind her, and she realized she could hear her own breathing again. The chimes above sang anew, their silvered designs reflecting the early glow of dawn on the horizon.

Slowly she pushed herself up and stood in the center of the rune circle, staring at the age-old designs and symbols surrounding her, carved by her grandmother's grandmother when the sanctuary had first been built. She looked to her own hands, full of lines and wrinkles carved by time and experience. Both had dug furrows into her brow, the reminders of years spent in thankless service. Looking to the double doors at the chamber's entrance, she once again dreaded opening them, allowing those young upstarts within to snicker and point at her failure behind smiles and seeming pieties.

She reached into a pocket of her pale yellow robes, pulling forth a handful of golden flower petals from a plant called the *fethra,* or "destiny," unique to the Qurth Forest and the western edge of Shandolphyn's Reach. These she squeezed between her palms, releasing their heady fragrance, then touched the small tattoo of the eye of Savras on her forehead with each forefinger. She began to speak the spell of sight, though her throat was raw and sore from earlier attempts.

Iron-gray hair lay matted to her scalp. Her eyes were puffy and dry, and her skin was chilled with sweat, but she would try, one last time before dawn, to contact her god. Weaving magic and prayer together, she sought his attention, his voice that granted her the truths and secrets of tomorrows to come. The spell hovered around her, a whirling translucent cloud sent spinning by her beseeching prayer and enhanced by the faintly glowing runes of the circle.

Her muscles ached as the magic grew, but she continued concentrating for as long as she could. Waiting and praying, she fought the slow return of frustrated rage. Nothing. Silence. She began to draw a breath, abandoning her prayer, preparing to scream and curse the fading, shimmering cloud around her.

But then it intensified.

The circle of magic flared brightly and closed on her, the force of its power hitting her full in the chest and sending her reeling to the steps of the altar behind her. She felt constricted and couldn't breathe as the vision rushed into her weary mind. Once again her heart hammered inside the frail cage of her chest. Blood rushed through her body as though attempting to escape, filling her with warmth and cold all at once.

She gasped for air as images formed before her eyes. Accompanied by tiny stars at their edges, she could faintly feel the pain they heralded, having hit her head on one of the dais steps when she fell. Visions forced themselves upon her mind, violent and powerful. Reeling, she watched, overwhelmed by this sudden return of the sight but unable to look away.

Storms ripped through the forests of her homeland and the lightning seemed to tingle down her arms and through her fingertips. She felt suffering and terrible pain, wails of unimaginable horror emanating from the trees as their trunks split and formed mouths full of splintered teeth. Blood flooded the forests as thunder rumbled overhead.

Nightmare upon nightmare flashed in her mind. Scenes

of absolute terror assailed her senses, but through it all, Sameska was full of joy.

⊛ ⊛ ⊛ ⊛ ⊛

Sunrise was a brief affair the next morning. The light disappeared quickly behind dark clouds and cast the scene below in shades of gray. A cool breeze blew through the empty streets and unshuttered windows of Logfell, an unnatural autumn breeze more than a month early.

Morgynn stood on the shore, dressed in red. Eyes closed, she breathed in the bittersweet scents of plague and wild flowers as they mingled in the air. As the slight chill in the wind caressed her tingling skin, she was reminded of summers in Narfell. The cold at Bildoobaris, a gathering of the Nar tribes each summer, never quite warmed to even the early autumn chill of the Border Kingdoms.

Her left arm felt as if it were on fire, a sensation she reveled in as the last remnants of magic danced on her skin and slowly faded, leaving clean white lines where the scars of her spell had once been. She sighed, reluctantly opening her eyes to lament the spent incantation. She loathed the blank flesh on her forearm and absently rubbed her shoulders and neck with her right hand, mollified somewhat by the remaining swirls of magic carved there.

She pulled her tattered red robes around her and walked to the low stone wall that marked the edge of the little town. She couldn't suppress a growing smile as she stood staring at the empty streets, doors left open and abandoned merchant carts crushed in the chaos of her magic. For a moment she fancied herself the last being alive in all Faerûn, looking upon the sad remains of a world that no longer held any meaning. In that moment she felt the cold eyes of death over her shoulder, a silent companion that rarely stood apart from her, a memory that hid beneath all others.

Her eyes settled on a patch of ground near the town gates, stained in the browns and rusts of old blood, and wondered at the memories of these folk. She briefly imagined she envied them, those swift heartbeats on the edge of oblivion where denial meets the inevitability of nature's design. She shook her head and stretched her neck, almost a spasm of movement as she righted her thoughts. Refocusing, she turned away from morbid curiosity, banishing the imagined specter.

She followed the sounds of her followers, their chanting and prayers echoing in the silent and empty avenues. Speaking the languages of the infernal realms in deep, sonorous voices, they gave praise to Gargauth, their devil god, violating the once peaceful and sleepy cottages that lined the streets. She enjoyed the contrast of dark worship and the still-life of rustic architecture around her, a composition of sight and sound that no artist's brush could render.

Turning a corner into a small square, she found the source of the comforting voices, chanting in a circle, sitting on the edges of a drawn symbol, their steady hands marking profane runes and designs as they lost themselves in a trance of unholy praise. They did not pause in their ceremony as she approached, nor did they reveal any awareness of her arrival. Though she led them, she was not Gargauth.

The high priest known as Talmen, named after one of Gargauth's many defeated enemies, a high honor among the order, remained standing and apart from the circle with a few others. All of them wore masks depicting the faces of devils, but only Talmen bore the mask of the broken horns, the traditional symbol of Gargauth. He awaited Morgynn's approach quietly.

She could feel his powerful lust for her, could see it in the dark eyes that stared at her from beneath his mask. She did not dissuade his affections, but rarely did she encourage them. The thought of his hands upon her sickened her far more than he would ever know.

Talmen watched Morgynn's every move, and she subconsciously graced his expectations. She walked as if she owned all that she surveyed, even him, and cared nothing for the wants and desires of anyone else. Her hair, a deep black, was worn wild and long but she controlled it like an extra limb to suit her whims. She wore tattered red robes that would have been indecent if not for the belts and scraps of leather armor that served only to accentuate what could not be seen.

Talmen had served Gargauth for many years before she'd met him one cold Nar summer. He had seen far more than potential in her, and she had returned as much of his attention as necessary to get what she wanted. Morgynn held no illusions about their partnership, and she held no qualms against maintaining his illusions.

She parted her lips slowly, gathering his attention. His eyes almost dulled beneath the mask, and she could barely hide her disgust at the ease with which she could control him. No spell had ever passed between them to precipitate such submission. None had been necessary.

"Where is Khaemil? Has he returned?"

He scowled as she mentioned the name of her beast, and she could sense his displeasure, had counted on it, in fact. The lines at the edges of his eyes deepened, and his head turned slightly away. She could almost hear his cursing thoughts and smiled demurely to frustrate him further.

"He awaits you in the temple of their witches, Lady. A blasphemous and dangerous act I could not persuade him from," the high priest replied. His annoyance with Khaemil was clear, as he was unwilling even to speak her favorite servant's name.

Morgynn's smile grew at the news, imagining her dark thrall in the hallowed halls of their enemy's place of worship.

"Come now, Talmen." She reached out, lightly brushing the cheek of his hideous mask, tracing its edge downward to rest a fingernail tip on his bare neck. "Blasphemy and danger are in our blood."

His pulse quickened at her brief touch. His blood rushed beneath her fingertips and she imagined its distress at being trapped within a frame as poor as his. Her touch could remedy his blood's imprisonment in mere moments, and she lingered a bit before pulling away.

"As you wish, Lady."

He bowed briefly and hastily returned to the circle of his brethren, seeming more content to watch the object of his unrequited lust from a safer distance.

As she made her way to meet Khaemil, Morgynn stopped to study an ancient statue in the central square. The stone—broken, cracked, and heavily weathered—depicted elf warriors defeating a faceless enemy on a pinnacle. It was of dwarven design and looked far older than the town which had grown around it, carved for the elves centuries before when they inhabited the Qurth forest and its distant sister, the Duskwood.

She'd studied much of the region's history while in Innarlith to the east. That was before its leader, Ransar Pristoleph, had ousted her nomadic Order of Twilight from his court. News of its current state she gained easily from contacts in Derlusk, as well as other beneficial services.

She quickened her step, eager to speak with Khaemil and be on her way. The near trees to the south waved and twisted in the growing wind as a pulsing sensation called to her from within the forest's thick branches and underbrush. Since she had discovered it, she hated to be apart from that kindred pulse for too long.

The Temple of the Hidden Circle sat alone in a large circular glade bordered by stout oak trees, their long and sheltering branches framing the simple stone building. Though the oracle-priestesses visited only a few times a year, the people of the little town kept up the grounds with pride. A cobbled path led through a once bright and flowered garden, now stripped of leaves and blooms. Morgynn gazed upon the broken stems in amusement. She'd heard them called "oracle bells" and "destinies," and she wondered how honest their auguries had been. Had they seen her, she wondered, huddled over their teacups, fevered and chilled as they looked for signs of the future?

The heavy wooden doors stood open before her, a stylized eye carved into the frame overhead. She walked in boldly, as much to spite Talmen's misgivings as to satisfy her own curiosity and audacious nature. Stained glass lined the walls to either side of the sanctuary, depicting scenes of daily life and terrible battles. None seemed relevant to the history she'd studied, but perhaps they were images of the future.

Before the altar, Khaemil stood like a shard of night, his thick black robes wrapped around him. He seemed almost a void amid the colorful glass and the bright marble floor, mirroring a small statue of a one-eyed sage set behind the altar, an image of the god Savras. Her darkening mood in the presence of the oracles' sanctuary brightened as she approached her favored champion.

She leaned in close, resting her head on his shoulder, breathing in his strange scent and soothed by its familiarity.

"Talmen says you shouldn't be here, pretty one, that you blaspheme against Gargauth." Her tone was mocking and light, but she enjoyed the tensing of his broad shoulders. No love was lost between him and Talmen, and neither cared to hide the fact much.

Khaemil did not move except to incline his head in supplication.

"I remain your servant as ever, Lady, and will obey no other. The high priest has no respect for the rewards of faithful service."

His voice was deep, rumbling from his large chest and seeming to shake the stained glass on either side.

Morgynn stepped back, studying his large frame, still amazed at his unwavering loyalty after so many years. He had become a symbol of her ambitions, a bold and dark knight sent by Gargauth as a blessing to the revived Order of Twilight.

"How went your hunting?"

The query hung like a blade in the air, razor-thin and cold, full of possibility. Morgynn did not enjoy disappointment and rarely tolerated failure. Though favored, Khaemil was not above her punishments, and she had earned his respect all the more for that fact.

Khaemil turned to her then, removing his hood and revealing pitch black skin, hairless and smooth. He was almost a head taller than Morgynn, but managed to look her in the eye without seeming disrespectful. His eyes were bright yellow, like a wolf's, and his wide smile exposed sharp teeth and prominent canines. He squared his broad shoulders proudly in her presence.

"Well, my lady. The sweetblood makes his way here as we speak."

Morgynn arched an eyebrow at this, satisfied with his success, but curious as to the nature of whom he spoke. Before she could question him further, they both sensed a disturbance outside. Looking to the door, they could see shadows fading as the sun rose. A strange yelping growl echoed from somewhere nearby, and Morgynn turned from Khaemil to meet the last of her followers returning from his own hunt.

Behind her, she could feel the heat of Khaemil's change, her blood responding empathically as his quickened. His form shifted and condensed, settling into the shape of a great black dog. Morgynn adored the protective nature of the canomorph, known as *shadurakul* among his kind.

She stood in the doorway, looking out at the giant figure standing in the dying garden, shrouded in deep blue robes. It stood twice as tall as Morgynn and nearly three times as wide as Khaemil. At its side it held a rune-covered glaive, decorated with arcane trappings and grisly trophies. Khaemil crept close behind her. Snarling quietly, he sniffed at the chill air, his keen senses picking up the scent of the ogre's monstrous companions to the south, a pack of gnolls on the edge of the deep forest, growling and clearly uneasy.

"Mahgra," Morgynn began, "you're almost late."

"Lady Morgynn," the ogre bowed slightly, a well-practiced and formal gesture, "I do apologize. We had some slight trouble evading the patrols farther south near Beldargan, of the old Blacksaddle Baronies, but fortunately, my magic brought us through unseen."

The ogre's voice made even Khaemil's deep baritone sound like a squeak, thundering in their ears like a growing headache. Morgynn dismissed his unnecessary explanation with a wave of her hand. She had no desire to engage the ogre's skill at prolonged discussion, typically a one-sided conversation centered on Mahgra's own exaggerated and colorful accomplishments.

Khaemil stood close to Morgynn, eyeing the robed ogre with unmasked suspicion, a mutual feeling between the two.

"All is prepared, then," Morgynn stated, paying attention to neither of them, her gaze lingering upon the silhouette of the forest's edge through the morning mist. She paused as if listening for something. Her eyes clouded slightly and tiny splotches of red appeared at their edges as she answered a quiet call.

Mahgra retreated a step as Morgynn became lost in a trance. Khaemil felt the pressure of her magic in his chest, his pulse unable to keep up with the storm of her wild blood. He growled and sidestepped, baring his fangs in pain as her brief lapse faded and released him.

She looked meaningfully at Khaemil and Mahgra both, and her eyes told them their time in Logfell was over. No command was needed; no reminders were necessary. They knew their parts. The time had come.

Khaemil padded swiftly back to Talmen and the droning circle of wizard-priests. His dark form disappeared in the shadows of a silent avenue as he went to gather the rest of their order. Mahgra turned to leave as well, in the opposite direction, to assemble his charges and continue east along the coast of the Lake of Steam.

Morgynn, left alone, stood staring at the tops of the trees, barely visible above the town's southern wall. Her blood sang in her veins, twisting languidly beneath her skin. Her bare left arm itched, the absence of scars still strange to her senses, while the pale shadows of a hundred past scars calmed her self-conscious musings.

She drew a dagger from her belt and walked toward the dark forest, no longer able to resist the pull of so many faded heartbeats, so many bright yet lifeless eyes, so many children born of plague-emptied villages, waiting among the twisted trees.

CHAPTER THREE

Evening approached, bringing more dark gray clouds. Birds began searching for steadier perches in the strong winds that rolled in from the Lake of Steam. A humid mist hung over the tall grass growing tenaciously on the hill between sea and forest, its mass interrupted only by the worn cart path that led to the town gates.

The mist shifted slightly, rolling in on itself, swirling in ephemeral drafts as a faint figure appeared in its depths. It was tall, this silhouette materializing in the agitated mist, a shadow taking form among shadows. He was wrapped in a gray cloak with a high collar and wore a long-used, wide-brimmed traveler's hat.

The spinning haze settled and revealed fair skin, a graceful jawline, silvered blond hair, and the light armor of a quick-footed warrior.

Reflexively, Quinsareth hid his pale eyes beneath the brim of his hat, never sure who might be present as he arrived from the phantom roads of the shadowalk. He stopped for a moment, allowing the icy chill to fade from his body, letting the gravity of the dirt road settle into his stiff muscles, and clearing his mind of the discordant voices that echoed in the Shadow Fringe. As his eyes adjusted, he saw that the mass of blurred darkness he'd seen was the ocean. Its appearance in the shadowalk had been hauntingly beautiful, a black velvet blanket of absolute nothing.

Quinsareth pulled the plated leather gauntlet from his right forearm and reached beneath his collar to trace the thin, jagged scar from Vesk's knife. It was tender but closed and healing quickly now, a benefit of the shadowalk's swift corridors.

The moisture in the air chilled him, driven by cool gusts of wind. He pulled his cloak tighter across his shoulders and surveyed his surroundings. He spotted the crude stone walls of the small town before him, noting the closed gates though it was barely sunset, or seemed so from the faint light illuminating the heavy clouds overhead. A signpost identified the town ahead as Logfell. A raven perching on the sign eyed him suspiciously, its wings raised.

Quinsareth replaced his gauntlet as he studied the town, something alarming him, triggering the abstract senses of his celestial blood and stirring the restless darkness in the pit of his stomach. He absently patted the scabbard of the slumbering Bedlam at his side. Although not truly asleep, the blade's magic lay inert and silent, allowing him a measure of stealth as he approached the gates.

The raven leaped into flight, flapping quickly against the wind and disappearing over the wall. No smoke curled from the chimneys beyond the low stone wall—a strange detail in a region where autumn was brief and winters brought more rain than snow or ice. In the early chill of the current season, Quinsareth expected warm fireplaces among those unaccustomed to such cold winds.

Standing before the wide gates, their surfaces eroded by years of exposure to the Lake of Steam's briny moisture, he could smell the familiar stench of death. Its aroma barely touched the air, but it confirmed his growing suspicions. As he laid his hand upon the wood, a hundred scenarios played through his mind, none of them worrisome. He had no expectation of a warm reception, or even of a peaceful street scene painted with curious onlookers. Those of his ilk rarely arrived in time to wield blade and will against injustice before harm was done. Like a scavenger to carrion, the ghostwalker came to balance the scales.

Quin banished all thought of what might be, emptying his mind to be filled with what would be. He had no liking for practiced swordplay—patterned strokes and thrusts could be too easily read and countered. Entering the unknown—this seemingly abandoned town, for example—with scripted preconceptions could be just as dangerous. He leaned into the gate, swinging it open slowly. The first stone in this Fate Fall was Chance. The next, he expected, would be Mystery.

His eyes darted left and right, searching for any movement, but nothing awaited him. He found only an empty street and several rats scurrying for cover. Tiny dervishes of dust skipped across the avenue, disappearing between houses.

He walked slowly, watching the open windows and doors of the stone and wood cottages, looking for the tips of arrows or the flash of readied blades. Or perhaps the frightened faces of hidden villagers waiting to learn the intentions of this silent stranger. No one met his shaded gaze. All seemed abandoned and overrun with rats and birds, no doubt feuding over forgotten crusts of bread. He heard the flutter of wings echo down the otherwise quiet street.

Quinsareth contemplated the vacant town. Unlike fellow aasimar he'd met in his travels, he enjoyed his isolation, and did not brood over the loneliness of such an existence. He typically saw only the worst in people when called by the shadows—the faint voice of Hoar, his patron deity—and preferred to spend as little time with others as possible. Thus, he feared those he hunted less than their victims, daunted by the ordeals of conversation and social etiquette.

He stared into a window, his eyes adjusting to the darkness within. Dim ambient light illuminated the cottage's interior in shades of gray. A table was laid out for dinner, the carcass of a chicken festering in its center, swarmed by flies and crawling with maggots. A loaf of stale bread was all but gone, devoured by rats and mice. A quick look into a few other homes revealed much the same, prepared meals left for vermin and any inhabitants utterly missing.

He wondered at the scene, uneasiness and dread settling in his blood. He knelt on one knee, listening to the distant rolling tide. Evening drew closer and weak sunlight faded behind ominously hushed storm clouds. Then he saw it—a dark stain spattered across a large garden stone, rust-colored and almost black, spilling across the wooden border of a flower bed. The sight of blood was almost comforting. Better a morbid clue than a complete mystery, he thought.

A strong draft blew down the avenue then, casting dust into Quinsareth's eyes and mouth. He coughed and spat as a loud clatter sounded behind him. Instantly, his hand went for Bedlam's hilt, drawing the first few inches of blade as he spun to face the source of the staccato noise that shattered the town's heavy silence.

As he watched the gates crash together, blown by the sudden gust, he eased Bedlam back into its scabbard. The garden stone forgotten, he stared at macabre splashes of blood and gore across the inside of the weathered gate.

Most recognizable were the hand prints. Some were clearly defined, others smeared downward as their owners were dragged beneath what could have been a sizeable crowd. The smears indicated a mob, all pushing on a gate that he had opened easily. Had the gates been sealed—by some force or magic—not to keep something out, but to keep it in?

He turned away, grimly searching for more and expecting the worst. It was a philosophy that had rarely failed him. "Prepare for the worst" matched his experiences better than "hope for the best." The empty streets suited him just fine as he strolled from house to house, relegating the possible fate of Logfell's population to the back of his mind. He would sort it out in time.

On his way to the eastern wall, Quinsareth paused, noticing something in a west-facing window at the end of a broad street. Looking in, he studied a small broken figure lying on the floor of a bedroom. Rather than lingering, he determined the town's secrets had moved on, and he must keep up to discover them.

He paused briefly to inspect the sanctuary of a small temple to Savras in the center of town, expecting any survivors to be there. In the company of its stained glass and marble floors, he felt something familiar, fleeting memories picking at his mind but dodging recognition. The temple itself seemed to be the only place untouched by spilled blood or signs of violence, yet it held the most ominous chill, as if any connection to its divine patron had been severed and replaced by a void.

Quinsareth was reminded of a monastery on the River of Swords, hundreds of miles away, similarly left hollow one day, its charred remains no doubt grown over by now. Those who walked the paths of Hoar rarely stayed in one place for long. That place though, had seemed hundreds of years old the first time he'd entered. The day he left was the last day he'd set eyes on any structure devoted to his god. Faith and service had come naturally to him, and Hoar was not a deity strict in the observance of rituals or rites. Though priesthood had never called to him, Hoar had.

Quinsareth found the eastern gate in the same condition as the western, except open and swinging, banging together like loose shutters on an open window. Logfell was desolate, displaying its wounds on every street corner, moaning as the windy breath of the coming storm blew among its orphaned lanes and austere buildings.

He studied the ground and the footprints he found there. The clawed prints of several gnolls and the heavy, sunken tread of an ogre confirmed the presence of possible attackers or even scavengers but did not explain the total lack of traces of them within the town. The prints showed them moving east, skirting the edges of the forest. His instinct was to follow them, as he'd always done, but something kept drawing his gaze to the forest, its dark depths hiding secrets, its twisted and misshapen trees calling to that dormant chill running in his blood.

He forced his eyes and thoughts away from the forest. Reaching within himself, he disappeared into the swift embrace of the Shadow Fringe. He followed his instincts and avoided that inexplicable dread of whatever lurked among the trees.

⊙ ⊙ ⊙ ⊙ ⊙

Sameska had seen to the daily tasks of the temple, forcing herself to remain awake, unable to even imagine sleeping. The others had noticed. She was wearing her hair loose and had let several rites go unsupervised. Normally she insisted on being present, seeming to take joy in the lesser oracles' minor and admittedly rare mistakes. Nothing could destroy her today. She was invincible and strode confidently through the corridors of the temple.

It was late afternoon, and she could not wait to be left alone again. The other oracles had worried and fussed after finding her unconscious in the rune circle that morning. She'd wanted nothing to do with them, refusing their help and their questions, stubbornly maintaining her composure and the secret of her visions.

The attitudes of those around her that day had changed. Things were different, somehow, and rumors wound their way among the members of the church and the citizenry alike. The blush was spreading, and those who'd always been looked to for guidance were silent.

Sameska pitied their blindness and looked forward to the morrow when she would make them see, but she needed time for the magic and communion with her god. She made her way to the sanctuary after closing the temple's doors. Dreslya, the most vocal of her young rivals, awaited her in the hallway, lit only by the dim gray of a suddenly overcast sky filtering through a window in the eastern wall.

"High Oracle," she addressed Sameska and bowed, touching her forehead lightly with both hands as she did so, "I offer my assistance with the Turning of the Circle and beg my lady to grant me such an honor."

Sameska stared at the top of Dreslya's bowed head, unable to suppress the subtle smile that turned the corners of her thin lips upward.

"No, Dreslya." She savored the sound of her answer, enjoying the shock on the lesser oracle's face as she rose from her bow.

"But High Oracle, this morning we found you unconscious. I and the other oracles fear for your health in these plague-ridden times."

It wasn't often that Sameska thought of her own age, one of frailty and senility in some, but she knew the tone of Dreslya's plea and did not appreciate being reminded of it.

"Young lady, you seek to stand with me in the Hidden Circle, to hear the whole and full voice of Savras? You fear I am too old to withstand the power of his sight?"

"N-no," she stammered, shaken by the tone in Sameska's voice and the steel in her gaze, "I did not mean to imply—"

"I have stood in the rune circle alone since I was but a slip of a girl well younger than you! You stand here stuttering and unsure in my eyes, hearing *my* voice. What will you do when *he* speaks fully to you? How will you stand when Savras pours his truth into your ears, child?"

"I beg your pardon, I have seen—"

"Yes! You have seen, haven't you? Seen the day a woman will bear her child, advising midwives to be prepared. You have seen the lives of lovers perhaps, where their paths might cross and for whom they are destined? These are but fragments! Bits handed down in his mercy so your soul will not be set on fire with the visions that await you in that circle!"

Dreslya was speechless, wide-eyed she looked away, unwilling to bear the indignant fury in Sameska's eyes. The high oracle looked her would-be successor up and down, once again feeling strength in her old blood. She reached out with one hand and turned Dreslya's face to hers, allowing a brief silence to settle on the young woman before speaking again.

"Child, I stand in the Hidden Circle for us all. Neither age nor burgeoning plague will end this." Her voice was softer, placating Dreslya's look of hurt and confusion. "Should Savras wish me to fall and another take my place, so be it, but until then I must do what my mother and her mother did before me. Alone."

Dreslya nodded and her quivering lip steadied. "Yes, forgive my intrusion. I did not mean to offend." She bowed and turned to leave.

Sameska's stern explanation belied the sudden rage that built within her, but she held it in check. As she watched Dreslya walk away, she wondered what new rumor or derisive comment might be made of this behind her back and decided she might have her hand in it as well.

"Wait." Sameska's voice echoed in the long hallway, sounding louder than it was. Dreslya stopped, cast in the darkness between two windows, but did not turn.

"Yes, High Oracle?"

"Instruct the oracles and the hunters to gather in the sanctuary at noon tomorrow."

Dreslya turned then, worry spread across her smooth features as the import of Sameska's words hit her.

"All of them? A gathering?"

"Yes, child, all of them," she replied, enjoying the moment, eager to proclaim her terrible secret and assert her authority once again over the whisperers and doubters of the church. Then she added, "Something is coming, and we must be prepared."

She left Dreslya standing in the dim hallway, mystified and frightened, and closed the heavy doors of the sanctuary, ending their conversation.

Sameska paused behind those doors, pleased with herself and feeling younger than ever as she straightened her robes and studied the circular chamber.

She stepped quickly to the edge of the rune circle. She recited a traditional prayer and cast a minor spell of seeing, a divination to guide her through the visions she hoped to receive, felt confident she would receive. She focused her mind, blocking out all but the circle from her thoughts, studying its edges, arcane symbols intertwined with the divine.

The Hidden Circle was the path of the oracle, the center of Savras's attention in the temple. She sighed and trembled as she placed one sandaled foot within its rings.

She had no chance to pray or meditate, or even to draw breath before she screamed in shock and pain. Sameska was thrown to the center of the circle as power flared around her, pulling her down and squeezing her mind. Torn free of her weak skull, her consciousness was sent beyond the temple, beyond her pain-wracked body. She fought feebly, attempting to wrest control by mere reflex, before giving in to the invisible thread of magic that wrapped itself about her spectral form.

Never had Savras been so forceful. He had been silent so long, had withheld his guidance and voice. Sameska had been as blind as the common people who looked to her for protection and truth.

I'm being tested, she thought. This is a test and I must pass, I must be vigilant.

Again she was thrust into the Qurth, flying through its perversions of nature, cursed so long ago by a Calishite sorcerer. His magic had survived centuries, winding its way into the soil and the roots, corrupting those that fed there. His curse was drawn into the forest's green embrace time and again to leave its lasting taint.

Miles sped by in moments, and as they did, she saw flashes of other places. Visions blurry and clear at once entered her traveling mind. The forest speeding by her was her present, but the fleeting images that appeared were the past. That same awareness one has in dreams told her she was seeing places and events that were already written in recent history. At one time, long ago, she might have been comforted by those things that were done and unchangeable, but the horror and fear she felt as she watched the unfolding scenes in her unblinking sight made her brutally aware of her mistakes and helplessness.

Dark ships gathered on a reddened sea. The gentle shores near the peaceful town of Logfell suffered a tide of plague and terror. Sameska felt a distant connection to her screaming body, but could hear nothing and saw only the blood, felt the press of bodies against her invisible form as she became part of what was shown to her. Though she could not touch what was no longer physical, the emotions in that place were a tangible mesh of accusation and betrayal. An aching stress infected her, catching her up in its urgent rush and soundless clawing.

She watched lives fade away, replaced with something else, something driven by passionless need. Something dark that pulsed and burned, leaving her numb and disoriented. Her vision moved and she stood on the edge of a clearing, looking into a bowl-like depression in the forest.

The ground was covered in fragments of worked stone, the ruins of an ancient place that she knew without knowing as dim familiarity blended with vague memory. The once-large city existed here as an outline of fallen walls, grown over with thick vines and the old roots of trees. Its only significant feature was a single tower untouched by time or weather. Sameska knew she saw a place of legend and myth, a tale she'd been told as a child and a story some said was as old as the Qurth itself.

The ruins of Jhareat and the tower that survived its fall.

At its base was a woman in red, a stark contrast to the dark greens and heavy grays around her. Sameska was mesmerized by the woman's stare, though she felt naked and humbled under its scrutiny. Then she realized the woman was looking directly at her, or at least seemed to be. Something else was moving in the forest behind Sameska's hovering, spiritlike form.

A muted pulse hummed in the air around her, followed by palpable heat that she knew could only be a construct of her mind. She imagined her body, chilled on the cold stone floor in the rune circle. The pulse grew stronger and closer, pushing through the undergrowth, heedless of thorns and razor vines. Sameska could not see them, yet in great numbers they arrived, out of sight, unbreathing, joining her in the long gaze of the woman in red.

The heat became nearly unbearable, its aura twisting the atmosphere and distorting the faint light. The high oracle wanted to gasp for air but had no mouth, no lungs with which to breathe, and the scene began to dissolve. The rippling air became dark waves as the tower and the strange woman disappeared and Sameska found herself floating above the coastline again, above another little town.

The confusion and vertigo of a dream stole over her as she tried to focus, wanted to yell and scream at the far-away guards on the outer wall, warn them to run, to avoid what was coming. She knew that she was witnessing the present yet nothing could impede the progress of whatever danger crawled toward those gates under the cover of darkness.

CHAPTER FOUR

No warning came, no war-cry to alert the lazy guards, no marching drum to crush the morale of the few defenders there were in Targris. Arrows struck down the five guards watching the western gate. The first crucial moments of the attack passed in quiet peace.

In the streets, people were hurrying home. Merchants packed up their wares. Those quarantined with the blush slept fitfully, disturbed by terrible dreams and fevered delirium. Only a few saw the western gates open—only a few casually turned from mundane tasks to see what merchant caravan or traveling adventurer sought refuge for the night. What they saw froze them in their steps; terror overtook them as bestial creatures rushed forward, baring white fangs and jagged blades.

Those few witnesses ran and hid, too frightened

even to scream out, to make themselves targets. The gnolls passed them by, unconcerned with the meek, determined to eliminate the strong. This strategy they were largely unfamiliar with, but their pack leader Gyusk had excelled in it.

The bodies of the guards atop the western gate had barely cooled before Mahgra's incursion fully began. Nearly the entire city watch had been struck down, and no surmountable defense seemed possible to those who watched from windows and prayed for salvation.

As his gnolls did their work, Mahgra walked the length of the city walls, lacing them with spells and minor magic, alarms and illusions to ward off attempts at escape. The gates he sealed as they had been in Logfell, though his spells were more effective than those cast from rocking longboats. He relished working his magic and seeing it up close, perfecting the slightest syllables and gestures.

Homes began to burn, citizens were thrown into the streets and herded together. A foolish few had been killed trying to defend against the numerous attackers, and those had been grizzled old warriors who still felt the lure of battle. Retired in the shadow of the Qurth and battling only the occasional bold beast that ventured out of its edges, they were unprepared for the assault, lulled into false security by their oracles' visions and the town's lack of strategic or economic value.

A group of gnolls began to destroy and burn the gardens around the Temple of the Hidden Circle. They spat on the ground of their enemies—the church had thwarted many such attacks in the past—before entering its sanctuary and continuing their enraged defilement.

Finishing his work, Mahgra breathed deeply the smoke-filled air, striding confidently down the main street. His well-kept robes fluttering in the wind, he cut for himself the image of a consummate conqueror. His attack had been swift, well planned, and made easy by perfect execution. That Targris had been an easy mark was of no concern; victims would scream with or without swords in their hands. Survivors would tell tales of the ogre's night of attack in awe and deep-seated fear. He always left a few survivors despite Morgynn's concerns.

His mistakes in Innarlith were far behind the Order now, ancient history as new vistas spread before them.

One day I might return to that city, he thought, to stand in the court of Ransar Pristoleph and commend his traitorous, smoking remains to Gargauth and the Order of Twilight.

Grinning, he approached the steps of a manor near the center of town, the home of some sort of leader, who peered out from behind sheer curtains in a darkened window. As a well-ordered chaos erupted in the streets and homes behind him, Mahgra called terrible spells to his smiling lips and met that fearful gaze behind such fragile and decadent glass.

The look in Morgynn's eyes—the sneer on Khaemil's face—their whispers and insults end *now,* he thought, as anger flared within him. All debts are paid, on my part at least.

Thunder rumbled overhead, the first sign of the storm that came not from the sea as the wind and clouds foretold, but from the forest. Distant lightning silhouetted flailing branches and illuminated curls of smoke as a long-held peace burned amid yelping howls from gnollish throats.

⊙ ⊙ ⊙ ⊙ ⊙

Sameska was forced to watch as her people suffered the attack. She screamed at the destruction of the temple by beasts and scavengers, but she could not look away. The force that held her was beyond resistance and full of what she felt was the wrath of Savras for her disservice, his punishment for her lack of humility. She pleaded with her god, begging to be shown how to stop this chaos, this betrayal of those who trusted in the oracles.

Savras did not answer. Something was wrong, horribly wrong, and she did not know what to do or how to make herself heard. She felt herself growing weak, her body crying out for her return, and she fought the urge to release her spell, afraid that Savras might abandon her completely should she give up. Yet the power that held her, that guided her spell, relaxed its grip on her floating form, and its waning strength eased her will to hold on.

Her vision became blurry. Smoke, flame, screams, and bestial howls merged as she limply floated on a phantom wind, losing her magic and beginning the fall that would bring her home.

Just as blackness crept into her sight, the shadows parted, and a warrior stepped out of the darkness. The warrior was shrouded in mist, exuding a bright light but surrounded by ghostly specters. Silhouetted by a winding road of shadows, his opalescent eyes smoldered in the dark. Lightning flashed across the clouds above him, a bright and terrible glow that faded quickly.

The image of the almost-translucent warrior held fast in her thoughts as her journey fell away and the weight of her gasping body returned. What was this man? Why had he come, this traveler of shadow roads? She'd felt the inherent goodness in the spectral light that surrounded him, along with the chill of the place he'd come from.

She fainted, her thoughts becoming dreams. Nightmares revisited all that she had seen, colored with the horror of what she'd felt, all of it ending with the vision of the ghost-walker who walked the road of shadows.

⊚ ⊚ ⊚ ⊚ ⊚

Through drifting smoke Quinsareth appeared in folds of shadow, looking down on the burning town of Targris dispassionately, fully expecting the nature of what awaited him, if not the method. He trembled in rage as the scene and its payback became clear to him. Hoar was strict about the protocols of his followers: swift vengeance, violence returned in the manner it was given, whether the intentions were good or evil. Such abstract notions meant little to Hoar. Injustice was the true foe, and all manner of beings, from goodly king to cruel tyrant, were capable of committing the offense. Though the good men Quin had faced may have regretted their hypocrisy, only fear had introduced them to the truth of what they'd done. True evil, in his experience, was at least honest in its intentions.

He was no priest or cleric. He held no services, taught no wayward souls. He had no temple to conduct such teachings in. His church was the road, his offerings were of blood, and his prayers were dark, silent, and infrequent.

Sitting down with his legs crossed, Quinsareth watched as Targris was subdued. He smelled the smoke and watched the fires. His celestial blood screamed for action, moved him to descend on these brigands and beasts. He waited, fighting himself as he focused on Hoar's blessing. The double lives of everything around him were visible, the real and the halo of shadows that flickered behind it all.

He closed his eyes to the flames and attempted to block out the screams and weeping that reached him. He knew he could do nothing for them now but wait for early morning. He held on to his emotions, gathered them, sharpening the edge of his desires, molding them into the forms of the predators below.

Quinsareth knew that in spite of everything—all that he'd done, all that he'd seen, and all that he might have once held himself to be—he was as much the killer as any of them.

◉ ◉ ◉ ◉ ◉

Dark clouds obscured the dim light of early morning. Gaining strength, thunder rumbled in the distance, lost in the trees of the Qurth Forest that filled the southern horizon. The twisted branches danced in the wind, as if reveling like savages around a growing fire. Small fishing boats in the town's harbor were tossed in the wild waves of the Lake of Steam.

Mahgra watched it all and smiled, his bejeweled tusks bared as he swept his gaze across the main street from the doorstep of the mayor's home. The mayor himself was long dead now, covered in the bloody sheets of his own bed, a diversion for Mahgra's cruelty while he awaited the report of his gnoll warriors.

He had thrown back his hood and heavy robes in order

to inspire fear in his captives as well as to satisfy his own sense of vanity. Mahgra was rare among his kind, born with an affinity for magic that was reflected in his strange appearance. His skin was a deep shade of blue and covered with tattoos, both tribal and arcane. Small ivory horns protruded from his forehead, and his eyes were orbs of solid black, matching his well-groomed long hair, a banner of shadow across his shoulders, flowing in the wild winds of the storm.

Gathered before him in the central square were the residents of Targris, guarded by gnolls wielding swords and axes. Others of their kind roamed the empty streets, ransacking homes for valuables and weapons.

The gnolls were edgy and anxious, only barely held in check by Gyusk, their commander and Mahgra's second. Gyusk was the fiercest of them, his fiendish parentage giving him a semblance of royalty among their tribe. His green eyes, common among his race, glowed with a hellish light. Mahgra valued his shrewd mind and keen control over the hyena-faced warriors.

Seeing that matters were in control, the ogre turned his thoughts to the Qurth Forest and wondered when the messenger might arrive with new orders, though he loathed Morgynn's silver-tongued lapdog, Khaemil. The sibilant tones of the *shadurakul*'s voice were enough to drive the ogre mage mad at times. He could already imagine the smell of wet dog Khaemil would invariably bring with him. He brushed at his cloak absently as if to ward off even the idea of the aroma.

Rain began to fall, the heavy clouds finally releasing their long-held burden, drops hissing in the dying embers of destroyed houses and the defiled remains of the oracles' temple. The sound added to Mahgra's mood and brought him back from the depth of his thoughts, back to the situation at hand. Gyusk loped forward, as formally as his slightly hunched form would allow, to stand before the ogre commander and await his attention.

Mahgra looked down into the dim light of Gyusk's eyes, almost daring the gnoll to report anything contrary to the success he demanded.

"Have your warriors finished their sweep?" His voice boomed over the noise of the storm, a second thunder that sent the gathered townsfolk to shaking as they huddled together on the cobblestones of the square.

"Yes, Lord Mahgra, but we've collected only a few trinkets of any value." Gyusk's voice was growling and deep as he haltingly spoke in the common tongue that Mahgra preferred over the feral sounds of the gnolls' language.

"Do what you will with the spoils. Disperse them among your warriors if it will help keep them in line. The Order wants no one harmed unless absolutely necessary. Understood?"

"Yes, Mahgra."

The ogre looked over the crowd of huddled fishermen and tradesmen. He frowned. "A pity these fisherfolk breed few warriors, Gyusk. A little resistance might have quelled the boredom of waiting."

Gyusk's brow furrowed at the statement and Mahgra smiled at the gnoll's obvious disagreement. He respected Gyusk's desire for swift victories and low casualties. Indeed, that very quality had compelled Mahgra to recruit the gnoll and his warriors for the Order. Gyusk's mind for strategy in the land of the Blacksaddle baronies had made him a thorn in Baron Thaltar's side for several months. They'd struck upon the weak swiftly and the strong warily, avoiding the armored patrols of Thaltar's soldiers. Mahgra, however, believed that such battles, while profitable, were ultimately hollow.

"Petty fear breeds anger in the hearts of one's enemies," he'd said to Gyusk. "The true battle lies in the heart of the strong foe. Destroy that and you will have won. Shying away from conflict in favor of survival will ultimately destroy you."

Lightning flashed and the rain fell harder. The wind whipped at Mahgra's cloak and hair. He could feel the magic of the storm like a singing in his blood.

This never could have occurred in Innarlith, he thought. *The best we could have hoped for there is pale compared to what we might accomplish in this place. Morgynn may think me a fool for insulting the puffed-up Ransar, but Innarlith* was never the place for the faithful of Gargauth. Morgynn merely uses the Order, stringing along the affections of Talmen to her own ends, but our ambitions will clash one day, and the Order will be free of her and her pet.

He stared at the roiling clouds. They were tinged with an eerie red glow. Mahgra's dark heart rejoiced as visions of conquest filled his mind. He could hear Gyusk speaking, saying his name and clearing his throat noisily. Reluctantly he turned from his reverie and faced the large gnoll.

"What is it?" he bellowed, causing everyone to flinch.

Gyusk pointed his clawed finger to the western end of the street, past the central square and toward the closed and sealed gate, where a lone figure stood in the darkness.

"Someone seems to be resisting." His tone was low and serious, a stark contrast to Mahgra's irritated yelling.

The ogre squinted his eyes, blinking through the heavy rain, but saw the figure only briefly before it seemed to disappear into thin air. A low growl, more common among his less civilized cousins, escaped him. "Someone is out there, Gyusk. It appears your warriors failed to find everyone."

Gyusk snarled, his hackles raising at Mahgra's mention of failure, but he focused that anger on his subordinates, barking orders in their bestial language. They loped into the streets in groups of three. Only ten remained behind to guard the hundred or so frightened prisoners.

Thunder rumbled as they waited. Mahgra was lost again in his thoughts of arcane ambition, clearly uninterested in the current effort. Gyusk, though, stared intently into the rain and darkness, his hand gripping a long serrated sword. Large puddles were forming in the streets as the rain grew heavier, pounding down with unnatural fury. A fierce cold infected the wind, freezing the blood and numbing the extremities.

Time passed slowly as Mahgra tried to ignore the gnoll's strict attention to the streets, as if an army had slipped past the town gates and threatened them all. He glared at Gyusk, annoyed by his battle-ready posture, and intently stared into the shadows and rain. Above the thunder, he yelled at the gnoll, "It is only one man!"

Then Mahgra saw him, closer this time, perhaps halfway between the west gate and the town square, materializing as quickly as he'd disappeared before.

The rain, reduced to a heavy drizzle, allowed the ogre and the gnoll to get a better look at the enshrouded figure.

His armor was an old style, an odd fashion uncommon in the southern realms, more suited for colder climes of the north. A high collar concealed the lower half of his face and a worn, broad-brimmed hat covered all but his eyes. Those eyes were chilling. Pearly and opalescent, they did not glow, but neither were they muted by shadow, darkness, or rain. His dark cloak was unmoved by the wind, wrapped tightly around him. He was silent and still, as if he were not a part of the world at all but a vision, a figment. Only a few loose strands of silvery-blond hair seemed to react to the cold gale that blew through the streets.

Gyusk nodded to two of his warriors. They nodded back and advanced on the still figure. Their loping gait was slow as they padded toward him with axes raised, growling as they neared.

His collar was blown aside for a moment, revealing a pale face. The man smiled. His bloodthirsty grin was discordant with Mahgra's observation of light behind the pale gaze. Those unblinking eyes fell on the two gnolls as they closed on him. Mahgra gripped the handle of his glaive, smelling blood on the air in spite of the wind and rain.

Mahgra narrowed his eyes, intrigued by this strange visitor but angered as well. Nothing assaulted his vanity more than an enemy who regarded his magnificence with indifference. He clenched his fists and waited to measure the skill of this unearthly warrior. Spells tumbled through his mind like the rain before his eyes. The thundering of his heart and the lightning he prepared on his lips manufactured a storm to match the arcane tempest around him.

CHAPTER FIVE

Quin had already stained his blade, killing eight gnolls he'd encountered in the abandoned streets. The rest he had allowed to escape, his menacing aura more than just an affectation of style. The shadows that surged through his spirit had an effect on those he encountered, and most were glad to be well away from it. These two approaching gnolls, fur wet from the rain, carrying weapons in hands that must have been chilled to ice in the unseasonable cold, began to sense the darkness that pervaded this lone warrior.

Quinsareth could see the indecision in their hyena faces. They looked at one another, then at him. He allowed the tip of Bedlam's long, curved blade to scrape against the cobbled street, making a slight screech. Its grating wail overpowered the sounds of thunder and rain.

The gnolls' eyes widened, long ears falling back against their heads. Each took a step backward. The man spoke, in their language: "Leave now." The translation was like a menacing growl. It proved enough. The pair turned and ran down a side street to escape the unnatural warrior and the imminent anger of their leader.

A large gnoll at their rear howled in rage, drawing a great-sword and barking for his warriors to attack. The stillness of the moment was shattered by sudden movement. The storm roared back to life as the remaining gnolls advanced.

Eight gnolls rushed Quinsareth, separating him from the townsfolk and their commander. Their leader followed, watching carefully, his massive blade held out before him. Quin waited for them to close, playing the element of surprise. He counted the heartbeats, ticked off the stones in his mind. The game continued, and the next stone was Blood.

Quinsareth charged the first three, releasing Bedlam's howling blade from beneath his cloak. He ducked the first attack, the center gnoll's scimitar whistling over his head. He sidestepped an axe from the right while raising Bedlam to deflect the broadsword on his left. Spinning on his knees, he was grateful for the protection of his greaves between him and the cobblestones of the street. Before the gnoll on his left could recover, he sliced through its abdomen. Gutted, the hyena warrior howled madly as it fell, struggling to keep its innards from pouring out of the wound.

Leaping to his feet, he met the attack of the axe-wielding gnoll. Hooking his sword beneath the head of the heavy weapon, he kicked forward into the gnoll's kneecap. The joint cracked and Quin swiftly disarmed the beast. As the unarmed gnoll fell to the ground, Quinsareth turned to face the scimitar, once again arcing toward his neck.

This time, he blocked the gnoll's crude slash. Bedlam screeched as it bit into the heavy-bladed sword, protesting the defensive maneuver and unconcerned by the threat of injury to its wielder. The blade was overcome by an arcane bloodlust, flaring to life its green-hued glow of battle. The gnoll flinched at the magic weapon's surge and pulled back in fear. Quinsareth seized that brief lapse to force the scimitar high with his block, bringing Bedlam down viciously through the gnoll's shoulder and upper chest. The nearly bisected beast toppled backward senselessly, splashing in the gathering puddles. Blank eyes stared at the dead gnoll's five companions, who had slowed their brash charge and circled more cautiously around the enraged ghostwalker.

The injured gnoll tried to stand and limp on his damaged knee, carefully eyeing the movements of the quick, silent warrior. Quinsareth looked at the injured beast cruelly, leveling his cold gaze on the wary gnoll.

He spoke low, growling under the heavy rain and powerful thunder. Only the gnollish words for "lame dog" rose above the storm. An insult to gnollkind, the title was for those unfit to run with the pack. The injured gnoll turned and limped away in shame and fear, unwilling to face his tribal brethren.

Quin observed the others, their cautious steps and trembling blades. The large gnoll once again barked orders to his subordinates. He commanded them to close and end the battle quickly. None seemed eager to comply, but they crept forward, their ears flat against their doglike heads, growling menacingly. Amid their murmuring threats, Quin picked out the name Gyusk, apparently their leader, not well loved by some of the squad. Beyond the backs of the gnolls, Quin spied an ogre, patiently watching the spectacle. The giant effortlessly held a massive black glaive as he watched the battle over the heads of the gathered crowd.

The townsfolk shivered in the cold rain, eyes darting between their captors and the dark warrior who fought them, waiting for a chance to run away from both. The sight of Quinsareth's fair skin, splattered with the gnolls' blood, and his intensely opalescent eyes, like the gaze of a dead man, was monstrous and horrifying. The captives waited breathlessly, as yet unsure of who was the savior and who the villain in the unfolding scenario.

Quin was certain of the villain, but had no taste for the title of savior. These people could have been dead, and he still would have fought. It was a rare day that his brand of justice saved the living. He flashed a feral grin at the gnolls' commander and charged recklessly. Bedlam led the advance, humming and flashing brightly, accompanying the lightning overhead.

The gnolls closed swiftly and he reached the center of the group, dodging and tumbling past clumsy attacks. Those attacks were made clumsier by freezing hands and shadow-born fear. Quinsareth quickly parried two blades that came close and rolled into a somersault to leap at the center gnoll. The beast yelped and tried to avoid the madman, but Bedlam sliced through the gnoll's shoulder and bit deep into its collar-bone. Quinsareth used the bone as a fulcrum in a tumbling jump. Flipping over the screaming gnoll's head, he landed in front of the startled but ready Gyusk.

They exchanged quick blows, blades ringing in a blur of steel and rage. Behind Quin, the other gnolls turned to catch up to the ghostwalker. Quinsareth pushed Gyusk's blade back just enough to land a kick into the gnoll commander's jaw. Gyusk staggered briefly, spitting teeth, and Quin spun to meet those behind him. Swinging a leg low to unbalance the stunned commander, Quin sent Gyusk splashing into the mud.

Two of the five remaining gnolls closed again, unconcerned for their leader. The other three, one of them bleeding, held back, clearly fearful of the thinning odds against them. Gyusk spat and sputtered on the ground behind Quin, slowly pushing himself up and searching the puddles for the hilt of his sword.

Quinsareth engaged the advancing pair. The fight had carried him closer to the frightened townsfolk, and he could hear the sobbing of widowed wives and the screams of inconsolable children above the clash of steel on steel. He fought harder, stalled briefly by the synchronized blades of the pair of gnolls. He held his ground patiently, waiting for the proper opening and listening carefully for the commander to rise or for the ogre to approach.

He landed two quick slices on the gnolls as he heard the growl of Gyusk behind him. Bedlam hummed a shrill warning as the injured pair yelped and hopped backward, beyond the reach of the biting blade. Quin spun, kicking Gyusk in the jaw again before the big gnoll could rise. Spotting the gnoll's greatsword, Quinsareth lowered into a crouch on one leg, the other kicking the loose sword away, flipping it into a deeper puddle at the street's edge.

He thrust Bedlam forward and leveled his piercing stare, testing the resolve of the gnolls. The bold pair stood bleeding from the deep wounds that had flayed open their furred jowls. They tilted their heads oddly, protecting their aching wounds from the stinging rain, but held their ground warily. Quin was amused by their newfound respect for the long reach and sharp edge of the eager Bedlam.

He gave them his feral smile once again, his ghostly face spattered with the blood of many gnolls. Bedlam, reacting to the thoughts of its master, gave a terrifying screech, mimicking the pained howls of the hyena warriors as rain dripped pink from its bloodied edge.

Before Quinsareth could renew his wild attack, powerful arms grabbed him from behind, pinning his own arms to his sides. Determinedly, he maintained his grip on the hilt of the still-howling Bedlam. Gyusk had recovered swiftly and taken advantage of Bedlam's screams to surprise the ghostwalker. The gnoll bit deeply into Quinsareth's shoulder and neck, piercing easily through the heavy cloak and leather armor.

Quinsareth gritted his teeth in pain and frustration, but remained focused on the two gnolls who now grinned as only their hyena faces could, more gruesome for their bleeding jaws and the bloodlust in their flashing eyes. Swaggering, they approached the helpless warrior, one raising a blade to cut Quinsareth's throat, the other drawing back to slice open his belly.

The trio of cowardly gnolls stood at the edge of the street, yipping and gnashing their teeth in anticipation of the easy kill.

⊙ ⊙ ⊙ ⊙ ⊙

Sameska trembled as she dreamed of savage teeth and violent battles. The temperature in the sanctuary had cooled despite what should have been a warm autumn morning. Her sweat felt like beads of ice on her delicate flesh. Her breath came in small, white puffs that were borne away by the swirling energies of the magic around her prone form.

Through a haze of misty images, the ghostwalker of her visions fought on, battling the grotesque, vile creatures that had so brutally taken the town of Targris. Or so she thought, still unable to focus through the dreamlike state as her body slumbered and her consciousness struggled to make sense of the nightmare. Her ears were full of the sounds of thunder, growling, and metal clashing metal.

Death cries howled around her and the rain washed across her in the dream sight, a cloud of reds and pinks, blurring her view of the scene. Between waves of falling rain and flashes of lightning, she saw the ghostwalker. Oozing light and shadow, both had become strong and battled within him for control. Sameska stared into the glowing green eyes of a fiendish creature, a warrior gnashing wicked fangs, but beyond all this, at the edges of the terrible battle, she sensed magic.

It stood like a tempest of living spells, watching and waiting, filled with anger and brutish rage. It had no form in those few moments when she glimpsed its presence, but it dominated the field of battle with a darkness of coiled power.

In that moment, Sameska could feel herself murmuring a soft prayer to Savras, begging for the safety of this ghostwalker who battled between light and dark. Then she realized he had come on her behalf, a gift from Savras to protect them all from evils that would come. The thought was fleeting and uncertain, but she clung to it in fear and weeping confusion.

She could do nothing else as the thunder pounded in her brain and the phantom rain threatened to drown her in the dream. Gasping and coughing, she fell further into the trance, unable to escape, trapped between dreaming and the shadows of unreadable prophecy.

⊙ ⊙ ⊙ ⊙ ⊙

Steel blades reflected lightning as they cut through the rain, rushing toward the immobilized Quinsareth. He did not struggle against Gyusk's thick arms and massive strength in that heartbeat before death. He merely whispered a quiet word, a focus for the power he summoned from within himself, and vanished.

Gyusk stumbled forward as the weight of his opponent left his locked arms. The gnoll aiming for Quinsareth's stomach snarled and pulled back his thrust, scraping his sword across Gyusk's studded vambraces. The other gnoll had been too zealous in his thrust and ran his blade through the side of Gyusk's unprotected neck, losing the weapon as the gnoll commander spasmed in surprise and jerked backward. His glowing eyes flared and widened, and he fell to his knees, clawing at the mortal wound and the sword embedded there. He tipped forward, kicking at the ground, then lay still.

Mahgra straightened, raising an eyebrow, certain only moments ago that the sport was ended. He looked around, as did the five gnolls, searching the rain for a glimpse of their enemy. The ogre raised the heavy glaive at his side, gripping the weapon tightly.

The gnolls did not notice a misty form that gathered behind them, taking shape and gaining mass as Quinsareth's ethereal body returned to solidity. The gnoll closest to him turned, catching a faint sound like wolves howling, before Bedlam removed his head.

The others flinched and turned but Quinsareth was already among them, swinging the heavy blade like a steel ribbon of screaming light. He stepped straight into the pair of his would-be assassins, who'd raised blades high to cut Quinsareth down. Instead, both dropped their weapons, Bedlam's howl muffled and gurgling as it ran the gnolls through.

Another gnoll scrambled to ready his weapon, but Quinsareth kicked and side-stepped, and with a backhand swing sent another head to the puddles.

The last gnoll, still bleeding, made a decision quickly and was already running past the captive townsfolk, preferring to brave the storm and the shame of defeat rather than the ghostly warrior and the screaming blade.

Quinsareth had barely turned his attention to the ogre when his vision was suddenly filled with bright blue light and his body was hit with the concussive force of Mahgra's spell. The ogre mage bared his ivory teeth and tusks as lightning arced from his outstretched hand, launching Quinsareth's body into the air to crash against the side of a nearby cottage.

The townsfolk began screaming and rising from the cobblestones, no longer threatened by the gnolls and overcome with fear of the devilish ogre. Parents gathered their children, soaked and shivering, to run and scatter from the mystical battle.

Quinsareth hit the ground face first. Pulling himself up on hands and knees, he gasped at the searing pain that burned behind his eyes and throughout his muscles. Tiny arcs of electricity raced along his arms and disappeared into the puddle he'd landed in. Bedlam had sailed free of his grip when he hit the wall of the cottage but lay within reach, rippling the surface of a puddle into concentric rings as it hummed in a childlike rage.

Quin's eyes, aching, began to clear. The burning in his muscles dissipated and he flexed his fingers in the water, regaining feeling in them. A slight resistance to electricity accompanied his angelic and unnerving eyes, but the ogre's powerful bolt had caught him off guard. The game was always unpredictable, but few stones could change its course as could the one called Magic.

The blue-skinned ogre approached with an arrogant swagger, smiling and gloating at his fallen foe, spinning the rune-covered glaive casually as rain hissed and steamed on the vile blade.

A wizard, Quinsareth thought. That explains much, but does me little good if I lie down and die now.

He winced as he rose to one knee, reaching behind him and grasping Bedlam's hilt, assured by the confidence in the ogre's eyes. The ogre clearly felt he had the advantage and was taking his time with his kill. This beast no doubt had a common ogre's penchant for cruelty.

"You fought well, little one. Your tricks were entertaining, to say the least." Mahgra's booming voice carried easily across the noise of the storm. His large fingers absently traced several symbols on the head of the glaive as he added distractedly, "I can show you true magic, better than phantoms and parlor tricks."

Quinsareth jumped at the ogre, closing the distance in a heartbeat and slashing at the steaming glaive. He disrupted Mahgra's spell but landed no blow. Mahgra gripped the glaive rigidly, blocking Bedlam's wailing edge with his strength as he whispered another spell. The arcane words flowed like a dark song in Quin's ears.

Unable to overcome the ogre's strength, Quinsareth rolled beneath it, twisting and slashing across Mahgra's massive rib cage. Ducking beneath the behemoth's left arm, he turned to complete another cut along the ogre mage's back.

Mahgra merely turned as he completed his incantation, nonplussed by the pain of Quinsareth's attacks.

The magic was invisible, but it fell on Quinsareth's shoulders like a crushing weight, pushing him to his knees and squeezing his body like a closed fist. Stars erupted before his eyes as he struggled to breathe. The spell continued, worming across his skin and up his neck, clawing at the edges of his skull and scraping at his thoughts.

He closed his eyes tightly and called on the shadows, fighting the invasive spell and resisting its urges to submit and give up his spirit. The shadows answered, bolstering his will and disassembling the unseen power around him.

As the pressure eased, Quinsareth doubled over, feigning defeat but carefully watching the rippling reflection of the mage standing over him in the rain. He waited for an opening. Mahgra laughed, a hideous roar that hurt Quin's ears, but the ghostwalker resisted the urge to cover them and maintained his submissive posture.

"I should like to punish you for what you've done to my allies, little one. But I have more pressing business, alas."

He raised the magical glaive high overhead.

Quinsareth did not wait for its descent. Springing forward at the startled ogre mage, he buried Bedlam in the giant's gut.

Mahgra bellowed in pain as the blade screamed inside him. He batted at the desperate aasimar with a clublike fist.

Quinsareth's arm nearly broke against the ogre's blow. He heard several ribs crack as he landed on his back and rolled onto his stomach. He watched as Mahgra tried unsuccessfully to pry Bedlam from the grievous wound. Each time he pulled, the blade grew louder and twirled like an auger to dig deeper.

Steam rose in clouds behind the howling ogre. Quinsareth saw that the glaive had been dropped and forgotten by the ogre wizard. Ignoring the pain in his arm and chest, he rose on all fours to help the ogre remove the embedded Bedlam. He stood and charged, drawing Mahgra's attention.

A spell leaped to the ogre's lips as he tenaciously cast through the pain, rage carrying him through the syllables and gestures of his most familiar spell. Quinsareth was ready this time and dived forward as a lightning bolt streaked over his head. It singed the trailing edge of his waterlogged cloak and ripped painfully down his spine.

He grabbed Bedlam's hilt before Mahgra could react. Roaring through gritted teeth, Quin pulled the blade free and swung wildly upward. He felt only brief resistance as it sliced nearly halfway through the ogre's throat. Rain and hot blood spilled down on the ghostwalker as Mahgra gurgled for air, trying to bring forth another spell despite his severed windpipe and tattered vocal cords.

Quinsareth stumbled backward, his face a mask of feral pain as he watched the ogre mage crash to the ground. Rolling thunder emphasized the ogre's fall, and the wind mocked his last gurgling breath. Satisfied that the ogre would not stand again, Quin sagged. Dropping limply to his knees, he languidly watched the blood of the wizard trickle away in the pounding rain.

⊛ ⊛ ⊛ ⊛ ⊛

The temple in Brookhollow was silent and still, disturbed only by distant thunder from the northwest. The storm had at last broken, and the citizens were grateful it had done so elsewhere. Enough trouble and dire news had affected their lives in the last few tendays, indeed in the last several months.

The blush had not yet taken a strong hold this far south, but it would. Only time stood between them and epidemic. The Temple of the Hidden Circle had been quiet, doling out only what minor divinations might reveal. The lesser oracles did their best, but growing whispers and rumors surrounded the subject of Sameska.

Dreslya was still awake when the thunder began and the horizon was lit by flashes of faraway lightning. She'd sent riders out to gather the Hunters of the Hidden Circle, warriors of Savras and champions of his church. The other oracles would be informed as they awoke for morning prayers and the breaking of their fasts.

Sameska's look and words haunted her.

After revealing nothing for months, for nearly a whole year, the high oracle called a meeting of the Hidden Circle. Dreslya knew something was wrong; something horrible hid in autumn's early chill and the gathering black clouds. She had never stepped within the rune circle itself, but she felt the changes in Brookhollow and in Sameska. Faith in the wisdom of Savras was all that held her together.

"His plan will be revealed as he sees fit, no sooner," she told herself several times throughout the night, wondering what would come next.

CHAPTER SIX

They gathered in the fog, riding across sodden ground in heavy cloaks and grim moods. Their mounts were bred from the horses of the Southern Shaar, a powerful breed coveted in many places across the Realms for their speed and stamina. These warriors, expert riders and archers, came in ones and twos to the gates of Brookhollow. The Hunters of the Hidden Circle arrived to heed the call of the high oracle, to gather and bear witness.

Such a call they had not received for as long as any of them cared to remember. By tradition, none would enter until all were accounted for. They called out their names to the gate master as they arrived, some embellishing their names with titles, boasts of recent victories, or family legacies. The majority remained silent and calm, patiently suffering the soft patter of a sprinkling rain.

Their numbers were large when judged against the small towns they protected, Brookhollow being the most populous as it was the home of the primary temple. Among this elite group rode the standard bearers, seven in all, wielding long spears with loops of braided rope hanging from their blades. The ropes were knotted four times along their length, the hunter's symbol for the Hidden Circle. The knots represented the four precepts of their faith—the past, present, future, and fate.

Hanging within each braid was a single dried fethra flower, its bell upside down in the belief that the blessing of Savras would pour out and give them luck in battle. The standards held no individual markings, no sign of clan or leadership. This was a new tradition and belied those ancient times when the hunters were of the Shaaryan tribes and fought amongst themselves for position and status. The lack of decoration made them all equal and reminded them of their oaths of service and the humility of their chosen profession.

Each hunter wore traditional archer's armor. The primary piece was a shoulder and arm guard called an *eshtahk*, made of layers of lacquered leather and decorative cloth. The opposite arm required free movement for drawing arrows from back-slung quivers. This side was protected by a special cloak woven from wool and the fibers of the ironvine plant that grew on the southern borders of the Qurth Forest. The cloaks were flexible but resistant to the bloodthorns and razorleaf bushes that thrived in the forest. They'd even been known to deflect a blade now and then, though this was often attributed to the oracles who blessed the garments.

Dreslya Loethe stood on the wall with the gate master, prepared to officiate the gathering. In truth, she awaited the arrival of her younger sister, Elisandrya. Some said the Loethe sisters would be the next high oracle and lord hunter, though only out of earshot of Sameska, who discouraged such wild rumors.

Dreslya grew more and more impatient, hurriedly acknowledging the calls from below with a sign of welcome as the other hunters announced themselves. She knew Eli was prone to tardiness, but she worried all the same. She did not understand her sister's love for the open plain and always tried to hide her concern when they met—with little success. Ever since the loss of their parents, Dreslya had withdrawn to service in the church and Eli had run wild, sparked by wanderlust and a sense of adventure inherited from their late father. They spoke little of their lost parents, though the subject seemed to hang between them like a net of thorns.

Soft thunder rumbled far to the west, beyond the edge of the forest. Dreslya pulled her cloak tight, turning her head to the east and the empty balcony outside the stained glass dome of the temple.

She imagined Sameska stood hidden behind that glass and watched as the hunters came from far and wide across the Reach. Dreslya shivered, remembering the cold in the high oracle's voice and demeanor. She needed no divination or cup of fethra petals to tell her that something was wrong.

⊕ ⊕ ⊕ ⊕ ⊕

Evil was coming to their doorstep, and a ghostwalker strolled behind it.

Sameska paced nervously in front of the glass dome of the temple, wringing her hands and revisiting her dreams and visions. A terrible prophecy had come, and the pain of it still ached her old bones and stiff joints. The vision had meaning—and the ghostwalker, probably a nomadic Hoarite, had some part to play. This was troubling, for the Hoarites' actions were often unpredictable, as were their allegiances. She'd watched him fight viciously against monstrous enemies, though she knew not if he lived still.

Surely he must, she thought. *Savras has shown him to me—surely this wanderer comes at the All-Seeing One's bidding to aid us, but why this one? A foreigner?*

Sameska rubbed her forehead with both hands, weary of contemplating her disjointed memories. She'd replayed them a thousand times, over and over, and still Savras's mystery eluded her. She would be cautious at the gathering, revealing only enough to make her followers aware of what might occur, not send them screaming into battle against an unknown foe.

She must remind them that the soul of prophecy is patience, though little of it soothed her growing anxiety. Flickering remnants of a greater power, the true voice of her god, brushed against her cheek or warmed the air during the past day. No words could be heard in those moments; no message of clarity came, nor even further confusion. It brought only the uncanny feeling that something was missing, some vital element was wrong and out of joint.

Below, she could see Dreslya descending the gate excitedly and the Loethe sisters reuniting in the field outside the gates. She narrowed her eyes at their reunion and happiness, then walked away, suddenly angry and needing something to distract her labored thoughts.

⊙ ⊙ ⊙ ⊙ ⊙

The slim blade carved smoothly the winding symbols of magic into her skin. Morgynn squeezed her eyes shut. She relished the pain, infusing her emotions into the magic. Her blood sang at the blade's touch, rushing up through the broken skin to gracefully caress its pointed tip before withdrawing into the channels of spidery wounds.

She bit her lip as waves of heat rolled through her body. Focusing hard to keep the ancient dagger moving, to complete the runic scars on her arm, she savored each moment of arcane creation. She did not bleed as she cut, for the bleeding was unnecessary. She did not bleed because she willed it. She was a blood magus, and each drop of her life was power. Her pulse alone could kill.

During the scarring, her mind always returned to the tundra of Narfell, where she had first tasted power. That homeland was where she had once lived and died. The memories came unbidden, burned in her mind to play themselves out each time she put blade to flesh. When the blood became stirred, so did the past stir.

Morgynn had learned much in her seven years with the Creel tribe. Taken at the age of five from her mother, the Creel had spared her life on the word of Yarrish, their war wizard, who sensed power in the young girl. She had always felt the strange tinglings of magic, but had not known what they were or what to call them. She was born with the gift, a sorceress, and Yarrish had envied her connection to the Weave.

He taught her what he knew, how to channel the energy into spells, how to shape it to do her bidding. From the rest of the tribe, who tolerated her presence, she learned to be cruel and to take what she wanted when she could. Yarrish had looked upon her with new eyes the day she had killed a man, an outlander, and stolen his horse. For one so young to have summoned a killing flame and to mount her prize without a second thought, she showed that she had accepted the ways of the Creel fully and without regret. Then her mother, Kaeless Sedras, leader of the Sedras tribe, had come to reclaim her.

Kaeless led her people at dawn on a charge into the camp of the Creel. Yarrish had concealed Morgynn from enemy eyes during trade meets and tribal councils, protective of the girl he now considered his own daughter and legacy in the world. It had been Haargrath, son of the chieftain, who had informed Kaeless of her daughter's whereabouts in fear of the girl's power and quiet ambition.

Through force of arms and godly magic, the Sedras tribe was successful in recapturing the screaming Morgynn and bearing her away from the life she had grown to know. The Sedras typically held lands far away from the Creel territory, and Morgynn was quickly lost to her adoptive tribe, held captive by an enemy, a mother she barely knew or remembered.

Years passed and Morgynn learned to function within the Sedras tribe, even calling Kaeless "Mother," but she never truly lost her identity as a Creel. Under the tutelage of a wizard in the tribe, Morgynn learned more about her magic, surpassing the skills of her peers by leaps and bounds. They envied her power and spread rumors behind her back, calling her a Creel witch. Morgynn always heard them and enjoyed their hatred of her, casting withering stares at them and baring her teeth when no one was looking.

Once a year, the tribe would attend the Bildoobaris, a trade meet and occasion for the tribal leaders to converse and settle disputes. Kaeless had forbidden Morgynn to attend for many years after rescuing her, as the Creel would also be in attendance. Eventually, seeking to gain her daughter's trust, Kaeless allowed Morgynn to participate.

Morgynn had grown into a beautiful young woman by then, and was well aware of her effect on men. She was learning to use that knowledge to her advantage, much to her mother's glowering disapproval. At those trade meets, Morgynn had first begun to learn more of the world beyond the tundra. There she had met Zhamiel, an aging priest of Gargauth and an outsider from the Great Dale to the south.

She had never taken to the worship of Lathander, like the rest of the Sedras, and found no interest in Zhamiel's talk of Gargauth, but she'd felt a kinship that day as he wove tales of older times and armies of demons. She learned of the Nar Empire and its war against Raumathar, learned the histories of the ruins that dotted the cold plains of her homeland. Zhamiel told her of the magic as well, hidden treasures lost, buried beneath stone and time.

Ruins in Narfell were numerous and easy to find but were approached only by the brave or the greedy. Morgynn and a few acolytes of Zhamiel set out to find the Well of Goorgian, an open pit in the ruins of a nameless city. Goorgian was once a Nar wizard who, it was rumored, had worshiped Gargauth and built the first true temple in Gargauth's name. He and his followers became known as the Order of Twilight.

Zhamiel promised Morgynn that powerful secrets lay hidden in Goorgian's grave, a crater where he'd been destroyed by his own foolishness. She'd left the Bildoobaris unannounced, knowing her mother would search for her, but Morgynn had no intention of returning to the Sedras or even the Creel. Her time walking in the paths of others was over.

Her group eventually found the edge of the pit where Goorgian had consumed his own life in dreams of power. Morgynn stared deep into that darkness and began to dream herself. For the first time, Morgynn imagined power, real power. She had no idea that the next three years would pass so quickly or that her mother would not only give up on her only daughter but would also seek to end her life.

With her ritual complete, the memories faded along with the pain that lessened to a dull ache in her forearm. Traced with the letters and secret language of her magic, she admired her skin for a moment, studying her work and feeling more confident with her scars restored. She sighed, shrugging off the haze of the pain-induced trance, and surveyed her surroundings.

The walls inside the lone tower of Jhareat were piled high with bones, shoved from the floors to clear them. Dusty skulls and fleshless limbs adorned each room in the narrow tower, its long-forgotten defenders well beyond caring about being conquered. Their weapons and armor lay rusting and tattered amid the bones. Through a small arched window, lightning flashed and powerful winds roared. She could almost hear the chanting Gargauthans below, weaving the storm spell into the base of the tower.

She found that she enjoyed the storms more as she'd traveled farther south. Their warmth was a welcome change from the chilling gales that blew across the tundra in Narfell. The more she beheld them, the more it seemed her thick blood demanded them. Lost in the chaos of thunder and roaring tornadoes, her memories were but a nagging whisper, where her blood was a raging tempest.

She peered through the darkness of the low-hanging clouds, across the fields of ruined walls and jutting bits of rubble, to the edge of the forest. She whispered a quick spell and her eyes became as sharp as an eagle's, focusing the forest with amazing clarity. After a few moments, she found what she'd been looking for, what she'd sensed coming closer. A massive, coal-black mastiff stared back at her, its muscles rippling as it prowled through the trees. She smiled at his savage beauty, his brute strength and stealth as he negotiated the shadows of the ruined clearing at a full run.

Khaemil was *shadurakul*, a breed of shapeshifter called from the realm of Avernus in the Nine Hells. Though released from his initial bond of servitude, Khaemil had bound himself to Morgynn willingly, remaining at her side ever since and considered a blessing by the Gargauthans. Morgynn stopped short of calling him a blessing. She'd tasted one of Gargauth's favors already. Though grateful, she felt no desire to entertain them in the future.

Morgynn could hear him entering the tower below. The heavy clicking of his paws became the familiar rustle of night robes as he ascended the twisting staircase along the tower's interior. Then Khaemil stood in the doorway to the uppermost floor, his head bowed and awaiting Morgynn's attention. She'd been casting recently, and she knew he could smell the scent of her as soon as he'd entered the tower. The aroma of blood and heat defied the open window and the cool air that blew outside.

She turned to him slowly, settling into her stone seat and dismissing her spell of vision, bringing the room back to a softer focus. Khaemil stepped into the candlelight, lowering his hood, as Morgynn watched him expectantly.

"What news from the forest?" Morgynn asked the question nonchalantly and looked down to inspect her skin once again, caressing and tracing the darkening designs.

"We have many potential allies deep in the woods, but they are mere beasts. Those more intelligent attempt to hide themselves from us, but they are there."

"No matter," Morgynn replied, "All is as it should be for now. The Gargauthans have begun their work on the tower and the storm grows by the moment. We have little to do but gather our strength and wait."

"Yes, my lady. The storm is magnificent." Khaemil walked to the window then, looking across the dampening ruins as she had moments before. "Talmen looks little pleased by our success so far." A smile crept into his voice, capturing Morgynn's attention with his implication of further news.

"Your voice is mischievous, Khaemil. What delights you so?"

Khaemil turned, sighing through his toothy grin. "Only that poor Talmen and his favorite pupil no longer serve Gargauth in the same manner. While Talmen seeks his god's favor in his daily works, Mahgra now petitions for mercy in the pits of the Nine Hells. He is dead."

Morgynn returned Khaemil's smile, but the look lasted only a moment before her mood changed and rage boiled in the back of her throat. Khaemil gasped, his heartbeat pounding as she stood and walked toward him. He couldn't breathe and stared wide-eyed at her, frantically clawing at his chest and shoulder as pain raced through them.

As she watched him struggle, her eyes welled with blood, red tears seeking to burst forth in a mockery of despair. At her belt she gripped a small silver vial. Within it was Khaemil's blood, taken long ago and used as a kind of leash against him. A leash—and, as now—a lash.

"Why does Talmen know the tale of Mahgra before me?" Her words were swift and forceful, wasting none of the time Khaemil had left before death might claim him. She eased her spell slightly, giving him a moment to answer with shallow breath.

"Scrying! My lady, please! He watches!"

Morgynn arched an eyebrow and looked to her side. "Ah, so the worm isn't as docile as I'd imagined him to be." She released the vial of blood and Khaemil fell to the floor, gulping at the air and allowing the pain to fade before standing again. "We must watch the dear malefactor more closely. He may be ready to accept that a wandering Hoarite has killed Mahgra, but if he suspects our hand in the matter, we may lose the support of the Gargauthans."

"Yes, my lady." Khaemil's voice was hoarse as he regained his footing. He staggered slightly as his pulse slowly fell into step with his actions. "I will watch him."

"No, Khaemil. He already knows you are not fond of him. I will keep an eye on dear Talmen. He is blind enough to accept my presence without question." She stared into the flame of a nearby candle, her mind racing to put all in order. "We have no more need of the Hoarite. His job is done here—make sure he crusades elsewhere."

Her voice softened and grew more detached as the flame transfixed her gaze.

"I will do as you command, Lady Morgynn, as always, but there is another matter of the forest. A ring of pale trees, a short distance beyond the edge of the woods—a strange scent lingers there, a feeling of defiance and power but also fear."

Morgynn did not answer right away, lost in thought. She tilted her head, her eyes nearly closing in the embrace of her own magic, her blood excited and dancing within her.

"My lady?"

"Yes," she pulled herself away for a moment, "yes, the pale trees. I will deal with them later. I must prepare—I have work to do soon. Leave me now."

She did not hear or see him leave, only felt the absence of his pulse in the room, a void where his warmth had once stood. In the candle's flame, she saw other flames, old fires in her memory. The divine inferno of Lathander burned in her past along with the face of her mother, twisted in righteous anger as the Well of Goorgian had been surrounded by the Sedras.

Beyond all desire for power, beyond blood and magic and vile spell, the ambition of a blood magus is not born in the study of ancient secrets and dusty tomes. The blood magus, a child of death, must appease that fickle parent—the grave—above all other concerns. Only in death, whether chosen or delivered, does the power first stir in the cold, still heart. And the memory of that death lasts forever.

The candle flickered in a strong gust from the window and guttered out. Morgynn blinked, watching the trailing smoke of the blackened wick disperse before her eyes. Immeasurable moments passed before she finally looked away.

CHAPTER SEVEN

Elisandrya was taller than her older sister, taking after their father's strong Shaaryan blood. She was long of limb and lithe, her skin an exotic blend of the yellowish Shaaryan and her mother's dark Arkaiun tones. Both sisters bore the thick auburn hair of their mother, long and curled in natural ringlets, but while Dreslya's was contained and pulled back, Elisandrya's was free and flowing, at the mercy of the wind.

As they approached one another on the crowded field of hunters, each reflected on their long separation from one another. Dreslya fairly ran to meet her sister. Elisandrya stood in place, half-smiling and even happy, but nervous. She had always felt the irony between the two of them more, that Dreslya was an oracle and saw far less than her hunter sister. Elisandrya had fallen far from the scared and skittish little girl she'd been before joining the hunters and seeing much of the harsh world beyond Brookhollow's well-ordered lanes.

Her eyes had become older than the face that framed them, like those of the hunters who had trained her in their ways. Those eyes were at peace with the world they viewed, but they understood that only the sword and bow procured that peace. Life and freedom on the edge of the Qurth, more often than not, was bought with death. Being called to Brookhollow in the midst of such storms and spreading plague brought that martial knowledge to the forefront of her thoughts. The mere idea of a gathering, tendays before the traditional Feast of the Moon, set her on edge, and she found she could focus on little else.

Dreslya's easy smile faded as she approached her sister, and Eli felt instantly guilty for banishing the spirit of their reunion. Years could not erase the events which had taken their parents, nor the vast difference with which Eli had dealt with the loss compared to Dres. Always, she felt burdened with secrets, though it was in Brookhollow where they seemed stored.

"It's good to see you, Eli," Dreslya said hesitantly, as if addressing a distant acquaintance.

"Would that it could be under better circumstances, Dres." Elisandrya heard the tone in her own voice and felt ashamed. "I—I'm sorry, Dres. It's been a long ride and things—"

"It's all right, Eli. I know . . . we all know."

"It's good to see you, too," Eli managed, but she struggled to reconcile the memory of her older sister with the woman she now saw. Was she truly happy to be back in Brookhollow?

The white walls of the temple loomed above the wooden and stone barrier of the main perimeter. Eli avoided looking at them, content to wrestle with matters of family and time before confronting those of memory and faith.

She instead studied Dreslya's face and almost smiled, seeing the image of their mother. That understanding look had driven her to indignant rage at times, and at others it had been all that she longed to see again. It was pleasant now but bittersweet. Only days ago had she visited their parents' graves to the north along an empty stretch of the Low Road to Littlewater. Turning away, she fidgeted at her horse's saddle and bags, avoiding that familiar emerald gaze.

"How are signs of the blush within the city?" Eli asked while working at a loose harness on the saddle.

"The plague is evident in some, but not so much as the rumors from the north are telling. We do what we can, but a cure is still elusive at best."

Eli was quiet for a moment, attempting to choose her words, but then felt little need to as the narrow line of darkness on the horizon rumbled with thunder.

Well-chosen words will do us no favors now, she thought.

"There are no rumors from the north, only truths." Eli stopped and stared blindly at the worn leather of her saddle, remembering. "I chanced upon a merchant caravan just north of Littlewater. It had been through Logfell and Targris and was turned away at the gates of Derlusk.

"The hired guards spoke to me when I rode near to inquire of their business and wares. They said Logfell was lost, completely overrun with the disease, and that Targris had its fair share of victims as well. Several of their own caravan weren't feeling well, and they suspected those at Derlusk knew something but would not even open the gates to them."

"Turned away at Derlusk? But surely the sages there have some information, some knowledge of a cure?"

Eli knew the defeated and confused tone in Dreslya's voice, had known the same when confronted by these horrible truths.

"The sages have their books and magic, Dres, but the merchant princes hold the gates and the money. They'll not see their decadence ruined by plague, and I suspect Littlewater will hold much the same opinion—too long have they courted Derlusk's nobles and favor."

Dres was quiet, absorbing the news as Eli thought a moment. Then the hunter leaned forward to whisper in her sister's ear, "What is happening here? Why have we not heard news from the high oracle?"

Dres pulled back quickly, her eyes darting in all directions. She shook her head as if to say, *Not here, not now.*

Eli's concern grew at her sister's strange reaction, though something within her already sensed the nature of her anxiety. After a moment, she nodded and dropped the subject. Dreslya calmed, then turned as the long horns on the walls began to trumpet across the field, announcing the arrival of the lord hunter.

In older times, the Lord Hunter of the Hidden Circle had been selected from the greatest and most respected warriors—those renowned for prowess on the field of battle and powerful devotion to Savras and his temple at Brookhollow. As the unarmored figure of Lord Hunter Baertah rode through the ranks of the assembled hunters, it was apparent that recent times had seen the rise of politics and finances as the measures of virtue and title.

Baertah had a slight build, thin and wiry. His hands were well manicured, as was the fashion among the nobility in larger cities. His pale, unblemished face, perfumed with oils, contrasted with his deep black eyes, making them appear larger and giving him a feral look. Across his back was slung a bow and a quiver of arrows. The blade he carried was a thin rapier, an impractical weapon for a hunter, but popular in Derlusk and Littlewater.

Dreslya nodded to Elisandrya and walked to meet Baertah at the gates. Eli continued to needlessly check her packs and saddle harness. She felt no desire to watch Baertah ride by. She'd been at odds with the lord hunter on more than one occasion and had no need to rekindle old conflicts. She did not envy her sister's duty. As the acting Sibylite of the temple, Dreslya would accompany the lord hunter in the procession through the streets.

Elisandrya waited for the horns to be sounded again, the signal for the gates to be opened so the hunters could enter the city. She mounted Morningstar, her loyal steed named for the bright patch of white on his otherwise pitch black forehead. Reigning him in line with the other hunters, they approached the gates to make their way slowly to the temple.

Her eyes focused on the looming white walls of the temple, the center of Savras's faith in Shandolphyn's Reach, and she hoped to end this ordeal as quickly as possible. Curiosity, though, made her anxious to hear the high oracle's message. Rumors held that Sameska would be stepping down and naming a new high oracle due to her long absence of true prophecy and vision. Eli, however, had no such illusions about the woman. She knew Sameska too well to expect anything but total piety and barely concealed arrogance.

Eli's patience and nerves were already on edge here, in such close proximity to the people and places of her worst memories. She had more than one reason for dreading this return—the primary one waiting at the end of the hunters' parade to the temple.

Dres must have the resolve and fortitude of a hundred hunters, she thought, to face these things on a daily basis. But then, Dres never really found out what had happened. Shouldn't find out.

Eli lowered her head and rode on. Taking a deep breath, she banished her demons and tried to calm herself amid the confining walls and rigid lanes of the populated city. She felt a mild claustrophobia away from the open grassland of the Reach. The eyes of Brookhollow's citizens seemed to bore into her as they stood alongside the route of the hunters, silently casting fethra petals in front of the horses' hooves.

The scattering of the flowers before the host of hunters was a sign of dark times, as if saying the petals were useless and the faithful sought the blessings of their leaders. Eli noted that the onlookers threw down the petals, but each home kept a bundle of the dried leaves by the door in preparation for the growing sickness and the debilitating fever that was no doubt coming.

⊙ ⊙ ⊙ ⊙ ⊙

The sky was an impenetrable pitch beneath the singular tower of Jhareat. Though small globes of bluish light floated in a wide circle around its base, Khaemil did not need them.

His eyes were well suited to the absolute darkness in the ruins and forest beyond. He flexed his fingers, still numb from Morgynn's interrogation, and approached one of Talmen's wizard-priests from behind.

The mumbling man, lost in the trance of spell and prayer, paid no attention to the canomorph. The priest's face was hidden behind a mask resembling a bone devil. The skeletal image was pressed close to the tower wall as the priest carefully and feverishly inscribed the runes that tied the storms to the tower in knots of magic. The metal stylus he used dripped with an acidic ink that burned the symbols into the aged stonework. The scratching sounds it made, in tandem with others who worked alongside him, caused Khaemil to imagine the knuckles of the long dead clawing at tomb walls for escape.

He sighed, memories of Thay and its skilled necromancers bringing a horrid smile to his lips. He looked to the forest, feeling the fevered stares from between the trees, and thought wryly, We've come a long way from dancing bones and playing in the dirt.

"Did you tell her? Does Morgynn know we demand the blood of the Hoarite?" Talmen appeared at Khaemil's side, following the canomorph's gaze into the forest's depths.

"Lady Morgynn has more things on her mind than petty vengeance, Malefactor Talmen. Especially concerning the death of Mahgra." Khaemil did not favor Talmen by reacting to his sudden and silent approach with anything less than nonchalance.

"Our Order is weakened and Morgynn does not react?" The Gargauthan was angry. There were few friends among those of his faith, and the death of a powerful ally was not to be taken lightly.

"Mahgra was a fool, Talmen. He had a pack of gnoll warriors and his own formidable magic. A single man tore apart Mahgra's foothold in Targris. Is this the ally you wish vengeance for? I had no idea loyalty was so strong among your kind. It borders on—compassion." Khaemil said the last to needle Talmen's growing suspicion into a more logical frame of thought. What he said of Mahgra was true, but

Talmen need not know the ghostwalker was drawn into the matter purposely.

"It is not loyalty I speak of, but caution. One man did cause Mahgra's fall and the loss of Targris. Imagine what else such a man might do."

"Hoarites are not known for their heroics. They kill when they are called and move on. He is likely miles away by now."

"We don't know for sure, do we? We have no idea who he is, and we are unable to scry upon him if he walks the shadow road. How can we be sure the oracles have not seen him—and Targris, or even Logfell?"

"You worry too much, Talmen."

"Do I? I've watched too many of our plans in the past become foiled by overconfidence and missed details. Why should this be any different?"

"Because this time, we do not hide."

Talmen looked around in confusion at the ruins and the forest, and huffed an incredulous reply. "I'd say we are smack in the middle of hidden, canomorph."

Khaemil smiled, enjoying Talmen's ignorance and paranoia.

"The oracles, Talmen."

"What of them? Why are you smiling?"

Khaemil enjoyed baiting Talmen with mysteries. The malefactor was nervous and easily pushed to anger.

"They know already. That we are here, and that we are coming."

The Gargauthan's eyes grew wide behind his mask. He was speechless at this news.

Khaemil chuckled deeply as thunder boomed overhead.

"All of our work has been for naught! We might have just as easily charged in as barbarians from the north! What good has creeping into these ruins done?"

Khaemil watched him curiously, wondering how the Gargauthan had managed to survive among the devil-god's faithful for so long. He looked ridiculous pacing about in his hideous mask, gesticulating wildly as he mumbled to himself.

"This is a dangerous game that Morgynn plays at. The Savrathans may appear complacent, but they are visionaries! Seers! We cannot surprise them or catch them off guard. They will anticipate our moves!" Talmen pointed at Khaemil and then to the east, roughly in the direction of Brookhollow and the oracles' temple. He yelled above the noise of the chanting wizard-priests and the grumbling storms they gathered.

"Precisely, fool," Khaemil answered calmly, but irritation in his voice let slip the hidden growl of his bestial nature.

Before Talmen could respond to the insult, both of them became aware of a vibration on the air, a voice that rose above everything else. Looking up at the tower, flashes of light could be seen in Morgynn's window as her voice navigated the winding corridors of magic, becoming a slow shriek of mind-numbing power. Red mist spilled from the window like a living waterfall, taking flight and dancing in a crimson ribbon around the top of the tower. Its sinuous movement matched the singsong quality of Morgynn's spell, and the cloud began to ripple with its own lightning.

Talmen stood in thrall to his lady's voice. Khaemil admired the calming effect Morgynn had on the malefactor, and waited for Talmen's attention to return to the present matter. Morgynn's voice faded away, but the red mist remained, settling in a halo around her room.

Without looking away, Talmen finally responded. "We are all fools, are we not? We follow her where she leads, and only Gargauth knows where we'll end up." He shook his head and turned to Khaemil. "Why, then? Why do we stand here in plain view of our enemies? What does she expect they'll do?"

Khaemil returned his gaze to the forest, spotting the skinned carcass of an untainted fawn hanging from a branch at its edge, an old tradition when fiendish parties desired parley with potential allies. He raised a hairless brow at the sight and turned toward it, then stopped. He looked at Talmen over his shoulder. "Nothing. She expects they'll do nothing at all."

⊛ ⊛ ⊛ ⊛ ⊛

The majority of the assembled hunters packed into the sanctuary and surrounding halls of the inner temple, awaiting the Rite of the Circle and the appearance of High Oracle Sameska. Dreslya stood at the front of the central altar, with Lord Hunter Baertah taking the foremost position in the crowd before her. The lesser oracles were arranged in a semicircle around Dreslya, their heads bowed as they prepared to channel the opening spells of the rite through the acting Sibylite.

Elisandrya knew Dreslya did not particularly like the title of Sibylite or the amount of attention it drew to her as the primary figure in the ceremony until Sameska's arrival. Dres had always been shy and reclusive, but tradition demanded this role of the most senior of the lesser oracles. Other churches devoted to the All-Seeing One referred to all those beneath the high oracle as Prophets and Sibylites, but the Hidden Circle considered the terms archaic. The use of the title of Sibylite was used only when tradition demanded it.

Eli watched from the upper balcony, proud of her sister, but still fidgety and eager to leave the crowded sanctuary and all that it represented. It was within these halls that, as a child, she'd been the first to hear of their parents' death. Under the care of the oracles, Eli and Dres had often studied the tapestries and frescoes of the main sanctuary, lost in the stories they told. Elisandrya had been alone that day when Sameska came to her with the news. As tragic as the day had been, it paled in comparison to the revelations of the following day. Eli had endeavored to become a hunter soon after, and vowed to return only upon Sameska's death.

It was a coward's oath, she thought.

"Sevrak deslotas, emuarte."

Dres's voice carried through the circular chamber, echoing off the walls and growing louder as it lingered near the high dome above and returned in an amplified wave. Eli shook her head to clear it of memories and focus on the ceremony.

A soft glow formed around Dreslya's eyes and drifted to

the oracles on either side of her, until all the oracles stared at the crowd through a white haze of light. Eli envied them at times. They all worshiped Savras in their own ways, but only the oracles might hear his voice, perhaps see through his eyes. The best a hunter could expect were brief and flashing insights, the shadow of a vision—vague hints to what might occur in the immediate future.

"Peshtak revallas, emuarte."

This the oracles said in unison, though Dreslya's voice, as the Sibylite, led the harmony of the rite's prayers, woven in a tapestry of supplication and old magic. The walls began to vibrate with the sound. Tiny lines appeared like cracks at first, unfolding into the wards and runes of spells hidden in the white stone and marble floors. The entire sanctuary became a shining scroll of stone covered in writings of power.

In dangerous times, these arcane and divine defenses fortified the temple and protected the oracles while enhancing their power. Only once in the history of Brookhollow had they been used, and that was long ago, shortly after the temple's completion, when life near the Qurth was more tumultuous. The forest had been calmer since those days, having tested the will of the border towns and finding them formidable. The hunters remained on guard though, patrolling the Qurth's edges and battling those tainted beasts that crawled from its entwined roots.

"Savras. All-Seeing One. As an infant, I opened my eyes and was blind until you showed me what to see. Let us now hear the voice of your sight."

Dreslya turned and lit a single candle at the foot of the altar. She faced Baertah again and sat, joining the other oracles in their semicircle. A veiled alcove behind the altar opened and revealed Sameska, standing proudly with her arms wide. The high oracle stepped forward, allowing all to witness her in her finest robes before speaking. She nodded to the lord hunter and cast her eyes across the gathered warriors and the oracles.

Eli was silent, clenching the rail in front of her and fighting to maintain her composure. The image of Sameska's face, looking down that hawkish nose at the little girl caught in the sanctuary after dark, was fresh in her mind. She looked away, grinding her teeth and attempting to quell her nearly unstrung emotions.

Movement caught her eye. The oracle at the far left of the circle kept rubbing her face with a stained sleeve. Her nose had begun to bleed and the sleeve bore a patch of reddish brown where her attempts to stanch the flow were evident. The glow around them all flickered slightly. The thunder outside, inaudible until now, crept ominously closer.

"Hear me!"

The high oracle's voice was shrill, but the gathered hunters answered, "We hear."

Sameska took a breath to continue, but it caught in her throat. Her voice froze and her face reddened as she struggled to exhale. The designs of magic on the walls and floors flared brightly, like a flash of lightning, then went out, leaving only the glow of the oracles' eyes and the single candle burning at the foot of the altar.

Everyone gasped. Several onlookers stepped forward to assist the high oracle. She waved them back breathlessly, though her arms shook and her legs wavered unsteadily as if she might fall. She grabbed the holy symbol around her neck, a talisman passed down from one high oracle to the next, and doubled over in obvious pain.

Dreslya, eyes closed, maintained her silent chant. Sameska was at the mercy of Savras's power, for good or ill. Elisandrya stood transfixed on the scene, unnerved by the sudden darkness and alert for signs of danger, though her stare never left the high oracle's trembling form.

When Sameska finally lifted her head to face the hushed assembly, her expression seemed detached, as if she were unaware of her surroundings. When she spoke, the voice that issued from her mouth was hollow and brushed across the skin like a swarm of gnats in the heat of summer.

CHAPTER EIGHT

Hear me now."

Sameska's voice buzzed through the crowd, familiar and distant, bereft of ceremony, gripping the nerves in a vice of rapt attention. None could look away, touched in that primal place between reason and wild alarm. All the oracles except one, a young woman on Sameska's right, had passed out. Whether from fear or exhaustion, none could say. The young woman's neck had broken out in a dark rash and her nose continued to spill crimson drops to the floor.

On her hands and knees, the high oracle raised her nearly vacant eyes, peering at her stunned followers through loosened tangles of gray hair.

"An enemy sits at your doorstep, scratching at the edges of your security. I have been shown things. Things that were, things that are, and things to come. We have been brought plague and storms, received silence to our pleading prayers, but Savras speaks now.

"He tells us of the forest and a river of blood, a flood of crimson to rot the soil and feed unnatural trees. He delivers prophecies of dark warriors and foul magic standing at our gates and demanding submission.

"In my visions, these secret truths whispered in my ear, I have seen and heard our fall. We will fail against that which we resist. This must be our test, a crucible from which we can hope to gain favor once again. Stay your swords, leave your gates, and let plague claim who it may. Such is the will of the All-Seeing One."

Her words horrified them all, but none responded except with breathless silence. Nothing in their greatest fears could have prepared them for this. Doom was coming to claim them all, and the greatest act of faith they could perform was to let it happen. Warriors, especially those of the temple, bristled at the thought of inaction and submission, despite prophecy. Elisandrya watched, enraptured as they all were by Sameska's strange behavior. The high oracle stared emotionlessly at them, aware, but lost in the power caught in her throat.

"Hope has not yet abandoned us, though."

The hollow undertones of the high oracle's voice lifted a little, and hope did indeed seem to brighten in the eyes of a few. The hunters listened carefully. None could fathom that Savras would see fit to condemn them all in prophecy without offering some foe to put bow and blade to.

"One man comes to us from the north, across many miles and haunted plains. He alone must see to the ruins deep in the forest. He alone must come to excise that which sits at the delta of decay and complacency. He shall walk on a road of shadow that skirts the borders of the afterlife, where the whispers of the fallen carry him on swift winds."

"Ghostwalker he is known to be, Hoarite and Knight of Old Assuran. We shall hold ourselves mute and incapable, unmoved by emotion or blasphemy, until he arrives to deliver us. Such is the will of Savras—such is his prophecy and the edict of the High Oracle of the Hidden Circle.

"It is done."

Sameska's head slumped for a moment, then lifted as she took a deep breath, gasping for air, wild-eyed and trembling. A torrent of words poured from her mouth, too fast and jumbled to make sense. Moments before the gathering, she had been prepared to deliver those words in triumph. Now they were ashes on her tongue, forgotten and useless. She stepped backward, pushing herself awkwardly and tangling her feet in the hem of her long robes. Several in the gathering ran forward to assist and calm her, still in shock and full of questions.

Hands and faces surrounded Sameska, filling her sight, all but blocking the view of the multi-hued glass dome above. She'd been helpless, trapped in her own body, fighting to speak past the power that had clutched her throat and used her voice. She wanted to scream, feeling as if raped. She wondered if Savras had been with her, within her. Deep down, a black flower of doubt blossomed in her heart. Its roots spread and were cold, twisting her gut as bile boiled in her throat.

How, she wondered—how, with all the wards and protections in the temple, could it have been anything but his voice?

The ceiling spun in her eyes, the dome becoming a swirl of sickening color as questions filled her ears and clawed at the core of her reasoning. She fought again, squeezing her eyes shut and breathing deeply, calming herself and avoiding the well of sorrow that yawned in the back of her mind.

Blinking, she looked closely at the faces above her, not yet hearing them, and saw their awe. They looked upon their high oracle, overcome by the power of their own faith. They sought the wisdom of she who had borne the voice of Savras, she who had spoken to them with his words. The horror that had so consumed her moments ago gave way to pride and wonder.

The questions slowed, becoming more distinct. All of them echoed the same words, the same query, over and over. "What do we do? What do we do?"

Doubt tugged beneath her gathering tears. Slow, swallowed sobs met with her inner exultation at being returned to her rightful place in their sight. She knew all that she had said, knew it all to be true, though it had not been delivered as she had planned. Who was she to question the wisdom of her god, here in this temple, shielded from his enemies?

Collecting herself and clearing her throat, she motioned for silence so she could speak. She sat up and pushed her words past the lump in her throat, past tears of amazement and the pervasive doubt that settled in her stomach like a ball of lead.

In a solemn voice of command and practiced wisdom, she responded.

"Nothing. We must do nothing."

Elisandrya stood at the balcony, clinging to the rail in white-knuckled anger and frustration. Dreslya knelt below, listening as Sameska finally answered the barrage of questions, her answers loud enough to be heard by all. Dres turned to look at her sister, worry and confusion etched in her face, tears trailing down her cheeks.

Eli looked away. Her eyes fell on a place to the left of the altar, shadowed, but just within the radius of newly lit candles close to Sameska. Others noticed as well. Those who had heard what they needed from Sameska turned to that spot, frightened and curious. Sameska eyed these, hunting for doubt in their whispered voices, seeking any hint of disbelief among them.

Glinting in that flickering light, a stain of dark crimson slowly turned brown, marking the place of the oracle who had bled when the temple went dark.

⊙ ⊙ ⊙ ⊙ ⊙

The people of Targris milled about the streets, searching for family and friends and retrieving possessions cast into flooded gutters. Most of the fires had been quenched by the heavy rain, but the damage had been done, leaving several structures blackened and shrouded in steamy mist. No one neared the scene of the terrible battle or looked too long at the warrior. Quinsareth slumbered for some time, having passed out on the porch of the late mayor's home.

Curious children had crept closer, hoping to catch a glimpse of the stranger. Seeing his half-closed eyes, with their thin slivers of milky white showing beneath fluttering lids, they ran away. Rumors of the "demon warrior" ran wild among the youngsters and were only partly dismissed by their parents and fearful older siblings.

After Mahgra's fall, Quinsareth had crawled to the steps of the house and attempted to dress his wounds with strips of cloth from his cloak and massage strained muscles. He'd been alert, certain that at any moment, his field of vision would liquefy and waver, showing him the distant shadows calling him elsewhere. He'd sat for some time, pretending that no one else existed, hoping that any thankful souls would leave him in peace. After a time, he saw that few were bold enough to even look in his direction.

The weather had improved in that time, leaving only the rain to patter loudly on the roof of the wooden porch. The shadows never came and the sound of the rain lulled him into a long-overdue slumber. His dreams, when he had them, were nearly the same. Always he stood on the edge of a great cliff, overlooking a lush valley growing wild with greenery, flowers, and massive trees. The air was charged with energy and creation. He would run all day, looking for a way down into that strange, dreaming home.

He had never reached that faraway land. Many times, he had considered jumping from the cliff, but silent hunters would appear at the edges of the forest below with bright blades in hand. Fey creatures regarded him curiously—lithe bodies sheathed in radiant armor, dark stares colored in shades of threat. They gave him pause as they watched him with pearly white eyes, so like his own.

The porch roof leaked, and before long, fat drops of water splashed into his upturned face, waking him from forbidden dreamscapes. He spat water from his mouth and wiped it from his eyes, flinching as his back complained at the sudden movement. His entire body ached as he rose to sit on the top step, rubbing his left shoulder gingerly beneath his armor. He had often slept on the ground without removing his armor, and it seemed so natural to him that he felt strange when afforded the opportunity to sleep in a real bed. Judging by the lack of onlookers, no offer would be forthcoming any time soon.

He looked at the people in the distance picking up their lives and casting off those bits destroyed or befouled. He shook his head, but could not feel the surprise he supposed he should feel at still being there. The call of shadow had not come, would not come until his work was complete.

Much as he wished it, the ogre mage was not powerful enough to have been the source of what he'd seen—or not seen—in Logfell. Something else held him here, though somewhere deep inside, he questioned his own motives. He could easily leave on his own. He had no covenant with Hoar, merely a vague understanding, a meeting of the god's purpose and Quin's lack of direction. Somewhere deep inside, in those places that dreamed of the verdant land he could not reach, there was a sense of shame. Much as he knew he could travel any road, only the shadowed one led him to the kill, to injustice and to blood.

He struggled to stand, but something on the porch caught his attention. A basket, laden with what food could be gathered, and a skin of wine were placed near to where he'd been sleeping. He looked around, but no one was near. Through the rain he saw a middle-aged man, standing just outside the charred remains of the small temple razed by the gnolls, who looked in Quin's direction. His face was expressionless, and he leaned on an oak staff. He nodded to Quin, acknowledging him. Quin, unsure, nodded back, taken off guard by the man's steady stare.

Quinsareth turned away, back to the food. He picked at it slowly at first, then allowed his hunger to take over. Dried fish wrapped in broad leaves, some stale bread and pieces of fruit, all of this he devoured, then washed it down with the salty-sweet berry wine. He spared most of the wine and used the leaves to collect drops of the falling rain, quenching his thirst without clouding his mind.

He stood slowly, favoring his left side and carefully stretching his tender back. The ogre's lightning had burned a scar down his spine and the skin felt seared as if from a hot skillet. His tunic and armor chafed against the wound like sack cloth. He would need the shadow road's healing touch soon. It looked as if Targris's temple was empty, or its clerics had burned along with it. So where would he go? This region was unknown to him. Where might he look to find those behind Logfell's and Targris's attacks?

He looked toward the old man, who still studied the ruins of the temple and the charred remains of its gardens. Steeling himself and checking his equipment, patting the scabbard of the sleeping Bedlam, he descended the steps and made his way to introduce himself.

Dreading interaction with someone who did not threaten his life, Quinsareth made sure to walk loudly through the puddles to avoid startling the man. An unnecessary concern, as the man was obviously aware of him. Absently, he rubbed at the patches of dried blood on his face and lamented the loss of his traveling hat, most likely washed away in the flood along the side of the road. He dipped his head low, allowing thick strands of wet hair to obscure his unnerving eyes.

The man saw Quinsareth coming near and didn't move aside or turn away. Quin sighed and cursed himself for not carrying at least one map.

The burnt smell of the temple was strong but tempered with the scent of rain on the cool air. Quin stood awkwardly, staring into the broken windows and the steaming blackness within. The old man regarded him for a few moments and turned back to the burned temple, as if sensing the aasimar's troubled demeanor. A low-hanging branch from within the temple's garden shielded them both from the worst of the downpour.

"You fought well." The man's voice was low and emotionless, but it startled Quinsareth all the same.

"It was what it was, little more." Not fond of compliments, he could not help the edge in his reply.

"As you say, stranger." The old man turned to the aasimar. "This attack was wild and unexpected—perhaps its end deserved to be so as well. You are injured?"

"I will heal," he said, adjusting his left arm behind his cloak. "See to your own, elder. I must be leaving soon."

"Fair enough. Where will you go? You'll find naught but

plague near the forest, and Derlusk is shut up tight for fear of it."

Plague. He'd sensed the familiar smell of it in Logfell, but hadn't placed it. There was indeed something else beyond ogres and gnolls at work. He doubted this was any ordinary plague.

"Where else does the forest run? South, to more towns?"

"Aye, south, where you'll find Littlewater, most likely as tight as Derlusk. Beyond that is Brookhollow, the city of the oracles and the Hidden Circle. This ruin was one of theirs, but it has been months since their last visit."

Quin studied the temple, still not comfortable meeting the elder's gaze. Beyond the burned wood and stone, he could feel the presence of the forest. South it would be. Whatever held him in this region would be close to that forest.

"You should leave this place, lest the rest of it fall to some strange foe as well."

"Perhaps, but we will stay. We will rebuild. It is the wisdom of the Qurth that keeps us going, along with our faith in the oracles."

"Where are your oracles now—where were they today?" Quin asked, snapping the question out before he could stop himself. This man's faith was none of his affair, despite his misgivings.

The elder thought a moment, then answered, "I honestly do not know. It is not my place to question the oracles, but Savras always provides despite hardship and danger. You came to us, and I no longer believe in coincidence."

This time, Quin did bite back his reply, angered by the complacency in the man's tone. He had seen towns destroyed for lack of help or preparedness. He simply motioned to the temple and the people in the distance, some crying, some dead in the street, and said, "I did not come soon enough."

"Sometimes it takes flame and death to awaken that which has lain dormant for too long. Occasionally, the destruction of that which we hold dear brings us closer to what we really are. I do not mourn a burned temple or momentary pain—I see opportunity. You came when it was necessary and no sooner."

Quinsareth turned to face the elder, ignoring his pain to stand straighter and brush the hair from his eyes. Dried blood still stained his fair skin, and his gaze of milky pearl settled on the old man. The elder met the stare, but he could not suppress a brief shudder. A few people nearby glanced at him but quickly regretted their boldness, scurrying away from Quin's menacing visage.

He focused on the chill again, the ice in his blood, calling the shadows to open his path, directing it south toward Littlewater. He did not know exactly where he went, but the shadows would carry him true, knowing the roads he did not.

The old man backed away, obeying the fear Quin carried about him. The puddles near Quin turned black as did the rain which fell upon his head and shoulders. The aura of a darker world haloed his body. Quinsareth spoke before turning to disappear in the shadowalk, shaking his head slightly and reaching a hesitant, though oddly troubling, conclusion. "I am not like you."

In a flash of distant lightning, he was gone.

For the first time that she could recall, Elisandrya had lied to her sister.

She gripped the reigns and spurred Morningstar to greater speed, galloping through the muddied plain beyond Brookhollow's walls, followed by several others. These few who doubted the high oracle had left secretly in the dead of night, flirting with blasphemy in the face of Sameska's edict.

Riding behind her was Rhaeme Fallow, with whom she'd discussed the late night ride after the gathering's disturbing conclusion. Though they agreed on the necessity of their actions, the pair's tumultuous history with one another had caused curious stares from passersby. Rhaeme had vehemently cautioned against speaking with Dreslya before leaving. Reluctantly, Eli had agreed.

She had left a note for Dreslya, attempting to explain her

absence, but guilt rode with her as she headed north along the forest's edge. There were more reasons than she could justify that spurred her to action. Most of these had little to do with Sameska's recent performance and much to do with that one day. The day Eli's world had died and after which nothing seemed right anymore.

Dres would not understand, she thought. I barely understand myself.

Rhaeme and the others had their own reasons, but all of them had agreed, soon after the gathering, that something was wrong. Lord Hunter Baertah was too trustful of the inconstant Sameska and would never violate her word, especially if it threatened to involve getting dirty.

They all watched the forest on their left warily, wondering what new horror lay within its tangles and thorns. None of them doubted Sameska's claim of encroaching evil, but these were warriors of action, unable to sit still.

Several moments passed in which Elisandrya had almost stopped to turn back, still unsure of her own instinct and fearful for Dres. She never pulled the reigns, however, never acted on fear or insecurity. She sought the guidance of Savras many times but did not truly expect an answer. His answer had already come—plague and evil and mysterious warriors from the north. All that was left for her in that answer was nothing, to do nothing.

No, she thought, I'll do what I can, prophecy or not, Savras forgive me.

She would seek the Hoarite, the ghostwalker.

New rain lashed her face as she rode. She felt a little freer, a little more in control of her own life as the ground rushed by beneath churning hooves, carrying her farther and farther from Brookhollow. Temple life would never be hers, not now and maybe never. She left those concerns to Dres and the oracles.

Her sister's green eyes came to mind, Dres's faith and fears, her words of caution in every endeavor. She loved her sister and respected her decisions, but quietly, under her breath and drowned by the noise around her, she said apologetically to the image in her mind, "I'm not like you."

The storm grumbled overhead, churning as she rode against its winds.

◉ ◉ ◉ ◉ ◉

Khaemil sat on a section of the fallen wall of Jhareat, proudly reflecting on his successful meeting in the forest while licking the blood of the offered fawn from his lips and teeth. The last he'd seen of the Order's new ally had been their yellow eyes, tiny pinpoints of light disappearing into the folds of twisted and cracked trees.

He raised his head and gargled as rain filled his open mouth, feeling wild and blooded on fresh kill. It had been many years since he'd conversed with a kindred spirit, even a half-breed, and he longed a little bit for the hunting in Avernus. The tracking and killing of lost souls, howling at a burning sky and playing assassin for devilish lords, were sports he would always remember. Perhaps one day to which he might return.

Much of the malice he saw in those long ago devils he also saw in Morgynn from time to time. He knew she was well versed in the Gargauthan dogma, but her heart never really invested in what might pass her lips to quell Talmen's doubts. Power was her thrall, though what use she intended to make of such dominion he was not sure. True evil did not seem to rest in her nature—it was simply an afterthought, the place where she could comfortably work toward her own ends.

The tower in the center of the wasted clearing had ceased its crimson dance. Khaemil knew Morgynn rested within or lay enraptured by her own blood and magic. He wondered if she actually slept this time.

He decided to wait a bit longer, to enjoy the view and his full stomach.

If Morgynn slumbered, it would be folly to wake her. Morgynn's nightmares rarely stayed in her own head, and her blood saw little difference between friend and foe.

CHAPTER NINE

Morgynn descended the spiraling stairway in a daze, feeling the tingle of magic across her skin and the heat of its passing in her veins. She cast as she skipped down the steps, twirling the words of her spell gracefully past her lips. The warmth of the magic flared on her bare throat, humming on her vocal cords. Her body trembled, flesh rippling as the power took shape. The tips of her fingers blackened, becoming shadowy and transparent. The transformation crawled up her arms, leaving an ephemeral darkness in its wake.

She smiled and gasped as the change reached her throat, turning her lips and mouth into a ragged hole and condensing her eyes into tiny points of white light. Her hair was a black flame tossed in unceasing winds in a realm beyond the tower. The change complete, she felt her bare feet escape gravity and she floated above the floor, an incorporeal shred of staring darkness. She was the very picture of the soul she imagined she still carried inside, lost in time, possibly still buried in the dirt of Narfell.

She looked to the distant ceiling, the floor of her chamber above, and remembered a time when she had been in another hole, looking up into the eyes of righteous barbarians. The Sedras had come to lay waste to all that she'd accomplished since leaving them. Her mother, brandishing mace and shield, summoned fires from that god of dawn and flame, Lathander.

She blinked, as best she could without true eyes or lids in her wraithlike form. Her vision adjusted back to the present shadows above, showing her old stone and the fine, spidery cracks of age. She looked down and floated toward the wall, melting through it and peering out its edge at the mumbling priest who drew smoking runes into the surface of the stone.

He could not see her. His eyes fluttered behind a mask of sinewy muscle and bone, lost in arcane mumbling and malignant prayers. She slunk downward and drifted along the ground beneath him like a stream of brackish water, barely a shadow among those cast by the glowing orbs of the wizard-priests.

She wished to avoid Talmen, keeping her secrets to herself. Taking the wraithform was less efficient than teleporting, but she enjoyed the sensation of weightlessness and the constant chill of its nature. The cold was as familiar and numbing as the windswept plains of her childhood.

Across the stones she flowed, under and through them, making her way to the forest and the pale trees Khaemil had told her about. She'd sensed them before and had thought of ignoring them, but her mind changed along with her mood. Their presence intrigued her more than their defiance made them a nuisance. A use could be found for such allies—their obvious fear of her made them perfect for service.

Well away from the eyes of the Gargauthans, and Talmen in particular, she glided past the first few trees, sliding through low-hanging limbs and clawlike branches. Tasting their bitter bark through her misty form, she sensed ancient magic still pulsing in the sap and roots. She envied the kind of power that had changed this once peaceful forest into a haven of monsters and perversions of nature.

A Calishite, she'd been told, had cursed the forest and the city of Qurth hundreds of years earlier during the Mage Purges of the Shoon Dynasty. That fallen wizard's spell had destroyed the cities now buried in the Qurth Forest. The forest's magic became centered on the city of Qurth, where the Calishite had been executed. The lingering potency of that magic clung like an invisible mist to everything around her. She swam in arcane currents that thrived and spread like a living creature, born of a mob's righteous vitriol and the Calishite's violent death.

Close to her destination, she stopped her vaporous travel and cancelled the spell, feeling well protected from prying eyes. She regretted ending the magic even as blood flooded her limbs and breast, an onslaught of beating warmth that blushed her skin for a moment as it returned. She stood on a thick carpet of dead leaves, dark green grass, and vines that flourished in the forest's interior.

Sprawling bushes of razorvine and bloodthorn surrounded her as she casually walked between their reaching tendrils. She brushed her hands across the tops of razorleaf bushes as she passed. Cousin to the razorvine, its leaves were hard and sharp, whipping against the flesh on stiff stems to open wounds that fed its thick, knotted root system. Bright yellow berries tempted the creatures of the forest to pass within reach. The addictive toxin in those berries assured the return of animals large enough to survive the wounds. Although scarred, some forest creatures returned often to sate themselves and the hungry plant.

Morgynn admired the simplicity of the plant's resources as she watched the leaves slice her hands and wrists, imagining the frustration when the wounds quickly closed, refusing to feed the plant's appetite. The razorvines and bloodthorns lashed her calves as she passed, receiving equal reward for their efforts. The forest, impassable for some, was to her a savage and malicious garden of delights and wonder. Her progress was unhindered where others might fall and become food for the vicious foliage. This thought gave her short and hidden journey purpose, bringing her to a solution that stood in the form of three white oak trees.

As Morgynn stepped into the semicircle of oaks in the small grove, pale leaves shook, creating a feline hiss, despite the wind being gentle this far into the forest. Their trunks were a blend of white and ash colors, looking almost petrified if not for the sharp-angled leaves that hung from gracefully twisting branches. Morgynn could feel their presence, hiding behind the bark, peering from knotholes and the healed cracks of old wounds. Her feet felt the shuddering of long roots beneath the ground, trembling at her approach.

The hissing turned to whispers. Syllables and voices hid in a cacophony of tiny noises, growing into a wave of sound and sylvan magic that carried the scents of decay and tainted soil. The bark writhed and flowed like liquid as the power sought to overcome her. A chorus of words and soothing chants filled her mind, flowing through her and seeking weaknesses in her spirit.

Her previous amusement with this encounter was gone.

Though she'd expected resistance, this outright assault made her angry. In kind, she cast a spell of her own. She wove her words around theirs, countering their effects and wrapping around those seeking songs with melodies of thorns. Her magic followed the charms back to the trees, to the roots, to branches and leaves, a burning and stinging surge of power.

The whispering stopped, and the grove was silent a moment before screams and shrieks shook the branches, sending a shower of autumn leaves down on Morgynn's feet. Bark erupted in violent movement. Twigs grew, sprouting clawed fingers, then withdrew back into the trunks. Mouths opened and closed around knotholes and veins in the wood, exposing needlelike fangs and tongues of pale green.

Agony permeated the oaks and subsided only at Morgynn's word, and she enjoyed feeling their suffering through the forced link between them. The power they had sought to work upon her retreated swiftly once freed. She had barely released the magic before a trio of rasping, feminine voices erupted from the trees.

"Why do you torment us? Leave us, and keep your ruins!"

The voices overlapped and echoed each other. Morgynn reined in her own emotions, adopting a tone of diplomacy.

"Why do you defy me when there is much we could share with one another?"

"The forest is ours!" The trees' branches shook with each word, emphasizing their rage and hatred at this mortal woman.

"This forest will belong to the hearths and homes of your enemies, should I so will it!"

The oaks fell silent, considering Morgynn's words and weighing her possible power. She knew she had struck a nerve by threatening the forest itself. Though they were of a darker nature, nature was still their life's blood. Finally they replied.

"Your boasts are hollow, human. Such magic has not walked the Realms for centuries."

Morgynn heard an edge of hesitation in their voices and noticed pale, red eyes blossoming like sick flowers from their trunks, looking her up and down.

"You are correct. Power such as I claim is old and forgotten, a relic sought and rarely found."

Laughter was their response, mocking her bluff and echoing through the forest like a swarm of insects and snapping twigs. Morgynn smiled back at them, enjoying the moment and cupping a hand next to a small pouch at her belt. At a word of command the pouch responded, sending its contents into her open palm. She closed her fingers around the object.

She held her fist forward, palm upward, fighting the trembling anger that hid behind her cool façade. Staring daggers into the trees, their pale crimson orbs regarded her curiously as they continued to giggle and chuckle. Opening her clenched fingers, she revealed an ebon object resting within them.

The trees' laughter slowed and hesitation returned to their chortling voices as they beheld her prize. A smooth stone of marble it seemed, black as night, with lightning veins of ivory shot through its surface. What they could not see were the minuscule writing, ancient runes, and spells inscribed on its surface in ivory ink. All was written in a language long feared and considered taboo by the superstitious of the Border Kingdoms and Calimshan.

It was the alphabet of the djinn, the ancient masters of the Old Empire that had stretched from the Shining Sea to the far edges of the Lake of Steam. Though the letters and meanings were invisible to them, the stone's power radiated like a cold sun, draining their mirth and sobering their attentions.

"Do you know what this is?" Morgynn stared at the three massive oaks over the top of the black bauble. Though smooth and glassy, it reflected nothing around it, not even the brief flashes of lightning through the branches above.

Their silence and trepidation answered her question as she stepped closer, bringing the stone's icy aura closer to them, letting its chill settle on their exposed roots, which squirmed almost imperceptibly, trying to sink further into the dirt, away from its touch.

"It is called the Stone of Memnon. Do not be fooled by the ice in its heart. It carries the flame of the fire djinn, the efreet."

"Take it away!" The voices returned fully to their fear and Morgynn saw the foliage at the perimeter of the grove shifting and crawling, the razorvines and bloodthorns responding to the sylvan call of the oaks' inhabitants. Their crimson eyes disappeared, folding closed and melting back into the security of the white bark and the wooded flesh beneath.

Sensing their intent, Morgynn called a sphere of force around herself, snapping the words of the spell out like a whip, just as the animated plants lunged, uncoiling their greenish black tentacles. They thrashed against the sphere's transparent surface and the grove grew darker as the living forest enshrouded the unbreakable magic. Only Morgynn and the three oaks stood within her sphere, with her threat still pulsing in the palm of her outstretched hand.

"This tiny stone will shrivel your roots, bleed you dry, and reduce this forest to a wasted desert. This is the relic sought and rarely found, a sample of that old magic that ruled kingdoms and laid them to rest." Morgynn turned the stone over and grasped it between her thumb and index finger. "Shall I plant it here with you?"

Only the serpentine wall of vines and thorns made any sound, creaking and rustling against the barrier, growing thicker and darker. Quietly, almost conspiratorially, one soft, dry voice spoke without the others, "Your tower will be exposed. Your threat still rings hollow."

The other two voices hissed from within their trees, attempting to silence the third.

"True, but I will be alive to deal with the consequences. You three will be dead, along with your oaks."

Several branches moved then and Morgynn tensed, prepared to punish them again for further defiance, but the white limbs shifted, entwining in each other's embrace. Their horrible whispers were quieter now, directed at one another, the sound of dry leaves blowing in a winter wind on a barren field.

As they conversed, the animated plants surrounding the grove retreated, falling away to their roots and shadows, resuming their passive roles and hungry waiting. A bloodthorn snapped behind her, ensnaring a screaming animal flushed out by the commotion. Its cries weakened as the thirsty plant drained its tainted blood.

Sensing growing wisdom in the strange discussion between the pale oaks, Morgynn lowered her arm but still held the stone in her fist. She had no desire to drain the artifact at that moment. She would sooner destroy the three with her own power than waste such a treasure.

Finally, a consensus reached, the branches untangled from one another and returned to their natural positions. The pale eyes appeared again, shyly from behind the trees, hiding themselves as they once again spoke in unison.

"We will comply. The pale sisters are at your service, but we keep our loyalty to ourselves."

Morgynn smiled and returned the stone to her pouch,

removing its chill from the already cool air. "A wise decision, ladies. Enjoy your forest for now, and hamper not my minions. I shall call upon you when the time comes."

She turned her back on them and returned to the deeper forest, still wary of treachery but trusting her instincts. As her shell of force dissolved, the winds of the storm rushed back to life in the grove. The treetops swayed as fallen leaves mumbled and spun in the pull of greater forces.

⊙ ⊙ ⊙ ⊙ ⊙

"Elisandrya! Stop!"

Rhaeme strained to be heard above the pounding hooves of the galloping steeds and the furious thunder overhead as they rode farther north. Eli had heard him the first three times, but had spurred Morningstar even faster. This time, though, she'd glanced back and caught his eye, banishing her attempt to pretend otherwise.

Reluctantly, she reined her tired horse to a stop, gripping the leather tightly and dreading what she knew would come.

Rhaeme pulled alongside her with concerned eyes. Of all the hunters, she'd been closest with him, but like most of her relationships, it had fizzled from her own lack of commitment. She felt too much danger in being involved, being too close. She raised her voice to be heard over the wind and rain.

"What is it?"

He waited, looking at the other seven hunters who sat stoically in their saddles, puffs of steam rising around their faces. She had no desire to hear his arguments, but he was persistent and stubborn, much like herself.

She looked up at him. Her eyes were set, her face a mask of resignation and hesitation. Rhaeme was handsome, as handsome as any man to whom she'd been attracted. Chestnut brown hair flowed to his shoulders and deep brown eyes cast perfect reflections of her own. His dress and ready bow reminded her too much of her father, though that face had blurred with time.

His dark eyes regarded her knowingly from beneath his

hood and she looked away, at the pommel of her saddle, to the ground and the heavy splatter of constant rain.

"We're going. You know that."

Eli didn't reply except to lift her head and stare north. Rain streamed down her face and she resisted the urge to shiver.

"I know what you seek, Eli, but the rest of us . . . the rest of us don't have your faith, such as it is." Rhaeme's tone was firm, but understanding. "We're going into the Qurth. Beyond all prophecy or oracle's madness, something is there!"

"I know," she answered, still not meeting his familiar gaze. "I have no doubt."

"Then come with us! Prove your own fears! Sameska is lost, you said so yourself."

His voice became urgent and insistent, almost angry with her, which dredged forth her bottled anger.

"What I said was not meant for you, Rhaeme! I've slept alone ever since then, if you remember correctly. What I feel about Sameska is my own business. You have no idea . . ."

"Exactly Eli, I don't have any idea! Whose fault is that?" He shook his head and looked away, clearly regretting his words. He continued more calmly. "Come with us, Eli. There's nothing for you to find this way."

Elisandrya's lip quivered with emotion, but she mastered it, refusing to let him think he'd affected her.

"No. I have to prove something else first, and that lies to the north."

"What's that?"

She looked him in the eye, at once thankful for the rain. "That I'm right."

Rhaeme pursed his lips and looked to the others, anxious to be on their way. Looking back, he said, "You'll find what you're looking for, then. We'll miss your bow."

He nodded to the remaining hunters and turned his mount west to face the forest. Over his shoulder, he called back to her. "Farewell, Elisandrya Loethe. Despite all, I hope you find him." He spurred his horse to meet the others. The Qurth yawned as a black silhouette before them, a splotch of waiting darkness.

Eli watched him until he disappeared behind sheets of rain, where even the lightning could not show him to her.

⊛ ⊛ ⊛ ⊛ ⊛

From a distance, the surviving tower of Jhareat pointed like a jagged bone into the black vortex of flashing thunderheads above. It rose from the center of a bowl-shaped depression, surrounded by the forest, which sloped steeply downhill toward the crumbled bits of stone, all that was left of Jhareat's once strong outer walls. Whether the slope was natural or some ancient crater made during the city's fall, Morgynn could not tell.

The strange tales of the ruin of the once mighty city were sketchy and fanciful at best, so she hadn't pressed her contacts in Derlusk for more than its location. She'd grown tired of sagelike explanation and speculation.

From behind a large stone, Khaemil appeared, slowly and deliberately making himself visible as he approached. He had learned not to surprise Morgynn, and made all effort to ignore his primal instinct to remain quiet and unseen.

Patiently, for the moment, she waited as he came closer, noting the grim look of bad tidings on his ebony face. Her mood froze in midswing, somewhere between her recent success with the pale sisters and whatever nerve Khaemil might choose to strike in the next few moments. Chaos boiled in her mind and she closed her eyes to take a deep breath, dreading her own wild emotions.

"My Lady Morgynn," Khaemil bowed slightly at the waist, his eyes never leaving hers.

"Yes, Khaemillenthranux, I hear you. Speak."

Her use of his true name caused him to wince as if jabbed by a dagger. A fiend's true name held power for those with the proper knowledge, and Morgynn's tone conveyed her growing impatience clearly. She knew something was wrong. Sweating in the chilly air, he obeyed her.

"Talmen and his followers have detected a presence in the forest, east of here." He swallowed and gritted his teeth, but kept his eyes level as he reported. "Hunters from

Brookhollow have entered the edge of the Qurth. They seek us even now, just past the fringes."

Words failed her and rage bloomed in her heart, racing through her body. Outwardly, she showed no signs of her turmoil, but Khaemil stepped back a pace. She could almost see his pulse beating in the air, fluttering to escape her anger. Morgynn looked to the east, sniffing the air and searching for those wayward heartbeats, foreign to her. She would know them.

"Hold still," she said, walking purposefully toward him as one might approach a door.

Such was her purpose.

Her hands entered his chest, splashing crimson as they disappeared. Her arms and torso followed, racing along his veins and through his body.

A vast plain of red opened before her eyes, crisscrossed with corridors and tunnels. This was the void of the blood's magic, one river leading to the next, the connection known only by those of her kind. Distance meant little here, and time even less. Instantly she was drawn to those faint heartbeats she imagined and could now see. Beacons of pulsing red light called her to their corridors, their tunnels.

⊙ ⊙ ⊙ ⊙ ⊙

As he felt Morgynn's presence pass into him then leave him, Khaemil gasped for breath. He was winded, but otherwise none the worse for wear. It was never pleasant to be the portal that initiated the bloodwalk, but it was a far less fearsome fate than befell the recepient.

CHAPTER TEN

The forest felt like a living, breathing beast, fighting the hunters' efforts to penetrate its depths. Rhaeme's curved blade hacked ceaselessly through the thick undergrowth of twisted vegetation. They marched in a sideways gait, their armored sword arms bent to push forward, wielding the curved blades typical of Hidden Circle warriors. Their shield arms held thick ironvine cloaks tightly to protect against lashing razor leaves and the seeking tendrils of bloodthorns.

The rain had eased since they'd passed beneath the almost-solid canopy of branches. Rhaeme was glad for the gloom of the sky beyond that wooded ceiling. In sunnier times, he'd witnessed the effect of the trees in silhouette. He knew they looked like giant arms and fingers, interlaced and huddled together like conspirators over their victims. The image was unsettling, as was the way the canopy moved as a single organism when the wind was strong.

He put such thoughts out of his mind and focused on the task at hand, locating an easier passage so the group might search in a more stealthy manner. The only saving grace of the heavy rain was that it covered the sound of their movement. Their noisy approach echoed in his ears.

Better to get in, discover the source of the region's troubles, and get out, he thought. Easier said than done.

The hunters were growing nervous. The improvised path they'd left behind them would soon begin to close itself as the forest's predatory foliage reset its traps and vicious intentions. Rhaeme stopped and waved the man behind him ahead to take point. He needed a moment to rest his weary arm and take stock of the situation.

Direction was a problem inside the Qurth. Landmarks were few, and, when found, were well hidden. He'd hoped to find a small clearing, some overgrown ruin or sign of intrusion, perhaps even the sound or sight of an enemy encampment. His prayers to Savras had so far yielded only confirmations of his own fears. The Hunters of the Hidden Circle were not as receptive as the oracles to visions and prognostication, but they were gifted with a sense of insight, usually manifesting as flashes or images.

Each time he'd attempted to focus his awareness on this ability, he'd smelled blood, stronger and stronger as they moved inward. He closed his eyes and again raised the small ring of dried fethra to his lips. The scent came again, this time accompanied by a warmth that covered his skin like a wave of fever. Sucking in a quick breath, he opened his eyes and looked past the men ahead of him. He sensed that they were being watched. The feeling of distant eyes on him was chilling. The darkness of the forest revealed nothing, but he was innately aware of something getting closer.

The three men at the rear recognized his alarm and froze. The four ahead continued moving. A young man called Laen, a hunter for barely a year, whispered, "What do you see?"

Rhaeme did not answer right away. He wasn't sure how, but he knew that whatever they sought had found them first.

As he prepared to alert those in the front, the point man who had replaced him moments ago lurched to a stop and groaned. The man's sword fell from his hand and he turned around, wide-eyed and clawing at his stomach furiously. The groan became a gurgling scream as blood streamed from beneath his leather breastplate. Then it was pushed outward violently, torn apart from the inside.

⊙ ⊙ ⊙ ⊙ ⊙

Though she had ridden Morningstar hard, Eli knew she might not reach Littlewater by morning. A frantic urgency had infected her since parting with Rhaeme several miles back. She had other means of travel, but she was always distrustful of magic, even when used for great benefit. She also knew that sitting in the rain, sinking in the mud, and cursing the road ahead would do nothing for her dilemma.

Magic it would be then, she thought.

She took a small pouch from her belt. Shielding it from the rain, Eli untied the leather thong to sniff the mixture of herbs and other unknown ingredients.

She'd obtained the dry potion from the druidic shamans who lived around Brookhollow, in the wilder parts of the Shandolphyn. Practitioners of the wizardly arts, they were a natural sort, loyal to the old traditions of the Shaaryan tribes. This appealed to Eli's love of the open grassland. Her father had introduced her to them when she was young. Many nights she had camped with the Ghedia, as they were known, a name meaning "grass witch" in the old Shaaran tongue. One of their number, Lesani, had been like a second mother to her ever since. She missed Lesani's stories, songs, and practical wisdom and wished she were with her, but the nomadic Ghedia were difficult to locate. She focused on Lesani's lessons as she continued her task.

From another bag, Eli pulled half a handful of sugar and carefully poured it into the mixture. Tying the pouch tightly, she shook it and began to hum an old song whose origins lay in the wide plains of the Shaar. She stroked Morningstar's soaked mane and neck as she hummed the tune, leaning close to his ear to be heard over the storm.

The effect was almost immediate. Morningstar's shivering stopped and she felt his tense neck and back relax as the familiar tune soothed him. Eli knew that the potion would take effect immediately, possibly unnerving her mount. Calming him first could save her a broken neck when the magic took hold.

Finally, she loosened the knot around the bag and leaned forward, proffering the contents to Morningstar. He licked suspiciously, but then the sugar caught his attention and he ate the mixture quickly, shoving his muzzle deep into the pouch as Eli gripped her saddle horn tightly. She let the empty pouch fall, and though Morningstar had been calmed by her humming, his relaxed muscles began to move, taking him from a trot to a full gallop.

Gritting her teeth, Eli lay against Morningstar's neck and tightened her legs at his sides. Gently, she kicked his flanks and his sudden, jarring leap forward tossed back her heavy hood, turning the lashing rain into a hail of needles on her skin. After adjusting to the horse's unnatural speed, she pulled the hood back over her head and watched as the world flew by in a dark, wet blur. She recalled the first time Lesani had allowed her to use the mixture and remembered the bruises she'd received falling off the racing horse. In those days, Lesani had been quiet about Eli's past, content to enjoy her company and show her the charms of the wild. When Eli grew older, they spoke about her parents.

Lesani's wizened voice had not spoken the affirmations that Eli wished to hear. The older woman had not told her to ride forth with bow and sword to claim justice. Eli hadn't even been sure there was justice to claim, but she had bristled at Lesani's caution and patience. She regretted that argument, and though forgiven for her youth, had never forgotten it. She rode now for Lesani as well, with bow and sword, to discover if justice did indeed exist.

Soon, she made out the walls and watch fires of Littlewater in the distance. The worst of the storm was behind her and she breathed a sigh of relief as the potion wore off. Morningstar slowed. Wild-eyed and prancing like a colt, he trembled excitedly in the aftermath of the magical swiftness.

Raising her head, the first thing Eli noticed were dark figures approaching, long spears held out defensively.

The soldiers spread out in a line before her, blocking her path to the city. She held her hands up to show she was unarmed and meant no harm. The commander approached from behind the line of spears, a rapier at his side. Eli resisted the urge to roll her eyes. The man was almost the spitting image of Lord Hunter Baertah, right down to his manicured hands and the heady scent of perfume.

"Who are you and what is your business here, Savrathan?"

His voice was high and nasal, his tone practically sneering the final word as he looked down his sharp nose at the fethra ring hanging from Morningstar's bridle. Elisandrya raised an eyebrow and nodded in the direction of the city.

"Are those of the Hidden Circle no longer welcome in Littlewater?"

"When profitable, but plague bears little profit unless one holds the cure. Since I see no oracles behind you, I assume your business is irrelevant?"

Eli almost laughed in disbelief. She'd received cold receptions in Littlewater before, but this was ridiculous. She considered it best to respond in kind.

"I bring no cure, nor promise of one. I am Elisandrya Loethe of the Hunters of the Hidden Circle and I travel alone. My business is my own."

The officer digested this nonchalantly, but he did not order the soldiers to lower their spears.

"Have you seen no others on the road? Foreigners, perhaps?" He posed the question almost innocently, then became serious, staring at her intently. "A lone, cloaked figure with fair hair and strange eyes traveling south?"

A lone traveler bound for the south. His physical description was unknown to her, but the rest . . .

How could they know? she wondered. *Unless this is coincidence, but something tells me otherwise.*

"No. No one of the sort. I'm bound for Derlusk and have

met nary a soul save for yourselves." She had no intention of going to Derlusk, but saw no reason to raise their already high suspicions by appearing directionless.

The officer studied her as she answered, as if seeking any falsehood behind her words. Apparently satisfied, he snorted a reply. "You may as well stand where you are and sink in the mud, but by all means, carry your hopes onward. You'll receive little else at those gates."

Eli smiled despite his tone and turned Morningstar onto the path around Littlewater's walls. Questions flew through her mind as she put the officer and his men to her back, but she resolved not to dwell on them yet.

If the traveler they'd described was the Hoarite of Sameska's vision, then things were even stranger than she'd guessed.

⊕ ⊕ ⊕ ⊕ ⊕

The leather breast plate split and gave way to crimson hands pushing through. A bloodstained torso crawled from the innards of the hunter who had become the road for Morgynn's bloodwalk. His broken body slumped to the ground like a second skin being sloughed off. In an instant, Morgynn stood before the circle of seven hunters, her wet lips casting a spell through the froth of her fallen victim's life. Spitting and gnashing her teeth in the harsh language of magic, she sneered as the hunters slowly recovered from the shock of her gruesome arrival.

Morgynn saw them scrambling to defend themselves, all to no avail. Those in the rear of the formation unslung their bows, dropping their swords point down into the dirt. Drawing arrows from quivers, they prepared to take aim.

The three hunters closest to her raised curved swords and charged, but they were too late as her spell caught them all full in the chest. A wave of power, like focused wind, slammed into them all, knocking the swordsmen to their backs and ruining the shots of the archers. Morgynn laughed, releasing herself to the magic and her frantic pulse. Her dark eyes welled to black pools of blood, spilling down her cheeks and dancing in symbols and runes as she cast another spell, waving her hand in the air between her and the fallen bowmen. Turning to the swordsmen, who'd recovered their footing, she winced as light spilled from a small stone one of them drew from a pouch, illuminating the cleared ground and broken plants.

Shaken, the swordsmen charged again, attempting to get close and disrupt her casting. Morgynn frowned and brushed her left hand across her collarbone. The scars burst into flames as they awoke and burned away, letting magic course down her right arm. A coppery scent filled the air and a reddened bolt arced from her fingertips, striking two of the hunters and forcing the third to abandon his attack.

The stricken hunters had no time to scream before their muscles convulsed and tensed, threatening to tear away from the bones beneath. One fell almost instantly, a young man with dusty brown hair and striking blue eyes, now clouded with blackened tissue. While the arc of energy still gripped him, she could taste him in her mouth, both his fear and the gamey taste of his cooking flesh.

The other man's eyes were lost to her, bursting within their sockets as the spell ended, showering his face in blood and pinkish fluids. He collapsed to the dirt as his muscles gave way. Trembling, he whimpered hoarsely, trying to give voice to his pain through a raw and bleeding throat.

The thrum of released bowstrings followed by hissing charges of energy drew her gaze back to the archers. The bowmen had risen to one knee to take aim. The arrows stopped short of their marks, bouncing away from an invisible barrier that crackled and flashed with each strike.

Smiling at their futile attacks, Morgynn brushed her right hand across the scars on her neck as she heard the last swordsman approach again, sword drawn, yelling fearfully. The magic responded. Scars disappeared in sizzling lines of thin smoke, following the runes inscribed in her flesh. Thrusting her left hand forward, a caustic scent accompanied the crawling spell as it sizzled across her skin harmlessly.

The swordsman's powerful stroke fell short as crimson

arrows of acid pierced his armor and buried themselves in his chest and side. The force of the missiles spun him around like a child. A wet gasp escaped him, and Morgynn could feel the flooding hole in his right lung, feel the impact of each arrow as it ate at tissue and muscle. His veins and arteries became inflamed, showing starkly against the skin on his neck and face. Her heart responded to his pounding pulse.

The bittersweet flavor of adrenaline danced ghostlike across her tongue, and her eyes rolled back. She moaned as he staggered backward, dropping his sword. His heartbeat slowed, and, pulse by pulse, she felt drawn into his death.

Gaping oblivion yawned in his mind and tempted her. That moment between life and final rest, the twilight of existence where she'd been the past decade called to her, but death would not have her. Buried once in soil that would not keep her, she had risen to a power bound only by her skin.

"Toys and playthings," she whispered. "They barely know they're alive."

Rage replaced her ecstasy as the man fell lifeless. She turned, furious, on the archers.

Rhaeme fired one last arrow in frustration, but again it was reflected just inches from Morgynn's breast. He rolled forward to grab his sword, abandoning his bow.

"Run! We can't win here!" he yelled to his fellow hunters, who gave no argument. They turned to escape, but in the dim glow of the light stone, they could see the edges of the path closing behind them. The tortured sound of another spell being cast hummed behind them, scratching at their ears and clawing at their spines.

One of the men turned back. Morgynn could see the fire of youth and anger in his eyes. Rhaeme attempted to stop the boy, grabbing at his cloak but missing. The boy drew his ready sword, still protruding from the ground where he'd first drawn his bow. His voice, raised above spell and storm, was full of the early pitch and tone of manhood.

"As Savras sees, so shall I see you fall!"

Morgynn finished her spell in a crescendo of sound, drowning the boy's voice and opening her mouth wide beyond its natural ability. Her scream became a buzz of noise as red-eyed insects flew in a mass from between her thin lips. Each locust was the color of dark wine and onyx. Their eyes glowed, giving the swarm a hellish light as it streamed forward to meet the charging hunter.

The boy met the mass head on, swinging his blade valiantly, but the locusts were too many and quickly found small openings in his armor and clothing, landing inside his hood and hungrily feasting on his scalp and neck. Morgynn sighed as her jaw popped and resumed its natural shape.

The boy's companions sprinted forward to retrieve their swords, determined to make their ends proud and honorable. Morgynn wondered what thoughts crawled through their minds as the dawning realization came that they would likely die here.

Ahead of their grim charge, the boy's writhing body was lifted into the air. His boots scraped the ground for a moment before the momentum of the swarm bore him down, stripping his flesh to the bone. The locusts' buzz drowned the young hunter's muffled screams.

Morgynn watched as the warriors advanced. She saw death in their eyes and hated them for their acceptance of it. Righteousness fueled their spirits, and the sight of it sickened her. Whispering a drone of grating syllables, she pulled the threads of the Weave to her will, determined to teach them the true nature of death and their foolish choice born of courage.

With a single word, the lead hunter's sword flashed and steamed as cold flames enveloped its length. He screamed as his fingers froze and became fused to the hilt, the flesh burning and brittle. He tried to push past the pain, to wield the weapon against the spell's mistress, but the sword cracked and split, shattering in an explosion of metal that left his arm a cauterized stump and blinded his eyes.

The next man was closer, and Morgynn had no time to cast again. She spun away, but his blade glanced across her left arm, opening a small wound that sent shudders throughout her body as her blood recoiled from the open skin. Growling another quick spell, she roared the words madly and swung her right arm around before the man could strike again.

•

Her fingers grew, extending into long, blackened claws like swords of shadow. She raked these across the hunter's face and chest. Like ephemeral knives of ice, they melted through flesh and bone, leaving gaping scars in his spirit and mind. The man's eyes rolled and his arms went limp. Dropping his sword, he spasmed but tried to maintain control of himself. Her claws had rent his mind and he babbled nonsense as he fell to his knees.

Rhaeme was last, just a few yards away, and she pitied him for a moment—a morbid, mocking pity as she whispered quietly to the dagger at her belt, freeing the clasp that held it in its sheath. She touched its jeweled pommel once and it flew at her command, slamming into the lone hunter's gut with a force born of old Nar magic. It knocked the wind from his lungs and laid him flat on his back. The carved figures on the dagger's handle squirmed against one another and mouthed quietly.

Picking up his dropped sword, she stopped to watch his slow agony. He refused to scream and met her gaze, grasping at the dagger planted in his stomach but unable to pull it free. Her black eyes looked straight through his, not really seeing him, focused on the branching rivers of blood beneath his skin. The bleeding streams of her eyes changed shape on her cheeks, mimicking what she saw inside him. They matched his swift pulse in a red image of twin trees, stripped of leaves and laid bare for winter.

"They barely know they're alive," she mumbled as the rage bled from her limbs, dispersed by her arcane tantrum, "then they die."

Around the pair, the locusts moved from body to body, devouring the fallen and eliciting howls from those not yet passed on. Long she stood, lost in thought as the swarm finished each body, leaving naught but bones under loose armor and clothing. Finally, they gathered in a cloud around her legs and she considered the command that would send them feasting on this last body.

Deciding quickly, Morgynn hissed a sibilant word and the swarm faded into thin air, returning to that foul realm that had spawned them.

"You serve the whores of Savras?" she asked emotionlessly, drained for the moment.

The hunter tried to spit, attempting to show some defiance to her face, but it was all he could do to breathe and force back the burning vomit in his throat. His pulse said so much about him. Strong and stubborn, righteous and honest. Qualities she could respect, but merely a nuisance for her current intentions.

The dagger responded to her twitching fingers, lifting and carrying the hunter's weight with it. His stoicism failed and he gasped, gurgling as a wave of vomit and blood flowed from his innards and into his mouth. She willed him to move slowly, allowing him a few moments to believe he would be disemboweled by the vile weapon, but it would not release him, however much he wished it might.

The blade pushed him against the trunk of a tree, pinning him to the wood. Morgynn followed closely with his lost sword. With a powerful thrust, she buried the blade just beneath his shoulder and deep into the tree. He gasped, his voice barely a whisper, his breath shallow and quick.

"You would die for peddlers of visions and prophecy? Does your life mean nothing?"

Morgynn twirled her fingers languidly and concentrated. The dagger worked itself free from his stomach and returned to her hand.

"Kill me, witch! F-finish it!" he spat through clenched teeth.

She glared at him and put a hand on his impaled shoulder. Caressing the bloodied flesh, she called to his pulse, feeling it roll and tumble in his distress. It pushed suddenly, fighting weakly against the walls of muscle and skin that bound it within him. She held it for a moment, exerting her control over its ebb and flow.

He tensed as his body tried to right itself. She felt his body as if it were her own, though his pain did not register as sharply within her. Pressure built behind his eyes, and his skull felt as if it would burst. Needlelike spasms caused his limbs to twitch. She could see the end looming in his mind, unreal and unbelievable. His thoughts wandered, trying to escape what was happening. She watched, reading his thoughts, observing the landscape of his retreat and the emotions that lingered there.

"You are Rhaeme, yes? And Elisandrya, that is her name." Morgynn spoke as if she stood beside him in that rain-drenched image in his head. "You still love her, but she seeks the Hoarite."

Unbidden primal panic stole over Rhaeme in a sudden chill at her words. Morgynn withdrew her fingers, ceasing her pull on his blood, satisfied that fear of death still hung with him on the tree. His head drooped and he managed a single sob.

Without a word, her hands melded into his chest painlessly, opening the doorway of the bloodwalk through his body. Rhaeme passed out. The warmth that her passing sent through him was gone almost in an instant and did little for the cold that would creep into his extremities.

Then he was alone.

CHAPTER ELEVEN

Alone. Mile after mile had passed and Elisandrya had not seen a soul.

Littlewater was far behind her, and an invisible dawn was fast approaching. She searched the eastern horizon for cracks in the cloud cover, seeking some sliver of elusive morning. Morningstar was slowing beneath her. His muscles trembled with wear, his breathing became more audible. She feared the Ghedia's magic of speed had taxed him more than she'd expected.

The ground was soaked with rain. Lightning lanced overhead, its branches stretching for miles, well beyond the perimeter of the powerful, southward-moving tempest.

Her stiff muscles complained, aching and demanding rest despite her willpower. With a gentle tug and a tap on Morningstar's sides, Eli slowed him to a walk. The sudden silence that fell in the absence of his hoof beats was oppressive. Her pulse pounded in her ears, an almost deafening cadence that rattled her eyes as heavy lids tried to steady them.

Resentment floated in her thoughts, of herself, of Rhaeme, and of Sameska.

I should have gone into the forest with Rhaeme, she thought. This is a fool's errand, chasing ghosts and the fears of an old woman.

Her head lolled back and she reached up to hold the threaded fethra around her neck, beseeching Savras one last time, one more chance. Then might she turn back to find Rhaeme's tracks and join him as she should have in the forest.

"Savras, I was blind—" the prayer passed listlessly across her lips, dry despite the damp all around her, and she could not finish. A wave of slumber rolled through her body and jolted her mind with an answer to her summons for aid. The vision was quick but awoke her in an instant of shock.

Wings, hundreds of wings flapped noiselessly in a small cage. A beast of feathers and wingtips, raging against the enclosed space, fluttered in her mind's eye.

Shaking her head and rubbing her eyes, the image faded, but remained burned on her memory.

"What could it mean?" she asked aloud. Morningstar huffed and snorted at her. "I wasn't actually asking you, Star."

As the vague vision played through her mind, rolling in the miasma of lost sleep, a tiny pinpoint of light became visible ahead. It winked like a firefly in the charcoal darkness that ruled the Reach.

Her hands immediately reached to touch the pommel of her sword, the bow at her back, and the stiff feathers on the arrows hanging across her shoulder. Though reassured of her own preparedness, the sense of alert brought her to full consciousness. Bandits were not unknown to lie in wait for merchants and lone travelers, but she had seen few of their like on this, the lesser used Low Road.

Angling toward the dancing light of the distant campfire, she straightened herself into the stance of a hunter. Exuding authority outwardly, she was inwardly enthralled by the many-winged beast in the cage in her head. Savras was rarely clear, but he was never arbitrary in those insights he gifted to his faithful. Briefly, she wished Dreslya had come with her, but touching her sword's hilt once again, she was grateful to be alone. The monster of wings continued to flutter and beat against its prison. Unexplained and unavoidable, the sound of its freakish limbs matched the pounding in her ears.

⊙ ⊙ ⊙ ⊙ ⊙

Khaemil knelt on the cracked flagstones of what had once been a courtyard. His bare arms hung loosely at his sides, palms up, in a mood of quiet meditation and supplication. He was not as knowledgeable in magic as Morgynn, nor so dutiful in prayer as Talmen, but Gargauth heard his call and answered his loyal servant.

Though he'd served many lords and minor powers in Avernus, he had taken to Gargauth the Exile quite readily upon being summoned to the Realms. Though Morgynn's face had been the first he remembered seeing, it was Gargauth's essence that drew him to stay in the world, to serve so strange a mistress. At first this had been by request, but Khaemil became enamored of Morgynn over time, trusting in the devil-god's instinct about her.

In the midst of his concentration, heat flushed his black skin, rising to a boil within him like a fever. Morgynn burned her way into his bloodstream, angry and prepared to tear her way out as she'd done with the first hunter she'd killed. It was not mercy that stayed her intention. Touching fresh air beyond his body, she emerged, fingertips and arms followed by the rest of her in a wet, warm rush.

She stood before Khaemil, quietly at first, stoic as he matched her gaze. He noticed the small wound on her left arm. It did not bleed, nor did it pain her, but it displayed her current mood. His moment of quiet meditation and prayer ended as she cast cold eyes on his kneeling form.

"Your crusader is neither gone nor dead. The Hoarite travels south even now, no doubt hiding in his shadows. Why is this, Khaemil?"

"I-I do not know, my lady, but surely—"

"They are looking for him!" Her anger was born anew as she witnessed his stammering and confusion. "Their hope gives them courage, makes them move beyond their walls, scouring our forest and riding north in search of the phantom!"

Khaemil could only bow his head in failure. Sharp claws tore into his palms and she smelled his infernal blood dripping to the ground. The aasimar would be a greater nuisance than she'd expected, more tenacious than others who walked the Hoarite roads.

"He will be dealt with directly, my lady, along with any who seek him."

"See to it." She turned as she said the last, looking to the tower and picturing the tiny box that lay within her chambers. The scroll within that ancient box, the Word of Goorgian, amended and altered in her own handwriting, would call its unholy plague again. The wards and protections of the Temple of the Hidden Circle were nothing to her. By proxy, she knew its secrets.

Whispering, she added, "I will deal with the oracles."

⊛ ⊛ ⊛ ⊛ ⊛

One of the secrets of the Temple of the Hidden Circle were its hidden chambers, rooms all but forgotten except in time of need. For the past few tendays, the oracles and younger priestesses, acolytes known as savants, frequented the chambers out of mercy and duty.

On the backside of the temple, in the Gardens of Thought, a spiraling stairway led down to these places, growing full with the weak and diseased. Though still in its infancy this far south, the blush had taken its toll on old and young alike. The rooms were kept dark, since the disease made the eyes sensitive to light and would form welts and rashes on the skin when exposed to brightness. Shuttered lanterns provided a dim glow by which caregivers could see and move from cot to cot, and victim to victim.

The smell of close, feverish bodies was overcome by incense and the scent of fethra leaves as they boiled to make a broth that eased pain and fever and seemed to stave off the worst of the symptoms. Delusional cries sometimes echoed down the corridors, carried by the curving walls and acoustics of the temple's architecture. Each cry found a fearful ear somewhere in the temple's silence, waiting in the dark for the storms to pass and for the deliverance of Savras's prophecy.

The newest patient in these suffering chambers was the young oracle stricken during the gathering. In her panic, Nivael had run from the gathering, frantically trying to stem the steady flow from her nose. She'd felt the fever but could not accept her own sickness. She collapsed in her small room, covered in her own blood. No one had sought her out, most still weighing the import of Sameska's prophecy and her edict of inaction against the encroaching evil.

Waking early and feeling little rested, Nivael had gone about her duties in the quarantined room. There, she stumbled and fell as the blush closed its grasp on her health. Her heart pounded and she breathed hoarsely, trying to cry out, but her voice was inaudible. Her throat was wet and tasted of blood. She didn't know how much time had passed while she lay there, delusional among the others.

Eventually a surge of strength filled her limbs, tensing them in spasms she could not control. Gnashing her teeth, her eyes rolled back in her head and her body heaved itself from the floor. She felt that she was dreaming and let go of her will, half-conscious and unaware of her wild charge at the wooden double doors. Her impact reverberated through the halls. Oracles and lingering hunters raised their heads in alarm, wondering what fresh terror came upon them.

Nivael could see the walls and floor of the temple passing beneath her bare feet, almost in slow motion, as if she floated rather than ran headlong toward the sanctuary. Her face was hot. The chill of the stone floors could not quell the heat of her blood as it again poured from her nose, and soon her mouth and eyes. An impossible strength sent her flying through the heavy doors of the sanctuary, gurgling a weary groan as she did so.

High Oracle Sameska, Lord Hunter Baertah, and several other oracles looked on in shock as Nivael made her way toward the altar, her arms outstretched. Dreslya raised a hand to her mouth as she saw the state her friend was in, covered in blood and swaying in a trancelike stagger.

No one moved, afraid to go near this walking plague, the blush in a form and face of one of their own.

Nivael stopped before the altar, standing on the top step of the dais, on even footing with the marble statue of Savras that stared calmly beyond her. Baertah raised a perfumed handkerchief to his nose as Nivael's stained hands gripped the shoulders of the statue. Rust-colored claws touched the image of their god. She turned reddened eyes on the small congregation and her voice spoke of its own accord. She could hear herself and wondered when this horrible dream might end. Blackness clouded the edges of her vision.

"Those who resist shall die. All of these are dead. It is done."

At those words, Nivael fell in a heap at the foot of the statue. As the others watched, the base of the statue cracked—a line webbed upward along the figure until two thin branches touched his peaceful eyes and gushed forth tears of blood.

Dreslya gasped as Nivael's words echoed in the chamber. *Those who resist . . . All of these are dead.* She reached carefully into a pocket of her robe and her fingertips brushed the edges of Elisandrya's letter.

Dimly, at the edge of her attention, someone screamed, but no one approached Nivael's limp body or the horrifying spectacle of the bleeding statue.

⊕ ⊕ ⊕ ⊕ ⊕

Morgynn gently closed the lid of the box and rested her hands upon it, mumbling the words of the warding spell to keep it safe. The secrets of the plague, written by the archmage Goorgian centuries ago and improved upon by herself, lay within. Admiring the skeletal carvings on its surface, she placed it upon the table with her other possessions.

She descended the stairs in a mixed mood, feeling lighter as the threads of the Weave responded to her presence, but more determined than ever not to leave anything to chance.

Talmen waited outside as Khaemil returned from an excursion to the forest. Talmen's eyes sparkled within his bony mask, detecting her look of command and standing up straighter as she approached. Khaemil appeared pleased with himself, possibly eager to deliver good news to make up for his previous failure.

Looking upon them both, she realized more than ever the scope of her own destiny. From the east came a resounding rush of need that filled her being, and she smiled at the eagerness of those dreadful creatures that awaited her command. She could sense their masses, shaking with uncontrollable desire, unfounded animosity held in check only by her will. Their sightless eyes glittered like a thousand stars, a ribbon of diamonds beseeching her to grace them with her wishes. They were so much more pliable, so much more useful, than they'd been in life.

"Soon," she whispered, her voice unheard as thunder crashed in the distance. It echoed in the droning chant of the Gargauthans at their task behind her.

"What would you have of us, Morgynn? The tower is nearly perfect, our control of the storm is unquestionable."

Talmen's words brought her back from her silent connection with her creations.

"Begin preparations for the attack. Have your followers summon what aid they can to bolster our forces. Call upon your own allies in the Lower Planes and make them ready."

While Talmen bowed in affirmation, Morgynn turned her attention to Khaemil, raising a brow to emphasize her unspoken question and expectation of his success.

"Our allies within the forest move even now, my lady. They promise the death of the Hoarite and the Savrathan by this evening or sooner."

"Well done."

Turning back to Talmen, she reached out to him, pointing with a red-nailed finger and whispering words of magic. Heat radiated down her arm as the spell grew, and the air became thick and wavered like a mirage around it. The wizard-priest did not move. Her eyes, black with rushing blood, met his.

"Hold out your arm."

Talmen rolled back the sleeve of his robe to expose his forearm, and she stretched her smoldering hand to touch his skin. Like a brand, the heat scorched him. Thin lines of fire trailed from her fingertip across his arm, emblazoning a symbol of magic on his flesh. The smell of burning skin filled the air and Morgynn could imagine the look on Talmen's face beneath the mask. She enjoyed his discomfort far too much.

When she pulled away, a blackened rune was left on his right forearm. Talmen studied the symbol curiously, then looked to Morgynn for explanation.

"This symbol will allow you to command those in the forest—the *bathor,* our hungry children, harvested from the undug graves of our enemies," she said, though it was partially a lie. The scar was capable of more than she let on. "Disobey or betray me, and the magic in the scar will lead them to you tirelessly. Do not test their willingness to serve."

She knew that no such thought lurked in his mind, but when called to arms, she doubted his enthusiasm. The scar would cement his role in the battle to come and ensure that his followers were committed alongside him. The idea of the coming conflict stirred her blood and she anxiously turned toward the tower. Final preparations loomed and she was not content to let the Weave rest for long while there was work to be done.

She called out, for all to hear, as she walked.

"Kavak bura sek liras. Furthad vel jerand, sul vel yefa. Sakrah suv awaret vel ros mar kellet dur."

She spoke in Old Nar, the words of an inscription found on the walls within the Pit of Goorgian shortly after her return so many years ago. In the common tongue, it roughly meant, "Call our powers to bear. Summon and gather, arm and prepare. Twilight comes to wake us and raise our standard there."

Talmen ran his left hand over the scars on his arm, repeating the ancient words of the Order to himself quietly, reverently. Like a whisper in her ear, Morgynn listened to him. The scar on his arm told her his thoughts, sending her his words when she wished.

"Brookhollow will fall," he said confidently, "then the whole of the Shandolphyn and the Border Kingdoms beyond. By Gargauth, be it so."

"Indeed," she answered softly, smiling.

⊕ ⊕ ⊕ ⊕ ⊕

Quinsareth sat shivering by his campfire. Still aching from half-healed wounds, he had dozed off more than once. Sleep did not remain long as the trees of the Qurth, maybe a half-mile away, swayed in the wind with noises unlike anything he'd ever heard from a natural forest. He'd traveled through many lands and seen many forests, even those that thrived in the north around the Dalelands and the Moonsea. Through them all, he'd slept comfortably in the warrior's rest, that half-sleep of soldiers and wanderers that broke at sounds of danger. The Qurth, though, held a menace all its own, almost a sentience, and his weary mind could not abide letting down its guard for long.

That same awareness had picked out the regular rhythm of horse's hooves plodding through the muddied grassland. Nonchalantly, he raised an arm across his knees, blocking the fire's light so his natural darkvision could focus on the approaching visitor. He saw a beautiful woman astride a dark stallion riding toward his camp. Her hands held the reins at an angle that suggested a simple traveler, but her stance in the saddle was straight and strong and her hips swayed with the steed in the manner of a practiced rider, possibly a warrior. As she came closer, he could see the curve of a long bow over her shoulder, confirming his guess.

She stopped just outside the firelight and held up her right palm, a gesture denoting a lack of hostility in most civilized lands. Quin lowered his head as if tired and looked away from the low fire, shielding his eyes for the moment.

"Well met, stranger," she said casually, though he detected a tension in her voice.

"Well met," he replied. "Do I camp on owned land? If so, I shall move on with all due speed."

"No, sir. These are free lands, such as they are of late. I merely hoped I might share the warmth of your camp. I have ridden all night and seek a moment of rest."

Quin was surprised at her manner of speech, as he had been several times since entering the Border Kingdoms. Tales abounded of a land rife with war and bickering over land, with cutthroats and thieves around every bend in the road, but the formality of their language and use of the common tongue belied these wild rumors for the most part.

"By all means, be welcome."

In truth, Quin did not wish to entertain visitors, but he required information. He had suspicions about this woman warrior and her arrival out of the darkness on an empty road in troubled times. He felt sure there was more to her journey than casual travel.

She dismounted gracefully, removing a well-worn pack from the saddle. Her mount lowered his head and began to graze on the hardy, wet grass, nosing the blades aside to reach the shallow puddles of water standing on the soaked ground. The woman wore armor, an archer's style guarding the bow arm but leaving the other free to draw arrows from the low-slung quiver he spied near her hip.

He wondered bemusedly at himself a moment, taking stock of the situation.

A beautiful woman wanders into my camp and I spend my time studying her weapons and armor, scrutinizing the cut of her jaw. He smiled at the thought. What a tragic life this is at times.

Turning, she spread a small blanket and sat cross-legged across from him.

"I am Elisandrya Loethe of Brookhollow. Forgive my rudeness for not saying so before."

"You may call me Quin," he said at length. "I am from many places, truth be told."

It occurred to Quin that he'd said that same phrase a thousand times or more in his travels. Almost by instinct, it had become a part of him to lie. He'd not uttered his true name to a soul in over seven years. He did not lament the fact, really, but he'd rarely considered his own comfort with the falsehood.

As she warmed her hands, it seemed she struggled to see his face without appearing overly curious. He wondered at what she saw, imagining how he looked after the last few days. Though self-conscious about his eyes, he cared little about his outward appearances. Keeping his eyes hidden, he studied her back, wondering at that searching look in her eyes.

What was she after?

"Well met, Quin. What brings you to these roads?"

The question sounded casual, but again he sensed a searching tone in her voice, something beyond small talk.

Another lie he'd grown attached to over the years was on the tip of his tongue, when a strange sound caught his attention. It stood out starkly from the wind and distant trees. Its familiarity froze his heart, and he snapped his head up, his muscles taught and ready to spring.

His visitor, too, heard the noise and spun, but not before catching a glimpse of Quin's face.

Her double-take at the sight of his eyes was more than telling. He had no more time to dwell on her intentions, and he focused on the darkness beyond the fire's light.

The grazing horse grunted and whinnied loudly as the first arrow struck his shoulder, followed by several more, whooshing out of the darkness and the surreal morning mist. The horse jumped forward, but was hit again. Missiles buried themselves in his neck and chest, the well-aimed shots of a practiced bow hunter.

"Morningstar!"

Elisandrya screamed in rage as she whirled to stand, her blade drawn in one quick pull. Morningstar fell heavily, thrashing in the mud before succumbing to the fatal wounds and releasing a shuddering final breath.

Quin was on his feet but had not yet drawn Bedlam. Looking down, he realized the fire made them both open targets for whoever hid in the thick mist between them and the forest. Lacking the time to put it out, he yelled to his new acquaintance.

"We must leave! We can't fight them here!"

She hesitated, aware of the flame's betrayal but unable to draw her eyes away from the fallen horse. Quin took several long steps out of the light's range, waiting a few heartbeats to see if Elisandrya would join him. There was no time to mourn horses, and he wouldn't get killed awaiting an impromptu funeral. Finally, she turned away, and they sprinted into the dark as more arrows landed in the mud where they'd stood.

The damp ground was like a sponge sucking at their boots and forcing them to push on harder. Quin veered toward the dark silhouette of a ruin he spotted, like so many he had seen in the past few tendays.

"No," Elisandrya panted as they ran. "Go around it. We'll wait for them on the other side."

"We need cover from those arrows! Inside those walls we stand a better chance."

"Those are the ruins of Char . . . they're cursed. They are . . . forbidden!"

Quin contemplated her words and admitted inwardly that she might know more about the local landmarks. An eerie howling erupted from behind them, quickening their stride and erasing any doubt in Quin's mind. Cursed, haunted, or worse, the ruins were their only option.

"Get over it," he growled and pushed on.

Elisandrya matched his stride. His survival instinct shut out distrust of this stranger for the time being. He focused on reaching defensible ground, but he could not forget the look on her face when she'd witnessed his eyes. It was not the shock of something horrible that she'd registered. It was as if she'd expected to see them.

As the ruins grew closer, Quin rested his hand on Bedlam's pommel and conjured the familiar game in his mind. He could not picture what stone those rusted gates might represent, and he considered the possibilities. An image of the Ghost came to mind—not for death, as many had played the piece, but worse: regret.

CHAPTER TWELVE

Nimble, cloven hooves raced across the sodden ground, leaping and gliding on black feathered wings. Elamiz shook his horned head and hissed in glee between needlelike fangs. The exhilaration of the hunt was intoxicating for him, to run wild across the guarded lands of the hunters and seek their blood for new masters.

His earrings jingled as he stalked his running prey, surrounded by the sliding and swift shadows of the pack. Jumping into the air, he tucked his furry legs beneath him and flew, raising his bow to harry the two companions as they made for the old ruins. That place his kind had known well once, before the oracles had driven them away and forged new roads, guarding them with their warrior-priests and prognostications, foiling all attempts to reclaim the unhallowed ground.

He snarled as he fired more arrows, eager to see them skip and jump at his will, smiling as the dark pack below spread out to surround the ruin's entrance. Landing again, he knelt and absently fingered the curling horns that grew from the sides of his head. He licked his lips with a forked tongue, anxious to make the kill, to make the Order of Twilight happy. Baby blue eyes watched the hunter and his companion slip between the rusted gates of the wall ahead. Long-clawed hands opened and closed, imagining the throats he might soon embrace.

⊙ ⊙ ⊙ ⊙ ⊙

Char was aptly named, as all of it was blackened and crumbling, the victim of some ancient conflagration. Quin and Eli took little time to examine their surroundings, disappearing around hollowed buildings and walls, seeking ground from which to retaliate against their mysterious attackers.

"Watch the gate," Quin said, indicating her bow. "I'll look for better ground."

Eli nodded and backed into the shadowed corner of what looked like an old tomb. She watched as Quin ran ahead, noticing his lithe and graceful movements. His surefooted stealth was a match for any hunter she'd known. She crouched and listened for movement in the direction of the rusted gate, her limited field of vision revealing little in the dim, dusky morning. The sight of Quin's eyes and the apparent ease with which he navigated the darkness remained fresh in her thoughts.

Those eyes! By Savras, those eyes! He must be the man sought after by the patrol in Littlewater, but is he the man I seek?

No sound had come from the gate as yet, and she determined to learn more about Quin if she survived the remainder of the morning. At first, she'd suspected that patrols from Littlewater had tracked her, hoping to discover this stranger she'd happened upon, but those chilling howls in the mist convinced her otherwise. Hunting dogs were uncommon in Savrathan towns, even one as cosmopolitan as Littlewater. Their bowmen would not have chosen to kill a fine horse, especially not the trained mount of a hunter.

No, but those howls were familiar, she thought. Something of the Qurth prowls the Shandolphyn.

Even as close as the Low Road was, it was rare for creatures to venture so far out of the forest. She had heard of such incidents in the south, near Owlhold and even in the west near Ondeeme, but here, the oracles and hunters kept the borders of the Qurth in tight check, anticipating the slightest dangers by favor of the sight of Savras.

Which, she thought discouragingly, makes these recent times all the more strange.

Her reflexes reacted to nearby movement, clenching the bow in her hand and darting her eyes forward. She saw nothing—merely a small section of fallen wall before her and more of the same all around. As she studied the blackness, she squinted, certain that the wall in front of her had shifted somehow. She had almost convinced herself she was imagining things when a low growl came from the same direction.

The shadow erupted and flew at her, blazing yellow eyes and ivory fangs rushing toward her face, pulling a rippling mass of darkness behind it. Rolling backward in surprise, she raised her bow and aimed at the center of the nearly invisible mass. The arrow struck something solid, drawing a canine yelp. The weight of the beast landed on Eli before she could draw again. It was heavy on her chest, gurgling a low growl before falling still and shuddering a final breath. Rolling it away and jumping to her feet, she detected the black outline of a massive hound. She backed into the corner again, looking all around, certain that every shadow held similar danger.

She wondered where Quin had gone and wished he'd bring his dark-seeing eyes back with him.

◎ ◎ ◎ ◎ ◎

Quinsareth was deep in the maze of black-stoned walls and old tombs. He stopped in a small, overgrown courtyard, staring at the only complete building in a mess of what must have been a terrible, unholy site at one time. Multi-winged gargoyles perched at the corners of the squat building, looking down on him with blind eyes. A bent steeple stood atop the structure, bearing a symbol—a circle of wings or feathers, the sign of some unknown or lesser god of ages past. The yawning temple entrance was anything but inviting, but Quin knew his options were limited, especially within the place's aura of festering evil. It repelled his senses, as if focusing its ire on the aasimar standing at its doorstep.

He tensed, sensing movement on either side. Looking down, he casually scanned the peripherals of his vision. Against the walls closest to him on either side were the skulking forms of two great dogs, barely outlines in the shadows but as visible to him as the walls themselves.

Their bodies were short and wide, powerfully built and crouched to attack. He slid his hand to Bedlam beneath the shoulder of his cloak. A tiny stitch of pain lanced across his left side where the bruised ribs were still not completely healed, and he cursed his previous exhaustion. Unable to maintain the shadowalk, he'd made camp and had uncharacteristically hoped for the best.

I should have known better, he thought.

As if sensing the mental cue, the hounds lunged, growling hideously as they abandoned the obscuring shadows.

Quinsareth moved to his right and drew Bedlam's scream into the morning air, slashing as he faced the charge of the lead dog. The beast yelped as the blade sliced its thick jowls, but fell silent as its head was sheared off above the jaw. Spinning, he brought the blade back around to meet the attack of the remaining hound.

The shadowy beast sidestepped the shrieking blade and snapped at Quin's extended leg, just missing his ankle. Quin judged the hound's eagerness to gain a hold with its massive jaws and watched for the second bite at his leg as he drew it back, meanwhile raising Bedlam over his shoulder.

When the growling beast snapped again, Bedlam howled through its bared back, severing its spine neatly. He finished off the mortally wounded creature before its low cries attracted others.

Considering their affinity for the shadows, Quinsareth imagined they were already quite near and just as invisible. Gently favoring his left side and the aching ribs, he made his way back to find Elisandrya, making sure to remember his path from the temple as he ran.

⊙ ⊙ ⊙ ⊙ ⊙

Eli abandoned the thought of drawing her sword in such tight quarters and wielded her bow. She trusted its supple wood and her ability more than the curved blade, which she considered more useful for hacking paths in the forest. Each time a shadow seemed to move, she aimed and waited, listening and watching for more of the hidden beasts, but no more came.

"Elisandrya."

Quin whispered the word from the edge of the wall, and Eli reacted swiftly, pointing her bow at his silhouette. Recognizing him, she relaxed the weapon and breathed deeply, relieved to know she was not alone. His eyes were visible in the dark, she noticed, not glowing, but bright in some indescribable way.

"We must move. I've found a building."

Eli nodded and followed him closely, trusting his sight but prepared to fire on any errant shadow foolish enough to come alive. As they made slow, stealthy progress, she saw that Quin favored his left side, as if injured. When he paused at a corner to survey the next length of ground, she questioned him.

"Are you hurt?"

"An old injury, nothing more. I'll survive."

"We are likely surrounded, you know. I killed a shadow mastiff back there."

"I found two of them myself."

Quietly he crossed an open space to reach the next wall.

She could see the outline of the temple now and scanned the courtyard for movement. She joined him at the wall and he motioned toward the doorway. Four shapes prowled there, sniffing the air, padding from one shadow to the next, waiting.

They know, she thought. Where is their master, I wonder?

As Quin peered around a corner, Eli heard the snap of a bowstring and saw the swift blur of an arrow just in front of Quin's face. He flinched back, and a fine scratch appeared on the bridge of his nose. An inch or two more, and the missile might have blinded him, or worse. Curling his lip and gritting his teeth, he placed a hand on his sword and took a breath.

"Stay close," he said.

He spun out in a crouch. Eli followed behind and fired in the direction of the unseen archer. She saw a dark figure disappear behind another wall, but nothing else of it before the shadow mastiffs charged from the darkness.

She was startled at first when Quin drew his screaming blade and slew the closest beast, but she recovered quickly as another creature appeared in front of her. Two quick shots flew from her bow, one landing in the hound's foreleg, slowing it, and the other piercing its neck. She and Quin circled back to back as they crossed the distance to the doorway of the temple.

Two more mastiffs fell to her bow and Quin had just finished off a third when a winged figure presented itself from behind a cracked column. The tip of an arrow was aimed at them from a black bow.

"Get down!" she yelled, and pushed toward the doorway.

Eli fired at the figure and heard a satisfying yet ominous hiss as her shot drove home. An arrow flew high and bounced off the stone lintel above them as they ducked inside and ran down a short hallway. Eli fired a few more arrows behind them to discourage any pursuers.

The hallway branched in two directions and opened into a large chamber beyond, lit with a smoldering green light. Satisfied their foes would not immediately follow, they entered cautiously to catch their breath and contemplate their next move.

⊛ ⊛ ⊛ ⊛ ⊛

Elamiz stepped from behind a wall, scowling and enraged. In his fist was the bloodied arrow he'd removed from his wing. The hunter's shot had been hasty but skilled. He could still smell her on the air, even through the strong wind and scent of old ashes all around. She was cornered, along with the stranger—the Hoarite whom Khaemil had sent him to find.

He cursed the aasimar's keen vision and lingered over the bodies of his fallen pets as the rest of the hounds gathered around him. Nine still survived. A small sacrifice if the promises of the Order were kept. Elamiz cared little for Derlusk or the eastern edges of Shandolphyn's Reach. Dominion over the Savrathans would be satisfying enough—those who survived, that is.

Around his wrist, Elamiz wore a cord of leather bearing a small whistle of polished onyx. Raising it to his lips, he blew three quick notes. Though too high for most ears, the mastiff pack responded immediately and encircled the temple entrance, sniffing and pawing at the ground excitedly.

The faint whiff of fresh blood wafted from within the doorway. Elamiz smiled, forgetting his aching wing and relishing the taste in his mouth. Celestial blood, even that of a mixed breed, was a rare find for those of the Qurth.

⊛ ⊛ ⊛ ⊛ ⊛

The temple's high ceiling was lost beyond the light of two glowing orbs set near a crude altar. Their permanent magic still burned, long after the mage who lit them was lost to history. Quinsareth was thankful for the light, trusting their illumination better than his darkvision in this place. Curved stone pews surrounded a central column carved to resemble scales. In those rough-hewn seats were the bones of the faithful who'd come to worship whatever dark god had been courted in those hidden years. The skeletons were charred and ashy, curled in upon themselves in response to the flames that had devoured them.

Not one of them lay near an exit. They had burned in their seats, unmoving save for twisting in the pain of a gruesome death.

Quinsareth moved quickly through the chamber, looking high and low, searching for their next advantage. He considered the bones briefly, taking special note of their presence, and moved to the altar. It was bare stone, a flat rock set on a dais, similar to offering rocks he'd seen in more superstitious areas of the world. Primal gods, such as the one revered in this place, rarely accepted prayers and piety alone.

Absently, Quin rubbed at his shoulder where the gnoll had bitten him the day before. His shadowalk had only partly healed the wound and it had begun to bleed, seeping from under his armor and staining the edges of his cloak. Kneeling to look more closely at the stone floor, he winced as his ribs ached with the motion. He squeezed his eyes shut and attempted to ignore the pain, focusing on the task at hand.

The altar was empty, and no bones of a leader lay with those of the doomed congregation. An idea began to form in his head as he examined the altar more closely. Memory guided his hands, but cynicism ruled his thoughts. Just beneath the slab, he found the edges of a raised stone set in the floor under the altar. Looking high above, he saw the bare ends of dangling chains in the darkness above.

He saw that Eli had cautiously approached the central column. Noticing that the scale carvings wound upward like a serpentine tail, he followed it up. At its top was a thing from out of the strangest of dreams, of oldest times and faiths. Carved in midflight, he counted at least eighteen detailed wings, their feathers looking ready to rustle in the slightest breeze. The body of the thing was merely a vehicle to house the many wings, having no head, eyes, or mouth. Eli stood enraptured, staring in horror at the thing as if she knew its name and expected it to swoop down upon her in a fluttering mass of stone feathers.

"Where is the cage?" Her whisper echoed through the room. Her eyes never left the stone beast.

The sound of clicking claws echoed from the hallway. Instantly, Eli was torn from her reverie and nocked an arrow to her bowstring in the space of a single breath. She looked to Quin, who met her stare across the pews that separated them. He motioned with his head toward the statue of the winged creature above her.

Nodding, she slung her bow over her shoulder, took the arrow between her teeth, and began to climb the snakelike tail to hide among the petrified wings.

Quin watched from the cover of the offering stone as several more of the nigh invisible hounds prowled into the chamber from both exits. He counted five on the left and four on the right. He centered his breathing and slowed his thoughts, waiting for their mysterious master to arrive. Unconsciously, he counted in his mind, ticking off a random list of the pieces of the Fate Fall. He found it strange that he was doing it, that after so many years of traveling, the game would return to him again and again.

Regardless, he made good use of the memory, his hand resting on the first stone, ready to tumble it into its brethren. The rest would fall as they would, and he would not regret the sequence, whatever it might reveal. This determination above all others hovered in his mind, for regret belonged to the Ghost and the Ghost destroyed all patterns that touched it.

Just yards away, he spotted the shifting shadows of the nearing hounds, baring white teeth as they rounded the edge of the sanctuary and noticed him. Their growls rumbled like hungry thunder as they smelled his blood. Their approach had been stealthier than he'd anticipated.

Damn, he thought, the first stone goes to the dogs.

Two arrows hissed into the growling darkness near him. One arrow cracked uselessly against the wall and the other brought a yelp of pain, causing a hound to appear. The green glow of the orbs highlighted its dark coat. Quin hoped more arrows would even the odds, but the clop of nimble hooves on stone announced Elisandrya's greater concern. She turned quickly to face the threat.

The winged creature leaped into the air, dodging Eli's reflexive shot, and fired back. The fiend's bow was now enveloped in an indigo flame, which it passed to the arrow it released. Eli ducked and the missile crumbled into a stone wing, leaving the lifelike feathers dusty and brittle in its wake.

Bedlam was half drawn as Quin observed the quick exchange between Elisandrya and some sort of devilish satyr. Moving swiftly, he pressed the stone abnormality in the floor, hearing a satisfying click that confirmed his suspicions. He rolled backward and unsheathed Bedlam as the mastiffs came at him, snarling and drooling. He leaped to his right, meeting their charge and screaming a warning, menacing with the great blade as he deftly spun among them, disrupting their organized attack.

Rusted pulleys spun among the rafters overhead, the ancient beams groaning under the weight of their descending burden. The whole building shook as its long-waiting task was demanded of it again. Two massive stone slabs lowered shakily on chains that snapped and popped. Dust shook from the ceiling as the entrance was sealed by the ancient device.

Squinting his eyes against a century's worth of dust, Quin realized the played stone may have been pure Luck. Squaring off against the pack, he hoped he was wrong, not wanting Luck to be played out just yet.

He stabbed and slashed at the snapping hounds, wounding several but unable to land a solid blow among them. Frustrated, he edged the closing pack closer to the pews, keeping them at bay with the shrieking Bedlam. The blade's pitch had lowered in an attempt to mimic the sounds of the surrounding beasts. It threatened them with their own growls and the sounds of gnashing teeth.

He cast a quick glance at Elisandrya's battle against the pack's leader. Another of her shots missed as the fiendish satyr twirled in the air, but Quin could tell it was having trouble flying in the cramped loft of the sanctuary. It flapped its black wings furiously to stay airborne. Reaching the nearest pew, Quin leaned hard and jumped to stand on the wide stone seat. Without thinking, he'd used his left arm. He almost slipped as the pain in his ribs stabbed through his chest. One mastiff tried to take advantage of the moment and lunged in, too close. It caught Bedlam's blade through its neck as Quin slashed the curved blade outward. Before its body hit the ground, Quin was running along the pew's seat. He circled toward the flying archer with the vicious pack snapping at his heels.

Finding cover in the wings of the statue, Eli ducked as another arrow hissed overhead. Quin ran at the satyr's right, hoping to distract or injure it and afford Elisandrya a better shot. Seeing it more clearly, he could distinguish the fiendish qualities of the fey creature in great detail. It bore the curling ram's horns of a satyr, but a second set sprouted behind the first. Black feathered wings held it aloft and glowing blue eyes aimed sorcerous arrows at Elisandrya. He'd faced devilish half-breeds before, but could only imagine this fey perversion as a child of rape.

Quin jumped across the narrow aisle between the pews, slicing at the satyr's legs as he passed. The fiend dropped sideways behind the blade's arc and kicked Quin in the small of the back. The blow sent the aasimar sprawling to the floor, soon to be at the mercy of the chasing pack. Before the satyr could harry Elisandrya, Quin saw an arrow strike the fiend in the shoulder. The satyr spun downward to land face first on the floor. Two more arrows pierced his back, one lodging in his left wing joint. He howled in pain as the feathered limb fell crookedly to his side.

The mastiffs scrambled and bit at one another as they fought for the prize of tearing into the fallen Hoarite first. Quin had rolled to a stop against the wall, enraged and in pain, but satisfied that his distraction had worked. Bedlam hummed on the floor just inches from his hand. Reaching for it, he felt the teeth of the lead mastiff seize his armored calf, squeezing so hard he feared the bone would break.

Arrows tore into the hound and two others, bringing them down with precise shots into the bases of their exposed necks, causing the others to turn and leap into the sheltering shadows nearby.

Quin took the satyr's moment of pain to capitalize on Elisandrya's well-timed barrage. Grabbing Bedlam, he thrust unmercifully into a hound nearby. He felt the pain of his aching ribs sharply as the stab landed. The skewered mastiff writhed a moment, biting at the growling metal in its side, then fell still.

Pulling the blade free, Quin rose on his uninjured right leg. He held Bedlam out before him, almost daring the four retreating mastiffs to finish their attack. Their ears were laid back against their squat skulls and low growls rumbled in their throats, but they were wary of the bow behind them. A savageness gleamed in their eyes and Quinsareth matched it.

Seeming to wait for their master's next move, their ears suddenly rose, hearing a sound far above Quin's range. Glancing up, he saw the satyr's face glaring at him, a small whistle pinched between its sharp fangs.

The mastiffs could not ignore the piercing command and leaped for the aasimar. Their master rose and fired at Elisandrya, the indigo arrow sizzling into stone, crumbling it at its touch. Though Elisandrya tried to return the favor, the satyr's arrow had loosened a joint between two of the statue's wings and they crumbled under her steadying knee. Her bow caught against another wing as she scrambled to grab hold of something. The bow fractured along its upper curve, unable to support her weight and sending her tumbling to the stone floor.

Quinsareth roared in unison with Bedlam as he met the mastiffs, fighting against his pain and viciously cutting the hounds down. He summoned a reserve of strength he felt certain would be his last as he swung the arcane sword through heavy muscles and tough sinew. The spark of shadow within him felt pale and weak, at its limits. The last of the mastiffs broke through his attack and bore him down, landing with massive paws on his chest. The wind knocked out of him, Quin was still able to swing his shoulder and land Bedlam, shrieking, in the mastiff's back before it could tear open his throat. His left hand pushed against the dog's neck, holding back the snapping jaws as Bedlam did its work.

Over the mastiff's shoulder, he could see the satyr grinning cruelly, arrows still embedded in its back. It walked calmly past the unconscious Elisandrya at the base of the column to stand over the aasimar, pinned beneath the dead weight of the mastiff.

Quinsareth watched dully as the satyr drew back the string of the black longbow and stared into his eyes down the arrow's shaft. Nauseated, the aasimar contemplated the creature's bright blue, almost human eyes, and would have laughed had he the strength for such cynicism. Those blue eyes widened in surprise, though, as the satyr's bow arm went limp and he hissed a scream.

The satyr turned and Quin saw Elisandrya gripping the bloodied arrow jutting from the fiend's wing joint. She yelled viciously as she plunged her curved blade through its chest. The satyr gazed at her in shock and fell to his knees, slumping back to stare sightlessly at the ceiling above.

Eli staggered over to Quin to shove the mastiff's body from his torso, but he was already slipping away, unconscious, lost in the bittersweet memory of a child's game.

CHAPTER THIRTEEN

The storm churned in the sky, growing wilder and more concentrated over the rune-covered tower. Those below ignored its fits and rages, oblivious to its lightning and waves of rain. Talmen and his followers carried out the commands of Morgynn in the name of Gargauth. The wizards and priests continued their labors, transforming the tower into the focal point of the tempest, while Morgynn retired above, as close to that chaos as possible.

Resting her head on her crossed arms on a cushioned divan, she was warmed by the dying embers of a brazier close by. She had brought with her across the Lake of Steam many of the luxuries she'd found in Innarlith. Apart from these amenities, the chamber remained unchanged, surprisingly intact and structurally sound despite the many years since it had last hosted guests.

The bones of Jhareat's combatants lay unmoved save for those that had cluttered the center of the room. Those had simply been shoved aside, enlarging the piles that lined the walls. The chamber was unnaturally quiet—the sounds of the storm were allowed in only when Morgynn permitted. As she rested, only a comfortable breeze passed through her wards on the window. All was still except for a single dancing shadow that flitted across the floor and walls.

The dagger spun in the air, diving and rising again. Each graceful move sliced another red line across Morgynn's lower back. She had been careless and angry in dispatching the hunters and chided herself for the brash attack. Her scars were nearly complete once more, cloaking her body in the Weave, which she wore more securely than clothing on her skin.

Slowing its macabre work, the dagger inscribed one last rune like a signature, connecting the lines of the spell in a seamless knot of dormant power. It descended to rest between her shoulder blades. Morgynn sighed as she released the dagger from her will.

The scent of cinnamon wafted from the cooling contents of the brazier, a spice she had grown fond of in Innarlith. Her eyelids fluttered as she stared at the tome in front of her, trying to put to memory those spells she would need in the coming days. Sleep came at unusually inopportune moments for her, stealing upon her waking mind and weary body after days of constant activity. She loathed that sleep and the dreams she relived over and over again.

⊙ ⊙ ⊙ ⊙ ⊙

Stones marked the edges where walls had once stood, a perimeter of ruin identifying the grounds of a nameless fortress. The herds did not approach the site, instinct carrying them far away from the ancient scents of magic and death. The Nar tribes typically ignored such places, leaving them to outsiders and adventurers foolhardy enough to enter. In the center of the ruin, a great pit stared like a black eye at the winter sky. The Well of Goorgian seemed unfavored by light, whether from sun or torches. It held the darkness of its own past in an ebon iris that would not fade, even in death.

Deep within, Morgynn traced loving hands across the inscriptions of Goorgian as the priests of the revived Order of Twilight excavated the tomes and secrets of their ancient progenitor.

"Twilight comes to wake us," she whispered to herself. "Is it prophecy? Perhaps dogma?"

The questions echoed in her mind, making her hungry to understand all of Goorgian's mysteries and madness. Hushed voices drew her attention to those behind her, laboring to shift a stone slab that had been carefully fitted in the wall.

Letting it crash to the floor, they stared in wonder at the artifacts buried in the rectangular hole. Morgynn knew these priests considered all that they found to be relics of an ancient order, sacred and holy. She saw naught but the magic and power she might wield and learn. Her eyes fell on a small wooden box carved with profane and cavorting figures. A wooden bowl bearing the same designs, stained with ancient blood, and a dagger sheathed in a scabbard of human skin also drew her attention.

Before she could even wonder what secrets these objects held, noises rang through the stones above, a deep pounding rumble as if an army passed overhead on the surface. She needed no spell of seeing to know what had come. Time had been against them, but Morgynn had never thought the day would come. It seemed shame and mercy had not stilled the spirit of her mother. Kaeless Sedras had arrived—with Lathander at her side and faith in her vengeful heart.

Artifacts were abandoned and secrets were left to collect dust as the Gargauthans assembled to dispel the disturbance. Morgynn calmly waited until the halls were cleared, collecting herself and her spells. Talmen walked ahead of her but far behind those more zealous to defend the pit with their lives.

The battle was joined in the upper courtyard as the Gargauthans rose from the depths of Goorgian's Well to defend their sacred ground. Even the upper courtyard was far below the opening to the surface, such was the state of the ruin and the destructiveness of Goorgian's last moments.

The Gargauthans acted quickly as the Sedras made their way down. Undead, controlled by the priests, slowed their enemies some, but the flames of dawn the Sedras brought with them reduced those shambling puppets to ashes. Morgynn's mother fought at the forefront, wildly swinging a heavy mace that burned with a divine light inside the cavern.

Profane magic shriveled limbs and left tribesmen breathless and dying, fodder to be animated and sent back at their comrades. So, too, did the spells and prayers of the Sedras decimate those before them. All the while, between one kill and the next, Kaeless called her daughter's name, searching for the doomed girl she had brought into the world, determined to erase the stain of guilt she bore with each day Morgynn still breathed.

Morgynn watched and listened from an alcove near the collapsed gate that led further into the ruined interior of the keep. She had no intention of satisfying her mother's desire to confront her. She was no longer the young girl her mother had rescued from the savage Creel. She was a woman and would choose her battles. The conflict between the Gargauthans and the Lathanderians was of no consequence to her, so long as she survived their fervent clash. The priests of the banished archdevil had been helpful to her, but were by no means integral to her destiny. She would keep them so long as they were useful or leave their smoldering bodies to rot in the wake of her mother's rage.

Yet something within her responded to Kaeless's demanding calls. Whether the rebellion of youth or the need to proclaim once and for all that she was not her mother's daughter, she felt compelled to answer. The need felt almost primal in its urging as she watched men die screaming and smoking under the bright weapon in her mother's hand. It would not be enough to destroy the righteous woman who'd birthed her. Kaeless needed to know, needed to understand.

"I'm not like you," she whispered, gritting her teeth and

boiling with sudden emotion and rage-filled passion. "I will walk my own path, even if it is paved in my own blood!"

She strode toward the battle, casting a spell and choosing a victim. The faces of the Sedras were indistinct and unimportant. She had little memory of the tribe, having purged names and events from her past to make room for more important knowledge. Flames flew from her fingertips, carving a smoking path through several warriors. The Weave wound itself about her body, a cloak that she pulled apart one thread at a time. Time ceased and she lost herself in the fight.

The battle did not favor the Gargauthans. Many fled, running deep into the sunken fortress to hide in the dark, cursing the vicious Nar warriors and their clerics. Bodies fell on both sides, and fueled by the Gargauthans' magic, most rose to fall again. The stench of fire and blood fed the pit with the scents of days gone by. Morgynn stood injured, struggling to cast her spells in the midst of the fray. She had precious few spells still stored and had eyed an escape route behind her several times.

Then Kaeless appeared before her. Similarly wounded and exhausted, her mother stoically strode forward to achieve what she'd come for. Morgynn's defiance returned in full fury, and those few remaining spells seemed just enough to destroy this woman who desired dominance over her fate.

The words of a spell flew across her tongue with a taste of ozone that left her body tingling. Her hands blazed with blue light and crackled with lightning. She stared down her mother but found only rage mixed with sorrow in Kaeless's eyes.

Mere yards separated them. A column of fire exploded nearby as a Gargauthan ended his life on the blade of a thrown spear, casting fiery magic blindly with his last breath. The force knocked Morgynn and Kaeless to the ground. Though Morgynn fell only to her knees, Kaeless lay on her side, shoving the sizzling corpse of a fellow warrior off her legs and grasping madly for her mace.

Morgynn jumped, landing on top of her mother and wrapping her sparking hands around Kaeless's throat. The magic burned and popped as she squeezed the shaking body of her parent, driving the lightning through Kaeless.

A blow from Morgynn's right released her hold and sent her rolling away in pain. A Sedras warrior had come to save their tribal leader and high priestess. His sword had bit deeply into her shoulder, exposing the bone. She felt a chill radiate from the wound. She shook her head to clear the haze of pain, but the world spun before her eyes.

Dimly she saw Kaeless regain her footing and lift the bright mace. Acting on reflex, Morgynn cast another spell, hurling a ball of fire. Weary with vertigo, she stumbled and the fiery sphere missed, exploding against the cavern wall behind her mother. Morgynn fell backward to the ground, screaming as her weight bore against her flayed right shoulder.

Silhouetted in flame, Kaeless approached her daughter and raised her weapon high. Morgynn spat the blood from her mouth and called yet another spell. Shouting the words, she felt the Weave respond. At the edge of its release, the spell evaporated and darkness overcame her. Raising a hand to her cheek, she felt something wet. Her blurry eyes showed the world turned on end, her face pressed to the ground and pain throbbing in the side of her head.

Her neck went limp and something pushed against her throat from within. She tried to move, to see her mother's fallen body, to witness the victory of her allies. She could see figures still fighting in the distance, but could not hear them over the pounding in her ears. Magic still hovered at the edge of her mind, tugging at her attention, demanding to be worked. Silently her lips moved, trying to comply with the instinct to complete the spell.

The only sound that triumphed over her failing senses was her mother's voice.

"Forgive me."

She felt a dull impact then succumbed to darkness.

⊙ ⊙ ⊙ ⊙ ⊙

Morgynn awoke with a start. Lying on the divan, she stared at the ancient text of a Theskan wizard she'd slain when he'd commanded her hand in marriage. She smiled at the memory, still picturing his body swinging from a post outside his home as she and the Order abandoned yet another realm to find a more fertile foothold on the continent. The smile did not last long, shadowed by the torment of old dreams.

Her stomach rumbled with much dreaded hunger. She had loathed food for years, only playing at its enjoyment while dining with powerful contacts and would-be suitors. Almost all sustenance tasted like ash and dirt in her mouth, save for strong elf wine and dwarven spirits—drinks she tended to consume in large quantities when available.

She turned her head to stare at her pack containing dried meat and fresh water. Bile rose in her throat at the thought of eating, which helped to quell the pangs in her stomach.

There would be time enough for eating later, she thought.

Waving her hand, the Theskan tome slammed shut and flew to the floor. Lifting another from beneath the divan, she caressed its red leather cover lovingly, carefully setting it upon the footstool in front of her. A haze of power surrounded the book like a web of thickened air, a threatening mirage of wards.

"*Suth vas bethed*," she whispered and ran a finger down its spine, disarming her seal upon its secrets.

This was the only book remaining from Goorgian's arcane library. Only half completed when she'd found it, now her own handwriting filled the remainder of its pages. Rumors hinted that several more tomes existed, stolen by looters and brave souls seeking quick profits. She had traced many of them to the possession of the Durthan witches of Erech Forest, just east of Goorgian's fallen stronghold in Narfell, but for now, the one would do.

She found the old wizard-priest to be insightful and imaginative, but his ideas were sometimes full of a madness born of his extended contact with creatures from the Lower Planes. Having traveled so long with the Gargauthans, Morgynn was quite aware of the dangers and pitfalls of favors and contracts with creatures of the Lower Planes.

Opening the cover, she turned to the book's center, where Goorgian's writing ended and hers began. His tight and obsessive script gave way to her flowing and hypnotic handwriting, a transition from one wizard's spells to the next, similar in theme and idea but vastly different in method and execution.

At the whisper of a cantrip, the brazier flared back to life, lighting the words on the open pages and reviving the scent of cinnamon around her. Adjusting her mind to an intense focus and awareness of the Weave, a state of concentration bordering on a trance, she devoured the text with her eyes. The study of magic was a different experience for her than for most wizards. Memorized spells merely filled the minds of other wizards, burning themselves in memory. For Morgynn, the words entered her eyes, settled in her mind, and were carried away in the space of a heartbeat to burn themselves throughout her body. Each spell she cast thereafter left her colder and wanting more.

Morgynn held vigil with the book until she no longer knew whether it was day or night. Raising her eyes from the final page, the arcane words swam in her vision. She stood and replaced the seal upon the book, then reluctantly reached for the pack of food. She grasped something hard and dry, not caring what it was, but made certain to take a bottle of wine. She walked to the window with the meager meal, warmth flowing in her veins as she contentedly gazed outside and forced herself to eat.

The field of stone below was illuminated in brief flashes of lightning as the Gargauthans still set to their task. Several summoning circles had been drawn to facilitate the Gargauthans' spells. A contingent of gnolls, no doubt survivors from Mahgra's failed attempt on Targris, loped in from the forest and met with Khaemil. She ate sparingly and drank freely until the bottle was emptied and tossed aside.

Half the stale bread still lay in her hand, its tasteless remainder sitting like lead in her stomach. The empty bottle of Derluskan wine lay shattered on the floor at her feet. Its taste did little to erase the dryness in her mouth and had reduced her hunger only slightly.

Her mind felt full and satisfied with the peaceful calm of magic that flowed through her blood and rested at her fingertips. She threw the bread among the bones beneath the window and walked back to the cushioned divan, unable to resist further rest. Sitting down, she stared into the glowing coals in the brazier, focusing on their light. Though she wanted to be prepared for the coming battle, she considered sleep a necessary evil, tolerated but unwanted.

"Wasted time," she murmured.

She wondered at her own words. Did they describe sleep, or her youth? Past and present were interchangeable at times, and she'd often feared waking up face down on the stone floor of the courtyard in Goorgian's pit. She scoffed at her foolishness and knew that worse fears lingered in the cloudy mists of her memory.

When she awoke next, the Order of Twilight would move against Brookhollow and the Oracles of the Hidden Circle. As she lay on the long couch, she imagined their faces as she strode into their sacred ground, as her minions took apart their defenses and brought low the primary obstacle against her ambitions. Flames licked at the walls of their temple as she drifted to sleep. Her waking thoughts faded as she slumbered, giving way to incessant memory. Marble walls became rough stone and peace became chaos.

⊕ ⊕ ⊕ ⊕ ⊕

Talmen had escaped the battle, hiding in the ruins and wringing his hands in anger and fear. He did not consider himself a coward, but he knew a losing situation when he saw one. The Sedras had come prepared to kill and die in their crusade against his kind. The Gargauthans had not been prepared for either, trusting in the natural fear the Nar tribesman bore for the abandoned cities and ruins of their ancestors.

They hadn't counted on Morgynn or a mother's desire to see a daughter dead.

As the remainder of the Gargauthans fled in a hail of arrows and spears, Talmen watched. The Sedras gathered around their high priestess, prying her away from the fallen form of Morgynn. Climbing up on ropes and bare stone, the Sedras left the pit known as the Well of Goorgian, taking with them their own dead and leaving the rest to rot.

Time passed and the malefactor saw no evidence that the Sedras would return, but he could still hear noises high above and he ordered the other priests to go below, deeper into the ruins. The light of numerous flames flickered from the mouth of the pit, growing brighter with each breath. Talmen could feel the heat that filled the chamber and watched in rage as stone melted and dripped. Crashing down in a glowing cascade, the magic of Lathander's priests sealed the entrance with molten rock, causing cave-ins that blocked any escape.

As the seal spread, compounding itself with fallen rocks and cold soil from beneath the tundra's surface, Talmen's eyes returned to the still and bloody body of Morgynn. Even in death he found her beautiful. Looking to the darkness behind him, to the safety in the lower depths, he was suddenly pulled by some unfathomable desire to that battered body staring at him with blank and half-closed eyes.

He was at her side in a few heartbeats, dodging the rocks and glowing bits of debris that tumbled down the steep sides of the collapsing pit. A heated rock landed on the hem of his robe, burning a neat hole through it and setting it aflame. He cursed and beat the fire away, glaring at the unseen presence of the Sedras above, swearing an oath to exact satisfaction for their incursion.

Looking down on Morgynn again, his oath took form and face, seeing the proper tool for such vengeance. Without delay, he pulled her legs away from the glowing, encroaching wall and lifted her limp form over his shoulder. He carried her, disappearing into the chilled corridors and fallen stairways of the ancient city.

Grimly, his mind was already beginning to imagine what bargaining it would take to gain Gargauth's favor in this endeavor. As he pushed on, deeper and deeper, he felt a sense of providence and strange destiny, a calm that strengthened his resolve to continue.

In spite of that feeling, uneasiness lurked somewhere behind it, like the waiting jaws of a trap from which he might never escape.

⊕ ⊕ ⊕ ⊕ ⊕

Morgynn's eyelids fluttered and she rolled uneasily in her sleep, but she did not awaken from her slumber on the divan.

CHAPTER FOURTEEN

Elisandrya sat on a boulder and stared.

She had done all she knew for Quin—bandaged his wounds, mixed healing herbs for poultices as the Ghedia had taught her, and collected rain water for him to drink when he stirred.

He'd slept peacefully the entire day. Night was once again dominating behind the clouds, banishing the misty, veiled light of the sun. In the flicker of the small campfire, she studied him and wondered if he was the one—if Savras had led her to him. The implications of that possibility boggled her mind in light of Sameska's prophecy.

She saw no symbols of Hoar on him, no sign that he followed the fickle lord of justice. He was attractive in an odd way. A pervading sense of goodness surrounded him, but something else lingered in his strange eyes, something dark. That curiosity held her gaze for a long time.

Eli had seen and heard of aasimar before, people touched by the blood of a celestial ancestor, but she had never come face to face with one or known their names. He had fought with an unexpected fierceness, a lust for battle that went far beyond mere necessity. She had not gone so far as to touch the screaming blade he'd wielded in battle, having wrapped it in his cloak and carried it carefully out of the temple through a secret passage beneath the altar.

Quin coughed in his sleep, disrupting her thoughts as he finally awoke. Groaning, he rolled away from the fire, shielding his eyes. His hand went to his side and he looked about, searching for the sword absent from his hip.

"Not to worry, stranger, your blade is safe."

Quin turned and stared at her for a few moments before recognition dawned. Their introduction had been interrupted so abruptly. She wasn't surprised he didn't know her at first. Though the events afterward had felt like days, he still knew her name.

"Elisandrya."

"Yes. You've been asleep for quite some time. I'm surprised to see you awake after the beating you took, and had obviously taken before. You lied to me when you said you were all right."

"I never said I was all right, just that I would survive." His wan smile belied the pain in his aching body. "I guess I was right, eh?"

"Just barely," she murmured, and leaned forward to check the bandages on his leg.

Quin's hand shot forward and grabbed her wrist, holding it inches above the injury. He looked at her in confusion and alarm. Eli froze, shocked by his reaction, but his grip relaxed as he realized her intent. He waited quietly while she inspected the wound.

"I don't think it's fractured, but the skin was broken and the bone is surely bruised. You were lucky. If the mastiff had held a moment longer, it could've been much worse."

An awkward silence came between them as Eli sat back and stoked the fire. Quin looked away, and she felt sorry for him. Though they were strangers to one another, despite fighting for their lives together, he seemed more vulnerable than she'd imagined. It did not seem a trait he was comfortable with. She knew herself that independence breeds a tough skin until broken by circumstance or injury. Not wanting to rely on others seemed a trait they shared.

"I'm sor—" he began.

"No need for apologies. I'd have reacted much the same had our situations been reversed." She turned to look at him. "Trust is a hard thing to come by."

"Indeed," he answered quietly.

Returning her attention to the fire, she changed the subject.

"How did you know how to seal the temple like that?"

"I've seen its like before." He pushed himself to a sitting position as he spoke, wincing. "Demon cults, usually. Their priests are fanatical about recruiting new followers into the fold, but not very attached when it comes to enacting suicide pacts for their unholy masters. When the time for poison, bleeding, or flames comes, measures are taken to ensure the souls reach their intended destination.

"Stone blocks, or locked or guarded doors keep the followers inside, while the priest himself escapes, extolling the virtues of spreading the faith."

Elisandrya shuddered, shocked that such practices occurred in the lands she knew so well.

"I gather you've traveled in many lands, then?"

"I've seen my share, yes."

His answer was guarded, but he seemed more comfortable speaking to her. She sensed a common liking for the freedom of the open road.

"You're traveling south now?"

"Possibly," he said, narrowing his eyes. "Why do you ask?"

She looked at him then, confused about how to answer. She had not thought about explaining Sameska's prophecy before that moment, or how to explain such a thing to someone outside the Hidden Circle's faith. She had witnessed unpleasant reactions before, in Derlusk a few times, when people were confronted with the idea of divinations and her faith's confidence in their knowledge of the future.

There was something in Quin, though, that she could not describe, a feeling bordering on contradiction that made him hard to place. It intrigued her, unlike most of the gruff men she had known throughout her life. Somehow, deep within, she knew Savras had guided her, but the implications of that feeling only disturbed her more. She dreaded what the future might hold for her people. Taking a deep breath and trusting instinct, she chose her path and forged ahead with the truth.

"Two evenings ago, my order gathered at the Temple of the Hidden Circle in Brookhollow, south of here, to heed the prophecies of the high oracle. Recent events, such as plague and this unseasonable chill, made the gathering an event surrounded by ill omens, but when the high oracle began to speak . . ." she hesitated. "We were told of a man like you."

She poured out the tale that had set her to riding through the storm. Quin did not so much as blink as she spoke. She considered it a testament to his self-control that he took in the story of prophecy, plague, and dark magic without renouncing her as completely insane.

◉ ◉ ◉ ◉ ◉

Stained glass rattled in the leaded frame of the dome above Dreslya as the storm hovered to the north of Brookhollow, growling and increasing its intensity. Though the high shutters had been closed against the wind, she still shivered in the chill that permeated the temple in spite of all attempts to make things seem normal.

She stared at the base of Savras's statue, unable to pull her gaze away from the streaks of brown that had dried into the stone after Nivael's strange and gruesome death. Until then, only the old and infirm had been threatened by the fatality of the blush. Denial now filled the halls of the temple like a hushed secret thrashing against constraints—unspoken, but known and feared.

Candles had been lit along the walls. They added to the shadows and whispers that crawled and floated from one person to the next, scurrying away to hide as Sameska and the oracles walked by, making their way to the inner chamber behind the sanctuary. Dreslya had not been summoned to gather with the others, but Baertah had arrived at her chamber to escort her to the sanctuary. Sameska desired her presence, he'd told her. She had no doubt what the high oracle wished to address.

"Tragic, is it not?"

Dreslya jumped, looking up from the dried remains of Nivael's blood to find Sameska at her side.

"Do not be so frightened, child. Surely you have nothing to fear here? Nothing to hide, perhaps?"

Shaken and somewhat uncomfortable under Sameska's scrutiny, Dres did not reply. Whatever the high oracle had called her for was most likely already known. Dres had no desire to play Sameska's game of rhetorical questions. Though she and the other oracles were priestesses and clerics of Savras, his was predominantly a faith of diviners and wizardly magic. Though able to call upon his power in prayer and meditation, it was in the Weave of magic where their true strengths lay.

Noting Dreslya's refusal to take her bait, Sameska continued more directly.

"Why did you not inform us immediately of your sister's absence and purpose?"

"I merely found a note, High Oracle. I did not open the town gates for her. She was gone and nothing could be done."

"The tone in your voice seems to say otherwise, *child.*"

She drew out the last word, as if to emphasize Dreslya's place in the order of things. Sameska was not accustomed to accepting even a hint of insolence from her lessers.

Dres quavered beneath what she now observed as madness in Sameska's eyes. Where there had once been an admittedly haughty yet wise countenance was now a fanatical dementia. Dark circles sagged beneath the high oracle's eyes and her face was drawn and tense.

"My tone does not change the fact, High Oracle. Elisandrya made her own decision."

"A decision that you knew about! A decision that threatens the lives of us all, that denies the very will of Savras and his prophecy!"

Sameska was livid, shaking with rage, more emotional than Dreslya had ever seen her. The young oracle looked away hopelessly, lost in confusion and knowing full well that reason was a futile tactic at this point. She could hear Baertah huffing in wordless and derisive agreement to Sameska's accusations, and she could almost feel his sneer of self-righteousness burning into the back of her head.

Straightening her robes and fixing her disheveled hair, Sameska softened her stare to a mild look of stern command.

"We have gathered here for five generations to venerate the teachings of Savras, to be carriers of truth and visions of what may come. You have kept truth from your sisters, and this is not acceptable.

"Dreslya Loethe, I banish you from attending the Council of the Hidden Circle this night, and until such time as your wayward sister returns to Brookhollow to face judgment before her peers. As Elisandrya is most likely already the victim of her own actions, I do not expect to see you at the council again."

Sameska turned away and disappeared behind the curtained alcove at the edge of the altar's dais, slamming the inner chamber's door behind her.

Dreslya's quiet fears for her sister were revealed in Sameska's words. She wept, heedless of Baertah's rolling eyes and disinterested sigh as he left her alone in the sanctuary. She was more alone than he knew. She felt the final loss of her family descend on her shoulders and bear her to the floor.

⊙ ⊙ ⊙ ⊙ ⊙

Quin glanced toward Elisandrya as she gathered her equipment, checking arrows and bowstrings for dampness.

She didn't look up at him as she fidgeted with her pack. He'd wandered to the edge of the road after her confession about the prophecy, unable to speak for the tempest that raged within him. He did not blame this warrior woman who'd helped him and fought by his side. Faith in and of itself was not an offense to him. This high oracle and so-called prophecy, however, he could not entirely accept. He didn't—couldn't—believe it.

Eli stood and kicked at the dying remnants of their campfire, the embers hissing as the wet soil smothered them. He watched as she double-checked her sword and her newly repaired bow. She chanced a look toward him, and he turned away, afraid that she might misunderstand his sudden silence. Still afraid that she might fear him.

Quietly she approached him from behind. Clearing her throat, she spoke first, breaking the awful quiet.

"You do not plan to continue on to Littlewater, do you?"

Quin shook his head slowly and fixed his gaze south along the curve of the Low Road. Though he was curious to know why he was being sought by Littlewater's guards, it was obvious they were not the reason he was called to the region. Elisandrya's tale of prophecy had proven that.

He held his tongue. He had seen towns disappear because of prophecy and complacent faith. The ruins of Char were still fresh in his mind, the blackened bones on ancient pews. The bloodied gates in Logfell were not far from his thoughts either.

His wounds still ached, having grown stiff while he rested. He needed the healing winds of the shadowalk to prepare him for what lay ahead. Sleep had returned the mystical current of darkness to his spirit, allowing him access to that supernatural ability. Despite his desire to feel whole again, the warrior woman stood behind him, her eyes full of questions.

He felt obligated to explain himself to her, for saving his life and tending to his wounds. He sensed a kindred spirit in her, a love of the road and a desire to act rather than wait for things to get better. She had defied her elders in coming to find him. He owed her as much as he could summon himself to admit.

Turning to face her, he forgot much of what he'd thought to say as their eyes met.

"I am no champion—barely a Hoarite, and certainly no priest. I am led by an oath I made long ago, and I place no weight in dangerous prophecies. I have been called ghost-walker, but this is just as often an insult as a description."

"What are you saying?"

He leveled his gaze once again to the south, narrowing his eyes and collecting his thoughts.

"I think this Sameska has endangered her people by giving them a false hope when they should be arming themselves against whatever lurks in those trees." He looked back to her. "And I'm saying that you feel the same way, otherwise you would not be here." Though his words were presumptuous considering the short time they had spent together, he felt confident they were true and awaited her response.

"Fair enough. What do you propose we do about it?"

His lips curved in a grim smile. "We're going to Brookhollow."

"But that will only strengthen Sameska's stance against defending the city. With your arrival there, the prophecy may go unopposed."

He placed a hand on her shoulder and his smile grew broader, a mischievous light dancing in his strange eyes. "Humor me."

His sudden change in demeanor startled her, and she looked at him curiously. Though dark forces seemed gathered against all she knew, she waited in his pearly gaze. He could not help but be astounded by her.

"Fine. But we must get moving quickly," she said. "It's almost three days to Brookhollow without horses or magic. With your injuries, we should try to get close to Littlewater so I can—"

"No," he said. "We don't need horses."

Quinsareth felt the situation fully and knew what they had to do. He could not leave her in the middle of the road, but the alternative felt almost shameful to him, exposing her to terrible dangers despite the necessity. He closed his eyes, reaching within himself until the shadow responded.

"Take my hand," he said.

Hesitantly, she agreed, and the world around them turned dark, wavering as the world beneath their world became visible in an array of shadows. He heard her whisper a quiet prayer as she stood closer to him, leaning into him. Though her prayer was finished and she did not speak, Quin still heard her voice somehow. In disbelief, he listened to what he assumed were her thoughts, quoting the words of her high oracle as she gazed on the blackened landscape of the shadow realm.

He shall walk on a road of shadow.

"How can this be?" he whispered.

The ground beneath them blurred, disappearing as they proceeded into a world of darkness that swallowed their steps.

◎ ◎ ◎ ◎ ◎

The inner chamber of the Hidden Circle represented the pinnacle of the history of the order since its founding in Brookhollow. It was lit by several waist-high columns. On top of each, a pool of glowing water shimmered like quicksilver. The floors were of rift marble, an especially hard stone whose mixture of swirling and geometric patterns was unique to the dwarf realm from which it had come.

In the center of the circular room lay a pool of placid water, a divining pool drained and filled daily by the savants. Most were aware that the pool was filled only as a formality, as it had not been used in years. Unlike her predecessors, Sameska did not approve of anyone displaying their powers in her presence, despite the Council of the Hidden Circle's long-held traditions.

The whole of the room was topped in a dome, a smaller version of that in the primary sanctuary. Its walls were carved with thousands of concentric circular patterns like ripples in a rainstorm. Their similarity to the unceasing storms outside was not lost on anyone in attendance.

Sameska sat in the polished oak chair at the head of the circle and glowered disapprovingly at her lessers. The twenty remaining oracles sat before their leader, avoiding her stare and deciding how best to continue their controversial inquiry into the fate of the other towns along the Qurth's border. In light of the edict against Brookhollow's resistance, none knew how to suggest that perhaps they could request aid from outside allies.

Sameska had all but accused them of blasphemy.

One young woman finally spoke, staring at her hands and attempting to resolve the situation calmly.

"We do not doubt you, High Oracle, or the words of Savras . . ."

"Questions of this nature are the very soul of doubt, are they not?"

The high oracle's voice had risen. Her eyes darted from one young woman to the next, seeking dissidence among them, alert to whispers and accusing eyes. Sameska had slept only fitfully since the evening of her chilling prophecy. Her nightmares had become amplified by her own fears. Her adamancy to stay the course, though, had been bolstered. There was no other way, in her mind, no doubt whatsoever—none that she might share with these rivals, in any case.

These girls are little better than Dreslya in hiding their obvious contempt and jealousy, she thought. *What do they know of prophecy? Of true divination?*

She stared through the door as if it were transparent, knowing that the statue still stood, stained with blood and tainted by death. She imagined its single eye upon her, the eye of Savras, dimmed in red and unblinking.

"Forgive us, High Oracle," another said, "we are afraid and our own spells have shown us nothing. Anything within the borders of the forest is invisible to us. We seek your sight and wisdom in these trying times, nothing more."

All stared at Sameska's back nervously. She had turned around completely in her chair, staring at the closed doors while wringing her hands and mumbling incoherently.

The words flitted through her mind, weaving between

her thoughts and imagined horrors until she realized she had actually heard them. She spun back around, narrowing her eyes at them, wondering if they had heard her, seen what she'd seen beyond the door. She felt it still—Savras's lidless gaze on her back—and she shuddered.

"What to say?" she whispered to herself, staring at their frightened and confused faces. Her mind teetered on the edge of inspiration, chasing the spark of her own reasoning through the fog of numerous thoughts that assailed her weary consciousness. She stretched herself straighter in her chair, grasping its arms and clawing absently at the smooth wood.

"Pardon, High Oracle?" the same woman asked quietly, a note of pity creeping into her voice.

Sameska held her breath, tensing as the answer revealed itself to her.

"The ruins of Jhareat," she said finally, formulating her words carefully so as not to reveal more than she felt prudent. "Beyond the edges of the Qurth, deep in the forest, lies Jhareat and its single tower. Do you remember its tale?"

Several in the room were visibly relieved by the high oracle's suddenly lucid voice as they recalled the story. It was a tale that most of them had heard as children, first gazing upon the walls of the Hidden Circle's sanctuary. A few nodded, sagelike, while most listened attentively, curious as to the nature of Sameska's obscure reference.

"All the oracles who came before us divined the history of this realm—the land, the forest, and the ruins that lay scattered across the fields and buried in the grip of the Qurth. The legends that they discovered decorate the walls of our sanctuary as reminders of history and how tenuous our survival is in this land if we lack foresight.

"Evil ruled within the walls of Jhareat in ancient times, during the days of the Shoon Dynasties."

She stood, looking down at them, almost smiling as she dangled her secrets before their blind eyes. She knew they would hear but a comforting tale while she held the truth in her grip, having seen that tower and the dark forces gathered around it. She did not trust their willful youth and would not see her prophecy disobeyed by brash actions and unthinking fear.

"One man. One man brought about the downfall of that terrible city. Savras sends us one man as well and asks only for our patience." Her scholarly tone disappeared, overcome by her earlier anger. "Think carefully on this before you question and doubt me again!"

She turned and left them, closing the doors behind her and ending all debate.

Standing in the alcove to the sanctuary, she listened for their voices and their whispers. Silence.

Turning her attention from the door, she gazed at the dark curtain that hung between her and the altar of Savras beyond. In her mind's eye she could see him, standing there in stone robes. She raised a hand to move the curtain aside and stopped. Her fingertips brushed lightly at the cloth, but fear held her in place. A chill such as only a god might inspire in the faithful kept her from moving for many heartbeats before she finally entered the sanctuary.

CHAPTER FIFTEEN

Talmen eyed his followers warily, studying their control of the creatures they had summoned from the Lower Planes. His senior acolytes had successfully gathered a small troop of malebranche devils, enticing them with promises of blood and destruction. The hulking brutes, four in all, shook their great horned heads and stamped the ground, gnashing their fangs and roaring in voices culled from the deepest nightmares of living men. The ground shook as they pounded the dirt with massive clawed fists in anticipation of the promised carnage.

The malefactor smiled at their ferocity. In their own realm, the malebranche served as shock troops and soldiers, but on Faerûn they were nothing less than living engines of war, towering above their foes. Turning back to the less capable of his wizard-priests, he watched with concern as five of them began the final ritual of their summoning.

Within their circle raged a dozen abyssal ghouls, thrashing and howling against the magical constraints of the arcane perimeter drawn on the ground. Undead were, as a rule, much easier to call and command, but these half-mad creatures were a test of will for even the more experienced Gargauthans. Talmen paid close attention to the efforts of the five as they sealed the controlling spell and made ready to release the bonds of the inscribed circle.

Already he could see that minor mistakes had been made, but he took no steps to interfere. Those who survived would be stronger and wiser for the experience.

In unison the five broke the circle, chanting the last of their binding and taking hold of the symbols of Gargauth about their necks, a gesture of control to denote themselves as the masters of the ghouls. The majority of the creatures stood still, swaying in an almost trancelike manner, with their unnaturally long fingers dragging the ground. Glowing white eyes looked blindly upon their summoners. They hungrily lashed long, whiplike tongues around their gaunt faces, the ends of the purplish tentacles trailing off into a dark mist.

One of the five acolytes, sensing something wrong, held his symbol higher and repeated the infernal language of command. The three ghouls before him shook their heads and tensed, crouched and growling, digging furrows into the dirt and mud as they leaned back on birdlike legs. Their blind eyes rolled and they sniffed at the air, smelling his fear. The priest's voice cracked as he desperately repeated the command again.

The change in his tone incensed the ghouls. They jumped, howling, and pounced on his screaming form, burying the misty ends of their proboscis tongues in his head and torso. His screams filled the clearing as they drank his mind and raked at his unarmored body, tearing his robes and flesh to bloody shreds.

Talmen casually glanced at all who stood nearby, including the four who had been successful in their summonings, making sure that all saw the consequences of failure. Once the man's screams faded, Talmen stepped forward and raised his own symbol, chanting a spell of command far beyond the ability of the fallen priest. The ghouls immediately took notice, turning their bald heads and dead eyes on this new voice, but continued to feed on the body, their smoky tongues reaching past mere flesh and bone to suck at the very marrow of the man's identity.

In the grating tones of an abyssal language, Talmen conferred command of the ghouls to the surviving four. The priests' masks hid faces of disgust as the creatures shambled away from the mess they had made of their meal. From the shoulders down, the man was unrecognizable as having been human, yet his neck and head were untouched. His unmasked face conveyed all too well the horror of his last moments.

Looking up to Morgynn's darkened window, Talmen wondered if she'd witnessed or enjoyed the spectacle. His scrying upon her had been unsuccessful of late, but this he attributed to the growing power of the storm that surrounded the tower. Part of the genius of Morgynn's ideas included an obscuring spell that foiled all attempts to scry upon Jhareat or even the surrounding forest. The dense magic around the tower was barely contained. He could sense the design of the Weave bending to accommodate the dense net of spells being laid to summon and control the tempest.

The symbol Morgynn had burned into his arm still throbbed, in tune to the restless host in the forest, the bathor, the undead of Logfell. Morgynn doted on her creations, calling them her children. He shuddered and rubbed at the scar, returning to his tasks and muttering prayers to Gargauth for a swift victory and an end to the whole affair.

◎ ◎ ◎ ◎ ◎

Time in the tower passed swiftly as Morgynn slumbered, tossing and turning in the throes of nightmares woven of old memory. Her skin was flushed by the swift current in her veins that had become agitated and heated as her dreams progressed, closer and closer, through battle and flame and darkness, to the chill of death. The dream, the memory, was relentless.

Darkness had become a vast landscape of bewildered faces, all meandering slowly toward a glittering spire of rock in the far distance. Lightning hung in her mind; the spell, not yet fully formed, clung to her thoughts. Kaeless was gone. The Well of Goorgian, the Sedras, the battle—all gone. She had no time to contemplate what had happened before powerful clawed hands gripped her shoulders and pulled her back into a swirling pit of crimson tornadoes. As she fell, a second landscape came into view, another sky she was falling through. Her back slammed into the surface, a ground that gave way like thick mud, knocking the breath from her lungs.

A red sky filled her vision as she sank in a black bog. A foul wind carried the scents of burning flesh and rot. She struggled to keep her head above the slime that had her in its grasp. Her limbs felt weak and sluggish, unable to fully obey her commands, her desire to pull free. Dark shapes flitted overhead and cavorted in the tempestuous sky. The silhouettes of what appeared to be giant mountains loomed in the distance.

Squirming in the strange bog were the wormlike forms of hideous creatures. Their pale skin was smooth and glistening as they flopped and splashed. Now and then, a head would emerge, bearing a humanoid face and smacking lips full of the dark ooze, gnashing toothless gums and wailing like a newborn infant.

Morgynn tried to scream as well, but her throat felt raw and she could manage only a weak croak. She freed one arm and reached outward, seeking something to hold onto. The flesh of her arm was loose and torn in several places. Her blood streamed into the thick, tarlike fluid and seemed to excite the wailing worms. She could feel them sliding against her body, biting her flesh and tasting her skin with cold tongues. Frantically she waved her arm and thrashed against the gnawing beasts, flexing fingers that were almost skinless as she clawed at the air. The soft beds of her fingernails lay exposed and the winds lashed across them, sending lances of fresh pain down her arms.

Loud voices roared and argued somewhere nearby. In the part of her mind that had not been lost to utter madness, she recognized their language with sickening horror. The unseen beasts argued in the language of demons, the tongue of the Abyss. They were fighting over the pleasure of owning her soul.

Fresh pain washed over her head as the memory of her mother's last blow returned. The sensation played itself slowly, her skull fracturing, the mace exposing the fragile tissue beneath to the open air. Again and again she died, ignominiously, in the courtyard of Goorgian's Well.

Moments stretched into years as, bit by bit, Morgynn lost hold of herself. Her flesh was dissolving in the muck, devoured by the maggoty things around her as it sloughed off. A fleeting realization that she was becoming one of them crossed her mind but was quickly forgotten as her eyelids drooped and a few teeth slipped away from her loosening gums.

The argument over her soul ended, and a night-skinned hag stood grinning with lion's teeth nearby, heating a branding iron over a venting crack in the ground. Behind the hag stood a massive creature with red skin and burning eyes, enveloped in massive batlike wings like a deep red cloak. The fiend's horned head nodded in approval as the hag held up the white-hot brand for his inspection.

Morgynn's eyes rolled back, barely seeing the blurred colors of the bruised sky above. Her body had begun to shrink. Her legs were numb and she wondered briefly if they were still there. Madness beckoned in her mind with the long trembling claws of a mania from which there could be no escape. Hope for death was lost to her now—that bridge had been crossed. Only oblivion awaited beyond this hellish afterlife.

An airy giggle passed her lips as the spell she'd left unfinished still floated through her mind, teasing her with that feeling of the living, the warmth and ecstasy of magic. Desperately, she clung to those arcane phrases, nearly weeping as she spoke them uncontrollably, feeling the emptiness that lurked behind them grow as they were lost. The lightning faded from her thoughts, but, strangely, its heat remained as if mocking her death.

The spell was gone. She knew she would never feel its power again. Never would she feel the Weave respond to her command and flow through her body, but despite her fears and lamentations, something strange happened. Her blood began to burn and a searing light assailed her eyes. The lightning returned. The magic tingled through her blood, summoning it back into a heart that beat more fiercely than she remembered.

She could still see the hag and its reaching brand, the worming souls around her and the ever-changing colors of the sky, but she also saw her arms rising in the air unhindered by the foul ooze.

New life flooded through her in waves of unspeakable heat and wild, pulsing magic such as she'd never felt before. A droning chant surrounded her, drowning out all other sounds as she rose, weightless, into the air. The night hag's fanged mouth opened in a stifled roar as she stabbed at Morgynn's rising form with the heated brand to no effect.

Morgynn ignored her, fixated on the warmth of life and magic that mingled in her body, growing stronger as the chant grew louder. Her heartbeat joined the relentless voices in her mind, and she flew upward into the tumultuous sky. Tiny bat-winged creatures swarmed toward her, and she screamed in horror as their claws lodged in her retreating heels. Looking back, she kicked at the little green-skinned demons. Her sanity swooned as she felt them pulling her down, into the pit, to the worms and the hag with her cruel brand.

Her screams continued for a long time, even as the walls of Goorgian's Well coalesced around her. Gargauthan priests in fearful masks stood gathered, ghostlike and somber, as her eyes fluttered open. Her flesh transformed and trails of blood receded into closing wounds. The bones of her misshapen face, disfigured by her mother's killing blow, cracked and popped, knitting together. Talmen held his ears as her ungodly wails echoed throughout the ruined halls of the Well.

As Morgynn opened eyes that streamed crimson tears, her laughter became maniacal. Somehow, she had evaded death. Goorgian's dark, battle-scarred well looked like a paradise. Kaeless had lost but still had much more to lose.

⊛ ⊛ ⊛ ⊛ ⊛

On the first day of autumn, the horses had grown sick, becoming weak then dying within days. The nomadic Sedras were at a loss to treat such a virulent disease. Magic and healing had availed them nothing. Rumors of a horse plague would make them outcasts among the scattered tribes of the Nar. Fear of a harsh winter, though, settled more deeply into the bones.

An autumn without productive hunting would make the colder months all the more difficult. They moved more and more slowly, until finally they stopped to construct a more permanent settlement for the safety of the tribe. Light gray skies blanketed the snow-covered permafrost when Morgynn and the Order of Twilight finally beheld their wandering foes.

The smell of smoke from the campfires drifted on the late afternoon air. The temperature had dropped considerably in the last few days, a constant reminder of colder days to come. The Gargauthans wore heavy cloaks and furs, while Morgynn had shed many of the usual trappings of the Nar plains, filled as she was with a feverish heat that coursed through her body. She was barefoot in the snow, wearing little more than a crimson robe and small pieces of found armor for modesty's sake against the bitter northern winds.

The day was drawing to a close, bringing thoughts of supper and sleep under the darkening gray of the clouded sky. The season's silence carried a young girl's voice across the plain, clear as the calling horns traditional among the Nar tribes.

Pieces of an old Lathanderian chant sought their ears,

ghostlike across the white fields, eerie as it twisted in the wind.

In the flames of his crown,
We give praise to the dawn.
In the fields where we hunt,
We give praise to the light.

Morgynn remembered the tune only vaguely, having heard it as a child, before she was taken away by the Creel. It was a song of ending, a light-hearted dirge for the setting sun. Its haunting melody had no meaning for her anymore, though her head ached to remember such things from before her untimely death.

Masked from sight by illusions, the newly formed Order awaited Morgynn's command, already viewing her as a sign of their god's favor. Morgynn surveyed the peaceful camp, settling in for the evening with only unmounted scouts on foot to watch for signs of danger. The smell of cooking horseflesh signaled the beginning of a mournful supper. They had slain one of the healthy to feed the tribe until they could catch up to the wild oxen in the foothills of the Giantspire Mountains.

The song drew to a close, the last lines awakening the burgeoning spirit of destiny that burned in the blood of Morgynn's restored body.

Night is yawning,
The Dusk is falling,
Twilight is dawning,
The Sun is calling
'Farewell 'til the morning's prayer.'

The last note disappeared in the wind. Morgynn narrowed her eyes and stretched her fingers out wide to her sides, touching those warm tendrils, the unseen connections from pulse to pulse in the hidden forces of the Order. Her silent command was clear and unmistakable.

"Kill them all."

The battle those words precluded was swift and brutal. The Sedras were weak, and the Order was prepared. There was no salvation for the tribe. Hunger gave them a desperation for survival but little else. The evening matured quickly as Morgynn waded through an ocean of chaos.

Sweat poured across her brow in pink rivulets. Her entire body was flushed with heat and pulsing with magic, an instrument of the Weave vibrating with power. The ground became soft and spongy beneath her feet. The permafrost of the tundra melted and became mud as fires raged across the Sedras camp.

All around her, magic seethed and slithered from vengeful Gargauthan throats. Unimaginable beasts howled in the ungodly pain of tortured existences as they heeded the bidding of the Order and fed on the flesh of the fallen and dying. Their hideous melodies sang in her mind, etching themselves in the depths of memory.

Morgynn drank in the moment, lived in the passing time of the night and early morning. She immersed herself in the final act of a former life, the first task of a spirit lost to blood and magic.

The sky was a halo of light, a false dawn to mock Lathander's breach of the eastern horizon. That sunrise would find only waste and char, carrion and silent screams whistling through mouths agape with voiceless tongues. Devilish visages, leering faces of crafted wood and painted metals, paced solemnly among the remains, witnesses to the death of one moment and the birth of another. They all looked north one by one to the girl they had wrought from injury and Abyss. A shadowy black dog slunk close to the hem of her crimson robes, casting bright and intelligent eyes on any who came near this new mistress.

Talmen, now the Grand Malefactor of the Order of Twilight, gazed upon Morgynn's dark beauty in awe. The light of flames danced across the broken horns of the skull-grinning mask he wore. Acolytes gathered behind him, following his lengthy stare as they whispered prayers of promise and offering.

Morgynn ignored them all, circling the prone form of a

final enemy, the first enemy she had ever known. Golden armor was battered and warped, blackened in spots and spattered by mud and blood. A heavy mace that had once glowed like the sun lay twisted and broken, beyond the reach of fingers too weak to lift it. Kaeless breathed raggedly, puffs of steam drifting lazily in the dying morning wind. Her eyes stared sightlessly into the gray sky. She shook her head in senseless denial, lost in a silent prayer. A plea for mercy or forgiveness, Morgynn could not tell.

Kaeless's head jerked to one side, suddenly alert to the noise of nearby footsteps.

"Forgive me! Forgive me!" she cried mournfully, pleading blindly. "I killed her! I killed her, and Lathander punishes us! My own daughter. . . ."

Her voice trailed away into nonsense, mere mumblings as the pain of mortal wounds slid like burning ice through her body.

Morgynn knelt closer, shaking with baleful animosity, to reach her mother's ear. "No. You didn't kill her." She kept her voice soft, soothing.

Kaeless squinted, trying to make out the dark blur against the lightening sky, trying to identify that familiar voice. She held her breath, waiting for that woman to speak again, to absolve her soul of wrongdoing.

"She isn't dead." Morgynn reached out to stroke her mother's matted hair, leaning in and whispering, "She is damned."

Morgynn's hand clamped over Kaeless's nose and mouth, foregoing magic or dagger so she could feel the life ebb between her fingers. In moments, her mother's eyes glazed over, her trembling stopped, and the battle was over.

A chant arose among the Gargauthans in the blasted field, a prayer to their devil-god. Morgynn heard them, but did not listen. She sat and stared at the hands she had felt melting away in a grave of ooze as demons had bargained over her soul. A gust of the north wind blew across the small hill, and she marveled at the gooseflesh that arose along arms covered in scars and blood.

⊕ ⊕ ⊕ ⊕ ⊕

Panting, Morgynn awoke. Recognizing her surroundings, she rubbed her forehead and her eyes, trying to clear the fog. The plains and the Sedras camp were gone, replaced by her chamber atop the tower of Jhareat. The dreams had ended.

Morgynn sat on the edge of the divan, bent at the waist, rubbing her temples and shutting out the phantom noises of her awakening. Khaemil was nearby; she felt the vial of his blood at her belt stir and churn. He could wait. She sat still for a long time, trembling as her emotions ran amok. No matter how much she slept, she always awoke exhausted.

⊕ ⊕ ⊕ ⊕ ⊕

Morgynn descended the stairs carefully, weary from dreaming too long. Near the bottom, she heard voices outside. Talmen's was one—his voice and emotions were known to her through the connection she'd forged on his forearm. Khaemil was the other. She stopped to listen before revealing herself. Tracing a finger lightly on the wall and whispering a spell, the stone became as clear as glass so she could watch them, though they could not see her.

"She sleeps still?" Talmen asked.

"No, she has awakened. Her screams stopped only moments ago."

"Ah, then she has rested. Good. Matters are grim enough without having to worry about her judgment."

Khaemil turned away from Talmen, facing the wall, smiling and shaking his head.

"Did you honestly think you would come to this point and not have your precious life threatened by some enemy? Or would you prefer that we choose a more fitting location for your Order, some place uninhabited and far away, perhaps?"

"I am no coward, shapechanger. My only fear is that our ambitions may exceed our ability. We have traveled across half of Faerûn, growing in numbers but dwindling in prospects. Any reservations I have concerning this one are well founded, I assure you."

Khaemil smirked and looked sidelong at Talmen.

"Your doubts will mark you, human. Leave them behind when we march or they will pierce your flesh and put your body in the grave where your mind already rests." He looked back to the tower's entrance as Morgynn appeared. "This, I assure *you*."

Morgynn stood with her fingertips pressed to her temples. Her eyes were closed as she walked, but her form was straight and her step was sure. Despite the lingering distress of her nightmare, she was confident in her bearing.

Talmen and Khaemil parted as she neared and passed between them. Her hands slowly left her aching head. Stretching her neck in a spasm that helped to separate physical action and wild emotion, she opened her eyes and beheld the monstrous troops that lay waiting on the field of stone. Although few in number compared to the garrison she hoped to command one day, the nature of the minions would be both horrific and daunting to any enemy.

"I commend you, Malefactor. Your wizards and priests have done well." She favored him with a look over her shoulder. "The malebranche will be interesting to observe in battle. What little there may be."

Talmen bowed. Morgynn was amused by the change in the priest's thoughts and actions now that she was in his presence.

"Thank-you, Lady Morgynn, but our servants are summoned merely to complement your own. The bathor numbers far outweigh my Order's meager contribution."

"Very good," she replied. "Go. Take your place and gather them. Our path will be prepared shortly."

"Yes, my Lady."

Talmen walked swiftly toward the forest's edge. He showed no emotions, but she felt him tremble beneath his mask as he stared into the trees and gripped the scar seared on his arm. Khaemil's words still echoed in his mind, and Talmen endeavored to bolster his feelings to match his show of courage. She left his mind then, confident that his fear of her was greater than his fear of death.

"I wager he will soil himself if the oracles have a guard posted at the gate, my lady," the *shadurakul* said over the droning work of the wizard-priests around the tower.

The humor in Khaemil's jest was not lost on her, but her mind was elsewhere as she scanned the damp ground.

"No doubt. But as long as he makes it that far, his fear is irrelevant."

Finding what she sought, Morgynn knelt on the ground, tracing long fingers around a puddle of water. She mumbled words of magic and waved one hand erratically over the water's surface while the other reached for a pouch at her side. A sliver of wood appeared in her hand from the pouch—a splinter from the ancient scrying bowl in Goorgian's Well. It would be a catalyst for her spell to allow her simple scrying to become more intrusive than her targets might enjoy. Completing the words of the spell, she finished the incantation by biting her lip and drawing blood. This she spat in the center of the puddle and it flashed with light, dimming to show a scene of swirling mist and impenetrable gray.

"Sisters," she whispered, focusing on the materializing image of the pale grove of oaks hidden in the forest.

Their leafy voices emanated from the water, sounding hollow and far away. Though their words were unintelligible, their tone of defiance was unmistakable.

From her pouch, Morgynn produced the Stone of Memnon and held the glossy black stone above the puddle, dipping it to brush the surface. Tiny ripples tore through the sylvan scene. Its effect on the trees was immediate, causing the branches to twist and writhe as they'd done before when confronted with the artifact.

"What do you want, blood-witch?"

She ignored their insult, admiring their tenacity and empathizing with their anger.

"A path. You three together have much control of the forest. I desire that you part the undergrowth and allow my followers to pass. East, if you please."

They did not respond, but the sounds of a disturbance

in the forest served as their answer. Morgynn watched eagerly. To her left, trees parted, roots shifted, and entangling vines and bushes pulled back, revealing a wide road of soft soil.

The leaves in the image of the grove shook and hissed as the sisters spoke.

"Our influence reaches far, but not to the other side. You must forge your own road beyond ours."

"We shall make do," Morgynn replied, and dismissed the image in the puddle.

Rising, she brushed mud from her red robes and discovered Talmen standing at the edge of the road, staring into the shadowy avenue that had seemingly appeared from nowhere. She touched a fingernail to her arm in a place corresponding with the dark glyph on his.

Morgynn revealed the true extent of the link she had forged into his skin and spoke, her words resoundingly loud in his mind. "Follow the path as far as it goes. The bathor will clear the rest."

He nodded, clearly unnerved by the sudden command, then shouted to those waiting behind him.

Morgynn smiled as they marched into the Qurth. She felt the weakening pulse of her children as they moved away from her, leading her army to the gates of Brookhollow and the doorstep of the Hidden Circle.

⊛ ⊛ ⊛ ⊛ ⊛

Sodden grass lay bent and broken across the western edge of the Reach in the wake of the heavy rain still moving southward along the Qurth's border. In the midst of the swamped plain, a solitary figure paused in her travels and gathered the ingredients of traditional magic. The ancient language of the Ghedia, the grass witches of the Shaar, sang in the air.

Mud sucked at the Ghedia's bare feet as she circled a pot of boiling water. Floating reeds churned and tumbled on its surface. Her loose clothing rippled in the wind and beaded bracelets dangled from her wrists, clicking like tiny wind chimes as she waved her arms and hummed, working the old magic of the Shaar.

As she hummed, she traced a stick through the mud every so often, writing down what she saw in the boiling pot. Her deep voice continued the casting song of her ancestors, but her mood grew grim as understanding dawned on her.

Her Ghedia sisters had already moved on, wandering the troubled grasslands of the Reach seeking answers and signs, protecting anything sacred as well as the ancestral ground of the Shaaryans. Their auguries had become erratic of late, showing danger and threat from every direction but not revealing the source. Lesani slowed her dance and stopped, her long brown hair falling from beneath her hooded cloak, framing the worried expression on her exotic and mature Shaaryan features. The flames of the fire danced in her deep brown eyes as she gazed upon the muddy runes.

For years, she and her fellow shamans had ignored the aura of darkness around the Qurth Forest, accustomed to its presence in the background of their seeing spells. Recently, it had begun to radiate with a strange magic—magic that grew stronger by the moment and moved sluggishly, as if just awakened.

Yet all the signs pointed south, to Brookhollow.

She narrowed her eyes, pursed her lips, and exhaled a long breath. Scanning the darkness and roiling mist on her left, she deliberated silently. She knew her duty, as all of the Ghedia did, but this would not be an easy decision. The Savrathans had long ago broken ties with the old magic of the Shaar and would not readily accept the assistance of those labeled heretics by the Hidden Circle.

If they still lived and had not succumbed to plague or secret foes by now, she thought.

Finding a cure for the blush had been a concentrated effort for the Ghedia lately. The runes Lesani had drawn, though, were clear: Plague, War, Twilight, Blood, and the eye-shaped symbol for Prophecy, the closest rune in the Dethek alphabet for Savras, not yet a god when the language was young.

Lesani thought of Elisandrya, one of the few hunters still friendly to the shaman sisters and acquainted with their ways. She knelt and grabbed a fistful of grass, twisting the blades together, breaking them in half and rubbing them between her palms, staining her hands green as she squeezed them. The spell of the green-fire sprang to her mind.

"If for no one else, then for young Elisandrya."

She stamped her foot in the mud, chanting the ancient call of the grass witches. The words of the magic were older than remembered time, lost in the history of the Shaar, older than the Shoon Dynasties, and older than the Calim Desert. Her voice was an echo from an age forgotten, passed down from shaman to shaman in the great oral history of the Shaaryan tribes.

Raising her folded hands to her lips, she blew upon them, igniting them with a flickering green light. She cast the crushed grass into the boiling pot, setting the water aflame. Using a stout stick, she upturned the pot's contents, pouring them onto the fire beneath. The flame sprang to life, whooshing upward in a blazing emerald bonfire.

Lesani stepped back from the heatless flame and began to gather her belongings, the sparse possessions of a nomadic life. The flame would reach beyond darkness and fog, beyond ruins and all obstacles, visible only to her sisters. They would return and they would follow, of this Lesani was sure. Whether they journeyed to war or a funeral, though, she could not say. The green-fire was a symbol of both.

CHAPTER SIXTEEN

A world of black mist and undulating fog surrounded Elisandrya, carrying winds that froze her flesh almost to the point of burning. The realm they traveled not only bore the shadows of the present—Eli glimpsed apparitions of the past, as if lurking in unknown corners. Her grasp on Quinsareth's hand had quickly evolved into a tight hug around his waist. She could not help feeling that if she lost contact with him she might tumble away forever into the company of half-seen ghosts. She did not look down—it was enough that she felt her feet walking upon a spongy, half-real surface that flew by at ungodly speed. Through squinting eyes, she could make out a tiny patch of darkness that came nearer as they journeyed through the hidden world.

Their eyes had met once during the swift

journey, each sensing the inexplicable connection they'd made, perhaps enhanced by the shadowalk. Her quiet prayer to Savras, finished in this shadowy realm, had given them both an insight they could neither control nor deny. She recognized the connection of consciousness and dream that accompanied her god's brief and sometimes confusing visions. The shadowalk had somehow awakened that spark of faith within her that called for Savras's wisdom and vision. Eli had turned quickly away, feeling exposed and vulnerable, but she connected again as Quin's thoughts and feelings washed over her, a warm wind in the otherwise harsh environment.

She could see both halves of him at once in her mind. The celestial light of his heritage was overlaid by the shadow of who he was in the world, the muted gray hues of the ghostwalker. She could feel ghostly tendrils passing through them both, like connections from one spirit to another. Lost in these thoughts and emotions, she closed her eyes and pressed her face closer to Quinsareth's chest, feeling the warmth on her cheek that hid behind his shadow and old armor.

⊙ ⊙ ⊙ ⊙ ⊙

Quin's heart pounded in his chest. Never before had he experienced such a bond in the shadows of his road. A few fleeting times he thought he could sense another's thoughts, but Elisandrya's soul had flooded through him, caressing his back and shoulders, flowing down his arms and into his fingertips. Almost immediately, he wondered if she could see him the same way. When their eyes had met moments after the shadowalk began, he knew she could, they both knew.

So much of himself was secret by necessity. Being unknown and near faceless to his enemies strengthened his powers in their presence. He had left his true name far behind him, in the dying ears of the Hoarite priest who'd inducted him to the lone lifestyle of the ghostwalker. It had become a ritual to him, each night before making camp, to reiterate who he was and remember his past, lest he become lost to sword and shadow. He feared abandoning the man he was and becoming like the mindless gemstone golems he'd heard of in legends as a boy in Mulhorand. He had begun this ritual on the banks of the River of Swords, as the small temple that had accepted this strange young man burned behind him. Ever since, the thought of his true name carried the smell of smoke from that fire.

Quin refused to look at Eli, afraid of what judgment he might see in her eyes. Instead, he focused on the shadow road. They had traveled for some time, and he expected to reach Brookhollow at any moment if Eli's prediction of a three-day journey had been correct. The shadows had grown swifter over the years as he traveled them more and more. Most times, he could complete a day's journey in less than half the time of this journey. He was anxious to meet this High Oracle Sameska and judge for himself the nature of her prophecy.

He dreaded the action he might take, afraid that the path laid out for him might alienate this woman with whom he felt momentarily bonded. He knew he could not abide, could not accept, the prophecy or the edict it had spawned. This gave him pause, cleared his mind, and made him afraid of a mission that might wield Bedlam against people she knew. The blood of the good was demanded more vehemently than that of evil, for it was often the blood of betrayal.

The shadows thinned around them. Objects became more distinct, inertia settled in their stomachs as they slowed. Each step became truer to the laws of nature. The walls of nearby homes appeared beneath the shadowy twins. Rain fell upon them like a tide and the shadows disappeared completely.

No one witnessed their arrival, no herald or watchman, no merchant packing his wares at the day's end. The streets were empty and still. Even the rats had sought shelter from the pounding rain, explosive thunder, and flickering lightning.

Quinsareth helped Elisandrya to her feet. The transition from shadow to gravity had unbalanced her and flipped her stomach. A flashing bolt above illuminated their faces as their eyes met.

Quin could feel her arms clinging to him. "Are you all right?" he asked.

She raised a hand to her cheek, catching her breath before answering. "I'll be fine."

They glanced about, taking stock of their position. The lightning showed them the curving ivory walls of the Temple of the Hidden Circle, mere blocks away. Both noticed that the storm had grown even stronger. It raged above the Qurth and it moved ever closer, a sure sign that little time remained for conversation concerning their shadowalk.

Quinsareth strode purposefully onward, splashing through the flooded streets. Elisandrya matched his stride toward the temple. They found the structure unguarded, the gates open and banging against the white walls in the icy wind.

The tall double doors at the top of the stairs stood unbarred. They opened easily to give the pair entrance to the long windowed hallway that led to the inner sanctuary.

⊚ ⊚ ⊚ ⊚ ⊚

The domed sanctuary of the temple was eerily quiet and full of dancing shadows as the lightning neared the outskirts of the city. A growing dread wracked Sameska's senses, and she paced the perimeter of the room, stopping to pause briefly each time she passed the murals depicting the city of Jhareat. She stared at the tower in the old paintings, surrounded by burning buildings and bloody warfare. The tower remained untouched by the fires and acts of war, pointing skyward as if to torture her with her own fears.

She glanced upward warily now and then, as if expecting to find Savras in the clouded sky, looking down upon her through the glass dome above.

"Foolishness," she told herself each time, knowing it was a commoner's idea that the gods lived among great cities in the sky. It was small comfort, though, as she strode on weary legs through his temple.

Wild thoughts swirled in her mind, unbidden, crashing into each other and rebounding with ever more questions and doubts concerning her prophecies. The voice in which she had spoken two nights ago made her shudder each time she remembered it, feeling like a violation of her will, but at the same time it was the truest sign of her ability as the high oracle.

"Savras spoke through me. Used me as his instrument," she said to herself over and over, but the words felt hollow. She wrung her hands almost constantly, the tactile sensation a welcome balm in a world that seemed to be slipping away with each passing moment.

The blood-stained statue of Savras had been covered with a black cloth, the body of Nivael burned in secret outside the walls of the city so as not to incite panic in the commoners. The statue stood like a black shadow of death over her shoulder, drops of blood still visible on its exposed, sandaled feet. Its image was burned in her mind and she had avoided looking at it directly since it had been obscured, but beneath the cloth she knew his eye was trained upon her.

Thus she also avoided the spells she had cast the day nightmares had begun, afraid to call upon the All-Seeing One. The screams and terror of Logfell and Targris still filled her waking moments. She had no wish to see again what could not be changed. The burning eyes of the Hoarite, as he fought viciously against the incursion at Targris, stared at her from memory, accusing in a righteous blend of light and dark. His sorcerous blade called her name as it cut and screamed, swathed in the blood of enemies she'd had no power against.

She feared the pain of experiencing what could be the rage of the All-Seeing One, but more so, she feared his silence. A solemn and unwanted judgment awaited her in the old power of the circle. Skirting its edges and blocking her view of the statue with a raised hand, she made for the darkness of the alcove behind the altar.

With one hand on the curtain, she paused as a sudden and inexplicable concern stole over her, as if she'd blinked and missed providence standing before her like a moment of pure and clear destiny. It was a familiar feeling, that uncanny notion of something greater taking place. One she'd thought lost many years ago.

She rushed into the alcove and down the hallway to the Council Chamber. With a whisper and a wave, she lit several candles, an effortless trick so reflexive that she couldn't recall when she had last laid hands on a torch, lantern, or candle. Kneeling before the scrying pool, she called a spell to mind and spoke the words breathlessly, fearful for several moments that even arcane sight might fail her, but the water's surface rippled and changed, obeying her magical command.

Images blurred and shifted as she searched the city streets outside, unsure of what she might find and uncertain that her instincts were not hindered by lack of sleep and the evil so close to Brookhollow. So obsessed in her search had she become that when the center of the pool darkened and clouded, she thought the storm clouds themselves had descended to lay siege. Only when the inky fog dispersed did she make out a familiar cloaked figure revealed in the heart of the shadow. Eyes of pearly white shone from beneath a heavy gray cowl and gripped her soul in talons of ice even as the image faded.

"He is here!" she said, covering her mouth as if betrayed by her own voice. She shook, trembling as vision became reality somewhere outside the temple doors.

She stood and walked back to the sanctuary, straightening her robes and hair to face this warrior of shadow, this ghostwalker of Hoar. She stood upon the dais behind the altar, expecting the doors of the sanctuary to burst open at any moment. She could not tear her eyes away from them.

A draft played at the edges of the old tapestries as candles wavered and dimmed. Footsteps echoed from the corridor beyond the doors, carrying with them the unknown and the knowing eyes that chastised everything she struggled to hold together. She must succeed in this, she knew. She must stand and face what fate had wrought for her, whether prophecy or nightmare.

The door opened and a howling wind entered, snuffing the candles and leaving two lone torches to light the sanctuary. Filing into the room, several oracles had come to attend the evening's council. They were shocked to find Sameska waiting for them, standing at the center of the dais as if prepared to speak. Huddling together in the chill, they stood confused, waiting in the high oracle's eerie silence.

One of them moved to close the door and quell the wind of the storm, but stopped short as she reached for the handle. She backed away slowly, frightened of the figure that sauntered in surrounded by a billowing gray cloak that resembled nothing less than tattered wings. The oracle joined her sisters, who had also moved away from the doors, gathering at the far edge of the dais and beseeching Sameska in whispered voices to escape, to run away.

The high oracle could not hear them, could not heed their unintelligible warnings as she was trapped by his eyes. The opalescent globes were shot through with black tendrils of swirling darkness, like ink dripped in milk. All she could manage was a staying hand for her followers, several of whom had begun to ascend the steps to lead her away. Her gesture was command enough and she was thankful, as her voice might have failed her. She wished to present no weakness before this walking killer from her dreams.

It came as no surprise when Elisandrya Loethe appeared in the doorway as well.

⊙ ⊙ ⊙ ⊙ ⊙

Dreslya sat in quiet meditation. She tried to calm her shattered nerves and focus her energies toward some spell, some magic that might penetrate the mysterious fog that obscured all vision into the forest and the evil entrenched in its depths. Her earlier sorrow had given way to anger and frustration at being unable to deal firsthand with the dangers that threatened the Reach.

Nivael had delivered the message of her sister's likely death. Dreslya felt compelled to do what Elisandrya might have done in her place, though it pained her to resist the desires of Savras as told by the high oracle.

For Sameska, she felt nothing but pity. The mad look in the high oracle's eyes had convinced her that the prophecy had driven Sameska mad, unstable with fear and anxiety over the terrible visions and words of the All-Seeing One. Never before had such a prediction shaken the church so, and Sameska was searching for enemies and heretics on all sides. Dreslya knew something had to be done, even if it meant her own death.

Elisandrya's sacrifice deserved at least that much.

Her mother's old spellbook lay at her side, its pages yellowed and the cover well worn, but the magic within was as potent as the day the ink had first been set to paper. The scrying she intended to cast was more powerful than any she'd done before. She hadn't had the need for such spells in the past, but her skill was more than she needed for the task.

Several oracles already believed she would succeed Sameska when the time came, but Dreslya took their praise in stride. She had not joined the faith to become its leader, but to honor the tradition, as had her mother.

She lit a candle on the windowsill and sat on the edge of her bed, closing her eyes and calling the words of the spell to the forefront of her mind. Out of habit she prefaced the spell by whispering a small prayer to Savras. Taking a deep breath, she gathered her will to speak the words of magic that would carry her sight beyond the walls of the temple to find the source of the threat that hung over them.

The breath was forced from her body as a bright and shining light burst behind her eyes, letting loose a dam of power that flooded through her mind. Her spell was lost, forgotten as she fell limply backward into the gentle grip of something unfamiliar. She tried to resist for a moment, frightened and unsure of what was happening, but she felt no pain and sensed no threat. Her breathing slowed as she gave in to the experience, accepting it. A peaceful warmth covered her body then, even as terrible visions began forming among her thoughts.

⊛ ⊛ ⊛ ⊛ ⊛

"Your people are dying, Sameska."

Quin's voice was a mere whisper, but it carried unnaturally above the raging storm outside. Sameska set her lips in a thin line and narrowed her eyes, fighting the fear that radiated from him in waves. He enjoyed her obvious discomfort.

"In this chamber," she said, "you shall refer to me as High Oracle."

"In this chamber," he replied, "I shall speak as I wish."

The oracles gasped at his audacious words, though several of them seemed intrigued by the scene that was playing out before them. They eyed him curiously in a manner he was accustomed to, though it was not altogether comfortable. Outwardly he ignored them, but in truth he despised their quiet perusal and hoped the power of his shadow led them to believe he was nothing less than a demon. He further confounded their judgment of his humanity as he pushed the hood from his head and let it rest upon his shoulders. His pale eyes found each of them as he swept his gaze across the group.

He wondered, briefly, if unfolding events would lead him to kill them and their high oracle.

"Why have you come here?"

Sameska's question disrupted his dark thoughts, and he shook off pondering what blood would be spilled to end his time in this affair. He had no desire to harm any of them, only the determination to do so if warranted.

"I assumed you might tell me, Lady Prophet." He smiled as he answered, though venom dripped from his words. "Your prediction seems certain about leaving your people defenseless, but it is lacking in details where I am concerned, eh?"

The high oracle flushed in anger and held her breath as his hand brushed against Bedlam's pommel. Though she was a mystery to him, she played to his suppositions easily.

"You have no right, warrior, to come in here and demand anything of me or my people!"

His smile disappeared.

"It seems I have every right, prophet! I have come here of my own accord. I have heard prophecy that labels me a savior, and I see a people who are aware of a coming destruction and do nothing!"

"This is who we are!"

"No!" His voice thundered through the room. "This is who you were. According to your own words, should I fail or walk away, your people will be obliterated!"

Elisandrya gasped behind him. He regretted the effect his words might have on her, but he could not allow the truth of the matter to be obscured by Sameska's righteousness. Should he choose to abandon this prophecy, then by her own words, Brookhollow would be destroyed. Deep down, he felt a spike of shame. Should that occur, he would mourn only one death among those many.

The long silence that followed felt like eternity, filling the sanctuary with its heavy import. Quin studied Sameska and noticed several oracles seemed intrigued by his argument rather than frightened. They nodded and looked to her for a response.

"You bring only disrespect into this temple, Elisandrya," Sameska said, ignoring Quin. "You tamper with prophecy and now seem shocked when your actions succeed?"

"You have not addressed his argument, High Oracle." Eli's gaze became steel and she stepped away from Quin. He could see the look of betrayal dawning in her eyes. "What of his choice?"

"Savras provides," Sameska began through clenched teeth. "Your presence here confirms his wisdom, his sight. We do not rely on your goodwill, Hoarite and have no faith in coincidence. Such is our way."

Quin shook his head, smiling bitterly as he looked at the floor.

"Yes, I know. I've heard this before."

Quin remembered that old man, standing in Targris beside the smoking ruin that had been the center of the town's faith. Under normal circumstances, he imagined their dogma might have merit, but death had infected that equation. In light of the prophecy and what he believed to be its purpose, he could not help but think they deserved what fate had in store for them.

"You cannot see because you are blind to the hidden circle around us all," Sameska said in a condescending tone. "Ripples of action preclude each moment and affect all whom we touch. If you could see just one ripple, you might see them all and what is to come."

Quin raised his head and met her eyes again in defiance.

"I have seen what prophecy accomplishes," he said, hardening his gaze. "In Logfell. In Targris. Do these circles reach only as far as the edge of your own safety, prophet?"

Sameska's eyes widened in fear and she shook her head as he spoke the names of those towns aloud. She looked away, breaking the stare between them. Her demeanor collapsed, leaving her looking as old and lost as her advanced years. Her voice, when it returned, cracked and shook, but conveyed her words clearly to all.

"You are an assassin, Hoarite. A killer without conscience who hunts for justice at the whim of a bitter god." She looked at him with red-rimmed eyes. "Your judgment carries no weight here."

"Agreed," he said matter-of-factly, stepping closer to her. "Now tell me all that you have seen, that I might finish my hunt and leave this place."

She stared a moment longer into his opal eyes. He gave back nothing but nonchalant acceptance of what she had obviously intended as an insult. He had no illusions about his place in the world. Though uncertain at times as to what his conscience would or would not accept, he felt sure he could endure her hasty judgment without shame.

"The Tower of Jhareat in the Qurth forest," she responded weakly. "There awaits a sorceress in blooded robes with a host of unseen creatures at her command. I felt their presence, nothing more. They have lain there several days at least."

She hung her head as she said the last, as if divulging the last of her secrets. He expected the full sum of her secrets remained hidden, but he had what he needed and cared little for the rest.

Quinsareth stood a moment longer, anger and pity in his eyes, then turned and walked out without a word. Elisandrya followed. He could hear her purposeful stride gaining on him. He quickened his step as much to escape the temple as to avoid the look he imagined in her eyes.

CHAPTER SEVENTEEN

Wait!"

Elisandrya yelled against the storm's fury, roaring through the open doors of the temple. Quinsareth would not listen, intent on leaving and tired of talk. He'd had enough exchanges in the last few days to realize he had forgotten himself. He had become involved, and it threatened to compromise his judgment. His business was in the Qurth, in Jhareat. For learning that one fact, he was thankful for this diversion to Brookhollow. The sooner done, the sooner he could go.

"Stop, dammit!"

Elisandrya grabbed his arm before he could step out the doors, her tone angry and desperate. Reflexively he reached for Bedlam and met her eyes. His hand never touched the blade, nor had he wanted to, but her eyes tore into him more effectively than any sword. In her eyes he saw a person he admired, a person he might have aspired to be like, who knew the difference between hope and despair and strove to act on that knowledge. He saw the humanity he had abandoned and the will to do good he had dismissed as the dreamings of wide-eyed children beset by the evils of the world.

He was crushed in her stare.

"An assassin, then? Is that all?"

He pulled away and turned, closing the heavy doors and shutting out the storm. They could hear the echo of the sanctuary doors slamming shut. The silence that followed was almost humbling. Alone in the small foyer, surrounded by high windows and flashes of lightning, they stared at each other, emotions unbalanced by uncertainty and the presence of each other.

"Well?"

Eli's question hung between them.

"An assassin is a better man than I, Elisandrya. An assassin acts on behalf of his employer and receives good coin. I act only on behalf of the dead and receive little more than good riddance."

"I don't believe that. We saw each other plainly in those shadows you call a road. The dark of that place could not hide the good I saw in you."

"A mere trick of blood. I bear the curse of any aasimar who desires to walk a normal life, to be human . . ." He searched her stare, seeking understanding. "To have a choice."

She didn't respond, softening her stare a little. He didn't watch her long, afraid to see any glimmer of the pity to which he had no right. Instead, he walked into a patch of darkness, untouched by the few weak torches that lit the room. He looked up at the windows and watched as clouds churned and spat white fire, growling as they deluged the city with rain. Inwardly, he sought a truce between what he knew and what he felt. Quin struggled to reconcile his level of involvement with this woman and what he must do.

"Tell me about the Tower of Jhareat," he asked nonchalantly.

"I gathered from Sameska's words that it is well known in this region?"

Eli stared into the distance, her thoughts miles away from his question. Pulling herself back, she answered. "That tale is from the end of the Calishite rule over the Border Kingdoms, and Shandolphyn's Reach in particular," she said, still staring blankly. "It begins with the death of a young woman.

"Her name was Zemaan. Captured and forced into slavery by the Calishite wizards who ruled Jhareat, she was the lover of a young Shaaryan warrior called Ossian. Many Shaaryans met the same fate as she, being fodder for the Calishites. It is said that Ossian swore an oath and vowed to destroy Jhareat. Many laughed at his wild boast, but the shamans of his tribe were not so dismissive.

"The tales are numerous about Ossian's exploits in gathering the scattered tribes over the following years, leading them into attacks against the eastern edges of the empire.

"The heart of the story is about Ossian's love for Zemaan and a powerful shield he wore into battle. Forged by Shaaryan shamans for his crusade, it protected him against the Calishites' magic. Its powers were invisible until tested, and then it was too late.

"The only thing the shield would not let Ossian hide was the love in his heart. Its face, which had been blank until he touched it, bore the image of Zemaan, so his enemies could see what he fought for.

"His war against the Calishites came to Jhareat, and the shamans and warriors of the Shaar caused a slave rebellion within the city. As his fellow tribesmen died around him, and protected against the wizards' spells, Ossian slew the lord sorcerer of Jhareat, fulfilling his oath and dying soon thereafter.

"Legend says that Ossian's spirit still guards the tower with his shield, standing vigilant against encroaching evil." Elisandrya smiled bitterly and added, "I guess it's just a legend—a hero's story to tell sleepy children at night."

Quinsareth listened quietly, observing Eli's love for the tale as she told it. He nodded gently at the end. "Legends and stories are usually preferable to the truth."

Eli pondered this and stared out the window at the storm's fury.

"Truth edges closer every moment," she sighed. Looking back toward the closed sanctuary, she narrowed her eyes. "I wonder what legends will come of our tale."

Quinsareth did not reply. He gathered his cloak around his shoulders and pulled the hood over his head. Walking toward the temple doors, he reached to open them, but Eli's voice stopped him.

"What did you speak of to Sameska? About Logfell and Targris?"

He let his hands fall to his sides. Closing his eyes, he remembered the rain and the growls, the taste of blood as the ogre's magic tore at his body, the old man standing calmly as his people picked up the pieces of their interrupted lives.

"Targris was attacked. A small force of gnolls led by an ogre wizard took the city by night." He turned and regarded her from beneath the cloak's cowl. "They were undefended and unprepared, a tempting target for a savage foe that did not fall easily."

"You fought them?"

"Yes, and I was nearly killed in the effort."

She nodded thoughtfully, and though he waited for her to question him again, he hoped she wouldn't. She looked up at him, questions in her eyes, but he waited. He sought the words, the explanation she needed. Truthfully, he did not know the entire answer, only what he'd seen. The silence between them became ominous, and finally she pushed him to continue.

"And Logfell?"

He reached again for the brass handles of the temple doors. He sighed forcefully, grinding his teeth as his jaw tightened. "There is no Logfell." He uttered the words quietly, nearly a whisper, but they seemed to fill the world with their weight. "There was nothing left but dried blood and the body of a little girl."

He saw her turn pale as the horror of his words settled in her gut. The realization was clear on her face, that Logfell's fate foretold the future of Brookhollow.

"I'm sorry," he added. "There was no prophecy to save them, nor prophets to deliver it."

"You're a liar," she said, but he saw the truth in her eyes. She wanted him to be a liar and he wished he was. She wiped the wetness from her eyes, her lip curled in anger. "No. I'm sorry. The liar," she said as if confessing a long held secret, "has been here all along."

She no longer looked at him, and he was thankful for that. He knew the look in her eyes. Blood hid in the future of her steady, blank stare, and he would leave her to what she must do. She turned toward the sanctuary, nodding sidelong at him—a solemn thanks before walking away. He threw open the doors, walked out into the driving rain and chill wind, and steadily made his way to the eastern gate.

He splashed through the streets, the city's details blurred by sheets of rain, all blended together in grays and darker grays. He wasn't looking, didn't care, and wouldn't allow himself to feel any more than he already did.

If nothing else, he thought, if my quarry has gone before I find Jhareat, then this city, its people, are bait. I'll know where to come back, to finish.

The eastern gate was unbarred and it creaked as the wind pushed against it. Nearby, the light of a lantern illuminated a game of dice and cards. Hunters whose minds were clearly somewhere else sat around a table beneath the roof of an open stable. Their weapons leaned against the stable wall, but their eyes were alert, their faces nervous, anxious.

Quinsareth almost blended into the scene of charcoal gray light and heavy rain, nearly invisible as he observed the undefended gate and distracted warriors. Homes nearby were locked tightly with curtains drawn. Not a soul peered out the darkened windows at the storm, the hunters, or the empty streets. Between the gates, through the gap, he could see the darkness of the Qurth Forest waiting for him.

He leaned against a wall in a narrow alley, staring at the puddles, the splashing rain, and the flashes of lightning. He felt the pit of his stomach grow cold as the shadows answered his silent call, filling his insides with ice and needles as they gathered. He did not open the shadow road right away, however, holding on to the power. Concern for Elisandrya held him in place.

It is not my place, he thought, to stay here and die with these people, with her.

He fought the selfish urge to turn around and return to the temple, to convince Eli to leave if no one else would. He knew she wouldn't listen, that she would rather stand alone and face what threatened her people and her home. He envied her.

Pushing away from the wall, he walked to the center of the street and faced the gates. Several of the gaming hunters noticed him then as he splashed through the rain. They narrowed their eyes at him, squinting through the storm suspiciously. Quinsareth noted that a few of them reached for their weapons resting against the wall.

He raised an eyebrow.

"Perhaps there is hope yet," he whispered.

Releasing the shadows, he watched the rain-filled air ripple with power as it was forced open, tearing wide to reveal his path. He focused on Jhareat, what he knew, what Eli had told him, and stepped forward, prepared to face the legend he'd heard in her voice.

As the swirling black doorway pulled him in, he thought of her tale about Ossian and his shield. He walked the shadows alone this time and was more aware of their chill than before. In moments, he knew Brookhollow and Elisandrya were far behind him, left alone to await what fate had been made for them. He closed his eyes against the darkness and put a steady hand on Bedlam's dormant pommel, concentrating on the task that lay ahead, leaving behind what was beyond him. The void that was the shadow of the forest enveloped him, comforted him in nothingness as his steady stride devoured the distance to his destination.

"There are no heroes in this tale, Elisandrya," he told himself, hearing his words echoing through the blurring shadows all around. "I'm sorry."

⊛ ⊛ ⊛ ⊛ ⊛

Morgynn gripped the sides of the wide wooden bowl set before her, tracing the designs on its sides with her thumbs and whispering their meanings as she awoke the device's power. Carved in the ancient days of the Nar Empire, legend held that it had been a gift to Goorgian from the Nentyarch of the time—a time long before the druids of the Great Dale took the title of Nentyarch for their own leaders. She admired the crimson stains of past use on its interior. Its bottom was set with a dark mirror, almost black, that reflected only shadows.

Khaemil walked into the chamber quietly, careful not to disturb Morgynn's casting. Morgynn saw his arrival but did not pause to admonish his poor timing.

The words of her spell completed, Morgynn released her grip on the bowl and picked up her dagger. She opened a small wound in the center of her palm, allowing herself to bleed freely. Setting aside the knife, she picked up a stoneware pitcher of rainwater and began to pour its contents into the bowl, letting it mix with the blood from her palm.

The bowl appeared no different once the spell was completed. She leaned on the table and peered into the depths of the pale red liquid, looking beyond the submerged dark mirror and willing the images to appear. Blurry shapes began to form, quickly growing more distinct. Morgynn sighed in satisfaction.

Before long, sounds emanated from the bowl and the noise filled the chamber, amplified by her will. She felt Khaemil shudder. During his years of service and his time in the Nine Hells, she knew he'd been privy to the many sounds humans make when in pain, but the tortured voices of the bathor had few equals among his experiences.

Their throats produced a cacophony of sounds that stemmed from a madness only the dead could comprehend. Morgynn's eyes closed and her head swayed as if hearing the hymns of a practiced choir. This was the sound of success, of victory. Though the lyrics lacked poetry, she knew no bard in all the Realms could have penned a greater tribute to her conquest. Beneath their voices were the twitchings and thrashings of strained muscles and cracking bones as her army tore its way through the Qurth, heedless of the limitations of living anatomy.

Lightning could not reveal them through the knotted trees. Thunder hid their cries and moans, their tearing of undergrowth as they progressed through the forest. Their steps were in tune to the rain, quick and scuttling, mindlessly hurried. Slack jaws opened and closed in a mockery of speech, physical habits that had no meaning or worth.

Even the harmful plants of the forest recoiled from their nearly impenetrable, leathery skin, smooth and unnaturally pale. The few wounds they received opened briefly like puckered mouths, but would not bleed and closed again in a few heartbeats. The rain washed away grime and clumps of thinning hair, matting what remained to their necks and shoulders.

An aura of heat surrounded them, feverish and sweaty, a fog of humidity created by their constant trembling movement, a blur of suffering and madness. Those who followed watched in awe and revulsion, sensing a terror unlike any they had felt before. Constantly, they whispered prayers to their devil-god, praising his wisdom and power.

Morgynn smirked as she watched through her scrying bowl. She allowed the wizard-priests their prayers and misguided praise, if only to keep them loyal, but wondered if even that vile god was capable of what she'd done, of what she'd birthed.

"Impossible," she said aloud, startling Khaemil. "What do the gods know of mortality?"

She sneered as she gazed, her face lit by a crimson glow, and mumbled her thoughts into the bowl, conversing with herself.

Finally, Morgynn stepped back from the scrying bowl with look of contentment. The light of candles danced in her eyes as she turned to Khaemil.

"Soon," she said. "Now, what news do you have?"

"It is the tower, Lady," he began, measuring his words

carefully. "The Gargauthans report that it is resisting their further attempts to strengthen the net of spells. The most recent runes, once written, begin to fade and must be applied again and again to maintain the magic's integrity."

"And what cause do they suspect?" she asked, her voice perilously close to anger.

"Only the tower itself," he answered. "The source of the obstruction is unknown but local."

Her eyes scanned the walls, searching for some trick or ward unnoticed before. Nothing. "They can maintain the control we currently hold?"

"Yes, Lady, long enough at any rate."

"Good," she answered, still peering at the tower walls, though she half-suspected the latent magic of the Qurth itself was at work somehow. "The storm and the obscuring shield should be necessary only for dealing with the oracles. I had wished to keep it longer, as we moved on the rest of the Reach, but I suppose. . . ."

Her words trailed off as she imagined the fruits of her ambition.

Khaemil did not reply. She didn't notice his silence, anyway, as she walked over to the window. Her eyes saw a horizon not yet born, a world under a twilit sky taken by the Order. The people who lived in her ambition were faceless, meaningless, casualties of her will and purpose. They were despairing throngs devoid of hope, lost between life and death, darkness and light.

They would know, she thought, what Gargauth could not. "It takes knowledge of a life lived," she whispered, "to know the nature of a life destroyed."

Though her outward demeanor was calm, she clawed at the stone window ledge, scraping her knuckles open on its rough surface. She allowed them to bleed, oblivious to the pain, and marveled at the sight of lightning reflected in the smeared drops of red.

Elisandrya stalked toward the sanctuary doors, assured of her path for the first time in her life. Her life had been a series of distractions, anything to escape the memory that chained her to what she could be and what she should be. The deaths of her parents had been shrouded in doubt that dissolved day by day. The more she lived, the more she knew, the more she was driven to act, regardless of consequence.

She opened the doors and stopped, looking for Sameska. The other oracles were gone, possibly in council, and for a moment she feared Sameska was with them. Then she noticed the high oracle, her back to the doors, staring at the curtain behind the altar and the dais.

Sameska gripped the soft fabric, exhaling long rasping breaths. She didn't notice Eli's arrival, lost in some fit or trance. The muted voices of the oracles could be heard from the chamber beyond. The arrival of the Hoarite had done much to solidify the truth of Sameska's predictions, but his words had sown seeds of doubt and discord among the more fertile minds of her lessers. The top of the curtain began to tear. Sameska wheezed through clenched teeth, squeezing her eyes shut as she turned toward Elisandrya.

"No," Sameska said as the episode passed, "this is not the time for anger. I will not add flame to their fires."

Calming, gathering her wits, she stared at the silhouette of Savras beneath its concealing cloth. She gasped as the black fabric fluttered and waved, but the open doors revealed the source of the breeze. She stood straighter, peering through the dim sanctuary with narrowed eyes.

Elisandrya stood outlined by the light of a torch in the hallway beyond. Her squared shoulders and hostile demeanor left no doubt as to her intention. "You killed them." Her voice was low, menacing.

"I fear your judgment has been influenced by honeyed words and a handsome face, child." Sameska's voice was clear and strong, a practiced tone perfected by years of speaking to her followers. "The only killer here is the one you escorted to this temple."

Eli walked closer, approaching the center of the room. She ignored Sameska's remark.

"Targris. Logfell . . ."

"Hold your tongue, girl!" Sameska shouted.

". . . my parents," Eli's tone did not change. She refused to be baited by the high oracle's condescension.

"Madness! Blasphemy!" Sameska's throat constricted, causing the words to issue forth in a screeching whisper. A shiver ran through her body and she was transfixed by Elisandrya's nearing form, her slow step and balled fists.

"You told me they were set upon by bandits while traveling to Littlewater." Eli huffed and shook her head. "You even managed to sound sorrowful."

"I told you the truth!"

"Oh, yes," Eli said, then yelled, "The day before it happened!"

Eli flung the words like a hammer, releasing the truth that had plagued her for years, had fed on her spirit, on her faith in all she'd been taught. The guilt of those long years of denial rose in her throat, demanding release.

Sameska flinched as if struck and raised an arm to protect herself as Eli edged closer still. Tears rimmed the hunter's eyes but held fast to their perches, making way for the steely-eyed assuredness of vindication.

"This has been a long time coming, High Oracle."

"You would draw that blade against me, here in this temple?"

Only then did Eli notice that her hand rested firmly on her sword's hilt, and she pondered Sameska's question. She struggled between rage and sorrow, flooded with both as years of quiet suspicion and youthful rebellion took root in the present. The once cold facade of the high oracle's face did not match the nervous and unstable woman who backed away from her, arms raised before eyes livid with indignant fury.

She did not remove her hand from the sword, but neither did she unsheathe it. Ignoring the high oracle's question, she continued.

"My mother defied you, accused you of using the sight to further your own power." Eli's words were focused on Sameska, but she spoke more for herself than for the high oracle. "She would have ruined you, and so, too, the traditions of the Setha'Mir.

"My father would not let her travel alone, guarding her as she went to Littlewater to speak with the oracles there, to plead her case against you. And you let them die."

"You are as naive as she was, Elisandrya Loethe! You believe rumor and hearsay before the words of your betters. She paid terribly for her hasty actions," she replied. "The Hidden Circle tolerated you for the sake of your mother. I see now that was a mistake." Sameska had lowered her arms and now attempted a more authoritative demeanor.

"One mistake among many, 'a blade of grass on the Shaar,' as our people once said."

"Further evidence, child, that you are living in the past."

Sameska turned away. Elisandrya stepped closer, inches from the high oracle. "I think being aware of the past has proven quite valuable in recent days." Eli stared daggers at Sameska's back. "Our present may depend on it."

Sameska looked sidelong at Eli over a trembling shoulder. "Your ignorance is no longer welcome here, child. You and your sister shall be arrested and charged with heresy before the Hidden Circle." Sameska's hidden smile was evident in her tone as she added, "Unless you intend to slay me, I have no doubt what conclusion will be drawn, I assure you."

Elisandrya breathed close to Sameska's ear, making up her mind and slowly drawing her sword. The high oracle trembled all the more, but made no move to defend herself. For all the favor of Savras she supposedly had, Elisandrya considered Sameska's helplessness quite telling. She savored the moment, then spoke, her sword freed. "Don't bother with your charges."

Elisandrya turned and walked toward the sanctuary doors, satisfied that she had said all she needed and heard all that was necessary.

"You renounce your faith, then?"

Eli slowed and stopped, but did not face the high oracle. Her words echoed easily in the round chamber. She had no need to look upon Sameska's face again.

"I do not question my faith." She adjusted her armor and bow as she added, "I renounce this prophecy and your foolish edict, but most of all, I renounce you. Savras willing, I will finish what my mother started."

She shoved the doors open and disappeared down the hallway, leaving Sameska to shiver and fume in the blasting winds of the storm that howled through the open temple doors.

CHAPTER EIGHTEEN

Dreslya blinked, opening her eyes and rising from the bed on weary legs. The room had grown cold—a strong draft blew from beneath the door. Resting her head in her hands, she tried to recapture all that she'd been shown, the horror and wonder of a strange dream. Taking a deep breath, she looked out the window. The candle had gone out, leaving the room in darkness save for flashes of lightning outside.

No, she thought. That was no dream.

"Elisandrya is alive," she whispered.

The moment of relief was quickly overcome as the vision reasserted itself in her mind's eye. She shivered, afraid of what was to come. Clenching her eyes shut, she squeezed her hands together. She steeled her nerves that had too often sought shelter behind the walls of the temple and the tenets of her faith. Exhaling a long, slow breath, she eased herself off the bed and knelt on the floor. Beneath the bed was a small box she'd touched almost every night but had never opened.

She cradled it in her arms and stood, setting it down on the windowsill beside the unlit candle. Unhooking the latch, she opened the container and gazed upon her birthright, the only items recovered from her mother's body. On top, wrapped in a soft cloth that had been the hem of her mother's robe, was a silver dagger, curved in the hunter's style and emblazoned with the eye of Savras at the center of the crossguard.

She felt its unfamiliar weight in her hand and wondered at its hidden power, tracing the tiny runes burned into the edge of the blade, careful not to cut herself. She placed it in the old leather sheath her father had made for it and thrust it beneath her belt. Turning her attention to the other object in the box, her hand wavered, feeling doubt clouding her judgment.

"I can do this. I have to," she told herself forcefully.

Wrapped in a small square of red velvet at the bottom of the box was a ring. It too was silver and bore Savras's eye in the center. She let it rest in her palm, feeling its warmth.

Placing it on the ring finger of her left hand, she looked east, picturing the unbarred gate and the forest beyond. The ring responded quickly, turning her thoughts into reality. The ring glowed white and heat traveled up to her wrist, searing and pure. Dreslya gasped and concentrated harder. The ring showed her what she sought, carried her sight to its target. The gates appeared and flew past her as she watched for movement through the rain. Lightning flashed and was reflected in a sliver of metal near the forest. A tiny figure stood at the edge of the tree line, wielding the curved blade of a hunter.

"No! Come back, Eli! They're coming!"

⊙ ⊙ ⊙ ⊙ ⊙

Elisandrya had raised her blade high, intent on following Quin into the forest. Her eyes were reddened but the rain had washed away her sorrow, and she felt only the need to act. To this need, she was more than just a willing slave. The razorvines would provide a difficult passage, but her hunter's blade was strong and sharp, accustomed to dealing with obstacles like the Qurth's formidable flora.

Before her sword could fall, her stomach lurched and a wave of nausea flowed through her. Her vision, already hindered by the rain and darkness, blurred and became foggy. The nearest trees loomed over her like black giants, shapeless masses that swayed and shook in the thrall of the storm.

She stumbled backward, nearly slipping in the loose mud and slick grass. The sounds of the rain and thunder diminished, fading as they were slowly replaced by other noises. Whispers came at first. The voices that spoke to her from the forest were inhuman, moaning cries and gibberings that froze her arms and legs. Rooted to the spot and trembling, she could not look away from the Qurth as phantom shapes appeared, hundreds of inconstant figures writhing and flailing boneless limbs as they murmured and gurgled.

A droning chant could be heard faintly, buzzing behind those tortured figures in a loathsome language of harsh syllables and vile tones. Their shapes were blindingly fast, frenzied and inconstant, spasms of movement like an unnatural tide. A faint sound like a distant heartbeat pulsed, shaking the ground beneath Eli's feet.

Black shapes darted overhead, beating massive wings. Eli ducked, flinching and covering her head. Try as she might, her darting eyes could not see what had flown by, but a stench like smoke and spoiled meat settled in their wake. She fumbled with numb hands to wield her blade, trying to see her foes through clouded vision and unequaled fear.

Bright, glistening eyes stared back at her from the forest as the horrible voices stopped all at once—a silence so profound that only her own wildly beating heart and short gasping breaths could be heard.

In a blink, it was all gone.

She found herself slumped to her knees, still on the edge of the forest with the storm roaring in her ears. Blinking back the rain, she looked behind her toward the dim silhouette of Brookhollow's walls. Her head throbbed and she nearly lost her balance as she stood up from the mud among the tall grass.

Casting one last look at the forest, she considered Quinsareth, no doubt far beyond her assistance by now. Pulling her feet from the muck, she turned and ran to the city, sword in hand. The distance seemed surreal, so great was her need to reach those gates. She couldn't run fast enough, couldn't pull at the old gate hard enough. It didn't seem real, as if it were already dead, along with Logfell.

She burst wide-eyed through the gates and immediately turned to heave the massive portal shut. Terror-filled moments ticked by in her mind as she envisioned hellish creatures on her heels and she pushed harder, slipping in the mud and digging into the wet clay beneath. The hunters in the stables stopped their gaming to stare in shock, wondering what madness had infected this frantic woman. One of the men pulled his cloak on and ran over to question her.

She only stared at him as he approached, still pushing on the gate, her eyes pleading, determined. Mere words wouldn't do. They'd all been living in the same place for days. Though swords and bows had been proclaimed useless in the prophecy, they still waited nearby. Hung within easy reach, full scabbards at the hip, quivers of arrows at the ready, true warriors did not just wait; fortunately, they prepared.

Hesitantly, the other hunter stepped closer and leaned a shoulder into the gate. Displacing water and mud that had collected in its path, the gate slammed shut. Without a word, Eli swiftly reached for the winch that would lower the bar and block the entrance.

The other men joined the pair and stood transfixed by the scene, uncertain, glancing at their weapons leaning against the stable wall. Eli strained at the winch. Rain had soaked the wood, tightening the braces. Heaving deep breaths, she looked over the device at the hunters who watched silently.

Meeting their eyes, searching for that warrior's instinct they had attempted to deny themselves since the night of the gathering, Eli spoke, shouting to be heard above the storm.

"Help me. It's coming."

The first hunter to join her, a solid, barrel-chested man called Zakar, turned to his fellows, pointing to each in turn as he spoke. "You two, help her bar this gate."

The younger of the two, called Arek, spoke up. "We cannot! The oracles forbade this. We shall die if we resist!"

The fear in his eyes belied the hopeful tone in his voice. He sounded like a man who wanted to be told he was wrong. Eli indulged him. "You can die defending people you have sworn to protect, or you can die at your dice and cards! Prophecy or not, death is coming!"

Elisandrya's voice was strong, angry, and inspiring. Zakar nodded, smiling grimly. Arek looked to his fellows and all seemed to be in awkward agreement.

In moments, the gates were barred and weapons were retrieved. Zakar and several others ran to secure the south and north gates and rally their brethren to the defense of the city.

Nary a soul, beset by plague, storm, and threat of imminent death, refused the call. Over fifty hunters had arrived at the eastern gate to find Elisandrya Loethe standing on the wall, vigilantly waiting, staring into the darkness beyond. Still more arrived as time wore on. Warriors came to claim an honor in death they might have missed in surrender. None questioned whether they might die, but rather how they would meet their end.

As more hunters arrived, Eli could hear them, feel them pointing up at her. Having begun this revolt, she was looked to as its commander. Shaken by the responsibility at first, she soon became comfortable giving orders. Zakar, whose booming voice carried much farther than her own, gladly assisted her.

All the while, her eyes never left the forest for long.

She wished Quinsareth could see them. She hoped Sameska watched from her temple. She hoped it would all be enough.

A familiar voice shouted from behind her. She and Zakar

turned to see Lord Hunter Baertah pushing through the crowd of warriors. Clearly enraged, Baertah growled through clenched teeth at the hunters who cleared a path for him. Eli could not hear what he said, but as the men looked up to her position, she knew this moment was bound to come sooner or later.

As their eyes met, Eli smiled slightly and leveled her gaze on the manicured fop of Littlewater. Clenching and unclenching her fists, she descended to meet Baertah on even ground. The crowd of hunters parted as the two neared each other. Lightning split the sky.

"Blasphemy!"

Baertah spat the word through the rain. Elisandrya waited calmly, glaring as the lord hunter approached her. She saw no rapier at his belt, no sign that he might be ready to face a true enemy, much less draw weapons in battle.

"All of you! Lay down your arms and return to your homes! The high oracle's edict forbids this!" He pointed at Eli with a trembling finger. "And arrest her for inciting a riot!"

"No!" Eli shouted. "Stand and defend your homes or die in them!"

No one moved, glancing at the adversaries in turn. Baertah narrowed his eyes and stepped forward, standing nose to nose with Eli, who did not budge. "You would let them die in vain?"

"Sameska is mad, lost in delusions," Eli replied in even tones. "I would let them die with honor, defending that which her prophecy would destroy."

He stepped back a half pace, staring in disbelief at her words and beckoning with a hand to the hunters behind him, who still had not budged.

"Just who do you think you are?" he asked, incredulous.

"I am a Hunter of the Hidden Circle. A warrior sworn to live and die in service to Savras and those faithful to him." Her voice lowered to a harsh growl. "Who do you think you are?"

Baertah looked over his shoulder, frustrated that no one had yet obeyed his commands. Turning back to Eli, he growled in reply, loud enough for all to hear. "I am the lord hunter!

And I want this yelping bitch in chains before . . . !"

He never saw the fist that found his jaw, only the spinning clouds overhead as his neck snapped backward. The barest hint of pain began to lance through his face as his back met the ground, splashing and sprawling in the mud like a rag doll.

Elisandrya did not stop to watch him gasp for lost breath. She ascended the ladder to the top of the wall and resumed her vigil. No one helped Baertah to stand, all going solemnly back to their tasks of mounting the city's defenses. More than a few found a moment to smile.

⊙ ⊙ ⊙ ⊙ ⊙

Dreslya walked with the slow gait of one who could not feel the floor beneath her feet. She felt the world tilting against her, could hear her own thoughts berating her as a foolish girl acting beyond her station in life.

But she continued anyway.

Dreslya had pulled back her straight, raven-black hair. Beneath the hem of her robes she wore sturdy leather boots instead of the sandals typically worn in the temple. The dagger in her belt felt strange against her hip, but its weight was comforting. She held a long, wrapped bundle in her arms gently, almost reverently, cradling it against her shoulder.

The sanctuary doors, lit by candlelight, loomed larger than they had ever seemed before. Shadows danced across the carvings of various stylized eyes, the traditional symbols of the All-Seeing One. Her mind raced through a hundred different scenarios of what might occur beyond those doors, all of them disastrous failures.

But she continued anyway.

A phantom sense of purpose pushed her on. Despite the doubt in herself, she struggled to trust her faith. Sameska's prophecy echoed in her mind, the words burned in her memory. That haunting voice trailed behind her, whispering in her ear, buzzing along her spine, and clawing at her robes. But a new voice had joined the chorus, far louder and more honest than Sameska had ever dreamed to be.

Just steps away from the door, she stopped, breathing deeply. For so long, she'd been the dutiful servant, the attentive and quiet student of faith. The silver ring on her hand glinted as the candle's glow touched it. She stared at the simple band, gathering herself to shatter the silence she'd clung to in safety.

She knew the prophecy would come to pass that night, unfurling its dark promises at the gates of the city. The sight of Savras would reveal its secrets and hidden meanings, ripples in the surface of time and chance.

The prophecy will prove true, she thought, like nothing we could have imagined.

Raising a hand, she whispered the words to a minor spell. The locks and seals on the door released at her command. She exhaled a deep breath and reached for the handle.

"Nothing is as it seems," she whispered to herself fearfully, and entered the sanctuary.

CHAPTER NINETEEN

Water reached the forest floor in a steady drip from the canopy of branches above. Dead leaves, early harbingers of winter, pooled the rain in brown cups, the overflow soaking the dark soil beneath. A mist flowed like a smoky river between the trees, climbing their trunks and then breaking like waves to curl back down into the current.

Bedlam's voice sang like the raging storm, flashing through the whipping tendrils of bloodthorns that sought Quin's legs. The ground was soaked in the sticky black ichor of the thirsty plants, their vines writhing and curling in on themselves at his feet. Pale snakes with multifaceted eyes slithered away as the sheltering bloodthorns were cut down. Insects with reptilian tails and eyes buried themselves beneath the leaves.

Panting and backing away from the high wall

of brush and deadfall, Quinsareth eased Bedlam's roar to a dull, metallic growl. The carnivorous plants pulled their vines back into the folds of thick roots and fallen limbs, displaying prominently their bright red berries in an effort to lure the aasimar closer again.

Quinsareth ignored the fruit and the sweet aroma it produced, taking the moment to scan his surroundings. The shadowalk was rarely accurate, even when he knew his destination well, but through the thick woods of the Qurth, he could see nothing of the tower he sought. Only a low hum that might have been a voice or a trick of the wind gave him any sense of direction.

Careful to skirt the edges of the bloodthorn and razorvine patches, he wound an uneven and slow path toward the sound, keeping his grip on Bedlam tight and his senses alert for the dangers that surrounded him. The sound grew louder, becoming more high pitched as he neared, picking out the notes in an unfamiliar tune. He stopped and looked closer, peering through the trees with his special darkseeing vision.

He could make out the edges of a small clearing just past the trunk of a large tree with unusually pale bark. The strange song drew him closer. The tension in his muscles faded as the smell of wildflowers wafted toward him on the whistling wind. Shaking his head, trying to shove away the unnatural calm that settled over him, he crouched lower and knelt at the perimeter of the inviting grove.

Three white oak trees dominated the clearing, their ivory branches gently swaying overhead. The scene was like a dream, so unusual and peaceful in such a dark and forbidding forest. The song was disorienting and Quin leaned forward, falling to his knees as he gazed on the beauty he found. Some part of him struggled to resist, maintaining his grip on the oddly quiet Bedlam, but he could not fathom why he might need a weapon in this place.

His head swam and swayed with the branches, in tune with the lilting and otherworldly song. Words began to form in the music, as if the leaves were speaking, hissing in the wind and whispering in his ear.

"So lost he is, Myrrium."

"Yes, Oerryn, so far from home."

"What do you think, Aellspath?"

Quin fought to keep his eyes open, rolling them from left to right, seeking the source of the dry, whispering voices. The grove became a blur of white wood and bone-yellow leaves. A shape began to form in the centermost tree. The surface of the trunk shifted and flowed like liquid to reveal misty white arms and an indistinct but beautiful face, framed by pale yellow locks of vines and leaves. The figure's milky skin was smooth and bare, unmistakably feminine as it crawled demurely toward him. Shimmering green eyes opened and closed like living flowers, capturing his will in a net of inescapable beauty and dark promise.

Her full lips moved out of sync with her voice, which was deeper and more lustful than the others.

"So beautiful he is. We must keep him, my sisters."

The grove grew darker as the plants and bushes closed together, sealing the clearing from the forest. The voices sighed in contentment as they viewed their catch. Aellspath smiled coyly and bit her lower lip with sharpened teeth as she reached out for the aasimar's arm.

Quin's breath was ragged and shallow, and he was only dimly aware of Bedlam's ponderous weight in his right hand.

Aellspath hissed pleasurably as she scraped her clawed fingertips across Quin's shoulder guard and down to his gauntlet. Her fingers crept casually toward his wrist to gently remove the glowing blue-green sword from his clenched fist. As she gently pried at his fingers, an errant claw brushed Bedlam's hilt, eliciting a hissing reply from the arcane weapon.

The dryads' enchanting song faltered as Aellspath gasped and recoiled from the sword. Quinsareth blinked, exhaling, as warmth flooded his paralyzed form. His vision was blurry but his will to live became razor sharp. He swung Bedlam wildly in front of him, cursing as the hazy form of the dryad ducked and scuttled backward on spindly, emaciated arms and legs.

The dirt beneath him shook and he rolled forward instinctively, swinging Bedlam behind him at a clawlike root that snatched at his cloak. The blade hissed, mimicking the dryads' voices as it sliced through the pale wood, leaving a smooth stump that oozed a thick red sap. The voice called Myrrium howled in agony from the trees above and she crashed through the branches toward the near-blind aasimar.

Quin rolled again, barely missing the screeching Myrrium as she landed. He continued to blink, rubbing his eyes with his free hand and gradually clearing more of his vision. Holding Bedlam before him, he studied his attackers, fiendish orphans of the Qurth Forest. The Fate Fall hovered in his mind, a ghostly sense of strategy collecting his thoughts.

Myrrium's eyes burned a dark yellow, no longer hidden behind the guise of sweet blossoms as Aellspath had done. Her face and skin were grained and knotted like the wood of the trees she lived in, a pale ash-gray. Tiny white fangs protruded from black gums as she crawled closer, favoring her left shoulder where a small wound had opened, bleeding the same thick red sap the root had.

Quin backed away slowly, waiting for the dryad to spring forward. He felt the roots of another oak behind him. Myrrium hummed as she crawled. The sweet tones of her song tried to calm his nerves, urging him to lay down his weapon and be as among friends. Shaking his head, fending off the dryad's spell to charm him, he lashed out, hacking at the trunk of the oak behind him. Myrrium winced as that oak began to bleed, halting her spell as Oerryn screamed in pain and appeared above Quinsareth.

He heard claws scratching against wood and glanced upward, catching only a brief glimpse of long black hair made of vines shading the orange light of fiendish eyes. He leaped sideways to avoid Myrrium's sudden charge. Both dryads stalked him, gnashing their teeth and tearing small ruts in the ground where their long claws touched. They continued their song, though its notes were harsher now, more insistent. Bedlam matched the sound discordantly, which helped Quin resist its call.

He backed away and the dryads herded him toward the middle tree. Though he considered turning the tables and attacking, he could not locate their absent sister. Aellspath had disappeared in the confusion.

Closer and closer he edged toward Aellspath's tree. The dryads' wounds bled freely, as did the tree and the root protruding from the ground. He was familiar with the fey creatures and their connection to the oaks in which they lived, though he'd never faced the creatures in battle. He raised Bedlam again, threatening the nearest oak. The sisters tensed, looking for Aellspath to come to her own defense. Quin raised an eyebrow at their reaction, flashing them his feral smile and preparing to strike.

Aellspath swam through the wood, flying through the bark and barreling into Quin's side. She shrieked words of magic as they fell to the ground in a tangle of limbs. Both were instantly blinded as her spell created a globe of impenetrable darkness around them.

Myrrium and Oerryn flinched backward to the edge of the darkness, listening to the struggles of the two within, waiting to witness the victor's emergence. Myrrium giggled nervously at Aellspath's frenzied screams of rage. Oerryn simply hid behind her thick hair, gnawing at the woody strands and wringing her gnarled hands feverishly.

In the dark, Quin fought to maintain his hold on Bedlam while attempting to fend off the claws and teeth of the enraged dryad. The darkness was calming to him, helping him to focus as an older instinct took over, the power of a birthright long denied. His knuckles brushed against a fist-sized stone as they rolled and he grasped at it, digging it from the moist dirt of the grove. The dryad's claws raked his upper arm as he diverted his attention.

Ignoring the pain, he did not call upon cold shadows to assist him but instead summoned the warmth of light. His hand grew hot as celestial blood rushed to answer the call, filling the rock with the bright and banishing light of day. Aellspath recoiled, hissing, as she was blinded by the sudden light. Her darkness melted swiftly away amid the beams that streamed through Quin's fingers.

Quinsareth took advantage of her confusion and planted a boot in her stomach, pinning her to the ground before she could scuttle away to her protective tree. He deftly brought Bedlam's tip to rest on her throat, eliciting a moan of pain from the fiendish dryad. Though forged in magic long ago by a mad wizard, Bedlam had been blessed by the hand of a god who'd taken pity upon the wizard. No mark or symbol identified the divine benefactor, but the holy touch was unmistakable, steaming as it burned against the dryad's neck.

Myrrium and Oerryn froze, squinting in the light. Oerryn moaned softly, the sound of her magic worming into Quin's mind and causing him to press Bedlam harder into Aellspath's neck. Frantically, the defeated dryad screamed to cease her sister's dangerous meddling. "Be silent, you fool!"

The moaning stopped and Quin breathed easier, staring into the dryad's green orbs.

"Good girl," Quin said, adjusting his stance to deal with the stand-off more comfortably.

"If you kill me, they will kill you, sweetblood!" Aellspath hissed.

"Possibly, but their victory cries will ring hollow in your dead ears," he jested back.

Aellspath considered this, apparently not as confident in her sisters as she boasted. "What do you want?"

"The Tower of Jhareat," he answered. "Where is it?"

"You seek the red sorceress and her priests? Certainly no sweetblood is a minion of that one? Tell her we kept our bargain. No one would suspect an aasimar to serve such an evil!"

"I serve only myself. This red sorceress will greet me with as much warmth as you three have."

Aellspath pointed an overlong finger in the direction of the ruined tower. "That way, sweetblood, and good riddance to you and the witch." Then she added, after a moment's thought, "Beware the priests that ring the tower and their pets in the field of stone."

Quinsareth relaxed Bedlam's pressure on her throat but kept the blade close, curious about the dryad's volunteered advice. "Helpful now, are we?"

"We share an enemy in the blood-witch, aasimar, that is all. This forest is ours to rule, not hers!"

Quinsareth was quiet for a moment, turning the gleaming stone end over end in his palm as he thought. Looking over his shoulder in the direction the dryad had indicated, he saw nothing but thick tangles of trees, bloodthorns, and razorvines. He considered the obstacles he'd face once he reached the ruins. He turned back to Aellspath, who writhed beneath Bedlam's touch.

He withdrew Bedlam from the dryad's throat, keeping it a hand's breadth away but sparing her the pain of its blessed blade. "Perhaps we might help one another," he offered mysteriously. The game piece he imagined tumbled through his thoughts, bearing the symbol of the Bargain.

The dryad, relieved by the absence of the sword, narrowed her emerald eyes and met his white gaze. "What do you propose, sweetblood?"

⊙ ⊙ ⊙ ⊙ ⊙

A gleaming black spider crawled cautiously across the window sill, pausing to inspect the pale obstacle of Morgynn's still hand. It reached out tentatively with its forelegs, tapping her skin lightly, testing the surface before continuing its slow progression. A short jump brought it to land on the knuckle of her index finger. Several black eyes glittered as it inspected this new terrain, searching for food.

She did not notice the intrusion, lost in thought, miles away from the tower she stood in and the battle she awaited that danced in the scrying bowl. The world in the bowl swirled and rippled, still displaying her last viewing despite her lack of concentration. Goorgian, who'd crafted the scrying bowl, was a mysterious figure in Nar's past, thanks in large part to such magic. Never leaving his fortress, he'd been able to send his magic across great distances. He preferred to watch the world pass him by, even up to that moment when the armies of Raumathar had come marching across the horizon.

The spider crawled cautiously, feeling the surface of her

skin grow warm as an unseen current flowed beneath its feet. Her pulse quickened and still she did not move, but the spider grew agitated as its new perch twitched. Feeling threatened, its fangs glistened with venom and its rose on its hind legs in a defensive posture, turning in tight circles.

Slowly the spider's world calmed, the soft ground it stood upon grew still and cooled.

"*Peskhas*," Morgynn whispered, and the spider's body stiffened and instantly turned to ash. With a quick puff of breath, it crumbled and blew away, joining the dust on the floor.

She turned and found Khaemil still guarding the doorway, though his eyes were closed and his lips whispered silent prayers. She did not begrudge his loyalty to Gargauth, but it annoyed her nonetheless. She was not accustomed to placing her faith in the gods or anything else except herself and the magic. Her servants' worship and granted powers were tools to her, nothing more.

Walking back to the reddened waters of the wooden bowl, she gazed into the black mirror at the bottom. "*Ravahlas su geska*," she muttered, and watched the liquid's surface boil and waver, casting shadows upon the mirror below. It pulsed in tune to her heartbeat, sensing her will and forming images to satisfy what she desired.

The scene changed and the silhouette of Brookhollow's walls coalesced, tinged in the crimson of the blooded water. Narrowing her eyes, the walls loomed into view, pulling near to the gates her forces would soon push through to gut the city. She bared her teeth as she noticed tiny figures moving along the crude battlements, carrying bows and spears. She searched their ranks, focusing on faces that were blind to her spying eyes. Those faces were set in determination—and some fear, she noted with slight satisfaction.

"Fear drives them to stand and fight, regardless of faith," she whispered. "I underestimated their instinct for survival."

Viewing their numbers for a few moments more, she leaned back and smiled despite her irritation. Khaemil had ceased his meditations and turned to watch her as she spread her hands over the bowl, creating ripples in the water's surface with her fingertips. Her eyes, sparkling with cruelty, met his steady gaze.

"Their warriors stand against us to defend the city," she said and he stood straighter, hefting his mace as if the battle were merely yards away. "Worry not, dear one. Their oracle witches do not stand with them."

He eased his stance but stepped closer, watching as the bowl began to glow with a red light. Morgynn lifted the carved box of bone that contained the secrets of her plague. She dispelled the seal on its lid and gently took the yellowed scrolls from within, tracing her thumbs over the arcane letters and symbols written on the parchments.

Leafing carefully through the brittle pages, she pulled one free and sighed in anticipation. Blood flooded to her fingertips, attracted to the magic that tingled along her arms in the scroll's presence. Her eyes became deep crimson orbs as she summoned the spell to her lips.

The scene in the bowl changed again. Gone were Brookhollow's walls, replaced by the marbled floors of the Hidden Circle's sanctuary. She smiled. No god interrupted her view of the sanctuary, no divine protection repelled her power. The image grew darker, the distorted and nightmarish forms of several figures moved in and out of view.

"The oracles will not act against their god's wishes," she said, slightly amused while choosing from among the shifting silhouettes. Her voice hollowed and hummed with power. "I will make sure they do not."

⊙ ⊙ ⊙ ⊙ ⊙

Dreslya stepped lightly, pushing through the gathered oracles who whispered and pointed. All were aware of her recent exile from such gatherings. Sameska paused in her speech extolling the virtues of those who refused to join the rebellious hunters at the eastern gate. The high oracle glared down upon this intrusion of her sanctuary, this interruption of her audience. Dreslya glared confidently back, just for a moment, before ignoring Sameska and turning to gather the attention of her fellow oracles.

She ascended the lowest step of the dais to address the others, but before she could speak, Sameska gripped her shoulder tightly in aged fingers of rigid iron. "You are unwanted in this chamber, child. Join your sister at the gates." She turned to the oracles. "Share in her blasphemy and none of you will darken this church's doorstep again!"

Dres calmly removed Sameska's hand from her shoulder, squeezing just hard enough to show the high oracle that her touch would not be tolerated again.

"For many months we have been without prophecy, relying on minor divinations and fethra petals to guide our lives. For a tenday or so, we have suffered the blush, watching loved ones succumb to fever and bleeding sores." She paused to allow her words to sink in. "And only two days ago, we were warned of approaching evil. Have you not wondered why prophecy did not come sooner?"

A few in the hushed crowd gasped at Dreslya's open defiance of Sameska's authority, but to the high oracle's growing irritation, many listened closely, while still others nodded quietly.

"Your words ring hollow, Dreslya Loethe. The plague, the storms, and the Hoarite have all come in accordance with the will of Savras and his divine wisdom. Do you now question the prophecy that unfolds before your very eyes?"

Dreslya turned and raised her emerald eyes to look upon Sameska as one might view a stubborn child. Her own recent visions gave her new understanding of the high oracle, erasing the old woman's façade of power and control, replacing it with a priestess full of fear and spite. She pitied Sameska, but tempered her pity with anger and concern for her people.

"I do not question Savras or his will," she began, her voice uncharacteristically strong and clear. "I question the shepherd of his temple, the seer that might destroy us all."

Sameska narrowed her eyes, speechless before this confirmation of betrayal within her own temple. Her anger seethed and boiled as the audience of oracles murmured and watched in shock.

Before the high oracle could respond, a cracking sound drew all eyes to the ceiling and the glass dome above.

Spider web fractures crawled through the glass like slow lightning captured in myriad colors. The largest cracks, near the center, grew dark and more defined as they began to bleed.

⊛ ⊛ ⊛ ⊛ ⊛

The water's surface bubbled and steamed as Morgynn chanted the words on the scroll. She stirred the bowl with a finger, churning the images into a swirl of shapes and colors. Beyond the sound of her own voice and the blood pounding in her ears, she could hear the dim buzz of words echoing from the scrying bowl—words that changed to screams as her magic took shape in the sanctuary.

Each shard of glass tumbled end over end in slow motion as she completed the first portion of the spell. She chanted, watching the reflections of the gathered oracles scattering in the flashing mirrors of the shattered dome. Her hands turned and pushed against the air, shaping the spell and focusing it. The mind of the creature she summoned was dull and shiftless, a slave to her will. Its airy body spun, snatching the shards from the air, making them one with its body.

A single shard caught the reflection of her chosen victim and froze in the tempest of falling glass. She stood alone, dark-haired with pale skin, a single pulse growing stronger as the spell gripped her heart and mind in its vile embrace. The blush was weak in her, only the root of the infection that would make her vulnerable to the spell Morgynn wove. Her blood-born voice roared in the girl's ears as the magic was completed.

The blood magus released the bowl from her power, panting and wringing her hands as the magic drained from her body. The scroll had burned away, leaving only a thin dusting of gray ash coating her hands. Gooseflesh rose and fell in waves across her flushed skin and she steadied herself before returning her gaze to the water.

"My lady." Khaemil's voice rang with concern as he stared out the tower's window into the darkness of the field and forest beyond. "Something is happening outside."

He held his mace in a tight grip, squinting to make out movement near the forest's edge and growling absently through slightly bared fangs.

Morgynn barely heard his voice above the torrent of her own heartbeat and was annoyed at the intrusion on her moment of pleasure. She watched the reflection in the bowl as her magic took effect, then reluctantly turned away from the image to join Khaemil at the window.

In the rippling waters of the scrying bowl, the young savant stared blindly into a twisting cyclone of crimson razors with eyes that grew clouded with red as cold sweat poured down her face and neck.

CHAPTER TWENTY

Most of the oracles retreated to the edges of the chamber, screaming and praying for release from the magic that descended from the ceiling. A glittering whirlwind of spinning glass forced the shards to crash into one another, pulverizing them into a fine dust of flying razors. Sameska took faltering steps backward, her mumbled prayers for forgiveness lost in the tempest of wind and glass.

Startled at first, Dreslya gathered her wits and concentrated to think of a spell to counter the intruding magic. She dropped her bundle to the floor and gripped her holy symbol tightly before her. A cold sweat broke out on her forehead as she watched one ensorcelled savant walk closer and closer to the falling doom of shredding glass. If the other oracles would add their power to mine, we might have a chance, she thought in despair. But most still accepted the prophecy and would not violate its edict.

The wheeling cloud centered itself over the ancient rune-inscribed circle of before the altar, the sacred place of the high oracle where the most powerful visions had been born in ages past. Large chunks of glass fell from the tempest's center, shattering as they crashed to the stone of the circle, covering it in sharp slivers. Something about the whirlwind's movement nudged Dreslya's memory and she quickly realized that the thing was not merely a magical wind, but an air elemental.

The dark-haired savant edged closer still to the perimeter of the circle, gazing upward into the spinning gale with blood-rimmed eyes and a blank stare. Dreslya held back an empathic gasp as the girl's foot crunched on the glass, her sandles merely padded cloth that offered little protection from injury. The imagined pain cleared Dreslya's head and she hurried to cast a spell. Conjuring a gust of swift wind, she directed it toward the circle, sweeping away the fallen glass, though it could not loosen the shards that already pierced the savant's bleeding foot.

The dark maelstrom lowered menacingly, hovering just above the girl's upturned face, bits of glass scratching her cheeks and forehead as they whipped past. The cloth that covered the blood-stained statue of Savras was ripped away and carried into the cyclone, fluttering as it was sliced apart and lost. The statue stared blankly upon the scene, dried rivers of brown blood trailing from its eyes. Sameska fell as the statue was revealed, and she scrambled backward weakly on hands and heels, averting her eyes.

Dreslya stepped as close to the circle as she dared and held her hands out at her sides, intoning an ancient rite. The duties and powers of acting Sybilite were still hers, and the temple's protections were formidable. A spell of command tumbled past her lips easily as she cast, stoically watching as several cuts appeared on the savant's face. Her voice was ragged and desperate as she shouted the last.

"*Peshtak revallas, emuarte*!"

The chamber shook with power, and the spinning wind slowed for a moment, recognizing a sudden threat. The sanctuary's runes glowed and burst to life, arcing across walls and floors like the lightning outside. Light beamed through the darkness of the foul wind, and the air creature writhed, surging upward to seek escape. Glass fell in a sparkling rain as the elemental abandoned its weapons and the helpless prey below. Trapped in the temple's net of spells, the wind quickly dissipated, destroyed by the magical wards of the temple.

Silence fell upon the chamber, broken only by sobs and the scraping feet of those rising from where they'd fallen. Rain splashed high above where the glass dome had been, the wards preventing the weather from penetrating. Dreslya rushed forward to catch the dark-haired savant as the temple's white light banished the girl's strange possession. She caught the wounded priestess and lowered her to the floor. Ignoring the sacred circle beneath them, she inspected the girl's bleeding cuts and whispered prayers of healing to close them.

Other oracles rushed forward to help. Dreslya rose, feeling slightly dizzy but relieved. Sameska stood as well, watching as rain slid across the invisible shield of power in the gaping hole above. Eyeing the chaos and disheveled oracles, she addressed the fearful and berated the blasphemous.

"This is what comes of our betrayal! This is his punishment, his wrath in answer to our doubt! We must—"

"No." Dres spoke quietly, but the runes in the chamber still pulsed to her command, amplifying her voice and vibrating in the floor. Sameska stumbled back as if struck. "Savras is not a god of blood and vengeance. We are taught to heed his words, not fear them." She turned to speak to the oracles, ignoring Sameska.

"I know that doubt still grips you, and I will not dismiss your fears as petty or trivial. I will ask none of you to join me at the gates to meet the evil that seeks to tear us apart." She paused, looking down at the blood staining the deep grooves of the circle and the shimmering glass spread across the floor. "But I will tell you this . . . I have been shown that a prophecy does indeed unfold before us, and we must decide for ourselves what parts we shall play in it."

Dres retrieved her bundle from the floor and turned to leave the chamber. Every oracle watched her go, still shaken and contemplating her words. Sameska stared wildly at the glowing walls of the chamber, as if unseen judgment lurked in the spiraling patterns around her.

⊛ ⊛ ⊛ ⊛ ⊛

The ground rumbled and trees swayed as the foliage parted at the forest's edge, a dark tunnel yawning through the Qurth's ravenous undergrowth. Quin charged toward the gray darkness at the end of the path, deftly keeping his balance as the earth threatened to throw him down among the writhing tendrils of bloodthorns.

Bedlam pealed a low scream amid bending wood and falling leaves. Its wail echoed down the wooded corridor, seeking wild freedom at its end. Massive shapes rose and fell in the darkness along the path, crashing through the forest and matching Quinsareth's speed.

At the tunnel's end, through the misty fog in the clearing beyond, Quin detected several pairs of cruel white eyes surrounding the dim silhouette of a forlorn tower. They were the eyes of the dead in the field of stone the Pale Sisters had warned him about, the pets of the blood-witch. As he neared the forest's edge, he heard the tortured shrieks of undead beasts summoning him to their playground. Bedlam changed its tune to match their challenge and Quin smiled, giving in to the wild of the shadows in his blood.

He leaped into open air above a steep incline, the forest exploding on either side of him in a hail of dirt, rock, and shattered wood. The long reach of the Pale Sisters' magic commanded the vines and roots that surrounded him. Twisting and lashing outward, they grew, summoning even more from deep beneath the field of stone. A wave of vines rippled across the ground and Quinsareth landed in the clearing between them. Running with Bedlam, he was ready to cut down anything that intruded upon the forged path.

The white eyes of fiendish ghouls surged forward to meet the charge, cackling and moaning in hellish madness as the aasimar neared. They bounded across the field, their bestial voices quickly turning to roars of rage as a thick mass of vines snatched them from their strides. The ghouls fell, entangled by the Pale Sisters' thorny minions, and were crushed against the hard ground and broken stone of the field. All around Quin, the undead were caught in the Pale Sisters' embrace, and still their network of vines and roots grew, pushing ahead of him in a wall of living foliage.

One fortunate ghoul landed safely on Quinsareth's clear path, hissing and lashing its long, smoke-tipped tongue as it loped toward him on back-swayed legs. It stared at him with blind eyes, tasting the air and smelling his scent. Quin steadily continued, staring the beast down and studying its strange movement. His hand tightened on Bedlam's hilt.

The ghoul pounced into the air, thrusting its head forward to reveal yellowed fangs and proboscis tongue. Quin stepped onto a large block of crumbled stone and jumped. Reversing his grip on Bedlam, he swung the blade forward to slam its pommel into the ghoul's jaw. The creature bit off its own tongue as its mouth slammed shut. The monster's head flew backward, snapping bones, and its long claws scratched and grasped at Quin's armor as they collided in midair. Blindly, it sought soft flesh to rend as the pair descended to the stony ground.

The aasimar ignored the ghoul's futile attempts to harm him. He continued his assault by sliding Bedlam's shrieking blade into the undead's emaciated torso. As the ghoul's back slammed to the ground, Quin rolled and thrust Bedlam up into the creature's chest. Regaining his footing, he turned to see the growth of a shorter tongue in the ghoul's mouth. Its claws scratched at the sword holding it in place, hissing as the metal rejected its fiendish touch. Quin sidestepped the flailing claws and withdrew the blade, spinning it to cleave the beast's skull and cease its shrieking cries.

The Pale Sisters' roots continued to surge, trapping the last of the Gargauthans' minions before quieting their entangling vines to a shuddering stop. Quin renewed his charge as the sound of a droning chant filled the air ahead of him. Ascending a low, fallen battlement, he stared down at the base of the tower to see hellish masks staring back—the gathered wizard-priests, surrounded by the black haze of spells inscribed on the tower's walls.

Wind and thunder formed a ceiling for the scene, punctuated by the muffled cries and impotent rage of ghouls trapped beneath the Pale Sisters' heavy foliage.

⊛ ⊛ ⊛ ⊛ ⊛

"I will deal with him," Khaemil said, turning for the door as the aasimar became visible among the crawling tentacles of vine and wood. Morgynn seized his arm, stopping him. Her fingernails pierced his skin as she watched the Hoarite's charge toward the tower and witnessed the insolence of the defiant Pale Sisters as they assisted the lone warrior. Khaemil winced at the wounds she made, but did not move.

She watched the scene with a mixture of subdued anger and fascination. Unblinking, Morgynn studied his foolhardy attack with calm eyes. Her fingers dug deeper into the *shadurakul*'s forearm, setting his blood on fire with the heat of roiling rage. He struggled to remain quiet, turning his attention to the aasimar. Morgynn released him at length, caressing his bloody wounds and keeping a hand on his massive shoulder.

"No," she said. "Let's have a closer look at him."

"But the priests below," he protested. "Surely they—"

"He might find a way to destroy them," she purred, a cruel curiosity in her voice. "They've performed their duties well enough. They can be spared now."

"And the storm?"

"Will last long enough with or without them!" she snapped, irritated by his questioning. "You have little faith in your Gargauthan brethren, Khaemil. Is that a flaw, or wisdom?"

The *shadurakul* did not answer, and Morgynn's attention remained on the field below. Her eyes danced as the warrior cut down the ghoul with his screaming blade. She enjoyed the weapon's discordant voice and bloody work in the aasimar's quick hands. She turned from the window and released Khaemil's shoulder, flexing her fingers and stretching her neck pleasurably.

"No," she said again, staring nonchalantly into the piles of bones and skulls around her chamber. "We will meet this Hoarite and have a good look at him. Before we ruin him."

⊛ ⊛ ⊛ ⊛ ⊛

Half a dozen Gargauthans joined blackened hands, weaving a spell to protect the tower from the aasimar and his unlikely allies. Quinsareth made no move to stop them, keeping their attention and hoping his alliance with the dryads had not yet ended. The net of vines in his wake was still and quiet, only brown leaves fluttering in the cold wind.

Deliberating quickly, he cursed himself for a fool. Too far from the priests to interrupt their chant, he was forced to rely on the fickle fey trio to honor a bargain made in mutual distrust. He braced himself to drop behind the stone he stood on, counting on the fallen block to protect him from whatever magic was being cast. Then his sharp eyes spotted movement on the ground near the priests' feet.

Tiny, dark green shoots sprouted and curled upward, unnoticed by the chanting priests. A carpet of new growth spread amid the spellcasters, hidden beneath their robes and twisting around their shoes. One by one, the tendrils brushed against skin, startling their victims and choking off the chanting. The priests frantically clawed at green thorns scraping against their flesh and tightening around their ankles and calves.

Relieved, Quinsareth watched, giving the Pale Sisters their due and allowing them their vengeance.

Several priests fell to the ground, roaring in frustration as their legs were wrapped together. Others, more level-headed, attempted to summon spells and prayers to dispel the wild plants. At the sound of hoarse voices rising to chant anew, the ground tore apart beneath them.

Vines and roots as thick as small trees burst from the dirt and cracked stone, shaking even the ruined wall on which Quinsareth stood. Priests screamed as several were impaled on roots and lifted into the air, only to stop suddenly as they were slammed back to the dirt. The rest became hopelessly entangled, thorny tendrils wrapping around their heads and crushing their masks, silencing their spells in a gagging vice.

Quinsareth skirted the edges of the Pale Sisters' chaos. He made his way to the open doorway at the base of the tower and ignored the eerily quiet work of the dryads. Faintly, he could hear their songs inside the tangle of roots and limbs. Though their magic was directed elsewhere, Quin felt a familiar peace steal over him briefly. He stopped at the doorway, glancing sidelong into the newborn thicket. The dryads flowed through the network of wood, their bodies sinuously melding in and out of roots, visiting each victim in turn.

Their bare bodies were hideously beautiful, lithe and graceful as they quietly stalked their helpless prey. Aellspath saw him pause and she smiled cruelly, winking her flowered eyes at him. The ease with which Quin felt he could succumb to their charms frightened him and jolted him out of his dangerous musing. He darted inside and ran to the stairs, eager to be away from the soothing voices and to finish his business above.

The tower was silent inside. Quin ascended the stairway warily but swiftly, expecting danger to come howling from the decayed building's hiding places. Nothing came to reward his alertness, which only made him more aware of his surroundings. Most of the inner chambers he passed were rotted through, wooden floors gaping with holes, some with no floors at all.

Near the top he could see the stone ceiling of the highest room and the soft glow of candlelight through an open door. With Bedlam ready, he took a shallow breath. Feeling the ice of shadows pulsing through his body, he prepared to face the source of the dark call he'd felt outside the Red Cup less than a tenday ago.

He smiled a killer's grin and rushed the last few steps, entering the chamber with Bedlam before him. A woman sat calmly watching him, reclined upon a red-cushioned divan.

Her dark eyes reflected the light of many candles, and her pale skin was radiant in their glow as she seductively rose to a sitting position and crossed her long legs, studying him. Dark red lips curved upward in amusement as something shifted in the deep darkness behind her.

Too late, Quinsareth heard the whispers of a spell being cast and made out the dim silhouette of a massive figure in the chamber's back corner. He ran forward, berating himself for being distracted, but was met head-on by the force of summoned magic. It slammed into his chest, an invisible gripping mass, spreading quickly across his body and denying his attempts to break free. In moments he was paralyzed. He could only watch as a black-skinned figure in dark robes approached from behind the sorceress's divan.

The bright eyes within the figure's hood tugged at some distant memory. The feeling was the same as what he'd felt before the call of shadows at the Red Cup, when the illusory red star begged him to the east, that same odd sense of a kindred spirit watching him slay the last of the Fallen Few. This figure had sought to summon him here, but to what purpose? The eyes were accompanied by a glittering smile of sharp, white teeth as Bedlam was knocked from his grasp to clatter on the stone floor.

⊙ ⊙ ⊙ ⊙ ⊙

Myrrium licked her lips with a forked tongue, stroking the bare chest of another quiet victim with her black claws. She had pushed through the thick tangle to lie in the open air, curious and a bit apprehensive about what might be occurring in the tower. The twisted vines rustled as Aellspath and Oerynn emerged, sated and sleepy-eyed, to stare up at the tower.

The churning clouds were flashing and rumbling more frequently, changing speed wildly. The arcane storm raged as its vortex above the tower grew larger and slid askew from the rune-inscribed spire. The Pale Sisters flinched and ducked as lightning struck the field of stone. Silently,

Oerynn crawled closer to the nearby wall, spying strange movements in its surface.

The dense net of symbols and spells rippled and unwound, some disappearing, others upending themselves as their tight order fell apart in the absence of the Gargauthan scribes. The dryads gathered close, sniffing the air and feeling the stone restored in those places once burned and scarred with controlling magic. Their heightened senses could feel unseen forces working against the carved tapestry of spells, tearing it apart and draining its power.

Nervously they edged away from the tower, wary and alert as nature turned mad in the skies. The ancient roots that bound their lives together called from the forest, tugging at their primal need and sense of survival. One by one, they dissolved into the thickest roots around them, casting fearful glances at the discordant storm before safely returning to the pale oaks they had strayed from.

Lesani pulled her cloak tight against the howling wind, peering from beneath her hood with eyes that reflected the green glow of the lantern she carried. In a small iron cage, hanging from the end of her hooked staff, burned a bit of the green flame she had summoned earlier. She could not yet see the walls of Brookhollow, though what magic she could spare had carried her close.

Unnatural sounds emanated from the forest's depths, noises from outside the material world that echoed in waves through the Weave. Lesani shuddered, sensing the imbalance that lurked somewhere within the Qurth. It shook the air, like an earthquake to those sensitive to nature's harmonies and rhythms. Lightning screamed like fabric being slowly torn. Thunder pounded like dwarven hammers in deep forges.

Reflexively, she bit her thumb and flicked her fingers at the disturbance, an ancient gesture of the Ghedia meant to ward away evil. She smiled in spite of herself, feeling comfort in the traditions her mother had observed, powerless though they might be. Traditions were greatly honored among her Shaaryan forebears, and she'd often contemplated returning south to the plains of her people.

"Perhaps this shall be the last," she said aloud. "We have strayed for too many generations among these Border Kingdoms, with its cities and ruins. All the signs point south, and perhaps we should continue that way."

She paused, looking behind her and searching the darkness for some sign of her sisters. Only darkness lay in her wake, as empty as the road ahead. Frowning, she pushed toward the flashing horizon and held the green flame higher as she walked, determined to honor the last vestiges of her bloodline's misplaced tribe one more time.

CHAPTER TWENTY-ONE

Hooded and cloaked men swung heavy scythes at the tall grass and bushes that had grown close to the outer walls of the city. Often they would peer over their shoulders toward the Qurth, watching for movement in the trees, fearful of being caught unawares. Two guard towers flanked the wall, protruding to provide archers with a swath of crossfire upon approaching attackers. Clearing the field of possible cover was difficult in the rain, but any precautions they could take before the impending attack might provide an advantage.

Atop the wall, gleaming spearheads glistened as rain trickled across their blades, propped against the battlements and waiting for warrior hands to wield them. Those warriors, Hunters of the Hidden Circle sworn to uphold the prophecies of the oracles, lined the walls, armed and armored in direct defiance of the most recent prophecy. Prayers for guidance had been whispered by them all. Doubt had brought them to this point, but faith would see them through, even at the cost of their lives.

On the ground, behind the barred gates, archers stood waiting for the call, shivering despite heavy cloaks and layers of leather armor. The wind had picked up, blowing colder and whipping their cloaks in every direction. Icy rain stabbed at exposed skin, the cold slicing straight to the bone.

Many citizens joined the hunters. They carried weapons of farm implements and polished old swords left behind by generations before. Many more stood bundled in open doorways, shouting for the defenders to lay down their arms and return to their homes. The hunters ignored these protests and maintained their posts. No one was faulted for following Sameska's edict of passiveness, and no one was forced to renounce it openly. More than a few defenders shook their heads and wrung their hands over the conflict that had seemingly sprung from nowhere. They had known for some time that things were off balance inside the temple. Obeying the instinct to defend themselves felt inherently right.

Elisandrya rode briskly through the streets on a brown mare, feeling the loss of Morningstar deeply. She inspected the north and south gates, observing more battle-ready hunters at both. Messengers had been sent on the fastest steeds to Splondar in the northeast and to Sprynt, the northernmost city of the Blacksaddle Baronies in the south. She knew that aid from either would be unlikely, considering the virulent reputation of the blush, and that any assistance might arrive too late to do any good.

As she rode, several people approached Elisandrya from their homes, pleading for surrender and pointing emphatically at the enraged and strengthening storm above as a sign of Savras's displeasure, then ducking back into cottages to attend to frightened children. Eli was speechless, newly realizing the damage Sameska's manipulations had caused and might continue to cause. She stood high in her saddle, looking east down the main road toward the temple, her eyes hopeful.

But she saw no oracles coming to join the defenders, no sign of her sister whose face she both longed and dreaded to see. She sensed the quiet rift between them deepening over the outcome of this battle. She still hoped that at any moment, Dreslya would appear with her fellow oracles, marching in a procession down the main street to solidify the defenses of Brookhollow by uniting sword and spell.

"Without their magic," she said under her breath, "one needn't be a prophet to foresee this battle's conclusion."

The strident tones of a watchman's horn split the air, dashing her thoughts apart. Three quick blasts pealed through the thunder and rain from the northern gate, a signal of movement outside; something approached the city under cover of darkness.

Eli patted the hilt of the sword at her side, checked the curve of her borrowed bow, and kicked the shivering mare's flanks. She took a moment to offer a prayer for guidance, indulging her diminishing doubt and seeking any sign that she had been wrong. Not expecting an answer, she was stunned when an image formed behind her eyes, appearing for an instant and then dissolving, leaving behind an inexplicable sense of calm.

She saw tall waves of wind-blown grass on an endless plain covered in an aura of emerald flame.

⊙ ⊙ ⊙ ⊙ ⊙

The room smelled strongly of cinnamon, concealing the dusty scent of old bones and burned wax. Morgynn had lit several candles with a wave of her hand and the barest of whispers. The aasimar struggled to break free of the enchantment that held him in place. She smiled at his attempts and waited until he seemed satisfied of their futility.

She circled, looking him up and down, admiring his strangely handsome features.

"You chose well, Khaemil," she said finally, stopping in front of him and exploring the depths of his pearly eyes. "Almost too well."

"Thank-you, Lady Morgynn," Khaemil said.

She leaned in close to him, brushing her cheek against his neck and listening to his heartbeat, calm and steady despite the situation. She reached up and touched his cheek, whispering arcane words in a deep voice, her breath warm against his throat.

Though the Hoarite could not resist her spell, something reacted to her magic, blurring her attempt to see his thoughts. Shadows cloaked her mind's eye like dark clouds in front of a high sun—faint beams of light sought to blind her in a celestial radiance. Through the bright and the dark she could choose wandering thoughts, fleeting emotions in a sea of experience, but only those floating near the surface. The depths of the aasimar's spirit shut out her dissecting sight, shifting and swimming in a pitch black fog that eluded her intrusive magic.

"Mysterious, aren't we, pretty one?" she said, withdrawing her hand and dismissing the spell. "No matter. Your secrets are unimportant. Though I am intrigued by the paradigm.

"Shadows and light," she said thoughtfully. "And only the barest hint of a man beneath them."

"The Pale Sisters have retreated, Lady Morgynn," Khaemil reported from the window, "but the storm is dissipating without the priests, far more quickly than it should. The tower could be in danger soon."

Unnaturally loud thunder roared in the sky outside, punctuating his words as stones shook and dust fell from the ceiling. Multicolored lightning ripped through the clouds, casting an eerie glow across the *shadurakul*'s deep black skin. He tapped his claws anxiously on the stone window sill.

"Worry not, all will be well. Besides," she replied sardonically, "we have a guest to entertain. A guest who'd have been wise to move on after slaying that oaf of an ogre for us, and even wiser to have ignored this prophecy business."

She moved closer to Quin again, gazing at his eyes and face, sniffing slightly and noting the faint lines of old scars running across his neck and disappearing beneath his breastplate.

"I sense no hero in you, Hoarite. There is cruelty lurking

behind those angelic eyes of yours, a coldness that belies any trace of charity or goodwill you might possess. Even the name your mind reveals is a lie, isn't it? Quinsareth? A term in Old Mulhorandi, is it not? Meaning 'falsehood,' I believe." She smiled, realizing some private humor, and added, "How quaint."

She studied his reaction though his pale eyes revealed little.

"Was it the girl who brought you here, I wonder? Oh yes, I know of her, this Elisandrya. I have tasted her name on the lips of two men now who reached the end of their time in the last few days." She thrilled to hear a slight change in Quin's pulse, momentary but telling. She traced a fingernail across the ancient designs in his armor, following the symbols and letters of an alphabet she did not recognize as she continued. "A hunter for the oracles of Savras, a warrior for her people, brave and beautiful, brash and wild. What a monster she must think you, eh?"

Then she leaned close again, breathing heavily against his ear. "You might have been better counseled to have pursued a darker mistress."

His eyes drifted to the floor and his sword, so close, lying against the deep pile of bones along the nearby wall. Skulls from Jhareat's last days leered at him with empty sockets and grins that never waned. She stepped aside, allowing him to see the weapon he so desperately wished to wield.

"Or was it the prophecy that guided your steps, aasimar?"

His gaze went to her at the words. Turning, she looked over her shoulder at him, searching for some spark of emotion in his eyes. Pleased to have his full attention, she coyly brushed a strand of dark hair from her face and drew a long dagger from her belt. She licked her lips and wiped absently at imagined spots on the blade.

"I imagine the old witch of Brookhollow must have spun quite a tale. Even now they hide in their temple, trusting in her words while steeped in the stench of plague and fear." She raised an eyebrow and regarded him conspiratorially. "Want to hear a secret?"

Thunder again shook the walls, sending bones to clatter on

the floor as the dusty piles shifted. Morgynn's eyes sparkled in dancing shadows as the candles died one by one, deepening the darkness of the chamber.

⊙ ⊙ ⊙ ⊙ ⊙

Horses pranced in place and snorted impatiently as Eli rode past, churning through the muddy puddles along the sides of the cobbled streets. Riders watched with grim countenances, holding back their steeds and awaiting the next call of the watchman's horn, the one that would send them to battle.

Elisandrya pulled hard on the reins, stopping at the wall and looking up to the nervous face of the young hornblower. Dismounting and ascending the ladder, she expected to see the worst beyond the wall. Though she tried to shove images of massive armies and mounted cavalry out of her mind, they marched in her thoughts anyway. The unlikelihood of such a force in the Reach was not enough to quell anxious fear, that passing terror that grips all warriors before combat and pushes them to exceed their own expectations.

Gripping the battlements, she peered into the dark, blinking past sheets of rain and racing lightning. What she saw in the distance was unlike anything she expected.

Bobbing slightly, teetering from left to right along what could have been an invisible horizon, were tiny lights, some closer and closing, others following behind. Some would blink out for a few moments and reappear, closer and more distinct as if jumping across miles in the space of a few heartbeats. Small flickers of green flame, swinging in time to a steady march, all converged toward the walls of Brookhollow.

"Should we sound the alarm, Lady Elisandrya? Prepare for battle?" The young watchman was shaking, though from fear or cold she could not tell.

"Not yet." Something was familiar about those green flames, and her brief vision a few moments ago did not fully explain the faint memory those lights sparked within her. "Wait until we can assess what we're actually seeing, then gauge the threat and decide."

The watchman nodded though he clearly disagreed. He was not a hunter, as Eli could see from his armor and bearing, but one of the city watch, a volunteer from among Brookhollow's citizens. She was glad to know that not everyone had abandoned the hunters for defying the oracles, and clapped the young man on the shoulder in reassurance, flashing him a calm smile and nodding.

The nearest flame winked out, then reappeared less than a hundred yards from the gates. Those on the wall could make out the robes and cloak of a figure walking against the wind and rain, holding a crooked staff from which hung a lantern, swinging in step and radiating a flickering emerald light. Eli immediately recognized the garb of the Ghedia, the light and dark brown robes of the druidic shamans that wandered the Reach.

Stepping within the light of the hooded lanterns of the watchmen, the figure pulled its hood back slightly, revealing a wrist that bore several bone and wood bracelets. Eli was pleased to see the stoic face of Lesani. She patted the watchman on the shoulder and ordered the signal for "all is well." Two sharp notes issued from the horn, followed by a mumbling curiosity from the warriors below.

Eli called down to the gatekeepers. "Open the gates!"

"No need!" came Lesani's quick reply, the accent of the Shaaran tongue thick in her speech. The Ghedia approached the gate and stroked the old wood, tracing the grain with a practiced hand and whispering a familiar spell. The gate rippled at her touch, the wood responding to the wild nature of her magic. Lesani turned and planted the crooked staff in the thick mud, leaving a green beacon for the others following in the darkness. Stepping over the iron braces across the lower portion of the gates, she melded through the awakened wood. The druid looked into the astonished eyes of the gate guards and smiled. "Save your arms for your weapons. No need to make a fuss over me." She glanced up on the wall. "Elisandrya!"

Eli leaped down the ladder to embrace her old friend. "It is good to see you, Lesani," she said over the surprised Ghedia's shoulders. "It has been too long."

"No such thing as too long or too short, child. We meet

when and where we are supposed to." She stood back and held Eli's shoulders, then took a cursory look around. "Though I admit I'm glad we meet in this world rather than the next, considering the times."

Elisandrya's smile waned slightly. Lesani's words weighed heavily on the hunter's shoulders. They stepped away from the gates, arm in arm, pulling hoods and cloaks tighter against the rain to speak of recent events.

"When the blush first came in the north, I thought little of it. Plague comes and goes—it is the way of things." Lesani's voice took on the tone of long-past nights spent around the Ghedia campfires, telling tales of dangerous times. Eli shivered, remembering the dark morals of many of those stories. "But this time, the storms began, the cold winds. Early autumns have been known, even winters, but nature seemed too much at war with itself.

"My auguries showed dark magic at work, a prophecy of ending." She looked at Eli from within her hood, rain dripping from its edges. "That seeing brought me here, Elisandrya, and as many of my order who would follow. What is happening here?"

Eli stared at Lesani's wise face, hearing the words from someone she trusted. Ending. She looked around at warriors huddled against the rain, facing a storm that hid whatever evil crawled toward the walls. She stared at the locked doors and shadowed faces of those who refused to take part in their defense.

"A prophecy has been given to us," she began, but she felt contradiction blurring the lines of what she'd seen and what she knew. She shook her head, trying to put the words together. "No, not a prophecy. Something else. Something wrong."

Lightning raced above them. Lesani waited patiently, her eyes understanding. Eli felt comfort in those eyes, knowing that all she'd ever been was known to that wise countenance.

"Sameska lied to us. To me," she said, borrowing the confidence she saw in Lesani. "She gave us a prophecy that told us to lie down, to do nothing and that all would be well. Before this vision, Targris was attacked and Logfell had already fallen." Her eyes darkened, looked knowingly into Lesani's as she repeated the word. "*Before.*"

"Ah," Lesani nodded, realization hardening her features. "A vision out of joint, like your parents."

Eli stared at those who stood with her, controlling the rage she felt at hearing another confirm her own knowledge. Lesani did not push the subject, for which Eli was grateful. They'd had that conversation many times in years past.

Both considered the import of the other's tale while more of the Ghedia gathered around them, stepping through the gates and exchanging greetings with one another. More than twenty nomadic shamans arrived, with several more still making their way toward Brookhollow. They awaited the attention of their sister Lesani, who was the initiator of the green flame.

Lesani quietly apologized that so few of the Ghedia had gathered, remarking that many still held ancient grudges against the Savrathan bordertowns.

"I understand," Eli replied. "We are glad to accept any assistance at all. We still haven't heard anything from the oracles themselves."

"In your youth, I remember, you wouldn't have wished to hear another word from those oracles ever again," Lesani said, pulling her hood back to meet Eli's gaze despite the rain. "I imagine it is more your sister that concerns you."

Elisandrya nodded. She hadn't mentioned Dreslya, still hoping her sister would appear to stand with her.

"I'm worried about Dres, I admit."

"Now that's odd. As I recall, Dreslya was the worrier." Lesani smiled. "Should I speak with this Sameska? Perhaps she can be persuaded to see things differently?"

Eli's face darkened and she looked at the ground, avoiding the looming silhouette of the temple to her right.

"That would be wasted breath, I'm afraid," she said coldly. "Sameska is lost to a madness of fear. Seeing a Ghedia in the temple might serve only to strengthen that fear."

"I see," Lesani replied, then added, "I'm sorry Eli. I should have listened with better ears when you were younger. You were right, then and now. Take strength from that."

Lesani turned to address her sisters. Elisandrya walked to the nearby street corner, staring toward the eastern gates though she could not see them, and felt ashamed for her people. She imagined how they must look in the eyes of the Ghedia, whose forebears had counseled long ago against the evils of abandoning the tribal lifestyle of the Shaar for this northern stretch of land.

As she stood in the pounding rain, staring sightlessly east, an odd noise filled the air. Quiet, almost whispering at first, it began to grow, droning deeply in her ears and filling her heart with a primal dread that chilled far more than any wind or rain. On the heels of the noise, three sharp horn blasts echoed through the storm once again, this time from the west, causing her stomach to lurch as the horn's urgent call faded.

⊙ ⊙ ⊙ ⊙ ⊙

"Let him answer, Khaemil," she said without looking at her servant. "I'm curious to hear his thoughts."

Quin felt his jaw loosen as Khaemil whispered and altered the spell that held him, allowing him to speak. He saw the anxious look in Morgynn's eyes, waiting for him to ask with baited breath for her secrets and intrigues. He didn't much care, but her talkativeness kept her focused on him so he decided to play along.

"The plague, perhaps? Or the storm? Your secrets aren't very well hidden."

Morgynn smiled all the wider, enjoying herself. "I suppose I could have been more subtle concerning the blush and the storms, but I really saw no need in the end." Her matter-of-fact tone was confident and proud as she continued. "I thought you might have guessed it all by now. You see, *I* am the prophecy."

Quin narrowed his eyes at her words, curious at this strange news, but not truly surprised. The ramifications of her claim, however incredulous, reverberated in his mind.

"When I first sent my agents into this land, they told me of the Oracles of the Hidden Circle and the powerful divinations and prophecies of which they were capable. Then they told me of High Oracle Sameska and I chose to study her from a distance. The old woman's thirst for power and influence was admirable and her control over her subjects was impressive, but her relationship with her god had dwindled almost to nothing. So, in her quiet moments alone, trying desperately to renew her faith and maintain her position among the oracles," Morgynn looked at Quin mischievously, "I gave Savras back to her. I shaped the landscape of my dominion over this Reach by eliminating the one threat that might have seen me coming.

"And you—well, you should have moved on after slaying Mahgra. Your part in the prophecy was to make it more palatable." She stood close to him, looking him up and down again. "Allowing room for hope makes it easier to keep a victim lying still, don't you agree?"

Once again, Quin looked away from Morgynn, staring into shadows that played along the floor, contemplating how he might escape his magical bonds and slay the haughty sorceress and her sharp-toothed servant. She spun away from him and lit several more candles close to the wooden bowl of reddish water.

The sudden light filled the spaces between the bones, bringing Quin's attention back to the chamber. His eyes rested on something shining beneath the remains of Jhareat's fallen combatants. A strange glow burned there that belied the rust and corrosion of the ruined weapons around it.

"Ah," Morgynn's voice was low and sonorous, filling the room as she watched the images in the bowl with rapt attention. "It begins even now."

An incessant chant echoed from the bowl, crawling through Quin's ears as he recalled Elisandrya telling him the legend of Jhareat's fate. Though he'd dismissed the tale as fanciful before, now he wondered. Thunder rumbled and shook the floor as he studied what appeared to be the exposed corner of a truly remarkable shield.

CHAPTER TWENTY-TWO

The wind felt alive, tearing at heavy cloaks and twisting around the hunters upon the west wall, threatening to toss them aside like weightless trifles in its fury. Many gripped the battlements as they waited to see the source of the deep chant that emanated from the trees, growing stronger by the heartbeat. One by one, pale faces began to emerge between the trunks, indistinct and blurry through the rain, but staring with bright, hungry eyes.

A cluster of trees shook violently and unholy roars pealed from the darkness. The sounds of the unseen beasts bespoke of huge throats and myriad imagined monsters in the minds of Brookhollow's defenders. Their grim reverie was interrupted, however, by a new chant that arose behind them, within the walls. Surprised faces turned in time to watch a solemn procession of the Ghedia walking toward the wall, their outstretched hands glowing deep green with summoned power.

The old language of the Shaar, intermingled and woven into their casting, was seldom heard among the border towns and evoked images of rolling grasslands and ritual hunting grounds. Few among the defenders had ever seen such a sight. The legends and tales of older times were told often enough to stir the blood with memories of savage warriors and proud leaders. The burgeoning fear was quelled by the chant of the Ghedia, and weapons were turned to face the unknown enemy.

Elisandrya leaped up a ladder, climbing quickly to stand by the stoic Zakar, who greeted her with little more than a silent nod. Breathing heavily, Eli unslung her bow and stood fast, ready to give face and form to those who would threaten her home. The concept of home struck her strangely at that moment. For so long, she had only run away from and denied her place in Brookhollow. Now, after so many years, the town was all she had, her only connection to a family destroyed by the ambitions and fears of an old woman.

Three of the Ghedia accompanied Lesani to the old gates. Completing a spell, they pressed their hands upon the wood, compelling the magic to fill its length and width, pushing power through its depth until the walls shook with force. The whorls and knots in the gate faded and thickened, groaning as they grew as strong and dense as stone, a barrier even a giant might not easily fell.

The other shamans divided into two groups. Standing an arm's length from one another, they did the same for the wooden and stone walls. They called roots from the ground to brace the battlements in a grip that creaked mightily as it took effect. Once-loose stones were wrapped in an immovable embrace, cracks sealed themselves, and thick masses of tough vines braced the edges along the ground. Mud bubbled and churned under the strain, but the thick clay beneath held strong.

Atop the wall, Eli watched as figures bearing devilish faces, like stylized helms or masks, appeared in two groups along the treeline. They stood far beyond bow range, and their droning chant drifted just beneath the sounds of thunder and rain. Bows were immediately trained in the spellcasters' direction, waiting for their advance, but the priests did not move. Eli wondered at their strategy, but at a nudge from Zakar, she turned to the stretch of woods between the two groups. A steamy mist had begun to slide from the brush beneath the trees.

The first tortured scream burst from the forest, clear and horrendous. Lightning flashed as the first of the undead tore through the briars and bushes. Its movements were awkward and unnaturally quick. Bare white flesh was crisscrossed with bright red splotches and branching veins. The wet ground steamed where the creature stood, shaking with uncontrollable spasms, swaying to some unknown cadence. Its bright eyes rolled in sunken sockets, while its mouth worked at some attempt to speak or shriek. Taut, quivering muscles and an obviously broken arm collected themselves and stilled. The thing rested its suffering gaze on the wall ahead and those standing upon it. Cruel purpose defined its visage. A mournful wail escaped its slack-jawed mouth and wisps of steam tumbled past its crimson gums in a mockery of true breath.

The forest came alive as more of them joined the first. Focusing their ghoulish stares on the living defenders, they gave voice to some wordless pain. Hundreds gathered at the edge of the forest and at least as many still ripped and tore at the foliage behind them.

Several hunters retched, emptying their stomachs over the wall as the scent of boiling blood wafted by on the wind. Others looked away from the once-human faces of the macabre assemblage and swiftly prayed for a peaceful end, a deliverance from such a fate. Many were thankful for the downpour that washed away most of the undead stink and left the smell of fresh rain. Some, Eli noticed, openly wept tears of a sorrowful rage, a saddened anger that was beyond mere words or reasoning. Of those undead who were familiar to her, all hailed from Logfell in the north.

Beside her, Zakar looked to the sky, squinting past the rain and searching the clouds. He nudged her arm with an elbow and Eli followed his gaze. Only then did she hear a strange, steady noise through the rain. Her eyes widened as the sound registered in her brain. She caught a glimpse of a dark shape, diving and turning through the sky on massive beating wings.

"The sky! Watch the sky!" she yelled, turning left and right, making sure that bows were up and spears were close at hand. The clouds churned above, easily hiding more of the flying creatures—several wing beats could be heard when Eli listened for them. She drew her bowstring back, an arrow already nocked and ready to let fly. One of the winged beasts was getting closer. Zakar cried out, his booming voice in her ear. She turned to match his aim.

It banked low, a dark silhouette of horns, batlike wings, dangling clawed arms, and burning feral eyes barely a heartbeat away. Arrows bounced off its tough gray hide and it roared in annoyance. The sound drowned out everything else, making even the thunder seem gentle. Zakar cursed as his arrow failed to puncture the devil's wing. Eli exhaled and loosed her own arrow, watching its flight, sucking in a breath as it bounced off a claw, useless.

Her field of vision became a blur of movement. Chaos erupted as the hunter to her left screamed and a splash of warmth washed across her face. The smell of blood and smoke, like burning rocks, filled her nose. She raised her bow, covering her face as the beast's lashing tail swung toward her. The bow splintered in her hand and the tail slammed into her chest. A multitude of streaming stars danced before her eyes as she fell from the wall.

⊙ ⊙ ⊙ ⊙ ⊙

"Look at them. Bows and blades against magic and death." Morgynn watched the battle's first moments dispassionately. "Pitiful. Their savage shamans summon wood and grass against me."

Quin barely heard the sorceress's words, his mind clinging to the dim hope that escape might still be possible. The spell had numbed his limbs, but his thoughts raced. Examining his surroundings, he searched for any advantage in the range of his limited vision. Each time he did so, his eyes came to rest on the gleam of polished metal beneath the bones. Eli's tale had flashed through his mind so many times that he'd come to call a nearby skull Ossian. But the dim hope of the shield was too fantastic and out of reach.

Not yet, Ossian, he thought. I'm not quite there yet.

Morgynn pulled herself closer to the images taking shape in the ripples of rain and her own blood. Concentric circles spread across the bowl's surface. Quin saw the scars along her arms and shoulders squirm slightly, vibrating in tune to her tapping against the sides of the bowl.

A tightness slipped into Quin's chest and his temples throbbed as warmth radiated from Morgynn. His breathing became shallow and quick. Tiny lances of pain stabbed at the back of his eyes.

"You can feel it, can you not? Her power, her blood calls to your own." Khaemil had quietly come to stand behind him, whispering as they both watched Morgynn in the throes of her magic. "She is no longer human, barely a woman anymore. She is the spell itself, a pulse in the Weave. You have accepted a fool's errand, sweetblood."

The tower shook again, this time more violently. Cracks appeared along the ceiling and walls. Morgynn's strange influence disappeared from Quin's body. He breathed as deeply as he could. The surreal silence of the storm outside added to the sense of vertigo and nausea he felt as the sorceress calmed and stood straighter.

Khaemil walked around Quin to observe the battle. Morgynn patted Khaemil's arm and turned back toward Quinsareth. He noticed that the bowl still revealed the battle, even without Morgynn's concentration. He committed that fact to memory and braced himself for her attention.

"It appears you have failed them, aasimar, or perhaps just her. Yes, you have failed her," Morgynn said, her nonchalant tone needling, seeking some weakness in Quin's blank opal eyes. "The false prophecy has come true and the Hidden Circle shall fall. Their only hope lies in the nightmares of an old woman."

She reached for his face with a graceful hand, whispering

words of magic that tingled across his skin as she rested a single fingernail on his lower lip. Her eyes were solid orbs of reddish black. Her voice, when she spoke again, echoed itself, each syllable chasing itself as it passed her lips.

"Speak, once more before you die. Let me hear you as I end you."

He felt his jaw loosen again, felt his throat rush with blood as the power to speak was restored to him. His muscles tightened, blood pounded in his ears, and he tried not to think of the death Morgynn had in mind for him. He felt as if he were boiling inside, or at least beginning to. Summoning the will to form words beyond the pain of her touch, he spat them through clenched teeth. He stared defiantly into twin pools of blood that darkened as he watched.

"Prophecy or not, witch," he began as spasms rolled through his chest and the cloying taste of copper spread across his tongue, "I am here!"

Morgynn tilted her head and smiled. The words of a spell rose to her lips just as Khaemil's voice interrupted her. The alarm in his deep baritone drew her attention reluctantly away from the aasimar's impending fate.

"Lady Morgynn, something is wrong." His eyes, reflecting the crimson glow of the scrying waters, looked to her in concern. "The bathor are not moving."

⊙ ⊙ ⊙ ⊙ ⊙

Zakar yelled orders above the sounds of battle. Archers ducked and continued to pepper the massive devils with their arrows, distracting them as the Ghedia cast spells from behind the wall. Tiny bright blue spheres burst across the devils' wings and chests, singeing where they touched and causing roars of pain that deafened all within earshot. Lesani took a handful of acorns from a pouch in her robes. Chanting the magic to change them into lightning missiles, she hurled them into the face of a diving devil.

The beast shook its horned head madly, nearly blind, and crashed into the top of the wall. Tumbling over the side, it screeched and clawed at its scorched flesh.

Armored men in dark robes and masks advanced from the enemy flanks. They guarded other men in similar garb, whose hands waved and voices chanted. Several had attempted to burn the gates and walls with balls of flame, to no avail. Zakar scowled as arrows fell just short of the spellcasters, stopped by an invisible barrier of whistling wind.

"This is a wizard's battle, not a warrior's!"

Another roar turned him around to see one of four devils hovering over a mass of upturned spears, looking for a place to land inside the walls. More of the Ghedia's ensorcelled acorns and seeds deterred the beast.

Elisandrya disappeared as the devils pressed their attack. A few hunters cast worried glances behind the wall, seeking her in the mud and rain. Zakar yelled to them.

"The time for honoring the dead will come," he bellowed. "Now is the time to avoid joining them!"

In a brief moment of silence between thunder and crackling spells, the gentler tones of a soft sound arose—something familiar and rhythmic, lost again as disorder resumed. Zakar turned at the sound. Something caught his eye, but he was forced to turn back. Firing an arrow beneath a passing devil, he cursed as it ignored the slight scratch and flew upward to dive again.

Elisandrya choked on rain as she gazed up at the battle through blurry eyes. Lightning blinded her and mud sucked at her body, foiling her weak attempts to pull herself up. She'd barely seen whatever had thumped her from the wall, but she was determined to face it again. A stabbing pain in her chest forced her to lie back in the mud for a few breaths.

Arms grabbed her shoulders, dragging her as she gasped for air. Her breath, knocked from her lungs by the devil's fearsome tail and her fall, came back slowly. Consciousness came and went. The stars faded from her eyes and left her nearly blind, wondering if she would recover. Blackness gave way to dazzling light, then streaks of blue flashing into the air nearby. She blinked and cautiously inhaled, wincing at the pain in her chest.

A strange sound filled her ears, like a singing chant,

a choir of voices speaking spidery words and harsh syllables. A hazy figure appeared before her, looking down and saying something unintelligible. Hands pressed against her stomach and warmth flowed through them. A burning passed through her torso, removing her pain and soothing her shaken nerves. The figure spoke again, becoming more distinct and more familiar, the voice making sense as it called her name.

"Eli! Are you all right? Eli!"

Dreslya! Eli thought, then pushed herself up. Her chest felt numb, but she was otherwise uninjured. Her sister helped her to stand and embraced her shoulders. Several hunters ran past the pair, shouting for reinforcement on the right. Devils pounded against the thickened walls, the impact of their fists shaking the ground but having little effect.

"I'm sorry! I'm so sorry!" Dres cried in Eli's ear then released her, looking about as the battle against the devils raged and spells were cast by the Ghedia. "We had to wait. It was the only way!"

Elisandrya looked about and saw the assembled oracles. A dozen of them stood in a circle, holding hands and lost in concentration, chanting softly and straining with the effort. Their white robes were wet and stained with mud, and they shivered in the cold, but they held their arcane rhythm. A dozen more stood close by, watching the sky warily with solemn attention.

"And Sameska? What of her, Dres?"

Dreslya nodded toward the temple, her face dark and expressionless.

"She hides there with several others. They stayed with her to keep the wards and protections of the temple active. She refuses to protect herself," she looked to Eli, a tone of contempt in her voice as she added, "or is no longer capable."

Elisandrya nodded grimly, understanding, but was pleased that the oracles had joined them in defending the city. She was elated that her sister was among them. She squeezed her hands together, rubbing her left hand that ached from the bow being wrenched from her grasp.

"Here," Dreslya said. Taking a wrapped bundle from her

shoulder, she handed it to Elisandrya. "I had a feeling you might need this."

Beneath the layers of wet cloth, Eli discovered the strong, dark shaft of a long bow. Her breath caught in her throat as she beheld the familiar runes etched in the wood alongside depictions of Shaaran steeds racing down its length. Rain chased the symbols and pictures, bringing them to life in her hands. Twelve years had passed since she'd last seen the bow. She recognized it as if it had been only yesterday when she and Dreslya had quietly packed it away.

"Make father proud," Dreslya said to her before joining the oracles in the circle.

Elisandrya held the bow in trembling hands, hesitant at first, but then reached into a leather pouch on her belt for a bowstring. Skillfully, she braced the weapon behind her left knee and strained to bend the shaft, stringing the bow with the deft speed of a trained soldier. She nocked an arrow and splashed through the street to stand with Lesani near the rear of the wall's defenses.

She cast one last look at her sister before danger loomed on black leather wings. The devil's sharp, curving horns swung left and right, batting away hurled spears. It rested menacing red eyes on the tiring Ghedia. Eli saw smoking wounds across its thickly muscled chest and arms. It dived again, roaring in imminent victory over the Shaaryan druids. Elisandrya fired her bow. The arrow's flight was quick and nearly invisible, embedding in the devil's exposed chest.

The malebranche pulled back, furiously flapping and grasping at the arrow's shaft as it howled in pain. A cheer rose up from the hunters at the sight of the wounded beast, but quickly died as three more devils flew overhead, roaring exultantly with the thunder as the pouring rain turned into fire.

⊙ ⊙ ⊙ ⊙ ⊙

Morgynn pushed Khaemil away from the bowl. He winced at her touch, and Quinsareth felt his magical bonds loosen.

With a quick and furious glance from the canomorph, the spell tightened again.

Despite the magic, Quin still found himself able to speak and move his head. The pain Morgynn had induced in him had faded at her release. Her touch would have been enough to kill, he realized. He stretched his jaw, tasting the warmth of blood on his lips.

"There they are," Morgynn said, studying the Savrathans in the scrying bowl. "They defy their own edict now, working against my prophecy."

Morgynn's eyes still swirled with living blood. Her hands gripped the small table, shaking it with fury though her expression and voice never changed, never lapsed into the rage that seemed to flood her senses.

"They can do little harm now, Lady Morgynn," Khaemil ventured. "Foresight cannot help them now."

"True," she snapped. "However, this does not quell their potency against the bathor, does it?"

Her brief control of her anger crumbled. She gripped the wooden bowl and hurled it at Khaemil, splashing him with the crimson waters. Khaemil raised his arms, but otherwise did not move, remaining still and avoiding Morgynn's accusing stare. Quin winced to see the bowl's visions banished. The game seemed at a stalemate, his options evaporating with each moment.

Quinsareth's voice broke the silence.

"It's a funny thing, prophecies," he began, smiling freely at Morgynn's tantrum. Her head slowly turned at his interruption. "Sometimes they come true."

She did not reply to the aasimar, but neither did she look away as she spoke again, quiet but commanding. "Deal with your mistake, Khaemil. End it. I will go and correct its consequences."

Before the *shadurakul* could protest, Morgynn strode forward into him, melding into his flesh and disappearing through his blood. In a blink she was gone, leaving Quin to wonder in awe at the gruesome trick. He did not know how she had done it, but he had no doubts as to where she had gone.

A low, grumbling growl rolled from Khaemil's throat as he beheld the aasimar. Long fangs grew in the canomorph's mouth, and he bared them. He hefted the mace at his side and stalked toward Quin. The chamber shook again, the storm's violence threatening to bring the tower down on their heads. Quin's bonds felt as strong as ever. Bedlam lay far out of reach, useless, and the game tumbled on in his mind. The only piece left, seemingly as useless as his sword, was the shield.

CHAPTER TWENTY-THREE

The canomorph's magic was insidious and subtle, leaving no scars or bloody wounds in its wake, only the memory of one pain and the continuous anticipation of the next. Quin's mind reeled, becoming more and more detached from the pain. He had been burned with invisible flames and sliced by blades that only his mind could give form and substance.

Through it all, through pain and paralysis, he could not summon or even fathom the rage he'd expected. It seemed to him that Khaemil carried rage for them both. He had been the canomorph's failure in Morgynn's eyes, the reason for whatever punishment the blood-witch had in store. So Khaemil drew out Quin's pain, keeping him alive to exorcize his rage. Both of them expected death in one form or another, one sooner, the other later.

The tower shook with each peal of thunder, rattling the bones and shaking dust from the ceiling. Only a blur of twisting wind, filled with lightning, could be seen through the small window. Whatever remained of the storm's power was just enough to keep it going.

One by one, the game pieces fell away in Quin's thoughts. He fought the urge to retreat into those memories of childhood. He wanted to be aware, strengthening his will on the present.

He had strained his muscles almost to exhaustion trying to break the bands of force that held him tight, to no avail. His only freedoms were to see and to speak, neither of which were useful under the circumstances. He had been at the mercy of boundless rage before on the long roads he'd traveled across Faerûn, and found it distasteful to witness such pursuits once more.

Khaemil growled and snarled as he cast, flinging Quin's mind into illusory landscapes filled with keening phantoms, then dismissing the images to deliver more direct torments. In the brief respite between spells, Quin allowed himself to respect Khaemil's instinct for torture. A man could live for tendays, even months, in such intricate and carefully doled out pain.

Only the occasional trembling of the tower, cracks widening along its walls, let them both know that such time would not be afforded to them. Khaemil would have to finish his games soon enough, lest the crumbling tower give in to the chaotic storm outside and crush them both.

The canomorph circled the aasimar as he contemplated the theme of each spell. Quin watched his face each time, seeing the familiar visage of a fellow killer, an assassin hired on faith to deliver bloody sermons to one's enemies. Through the fog of pain, Quin contemplated scenarios of escape, miracles beyond hope by which he might slay this dark preacher of vile magic and follow Morgynn to Brookhollow. Occasionally his eyes drifted to Bedlam, still lying on the floor, so close to the strange shield beneath the bones.

He focused on the dormant blade, the dull shine of its

screaming steel. Something stirred in his stomach, rising to pound in his heart and remind him of aching limbs still frozen in magic. Fresh pain surged as daggers of air pushed through his legs and knees. Nerves screamed in his brain for movement, a primal instinct to resist or flee, fight or run. He found anger again as he imagined his fingers closing on Bedlam's hilt. He longed to wield the blade and teach Khaemil his own form of vengeance, a lesson that, once dealt, could not be unlearned or ever put to use again.

Khaemil crossed in front of him again and he studied the heavy black mace in the *shadurakul*'s hands, gripped tightly and held close. The tower shook again, and only the canomorph's magic kept him standing. A gamble eased into his mind comfortably, the intricacies of the game spinning once again. He had little to lose, and only one piece of the pattern was left unplayed. He listened carefully, counting the canomorph's rhythmic step, and summoned his voice through a raw and scratchy throat.

"Dog," he said, coughing slightly with the effort, but not so much that he did not hear Khaemil stop to listen, just a stride away behind his left shoulder.

"What's that, sweetblood? Some plea for mercy, perhaps?"

He leaned closer, almost half a head taller than Quin, eagerly listening to catch the sweet sound of begging from his captive. Quin smiled slyly, choosing the words of his own spell, far more primitive than Khaemil's chanting or prayers, but just as effective.

"Dead dog," he continued. "Nothing more pitiful than watching the kicking and scratching of a dying dog beaten by its own master. Least of all one like you, that doesn't even know it yet."

Quin braced himself, daring to place hope in the rage that he attempted to evoke. It was a simple kind of magic, targeting pride, and he knew that even devils—especially devils—valued a certain amount of pride.

The effect was immediate. Quin heard robes rustle and a deep breath being inhaled. He squeezed his eyes shut in the instant that the mace slammed into the backplate of his armor. The solid pain of the impact was refreshing as he was thrown to his right, a physical pain more easily accepted than that induced by magic.

His legs fell across the flat of Bedlam's blade. His torso crashed into the heap of bones, shattering old skulls and rib cages. His right arm, outstretched and bound by the spell of paralysis, fell flat on the face of the hidden shield. Sudden and unmistakable warmth washed over his body. He flexed his fingers and gripped the shield's edge, careful to hide the movement from the seething Khaemil. Patterns of stones spiraled and flourished in his mind, the game restored by the simple Shield. Such was the Fate Fall, that even gods could not thwart the smallest details.

A feral smile graced Quin's features as he quietly gave thanks to the foresight of long dead Shaaryan wizards and the legends they spawned. The grinning skull he'd dubbed Ossian lay nearby, and he was suddenly curious to observe the shield, to see the face of the fallen warrior's love, Zemaan. His left hand was only inches from Bedlam's hilt and once again, he counted the steps of Khaemil's familiar stride approaching from behind.

⊙ ⊙ ⊙ ⊙ ⊙

The hunters worked feverishly to man the walls and fight growing fires inside the city. Some covered themselves as best they could with their ironvine cloaks, protected from the falling flames but unable to see the enemy clearly. The sky was brilliantly lit, as if the stars themselves fell from the sky to burn and destroy the city. Puddles of water hissed and boiled as globs of fire landed in the streets. Steam filled the air, rain vaporizing before it reached the ground. Black smoke billowed from empty homes as they were set ablaze.

Lesani was exhausted from fighting the flying devils and ducked beneath a slate overhang not touched by the flames. The devils reveled in the fiery rain, taking advantage of blind archers and crushing them in powerful claws or impaling them on their curved horns. The ravaged bodies of the fallen landed among their fellows with sickening splashes in the mud, broken harbingers of the horrifying fate that flew overhead.

The magic of the Ghedia was cut to half, as many of the shamans turned to the wounded, leaving only handfuls of the druids to dispel the rain of fire. Their voices shouted words of magic above the noise of storm and battle, raising clouds of icy mist over the defending forces. The fires hissed and fizzled in the cold white fog, creating havens of safety for the hunters and oracles.

Elisandrya ran from shadow to shadow, ducking as devils swooped by, the leathery beasts snatching up those too slow to avoid them. Their victims' screams trailed off into the sky then stopped abruptly. Eli ran to join Zakar, silently thanking the wisdom of the Ghedia for summoning the cold clouds over the wall. Zakar's face was grim when she reached the battlements, but he raised an eyebrow in surprise when he saw her alive. "Still kicking, are we?"

"Just enough," she replied, and scanned the field below, glowing in the falling flames, her eyes stopping on the mass of undead, halted by some invisible line beyond the trees. "Should we summon the mounted warriors? Try to harry their flanks and stop these damnable spells?"

"Not yet," Zakar answered. "They have no flanks to speak of, really. They'd pull back into the forest and leave our men exposed and vulnerable. Spells from within and those devils above—it'd be a massacre. There, look."

He pointed to the southern fringe of the enemy line, where the spellcasting ranks were thickest. Though some wore robes, others were fully armed and armored, bearing strange symbols on breastplates or tabards.

"Priests, most likely," he said. "From the masks, I'd guess they follow Gargauth the Exile. Our arrows can't reach them—or they could, if they weren't scattered by this foul wind."

"Dreslya and the oracles—they'll think of something."

"The oracles? Well, they'd better be quick. Much more of this and we'll end up looking like that poor lot." He gestured toward the stilled masses of bathor, intensely staring and eerily quiet. "Only without the walking around part, Savras willing."

⊛ ⊛ ⊛ ⊛ ⊛

Beyond the edge of the forest, beyond the mob of suffering bathor, a single figure sat in silence, fighting to put right all that had gone wrong. On his knees, Talmen held the symbol of Gargauth on its silver chain, praying for the god's blessings. Every breath that passed was a strategic moment lost, a chance for the oracles and the Shaaryan Ghedia to collect themselves and resist him further. Rain dripped from branches as the storm grew stronger, water pouring across his mask and down his neck. He lowered his arms as dark energy crept from the talisman of his god, encircling his body in a crackling black cloud.

He placed the symbol in the mud and whispered the final syllables of his spell, watching as the cloud shifted and swirled around him. The mist rushed forward, covering the ground and slipping between the bodies of the twitching undead. Where the smoky tendrils of magic touched, the ground blackened. Plants rotted at their roots and exuded a stench of death worse than a disturbed grave. Driven by his will, the fog spread through the vile host. Desecration settled over the area, a dark energy that gave purpose and movement to the undead, strengthening them and their ties to the magic that made them.

The scarred symbol on his arm throbbed with the renewed pulse of the bathor and he cried out, sharing their infinite pain for heartbeats that seemed to stretch into lifetimes. Through it all, he rejoiced in Gargauth's power and raised his scar high, commanding with his will for the undead to advance. Though the nearest few moaned and pushed against their fellows, clawing deep gouges in their backs, the force still did not move.

Exasperated, Talmen fumed and cursed, rising to his feet and staring daggers through the trees at the immovable gates and unbreached walls of Brookhollow. He imagined the oracles, safe and sound, thwarting his army with magic he'd been assured would be absent from the walls and field. The malebranche wheeled in the skies, delivering death in spurts, but the Ghedia were constant in their defense, even placing magic on the bows and spears of warriors. Blazing blue arrows trailed across the sky, causing the malebranche to screech in pain when they struck home. Though far from mortally wounded, the tough hides of the devils were unexpectedly vulnerable, and their attacks were less effective without support from the ground.

Snatching his talisman, Talmen gathered his robes and made his way to the south flank, where an equally exasperated lieutenant awaited his arrival. The lieutenant's horned silver helm reflected the last sputtering drops of flaming rain as he nodded.

"Nothing, Malefactor," he said, answering Talmen's unspoken question. "We have reached a stalemate."

"Yes," Talmen answered, disgusted. "Easy victory indeed, eh? Well, no matter. Let's test them more directly. Send forth the gnolls on the north side."

"The gnolls, sir? They are too few! They'll be cut down before they even reach the wall, much less the top of the battlements!"

"I'm willing to sacrifice the smell of wet dog in order to see something set foot on that field before we're forced to retreat!" Talmen's anger burst forth as he shoved the lieutenant into the mud, fully prepared to kick the life out of the man, but he stopped at the intrusion of a voice into his enraged thoughts.

"There will be no retreat, Malefactor."

He froze at the sound of her voice, gasping as his scar flashed with pain and an unexpected warmth flooded his body. He smelled her before he saw her. The cloying scents of cinnamon and blood filled his nose even as delicate, pale arms stretched from his chest, sheathed in blood that receded as they pushed through him. The pain in his arm subsided, and when he looked up, Morgynn was there, surveying the field. Her cold red eyes spilled blood onto her cheeks, squirming and trailing across her skin. Her gaze lingered on the bathor, halted at the edge of an invisible barrier and steaming in the chill rain.

She turned to Talmen, who quavered under her stare.

"The oracles, my lady," was all he could manage as her pulsing aura enveloped him.

The wind picked up again, growing wilder still, whipping cloaks and robes in a frenzied gale. Morgynn stood unaffected by the icy blast, not a single raven strand of hair or fold of her crimson robe defying her as she walked past Talmen toward the frozen bathor.

Again her voice invaded his mind, her simple command leaving him near exhausted and full of dread as roars of pain echoed from the skies above the city's walls.

"Ready yourselves. Prepare to advance," she said, and disappeared among the twitching bodies of her mindless creations.

⊙ ⊙ ⊙ ⊙ ⊙

Morgynn wove in and around the bathor, petting their skin. They took no notice of her presence, though their feverish trembling increased as she passed among them. She made her way to the center of the mindless horde. Exulting in the pulse of the Weave, hundreds of heartbeats long past death's door resounded in her senses like the drums of a long-sought conquest.

She imagined the oracles, hiding behind their walls, defying all she laid before them through the voice of Sameska.

"So fragile they must be," she said contemplatively. "Such precious things they sacrifice to make up for their lack of wisdom. So naive."

Making her way to the front of the crowded field of undead, she raised her fingers, tapping at the air. Imagining the Weave as an instrument, she tuned its fine threads, infusing the air with the sorcery she would exult in releasing. The gates of Brookhollow were visible to her, glowing slightly in her ensorcelled vision, her blooded eyes making out the faint dweomers of pale magic defending the walls.

"Borrowed power. Nature cannot give you the protection you seek, little Ghedia," she shouted, striding ahead of the bathor. "Power must be taken and commanded, not asked for!"

Easily within range of the archers, several arrows arced through the air toward her. Raising her arms in front of her, she balled her left hand into a tight fist and traced the ridges of her knuckles with her right. Muttering her spell, she stopped within a hundred paces of the gates. She watched the arrows as they sailed toward her, holding her fist tighter as they neared.

"Invesas!"

She opened her fist as she finished the incantation. A dozen arrows, a heartbeat from striking her, froze in midair. The magic, once released, pulsed outward audibly. The tall grass was bent away from her in a wide circle and even the rain stopped, streaming around the perimeter of her invisible sphere. Her body rose, lifting her feet from muddy puddles.

More arrows were loosed as she chanted again, and several were caught in the sphere's edges. With one hand, she pointed to each of the frozen missiles caught by her magic, surrounding them in a ghostly light. Frost formed on their heads and along their shafts. More arrows, still streaking toward her, were deflected along with the rain, splashing into the grass. Her skin tingled with power, her blood burned, and her cheeks grew slick as blood spilled over her eyelids and writhed into arcane symbols in tune with the discordant tones of her voice.

Most of the defenders ceased firing, seeing the futility of their attacks. Only slightly disappointed, Morgynn twirled her hands, and the arrows in her sphere of magic turned in time to her will, redirecting themselves toward the gates. The burning white arrows slowly spun in midair as she raised her right hand, curled in a tight fist.

She held the magic for several breaths, biting her lip on the final word, tasting it on her tongue like a snowflake in a Narrish blizzard. Her temples throbbed and sweat beaded on her forehead. Steam billowed from her mouth as she whispered the syllables and opened her fist.

"Veseras ingellas."

The captured arrows streaked forward, trailing wispy lines of frost as they sped toward the gates. Archers dived from the walls while others braced for impact against the battlements. Morgynn slowly exhaled the breath that carried the last of her spell. She brought to mind another, dismissing the last in favor of the next.

Such precious things, she thought, as the arrows struck home.

⊛ ⊛ ⊛ ⊛ ⊛

Elisandrya cursed as she ran along the wall with Zakar just steps behind. The relentless devils had ascended to greater heights, and a red-robed woman was approaching the gates. The archers closest to her had watched as their arrows failed, as the grass around the woman had writhed in rhythm to the sound of an echoing heartbeat. Many had almost cheered when they'd seen blood running down the wizard's face, certain that an arrow had found its mark. The hunters had paled as they'd learned otherwise.

The first of the glowing arrows struck as Eli leaped toward a short stairway leading to the guard tower. Sharp and stinging, the sound was quickly followed by dozens more. She landed hard, jarring her elbow on a middle step. Zakar landed beside her. The storm raged overhead, infected by some unknown chaos, and they waited for the attack to stop. Sitting up, Eli peered over the side of the wall.

Several arrows struck the walls, with the rest burying themselves in the gates. Each disappeared in a puff of white mist, leaving a frosty mark where they'd landed. An uncomfortable silence fell as the hunters studied the inner walls, wondering if the defenses of the Ghedia had repelled the wizard's attack. Curious as well, Eli pulled herself up and leaned over to see the inside of the gates. At first nothing seemed amiss, but then the white tips of the arrows, hissing and steaming in the rain, released the magic that imbued them.

Her eyes widened, imagining the force that had driven the arrowheads completely through the enchanted gates. The ice on the arrows melted before her eyes, leaving the shafts fully exposed. A cracking noise split the air and Zakar swore behind her. She turned and joined him at the battlements, her stomach sinking as she saw white sheets of ice growing from the tiny holes in wood and stone. The pounding rain fed the ice, freezing in a multitude of tiny drops.

Frost formed on the wet planks around Eli's feet as the voice of the red sorceress rose again in the dissonant drone of another spell.

Khaemil's reflection was a dark blur on the polished surface of the shield, silhouetted before the dazzling lightning outside the window. Quin watched as his tormentor raised an arm, the mace clutched in his hand. At the zenith of the swing, Quin pushed up on his hands and kicked Khaemil's knee out from under him.

Khaemil gasped in shock and fell to his other knee. Quinsareth picked up Bedlam, the noisome blade instantly springing to life in a blend of thunder and wolfish growls. He flipped the shield up on its edge, scattering bones and dust to the floor, and slid his arm through the braces. He spun around to face the canomorph as tremors shook the tower.

Wooden beams creaked below and both combatants felt the floor tilt. Water dripped through the ceiling as the structure shuddered beneath its own weight. Khaemil bared his fangs. Rising to his feet and stepping backward, he raised the mace in both hands and spat out the words of a spell. Quinsareth took faltering steps forward, the stone floor splitting between his boots. The pain of Khaemil's torture still filled his body, but survival pushed him on. Holding the shield before him, he was surprised at its lightness. Strangely, the shield seemed to pull him forward, reacting to the Gargauthan's voice and drawing its new bearer closer to the spellcaster.

The *shadurakul*'s voice roared to a crescendo and several smoky black swords materialized in the air around him. At his command, the ghostly blades darted forward to assault the aasimar. A sound like tearing metal rang in their ears as the ethereal blades sank into the shield. Even those aimed at Quin's legs were pulled upward to meet the shield's face. All were swallowed into the steel, the sound of their destruction clanging in Quin's head. The shield's braces tightened around his arm, fitting to his grip as if pleased.

Catching his balance on the tilted floor, Quinsareth charged forward to meet Khaemil's grimace. Bedlam wailed through the air and crashed into the haft of the canomorph's mace. Quin pushed against Khaemil's strength. He smiled wickedly as the weapons scraped against one another, Bedlam drawing a deep gouge in the mace's haft. Khaemil pushed back, cursing as Quin ducked the shove and let him stumble forward.

He's too strong for his own good, Quin thought, and stepped sideways, making a show of raising the growling sword high. Khaemil reacted quickly, bringing his mace to bear against the intended cut, but Quinsareth spun to his right instead. The shield slammed against the Gargauthan's weapon and extended Khaemil's reach for a heartbeat or two.

Bedlam screamed downward in that moment, shearing through the canomorph's wrist and neatly severing his hand. Khaemil roared in pain as the mace clattered to the floor along with the lost hand. He drew the stump of his wrist to his chest, squeezing it tightly as blood streamed across his robes. His sharp teeth clenched as he mumbled through them in a grating language, cursing in one of the many tongues of the Lower Planes. He stepped back from the aasimar, who calmly observed the *shadurakul*'s disfigurement. Khaemil's face twisted in agony, his features blending with those of the shadow mastiff that hid beneath his humanoid façade. Narrowing his pearly eyes, Quin's stare was every bit the match for the predatory gleam of his opponent.

The tremors repeated more violently than before, as if some crucial support had been removed. The tower stood at the mercy of the chaos of magic outside. Khaemil stumbled as he walked backward, falling to his knees. The shadows flooded Quin's body at his slightest call, his eyes murky with their color after only a few blinks.

"I spare you your mistress's beating, dog!" he shouted. "I shall collect my fee from her directly!"

He kicked Khaemil full in the chest, sending the shapechanger backward against the window sill. The mortar crumbled weakly under the impact, stones shifting under his weight. Ancient stones and *shadurakul* were snatched away, tumbling into the whirlwind of the hungry storm. Khaemil's screams were quickly lost in the gales and ripping lightning. Rain poured in through the yawning hole in the wall and seeped between the cracks in the stone beneath Quin's boots.

Stepping away from the gaping hole, Quin caught sight of movement to his right and saw himself reflected in a tall silver mirror. The shield he carried wore the profile of a proud Shaaryan woman with fiery hair and blazing eyes. The face of Ossian's lover faded slightly as he watched, the image rippling through the metal by some strange power. He nodded quietly to the image of Zemaan before the mirror was tossed by the wind to shatter on the floor.

He closed his eyes and willed forth the shadow road, turning translucent and blurry as it accepted him. Behind him, the tower collapsed stone by stone, burying the bones and legends it had kept secret for centuries under a mound of ruin.

CHAPTER TWENTY-FOUR

Lightning forked wildly over the city, setting fires, deafening those too close, and killing those it touched. The roars of eager devils in the clouds were joined by the howls of bloodthirsty gnolls waiting for a breach to open in the walls. The hyena-faced brutes' eyes glowed in the tall grass, just beyond the hunters' deadly arrows. Gargauthan warriors gathered in front of the war wizards among them. Like armored devils, they watched Morgynn's spellcraft through masks frozen in toothy snarls and leering skull grins.

Sheets of rain and icy wind never touched the blood mage within the invisible sphere she'd woven. She hovered inside it, just above the muck and mud.

Morgynn drew her dagger and sliced open the palm of her right hand. Holding the wound high, she willed her blood to drip freely. The blood was caught by her spell, collecting into a perfect sphere drop by drop. Her breath spun the red orb in place, enchanting and boiling it as she deftly directed the spin with her dagger.

The globe grew to the size of a fist, glowing with an inner, flickering light, and she let the sphere rest on the tip of her dagger. Through its glossy translucence, she admired the burning image of the crimson city captured in the spinning globe.

"Open them," she told it. "Bring them my blessings."

She blew on the sphere and sent it flying. It swelled as it neared the gates, gathering a tail of red flames as it grew larger and faster. She watched as warriors jumped and skipped away from the death she sent to them, abandoning their walls and shouting unintelligible curses. Morgynn imagined she heard swift and whispered prayers as well, but these were only a faint descant above the orchestra of storm, magic, and the pulse of the Weave.

⊛ ⊛ ⊛ ⊛ ⊛

The red fireball exploded like a dying star as it made contact in the center of the gates. Shattering ice disintegrated the walls embedded with frozen sorcery. The force and heat of the impact spread outward, burning everything in its path. Weapons and objects were charred or melted. The living were burned from within. Infused by Morgynn's blood, they twisted unnaturally in bloody flames before falling still. Those outside the blast watched with eyes watering from the incredible heat. Noses stung with the smell of char and cooked flesh. Even the freezing rain and biting winds could not quell the flames. Warily, the hunters raised their weapons at billowing clouds of smoke and steam. Some broke ranks and ran ahead of the racing cloud, slipping in puddles and falling over those in their path. All knew that the gates were gone and that the true battle was upon them.

⊛ ⊛ ⊛ ⊛ ⊛

Morgynn's heart skipped a beat, shock passing through her body as a wave of brief freedom shook the bathor behind her. A series of spasms rolled through the undead host and she felt her muscles flutter and quake, responding to the mindless will of her creations. She exhaled, closing her eyes and willing them to advance, but they did not move.

She screamed in rage, arching her back and raising her voice to a thunderous roar. The gnolls ceased their howling and covered their canine ears, yelping in pain. Even the malebranche paused as her voice reached them, feeling the tingle of magic itching across their hides. Out of breath, she inhaled and lowered her head, curling her lip as she observed the gaping hole in the wall where the gates had been, where her minions should be crawling and clawing their way into the city at her command.

"Nothing," she muttered, "only little deaths and—"

She stopped, detecting the lilting tones of the oracles. Their prayers and spells rose unhindered, drifting through the dissolving cloud of her destructive spell. Gritting her teeth in frustration, she flexed her right hand, opening the fresh wound on her palm.

Blood pooled in the jagged fissure and she whipped her arm left and right, spattering the grass and mud with crimson drops. Sheathing her dagger, she dipped into a small pouch, grasping a fistful of black insect wings. She crushed them in her fist and muttered quick words over them.

"Ixelteth suranyat!"

The dried wings turned to fine dust, released to the wind as she opened her fist. The sooty cloud peppered the ground around her, hissing where it met the waiting droplets of her blood. Each drop turned solid and bulbous. Clusters of pale pink sacs formed, splitting open soon after, hatching hundreds of writhing red larvae. The larvae split open as well, giving birth to shiny crimson wasps on buzzing black wings.

She held her arms out lovingly and several insects landed on her fingertips and wrists. They crawled across her skin on thin, chitinous legs.

"Seek them out," she whispered to them. "Sting their wretched tongues and fill their mouths with wings."

The swarm gathered and flew at her command, buzzing through the rain like a red mist to find the source of their mistress's displeasure.

◎ ◎ ◎ ◎ ◎

Dreslya could not take her eyes from the smoking remains of the gates and those unlucky enough to have been caught in the blast. Black water, thick with ash, streamed along the street and around her feet. Several times, Lesani held her back from searching through the ash and char to find Elisandrya.

"Mourning will come," she said to the oracle, "but not now."

Dres gasped at the words, a lump forming in her throat. Her vision from earlier had carried voices and snippets of conversation drifting in and out of focus. The vision had been a warning, showing her the consequences of inaction. She remembered Lesani's voice telling her of mourning, but she had thought the Ghedia spoke of the coming sunrise, of hope, not the death of her sister.

Lesani took her by the arm, leading her away from the defenders. The Ghedia searched inside empty doors and dark windows, though Dres did not know why. She followed in a daze, her eyes burning, trying to summon the courage to look away from the clouds of steam on the western end of Brookhollow. She tried to focus on the present despite the uncertainty of her vision. Rain soaked her robes and hair, and a numbness from the cold crept through her hands.

"Here!" Lesani shouted over a fresh round of monstrous thunder, pointing to the doorway of a stonework hovel. Low and sturdy, it stood abandoned and lifeless. "Come, I need your help!"

"Yes, you do," Dres mumbled, confused. Cold and shivering, she was having greater difficulty discerning between present and future. "I mean, I know. At least I think I know."

As the pair ducked inside, Lesani cleared a space on the floor, pushing a modest table and chairs against the wall.

She took several items from hidden pouches within her robes and sat cross-legged on the floor. Dres wandered to the lone window. Facing north, she could no longer see the steam and smoke, but she could smell them.

"Sit down, Oracle," Lesani said, the edge in her voice catching Dreslya's attention. "Elisandrya is a great warrior. I do not doubt you may see her again, but I need you here and now."

Dreslya turned away from the window and the sounds of battle. At Lesani's gesture, she sat across from the Ghedia. Though focused on the items she laid out in front of her, even Lesani glanced up at the window, like Dreslya, when the thunder died. In that moment of silence, filled only with falling rain, horrendous screams echoed through the streets. A furious buzzing filled the quiet. This, too, Dreslya remembered, and she paled in fear.

⊙ ⊙ ⊙ ⊙ ⊙

Sudden and untamed chaos jolted Morgynn's body as the bathor were released from the oracles' spell. She lowered her protective bubble, her feet dipping into the mud as the sensation overwhelmed her. Hundreds of feverish pulses rivaled the fury of the storm, drowning out all else. She stood still as the undead surged around her. Unnatural heat drew beads of sweat across her brow and down her back. She dismissed her protective sphere, allowing the rain and wind to cool her.

Searching left and right, over the backs of the hunched bathor, she watched as the Gargauthans advanced alongside the tortured throng of her creations. She stood quietly as they raced past her toward the ruined wall.

"Prophecies be damned, now," she said. "This is the beginning of my vision, my Order of Twilight. Woe to those who stand against it."

She fell into step with the undead. Magic itched along her arms to the tips of her fingers. Rain flowed in rivulets across her scars, following their patterns before dripping to the ground. Her crimson gaze fixed on the Temple of the Hidden Circle, and on the pitiful old woman who cowered within. A moment later, the broken gates became the vision she'd imagined. The bathor crowded into Brookhollow, pushing debris and bodies aside in their haste.

Drawing closer, she saw that beyond the destruction, Brookhollow's defenders had rallied admirably. They presented an impressive wall of flesh for her bathor to rend and tear. Bows and spears were prepared to meet her horde.

They fired arrows first, piercing the pale skin of the bathor with no visible effect. The undead did not bleed or scream in pain. A few paused and stared curiously at the feathered sticks that seemed to spring from them. Flickers of intelligence hung like cobwebs in the attics of their eroded minds, but they soon pushed forward, shaking off confusion.

Long spears stood propped between the archers, ready for combat face to face, and the bathor sprang forward mindlessly, some impaling themselves. They ran down the hafts of the spears, skewering themselves through their abdomens or chests to claw at their shocked opponents. Horrified, archers and spearmen dropped their weapons, drawing swords and axes more suitable for close combat. The bathor knew only claws and teeth, and a single-minded urge to kill what they no longer understood.

The heat surrounding Morgynn's horde burned eyes and lungs. The carrion stench forced more than a few weak-stomached defenders away to retch and cough. Some averted their eyes, afraid of seeing a relative or friend among the undead. Most held their ground and fought, and many defenders died in the first few moments.

The bathor were relentless, wailing horribly and dragging down the weak. They spat boiling blood on their victims, scalding skin as they tore at exposed throats. Slowly, the defenders were pushed back, making way for impossible numbers of feral opponents.

Morgynn watched their progress, glancing at the fallen hunters with interest, eventually finding what she sought. Lying against a half-burned stable was a young warrior with striking green eyes and wavy brown hair. The blood mage extended a hand toward him, gesturing at his chest.

She felt his slow heartbeat plodding toward death. Several bathor noticed him as well and crawled forward, splashing through the mud to claim their prize.

Morgynn approached the young man and waved a hand at the undead, sending them away with a glance. The bathor stopped, but could not tear their lifeless eyes away from the scene. Whimpering, they clawed at themselves as each puff of breath escaped the hunter's lips. Morgynn knelt in front of the warrior, observing the wound in his stomach that gushed dark, almost black blood through his clenched fingers. His other hand gripped his weapon, the curved blade traditional to his order, but he was too weak to lift the sword.

"What is your name, boy?" she asked, laying a hand on his knee in a gesture of comfort.

He tried to speak but only coughed, his throat wet. After a second try, he answered weakly, "Arek."

Morgynn heard him, but her mind was elsewhere. The young hunter's blood flowed beneath her touch, a conduit showing her the battle within the city. Blood called to blood, forming a crimson map in her mind. One lonely trail stood apart from the others, moving swiftly under cover of darkness, hiding and running, then hiding again. She smiled and returned her gaze to the dying hunter.

"Well, then. Farewell, Arek."

She crawled forward, over him then through him, merging with his flesh and fading to nothing. The impatient bathor loosed keening wails as they closed their circle and took what she'd denied them.

⊙ ⊙ ⊙ ⊙ ⊙

Lying in the guard tower, Elisandrya coughed, spitting blood and ash from her mouth. Rain washed over her and she flexed her muscles to warm them. She rubbed gingerly at her eyes, trying to restore her vision, blurred by smoke and unconsciousness. A heavy weight lay across her legs and she reached down to move it away. The coarse fabric of an ironvine cloak gave her pause. She raised herself to one elbow and blearily made out the fallen body of Zakar.

From his appearance and clouded eyes, he was far beyond her help.

As she pulled herself free, she noticed the clouds of steam growing thicker. Water streamed down her face and neck. Listening, she tried to make out voices she could hear close by. Their words were soft and unintelligible, a mumbling she could not understand, but she was certain they were children. Nearly panicking at the thought of children caught in the battle, she quickly escaped from beneath Zakar. Inwardly, she apologized to the fallen hunter for the rough treatment of his remains as she scrambled to her feet.

Eli found her bow and glanced at the ruined, tumbled wall where the gates had been. She knelt at the wall's edge to leap down and find the stranded children. Looking down, she stopped herself before jumping. Her gaze froze as she looked into the glistening eyes of several young boys, their cherubic faces ruined by a maze of bluish veins and trembling spasms. They whispered and mumbled horrible nothings as she stepped back from the edge. Her hand brushed against the arrow fletchings in her quiver as a low growl over her shoulder caused her to whip around.

Next to the watchman's tower, the top of a ladder rested against the wall. On the battlement, she met the murderous stare of an armed gnoll. Eli nocked an arrow and fired. The missile found its mark, killing the beast. She heard it fall among annoyed yelps and growls from its fellows below. Behind her, the children scratched and wailed at the wall, climbing over one another to reach her even as more undead crowded toward the breach on her right.

Wildly, she looked about for some escape. Her eyes fell on the dropped horn of a crushed watchman, a victim of the flying devils. The signal for a charge by the riders at the north and south gates played in her mind. She rose to her feet and saw the raised axe of another gnoll as it ascended the ladder. A few feet away, another ladder slammed against the wall. The signal horn might as well have been leagues away as the situation worsened.

Taking a deep breath, she nocked an arrow and raised her bow alone.

⊕ ⊕ ⊕ ⊕ ⊕

"Sanctuary." Sameska's voice broke the awkward silence. She sat on the steps, her back to the altar, pointedly avoiding the sight of it and the rune circle.

"Means nothing," she added, her tone full of venom and contempt.

The oracles who stayed behind to maintain the temple's arcane defenses ignored her. They focused on protecting the center of their faith, the foundation upon which their way of life had been built. A few refused to take any action, still convinced of the prophecy, though they wondered at Sameska's sanity.

The high oracle rocked back and forth slowly, holding her knees. Occasionally, she spoke to the semicircle of meditating young women around the altar's edge. Mostly, she whispered to herself, trying to make sense of where her followers had gone wrong, how they had fallen away from her wisdom.

"They don't see her coming," she mumbled. "All of them throw away their faith and their lives for fear. I see her, I have seen her blood."

She narrowed her eyes, peering suspiciously at the silent oracles.

They'll see us all dead, they will, she thought. They defy me, defy the words of their own god.

She blinked away the pain in her eyes. The soft glow of the chamber's wards seeped through her closed lids and she pulled her cloak's hood lower. She viewed the intrusion of the light as an affront to her leadership. It showed disregard for her bloodline and the respect the name of her family deserved. She bit her lip in frustration.

"Wayward souls, all of them, hiding in the dark." She stared at the floor. "It shall fall to me. I must protect them from themselves. What must I do?"

She looked up then, to the broken dome above. Chaos boiled beyond the gaping hole, turning and flashing in the clouds, growling through the thunder. Savras did not answer her. She flexed the chill fingers of her right hand. Hidden beneath her robes, she gripped the hilt of a bejeweled dagger.

Lowering her head again, still listening for an answer, she returned her attention to the oracles before her, to their still backs and exposed necks.

⊙ ⊙ ⊙ ⊙ ⊙

A thin trail of evaporating shadow clung to the edges of Quinsareth's cloak. The shadow of Brookhollow slowly gained detail as his eyes adjusted to the real world. He had emerged just north of the writhing mob that pushed its way through the western wall of the city. Invigorated and nearly healed by the shadow road, he ran toward the city. Bedlam hummed in the rain, screeching at each blade of grass that brushed along its length.

His keen vision picked out a group of robed figures in devilish masks. Solemnly watching the grim procession of undead, the Gargauthans made their way around the north side of an abandoned watch tower.

The city was a blur of flame and smoke. Hellish beasts roared in the sky even as the dead wailed and screamed on the ground. Quin consciously controlled his breathing as he ran, remaining steady and calm, observing the details of the terrain. He knew he was no soldier. He had never fought against armies. Morgynn alone was his chosen enemy, chosen by the shadows and the will of Hoar, a will for vengeance. He thought of what Sameska had called him, morbidly remembering his own reply.

"I am the assassin," he said under his breath. Some part of him rejected the concept, but the feel of a sword in his hand and his single-minded purpose drowned out the nobler parts of himself, putting them away until they could be afforded. "Only that and nothing more."

His thoughts fell silent as a familiar cry seized his attention.

A gnoll howled as it fell from the tower, splashing to the ground near the priests. A handful of its companions had already met similar ends. The Gargauthans approached and circled around the bodies. Their voices intoned a deep spidery chant over the corpses as they summoned the power of necromancy to command the gnollish warriors to fight again.

Quinsareth sped forward, raising his sword as the first of the dead gnolls began to twitch in the mud. One of the Gargauthans heard the scream of Quin's sword and looked up as it descended to cleave through his horned mask.

⊙ ⊙ ⊙ ⊙ ⊙

Baertah fell against a wall in the dark alleyway, gasping as warmth covered his flesh and a sudden pressure grew in his chest. The scents of cinnamon and rot filled his nose as his eyes failed, changing the gloom of the heavy clouds into impenetrable darkness. Blinded, he fell to his knees and whimpered, flinching as the ominous sound of beating wings passed over him. The warmth faded and his eyes adjusted to the dark. He blinked against the blur of the shadows, turning pale as he made out a familiar form standing over him.

"There's my little failure," Morgynn said, her voice sinuous and scolding, enveloping his fear in the intimate tones of a scorned lover. "What happened, I wonder? Not enough coin in your coffers, perhaps? The safety and rulership of Littlewater no longer desirable? Or maybe your abilities didn't quite match your claims?"

Baertah was speechless, backing into the street on his hands and knees, slipping to his elbows in the rain. Morgynn stepped from the shadows, the flushed color of her skin fading from the bloodwalk that had carried her through the lord hunter. She studied him a moment, raising an eyebrow at his silence.

"What's this? No excuses? No begging?" she asked, truly surprised. "If I didn't already know you were a complete coward, I'd have thought you were being brave, Lord Hunter. I thought your betrayal admirable before, but now I see why the hunters defy you."

"I-I'm sorry, Lady Morgynn," he stammered while warily rising to his feet. "Please accept my—"

"Ah, there it is," she said, amused. "Do not bother. I've heard your words on many tongues throughout the years and I still can't understand the tastes that put them there. Let's dispense with formality, shall we?"

Morgynn lightly touched the scars across her collarbone, shuddering as they burned away and released their power. Baertah was hurled into the air by her magic. Thrown down the street, he splashed in a crumpled heap on the cobblestones, the wind knocked from his lungs. He choked and struggled for air as he was lifted and thrown again, this time slamming against a wall and breaking his leg. She scowled at the need for such recreation, but Baertah was an ally courted by the fallen Mahgra and she was not surprised at the similarities between them. Both were vain and preening, and though the ogre had a streak of defiance, Baertah was little more than a fop.

She toyed with his body, carrying him closer and closer to the temple, battering his twisted limbs against any convenient obstacle. Only occasionally did he find the breath to scream. Even then, his voice was ragged and raw as if his throat had been scoured with gravel.

The battle raged far behind them. The sky was lit by the glow of distant fires when Baertah landed on his back only a few dozen paces from the temple's doors. Morgynn dismissed her spell and walked over to straddle his legs, crouching over him and whispering in his ear.

Baertah's eyes twitched behind bruised and broken skin. His jaw rested at an odd angle and several teeth hung in his gums by threads. A thin, wheezing breath escaped him and he coughed weakly as the rain spattered against the back of his throat.

"I will give you one last chance to redeem yourself, Lord Hunter," she said, her eyes fixed on the front doors of the temple. She smiled cruelly as several guards stepped out of hiding with weapons drawn. She slid her dagger from its sheath and traced the scars along her left arm with the blade's point. The runes squirmed to life as she chanted softly and placed a hand over the lord hunter's bleeding lips.

CHAPTER TWENTY-FIVE

Gnolls moved in single file down the north wall, eager to join the fray inside Brookhollow. Jagged battle-axes in hand, they growled at the frenzied waves of bathor below, pawing their noses and spitting at the stench of the undead.

Elisandrya fired a carefully aimed arrow into the throat of a gnoll as he scaled the wall, toppling him to join the others she'd felled. His companions ducked and quickly crawled into hiding. She screamed in protest as they escaped her bow, firing into the shields of the remaining pair. They waited for her bloodlust to wane or her attention to become distracted by the undead climbing the wall beside her.

Seeing the last of the pack loping out to join the battle, one of the gnolls edged forward with its shield raised. Closing the distance with her, he snarled, eager to meet her blade to blade. Elisandrya was tired and only dimly aware of the advancing gnoll. Over her shoulder, the sobs of the undead children neared the top of the wall. Tiny pale fingers, bleeding on the wet stone, gripped its edge.

Eli's throat and nose ached from the cold air. The steady sound of rain on her hood made everything seem unreal, like a dream. A sense of doom fell over her as a pair of glossy eyes crested the wall. Loping footfalls turned her attention to the gnoll, axe held high, charging across the wall.

Her readied arrow slammed into the gnoll's gut. He loosed a horrific howl but carried on, ignoring the pain. Behind the gnoll, Eli could still see the signal horn lying untouched at the dead watchman's feet. It taunted her and she raised her bow to deflect the descending axe. The contact awakened her numb reflexes and sent shockwaves of pain through her stiff arms. She growled at the gnoll wildly, losing herself in what she believed would be the last moments of her life.

The gnoll grabbed her bow and pulled his axe back to strike again, baring his teeth. Eli stepped back on one foot and kicked at the arrow protruding from the gnoll's abdomen. The wound gushed dark blood as he staggered back and released her bow, roaring in pain. Eli reached for her nearly empty quiver, and her leg was pulled out from under her.

Her back slammed against the battlement, jarring her neck as she kicked at the undead child that had grabbed her foot. The world spun before her eyes and freezing rain stung her face. Her mind reeled at the cacophony of sounds that pounded in her ears. The menacing growls of two gnolls echoed in her head as they approached her. Warily, they eyed the bathor that climbed and crawled over one another to reach her. She saw death in the eyes of the unfortunate child at her feet and screamed at it, challenging it as she kicked again and struggled to draw her sword.

Thunder crashed and the rain slackened. The wind slowed, but even as the thunder faded, a new voice picked up the sound. The thunder was echoed by a metallic hum. The injured gnoll, ducking behind its companion, snapped off the shaft of the arrow in its stomach. It looked up to view a man with fair skin splashed with blood and murderous pearly eyes. The beast was cut down by a green flashing blade and kicked over the side of the wall.

The other gnoll whirled at the noise. It sniffed the air and scowled at the scent of the cloaked warrior that faced him. A primal chill filled the warrior's eyes and the growling sword he carried. The gnoll raised his axe and abandoned the fallen hunter to the undead, baring his teeth in challenge at the shadowy aasimar.

Eli freed her blade and hacked at the numerous arms yanking on her legs. The blood she drew hissed and burned on her leggings and boots, the smell caustic and nauseating. Another bathor, a woman, had crawled up the wall on Eli's right and lay flat against the stone. The woman's head and neck twisted from side to side as she pulled herself closer.

Looking down the wall, Eli watched the assimar approach the gnoll like a deadly dancer. Waves of fear emanated from Quin, a tide of terror that made her shiver.

Quinsareth stepped forward, turning to his right as the gnoll's axe passed within a hand's breadth of his face. He continued to spin, pushing his shoulder into the gnoll's ribs and hooking his right leg behind his opponent. As the gnoll struggled to angle its axe at the aasimar, Quin grabbed the gnoll's right arm and pushed as he spun again. He slammed Bedlam's pommel between the beast's shoulder blades, then followed the strike with Bedlam's blade. He severed the stumbling gnoll's right leg at the knee and left him to fall over the edge into the undead below.

Elisandrya's sword arm was pinned, held down by the viselike grip of an undead woman who whispered nonsense as she dug her fingers into Eli's flesh. The bathor's touch sent arcs of pain down Eli's arm and across her chest. She fumbled with her left hand, searching for anything to beat the ghoulish woman away, refusing to give up.

The tortured moans of Eli's attacker suddenly turned to shrieks. More sizzling blood spattered across Eli's legs and face. Blue-green lightning flashed with each splash of putrid blood. A gloved hand seized her arm and suddenly she was being pulled across the wall. She watched as the woman, armless, squirmed and beat herself against the battlements before rolling into the masses at the wall's edge.

Eli felt strong arms lifting her to her feet and she instinctively fought back. Flailing her fists, she tried to kick the legs out from under her captor. Turning, she raised a fist and saw Quinsareth's face, grim and covered in blood. She almost fainted in relief, but he held her steady and lifted her chin, brushing his hand across the red welts that formed where the bathor's blood had scalded her face.

"Will you be all right?" he asked with concern in his voice. He backed them toward the guard tower.

"I'll survive," she said, managing a smile as she met his gaze.

She was stunned by the depth of feeling his presence suddenly stirred in her. The battle was blocked from her senses for a few moments. Unspoken words hung in her mind, then fell to their deaths in the awkward silence between them. Eli's eyes said things her mouth and lips could not.

In a daze, she stepped away from Quin and leaped up the steps into the guard tower. She retrieved the watchman's horn and glared down upon the gruesome army that assaulted her home. The devil-masked Gargauthans kept a safe distance along the flanks of the advancing throng.

Taking a deep breath, she blew one long piercing note that carried across the whole of the city. Flaming arrows were fired high into the air from the north and south gates, signaling their receipt of the order. When Eli turned back, Quinsareth was gone. She caught sight of his shadow moving swiftly and with purpose along the north wall.

Kneeling, she took Zakar's quiver of arrows and quietly promised him a warrior's funeral. With the quiver slung over her shoulder, she followed the aasimar.

⊙ ⊙ ⊙ ⊙ ⊙

The prized Shaaran warhorses stamped their hooves and shook their wild manes in the spacious stables reserved for the Hunters of the Hidden Circle. The warriors patted their mounts' necks and whispered encouraging words in their ears. The horses were uncharacteristically jittery. The smell of smoke and decay in the air had reached them, and tension grew as they waited for the call to charge.

Armor and weapons had been readied before the first sounds of battle, and the fray was still several blocks away, growing louder as it neared the stable. Some of the riders suspected that something horrible had happened, and the commanders were preparing to signal their own charge when the call came through the storm. The warriors' hearts jumped as the wide stable doors opened.

They rode hard, the surefooted warhorses pounding effortlessly through the mud. The two groups of mounted archers split, heading north and south. Once outside the city gates, they angled west with bows drawn. Exposed to the cruel elements, they breathed the fouled air like a drug, becoming intoxicated with bloodlust for the enemy. They spat the cold rain back into the faces of the clouds, reveling in the downpour. Their expectations of the battle were quickly rewarded as devils roared in the sky and gnolls howled and barked savagely from the walls.

"Hush!"

Sameska's voice startled everyone in the sanctuary, echoing in the silence as all paid wary attention to the broken woman. Her head was cocked to one side, listening for something, her eyes closed against the light of the chamber's runes. A few of the priestesses edged closer to Sameska, concerned and frightened by her behavior. They listened with her.

Moments passed and they heard nothing. Shaking their heads, they whispered prayers for the high oracle's broken mind. A slight gasp from the semicircle of oracles startled them again. Nerves were stretched taut as the evening wore on. Those present followed the oracle's stare to the far wall.

Several lines of runes had faded, and some had winked out altogether.

"It is coming. She is closer now," the high oracle muttered. Patches of the arcane architecture died before their eyes, dismantled and dispelled by unseen hands. An encroaching darkness crawled through the chamber little by little, leaving only a single light within the half-circle. The altar, the rune circle, and the dais of the high oracle became islands of misty light stranded in the dark. "She is here to fulfill the words of Savras, girls. To drown us along with the forest in her wake."

"Be quiet!" a young woman on her right said. Shaking, she searched the blackness outside the circle for movement. She held a dagger, the traditional weapon of Savrathans, close to her breast. Sameska scowled and clenched her own hidden blade.

"Heed what she says, child," Morgynn said as she stepped into the boundary of the circle's glow. "There is a certain wisdom in madness that should not be dismissed so readily."

The oracles looked in horror upon the sorceress, her face like a portrait painted in blood on an ivory slate. Blood dripped from her fingertips, covering her arms up to her elbows. She noticed the oracles' attention to the mess dripping from her hands and held them forward, palms up.

"Fear not," she said mockingly, "it's not mine."

⊙ ⊙ ⊙ ⊙ ⊙

Quinsareth sheathed Bedlam and ran, avoiding the clash of forces in the streets and making his way toward the temple. He jumped off the wall before the gnolls spotted him. He had no time to relive his battle in Targris, and he struggled to keep Logfell from his thoughts as suffering wails and keening moans erupted from the undead, only blocks behind him. He focused on the rain, imagining himself weaving between the drops. He dashed between buildings like the lightning, becoming part of the storm and not the battle. The battle itself was beyond him now, beyond the works of a single warrior, and would play itself out as such.

"Their fates must be their own," he whispered under his breath. He slipped between darkened, undisturbed homes and past the smoldering, steaming remains of others. Inside himself, he could feel the lie even if he couldn't admit it, but it was familiar and necessary to his task. It was a half-truth he maintained to keep moving, to stay focused. Nobility, he thought, forges more martyrs than it does victories.

The malebranche passed overhead, intent on destruction and reveling in their play. Their nearness called to his blood. He buried deep his instinct for battle and wars fought long before the elven nations were born. He'd felt the same call in the High Forest near Hellgate Keep, the forests of Cormanthor near Myth Drannor, and in the snows and tundra of Narfell. This, too, he buried, though he absorbed that primal bloodlust for his own use, bending his celestial nature to his own ends and means.

Seeing his objective ahead, he entered the last stretch of flooded street and crouched behind an overturned merchant's chart, its single wheel turning lazily in the wind over loaves of sodden bread. The wide square before the Temple of the Hidden Circle was paved in cobblestones laid in concentric circles, their pattern highlighted by rivers of water that flowed between the cracks and reflected the lightning flashes.

He needed no lightning to see the five figures standing in a line across the center of those circles of stones. All save one wore hunters' armor and weapons. They did not move or blink; no puffs of breath steamed from their open mouths. Their bodies rippled and shimmered like mirages. What wounds they bore had ceased bleeding, open and empty.

Narrowing his eyes, Quinsareth strode from his hiding place, in full view and no longer concerned with stealth. The glazed and lifeless eyes of the sentries had found him with preternatural senses that reached beyond darkness, rain, and man-made obstacles.

The very fact that he lived had given him away.

"This is foolishness, High Oracle. You know that, don't you?" Morgynn asked while observing the translucent veil of force separating her from the oracles. "This barrier will not hold forever against me. Meanwhile, your people are dying as we speak."

Sameska did not answer. The other oracles stood ready to act, though Morgynn felt none of them were a match for her magic. Those who sat in the semicircle concentrated on their barrier all the harder. Though their minds focused on the magic, she could sense their fear. Something was hidden in that rhythm beneath their breasts, some secret they held from her. Curious, she raised her hands to test their barrier.

Weaving her spell, she sent waves of light against the translucent veil of magic. Screaming as she pushed herself harder, she fought the combined wills of the oracles and the old magic they wielded. She stumbled backward as her spell failed and the light faded. Breathing heavily, she glared at her hands as if betrayed. She slowed her pulse and stretched her neck. Her muscles spasmed as she collected herself. "I can feel each of you," she said quietly, her words amplified in the chamber. "You're hiding something from me."

Sameska looked up then, peering at Morgynn over her shoulder, trembling. "Idiots!" Sameska hissed at them, but they ignored her still.

Morgynn raised an eyebrow at her outburst and cast another spell, calling forth a sphere of mist above her palm which she hurled at the barrier. It burst in a puff of smoke and tendrils of shadow spread across the invisible wall like a web, probing at the magic. Morgynn touched the shadows with her fingertips, shutting her eyes and listening to the spell as it sang in her blood, feeding her what she wanted to know.

"Calm yourself, dear Sameska," she said as the shadowy web melted away, slowly retracing its course back to her outstretched hand. "I once knew an old woman, many years ago, whose faith had outgrown her humanity. In the end, she lost both."

She smiled grimly at the memory of her mother, disgusted by the similarities she saw in the high oracle. The shadows ceased their movements and froze at her will as she sensed something unexpected. The oracles' heartbeats pounded in her mind, a cadence within the harmonies of the Weave that flowed through her, but another rhythm pulsed there as well. A multitude of hearts seemed to thunder together, dispersed and hidden.

She dismissed the shadows and opened her eyes knowingly, realizing the true source of their fear and sickening righteousness. Demurely, she approached the centermost oracle and knelt down to speak to her eye to eye, only the shimmering veil of magic between them.

"They're hiding here, aren't they?" she said, seeking some reaction in the young woman's solemn expression. "Those too old or too weak to fight. You're protecting them, hiding them somewhere in this place while you sit here and wonder if you've made the right decision. Defying prophecy, betraying the faith of your high oracle, and gambling with the lives of your people."

The oracle remained outwardly stoic, but Morgynn could feel her quickened pulse. She knew that if she had learned any lesson from her mother, it was that faith did not exist without doubt.

Morgynn noted that Sameska watched the exchange with rapt attention.

"It is a thin line you walk," Morgynn continued, "between honor and oblivion. I have seen the Abyss where doomed souls go. I know the fate that awaits you there."

For a fleeting moment, Morgynn saw the oracle's face flinch and relax, a hint of grudging resignation. She scowled as the girl tightened her fists and raised her chin, resolute and unmoving. Wordless, Morgynn stood, shaking with anger and backing away. She drew her dagger and gripped the blade as she summoned the words to another spell.

Sameska, wild-eyed, leaned forward, gritting her teeth. The high oracle pulled a dagger from beneath her robes.

"May Savras have mercy on your soul!" she cried, drawing everyone's attention. Morgynn tilted her head and halted her spell, intrigued by this development as Sameska brandished the hidden blade and lunged for the young oracle's throat.

⊙ ⊙ ⊙ ⊙ ⊙

Misty blades flashed and rippled in the rain, driving Quinsareth back, hard pressed to deflect the attacks of the wraithlike creatures Morgynn had placed outside the temple. He cursed her name with each parry, spitting words that might have raised eyebrows even among the pirates and rogues of the Dragon Coast. The undead pressed on, nearly mindless but amazingly quick. Their bodies alternated between solid and ephemeral states. Their shifting had foiled Quin's initial charge, Bedlam's blade only serving to disrupt their spiritual forms harmlessly.

With luck, he'd managed to fell two of them, swinging in anticipation of their attack and cleaving the things as they'd materialized. Though fallen, their forms still writhed on the ground, wailing as their semisolid bodies twisted and malformed. Their souls seemed bound to their dead bodies, wraiths bearing the cumbersome weight of undead flesh. The remaining three sentries worked in unison to break Quin's swift defense and stab beneath his hissing blade.

Quinsareth fought to control his breathing, reining in his anger as he skipped backward. He tried to recognize a cycle to his opponents' unstable corporeality. Patterns rose and fell in his mind, found but quickly abandoned. He counted the breaths carefully, numbering each parry, deftly wielding the large shield and Bedlam as if they were a buckler and foil.

Indeed, the unarmored opponent carried such a blade, looking more like a dandified fop than a warrior. The fop's blade passed within a hair's breadth of his neck as he arched backward to avoid the slice. Angrily, he began to count out loud, slowing his backward motion and quickening his defense.

"One . . . two . . . three . . ." he breathed, then crouched, rolled forward, and slashed left and right. The hunters' blades thrust harmlessly over his head as he carved through flesh and bone, crippling the two along their upper thighs. He knew he could not kill what was already dead, but he could slow them. He sought to immobilize them that he might bypass Morgynn's guards and follow her into the temple.

Leaning back on his left leg, he swept his right in a wide arc to trip the third sentry as it materialized, but he was a heartbeat too fast. His boot passed through the legs of the fop just before it took solid form, and its foil sliced down on Quin's low position.

Two arrows hissed into the dandy's chest, followed quickly by a third that found its sword arm, halting the swing and burning its undead flesh. The creature reeled backward, wailing in agony. The pale shadow of its spirit clawed at the arrows, as if suddenly nailed to corporeality. Quinsareth rolled back to his feet, casting a glance over his shoulder to see Elisandrya nocking another arrow, a look of grim satisfaction on her face as she fired.

The arcane missile seared into the fop's neck, quieting its cries to a wet gurgle as it fell on its back, shaking as its spirit turned to a pungent, thick smoke and dissipated on the wind. The body left behind flopped in the rain like a landed fish gasping for air.

Quickly scanning the area, Quin noted that the temple doors were unobstructed. Turning to Elisandrya, he could not read the strange look in her eye. Her defensive stance and firmly set jaw seemed at odds with her beauty, but at the same time complimented her strength. He could forget himself in her face, he realized, and he forced himself to turn away from her.

In that moment, Eli's eyes were eclipsed in a rushing darkness as chaos broke their brief glance. Quin found himself running toward her as time crawled and a black shape crashed to the ground near her. Through the rain, the scene was a blur of splashing water and massive leathery wings. A roar cut off Elisandrya's yell of surprise, turning it into a sharp scream as she was slammed into the side of a building. The force of the blow cracked the wall and she crumpled to the ground.

Quinsareth saw a flash of red as Bedlam took on the devil's roar as its own. The battleworn beast turned and glared at the charging aasimar with burning coal eyes. One of its forward horns had been snapped off and several arrows protruded from its arms and chest. Thick, black blood oozed from wounds across its stomach and from rips in its wings. Its face was twisted into a mocking grin by a jutting, underslung jaw filled with fangs and two large tusks. Rain steamed as it poured over the devil's hard skin, boiling in its hell-born heat.

The malebranche roared weakly at the mocking sword. Wracked with pain from its injuries, it tried to turn and meet its enraged attacker. A massive fist crashed into Quin's shoulder, sending waves of pain through his chest. He rolled with the blow, bringing Bedlam inside the devil's reach. The beast snapped its head up, raking its single horn along Quin's breastplate and cutting a jagged gash through the Hoarite's jaw.

Quinsareth, oblivious to the pain, swung his sword up in a vicious cut. Bedlam sliced off the remaining horn and bit deep into the side of the beast's head. His arm ached with the impact, but Quin held on as Bedlam screamed and cut deeper. Burning in contact with its flesh, Bedlam howled until the devil's struggles ceased.

The aasimar jumped backward, wrenching his sword free as the hulking body of the malebranche slumped forward, shaking the ground with its weight. Its spilled blood hissed in the puddles, the sounds merging with the deluge. Quin's shoulder stabbed with pain as he hobbled over to Elisandrya, his gut chilled with fear.

Kneeling beside her, he inspected the deep gouges in her side. She gasped in pain as he pressed against them to slow her bleeding. Her eyes wide, she gulped for air and winced. Though relieved to see her conscious, she grabbed at his wrist before he could speak. He trembled as she slid her other hand across his cheek.

"Go, finish it," was all she said, her eyelids heavy as she released him. She pulled her cloak around herself tightly, but never looked away from him.

Wordlessly, he nodded and stood, turning toward the temple doors. Her words and brief touch were seared into his mind, not for their sentiment or the feelings they conveyed, but for what he knew, in his heart of hearts. With or without her permission, whether or not he might have been able to heal her wounds, he'd have gone and left her anyway, to finish what he'd begun.

And he hated himself for it.

CHAPTER TWENTY-SIX

Splotches of red covered her hands and arms.

She could feel herself screaming in the candlelight, crying and trying to wipe the stains away, but they stubbornly remained. Her grandmother opened the bedroom door calmly and knowingly, waiting for the vision to pass, not wanting to interfere with the child's destiny.

In moments, the blood was gone as if blown away by her own breath, and she looked to her grandmother, the High Oracle of the Hidden Circle, with pleading in her eyes.

"Make it go away, Nanna! I don't want it!"

The old woman merely crossed the room and sat by Sameska's side, holding her hands and looking gravely into her eyes.

"That I cannot do, Sameska. Would not if I could," she said, her voice deep and comforting. "It is a blessing of Savras, to see that which will be. You have been chosen, just as your mother and I were chosen."

Chosen. She contemplated the word later as she slept, bundled in soft blankets against an early autumn chill. The visions had only recently begun, making her feel special at first, but then they had come more often. In quiet moments, in the middle of daily chores, and, that day, among her friends. She sobbed, still able to see the looks of horror on their faces as she'd rambled, telling each about the day they would die. Horror turned to anger and hatred, and the cruelty of children became isolation. She was hidden indoors to await her mother, still among her peers at the temple.

Alone in her room, staring into the darkness, smelling the smoke of a cooling candle, she listened to the muffled voices of her mother and grandmother through the door. She drew up the stone cold courage of her mother and stoically pulled her arms out from beneath the covers, holding them up to the moonlight that shone through the dark curtains.

It was there. She could not truly see it, the vision having passed, but the blood was still there. Imagining it across her hands and fingers, wrinkled and old as they'd been, she wondered at what she'd seen. Savras demanded truth in all things, an accounting of each vision or prophecy for all to hear. This one she had not told, not to Nanna or her mother. A sickening guilt had haunted her about the vision, for the blood was not hers, and she knew that someone had died.

She lay awake all night, eventually rising, still wrapped in blankets, to pace the floor in front of the window. Each time she passed, the moonlight splashed blood across her hands.

⊙ ⊙ ⊙ ⊙ ⊙

Rough hands dragged her backward, clutching at her robes and prying the bloody dagger from her fingers. She studied her arms when the oracles finally released her, covered in blood. She felt older than she'd felt in the last several tendays. The faces that watched her bore a mixture of horror, pity, and anger. She sobbed and squeezed her eyes shut, wringing her hands in her robes and falling to the floor, choking out words past the lump in her throat.

"Make it go away, Nanna. I don't want it."

Behind her intended victim lay the young oracle's savior. Pale, staring up with sightless eyes, Sameska could not remember her name. The girl had dived between the two, receiving the fatal wound in her throat that now flooded the marble with the high oracle's crime. Looking over the girl's shoulder, Morgynn crouched, like a cat waiting for a mouse to come out of its hole. Staring at the high oracle, she blankly observed the effects of what she had wrought in Sameska's mind.

Morgynn studied the brave oracle's lifeless body. She pursed her lips in disgust at such a selfless act, but was amused by the chaos of the scene. Sameska squirmed as Morgynn paced along her barrier's edge, studying the dense network of Dethek runes that glowed brighter when she neared. Similar spells had been in place along the corridors and entrance to the sanctuary, dormant sentinels set against evil threats. They had been interesting puzzles, but less effective than these in the heart of the temple.

Smiling, she faced her captive audience, enjoying the variety of expressions on their faces. Defiance, fear, and hopelessness, she favored them all as validation of her existence. Whispers slipped among them, prayers to Savras to deliver them from evil. She paused in her pacing and looked around curiously as if staring through the walls at the whole of Faerûn.

"It's not about good or evil," she said, "higher powers or faith. None of it matters in the end. It's about blood, who spills it and who owns it . . . that's all."

Drawing her dagger, she sliced a small cut in her left palm to match the wound on her right. Clasping them together, she willed her blood to flow for her magic. Although she had the knowledge and means to cast spells as other wizards did, she had no taste for their primitive ingredients. Bits of spider web or bat guano had their places in shaping the Weave, but the crimson stream of her own pulse brought the magic closer, made it more intimate. It was an arcane taboo that was regarded by some magic-wielders as a form of cannibalism.

They spend their lives fighting the magic, she thought, *addicted to its power, but unwilling to risk their vanity or health, seeking out spells of long life or even immortality. They will never know what it means to be consumed.*

The words of the spell were quick and simple, uttered and gone in a single short breath as she spread her hands apart. The blood from her palms flowed toward her fingertips, setting each alight with a red energy. Lowering her arms, she pointed each glowing finger at a design on the floor. Tracing them in the air, she followed their twisting threads until they met the barrier and passed beyond.

The energy of the spell throbbed through her arms, aching for release as she focused. Sighing, she let the magic fall, gently drifting to the floor like snowflakes. The marble darkened where it touched, slipping between the edges of the runes and hissing on contact. The glow flared and pulsated in tune to Morgynn's will, growing and filling the room with a thundering hum that shook the floor. Minuscule cracks appeared in the marble. The oracles covered their ears and watched as light flowed through the patterns, inexorably following the whorls of the arcane alphabet toward them.

The hum reached a powerful crescendo, shaking the walls. Fractures appeared all over the chamber on Morgynn's side of the barrier as the thin lines of light flashed and raced toward the warded wall of energy. The crimson bolts slammed into the barrier, crackling and straining against its resisting power. Morgynn stood back and watched as the oracles fought against the spell's intrusion. She took care to note the patterns of the wards where they grew the brightest, memorizing the places of strength and contemplating how to weaken them.

Her mind drifted as she watched. Part of her imagined taking apart the temple's magic, while the rest of her imagined conquest beyond this simple town and its troublesome soothsayers. She envisioned her Order of Twilight crawling across Shandolphyn's Reach, her plague directed against Derlusk. She saw the Gargauthans inserting themselves in the port city, making way for her rule over the vast libraries within. Trade ships would become her secret armada, sailing the Lake of Steam to the cities along its coast, bringing them plague and inner turmoil, ripening them for her arrival.

Innarlith would be last, she decided. Ransar Pristoleph must know of her return long before her ships turn on his rule.

Idle thoughts faded as her spell died, having served its purpose, leaving the sanctuary in silence once more. She knew that nothing could be gained by wasting her magic on the oracles' defenses. Those weaknesses she might have exploited were defended by strengths other than the pattern of woven runes. Briefly, she wondered if her coming had been foreseen when those runes were crafted. She smiled at the thought as she stared at the layer of fine dust on the floor and the weblike cracks through the walls.

"I am impressed, ladies," she said suddenly, startling those whose ears still rung from the noise of the spell. "Though I trust none of you had a hand in their creation, the defenses here are quite astounding . . ."

She knelt and scooped up a handful of dust from the floor, letting it sift through her fingers before continuing.

". . . if not for one minor flaw. This would be Rift marble, I assume? I've read about this, very strong and . . ." she looked up to the ceiling knowingly, ". . . heavy. It has traveled many miles to this place. Such a distance to serve as your tomb. You may keep your barriers and wards. Hold them as long as you are able. When I bring this temple down about your heads, your wall will be your only protection against being crushed."

Turning to carry out her threat, Morgynn caught the sharp scent of moisture and blood on a chill breeze across her back. Facing the doorway, she glared at the figure that stood there, silhouetted in flashing lightning from the windowed corridors beyond. The scars across her body itched as she tensed. Several vile spells came to mind as her blooded eyes met his opalescent gaze.

He smiled grimly and broke the silence between them.

"Funny things, prophecies," he said sardonically. "Sometimes they even come true."

⊙ ⊙ ⊙ ⊙ ⊙

"I remember this," Dreslya spoke under her breath, careful not to disturb the Ghedia's chant as they sheltered in the stone hut.

They sat within the confines of a rough circle of grass blades, in the dark, only dimly aware of the battle and storm so dangerously close. Dres felt weak, lending her strength to Lesani, whose casting had seemed to go on for days. Time was lost to her, but Lesani's voice made time, bringing images to her mind of a savage era. The rolling grasslands of the Shaar stretched out beneath her as she drifted with the chant. The smell of dry grass under a hot sun produced a primal awareness in her, a desire to hunt and ride free, to give thanks to the land as it gave her what she needed. And in her dreaming eye was the magic.

Pressed into the grass, overlaid with twigs forming symbols of the Dethek runes, was the most basic element of the Ghedia way: the circle.

Within the circle sat a hooded figure, chanting in Lesani's voice with hands much like Lesani's, but it was not her. The eyes were older, wiser, and more fierce than any she had seen. She sat across from the woman, this Ghedia of another time, alone on the wild grasslands, and watched as dark clouds rose in the north over a hazy red sunset.

On that horizon, rising from the grass, pulling themselves from the ground, were the shapes of massive beasts. So far away, Dreslya could not make out much detail in the strange creatures, save that they bore manes of jagged spines and stood on six legs as they swiveled their ponderous bulks to face the circle.

The bearer of Lesani's voice spoke then in the Shaaran

tongue, one which Dreslya had not used often in her life, but knew well enough to understand.

"We bring the teeth of your forebears," she said to the silent pack. Dreslya reached beside her to lift a bundle of large thorns tied with leather thongs. Each was the size of a large dagger and razor sharp.

"We call you from their womb and their grave," Dreslya said, acting on blind instinct, unsure if the voice she heard was her own. The fierce Ghedia raised handfuls of dirt and grass.

"We ask that you honor us with your power. Aid us in defending our ancestral lands and we will ask of you no more."

The strange beasts bristled their spiky manes and tossed their heads, posturing and pawing at the ground with trunk-like forelegs ending in long claws. A note of alarm passed through Dreslya, and the Ghedia's eyes widened in sudden fear. The beasts lowered their heads in a predatory crouch, looking like giant lions as they whipped their spined tails across the grass. The storm rose behind them, thundering and scorching the ground with lightning.

Dreslya's sense of alarm faded as the creatures turned to face the storm and shook their bodies violently, producing a reedy hissing sound not unlike seeds in a thin gourd. The ground rumbled as they charged, moving away from the pair and into the darkness.

Lesani sighed and slumped forward, exhausted. Dreslya blinked several times, adjusting her eyes to the darkness of the hovel, disoriented and weak from the strange, but somehow familiar spell. The Ghedia had passed out and Dreslya tried to stand, but the ground still shook, vibrating beneath them as thunder rumbled outside.

The image of the Shaar remained in her mind, dream-like and indistinct.

"I remember all of this," she whispered, and though she did not know their true names, those beasts charging the horizon with whipping tails and spiny manes, she knew what the tribes knew, heard the name they were called out of fear and respect.

The word rested on her tongue, foreign and savage in the Shaaran language and no less so in its translation to Common.

"Battlebriar," she said out loud and shivered, instinctively drawing her dagger. She touched Lesani's unconscious face, then leaned back to rest and listen.

⊕ ⊕ ⊕ ⊕ ⊕

Makeshift barricades were erected near the center of town out of debris and anything that wasn't nailed or mortared down. Archers climbed onto rooftops, exposed to the diving malebranche, but gaining vantage points from which to fire into the endless ranks of ravenous undead that threw themselves at any and all opponents. Quivers of arrows were blessed by the surviving oracles, and the hunter's missiles sizzled into the writhing horde. The carrion stench of the steaming bathor wafted to those who waited their turns to face what were rumored to be the dead citizens of Logfell.

At first, Talmen had scowled in anger as the mounted hunters charged the rear of the advancing Gargauthans, but Morgynn's creations kept the defenders well occupied. They dragged down prized steeds into the mud while wizard-priests hurled spells of fire and lightning. The malebranche took their share of the Savrathan warriors, plucking them from their mounts and slinging their bodies into the barricades at the front of the assault.

Though far too many of the skilled riders still circled the field with their deadly Shaaran bows, Talmen had to admit he'd underestimated Morgynn. Still close to the treeline, Talmen had little cause to use the command he'd been given over the bathor; simply willing them to attack had been enough. He typically did not favor the use of undead beyond menial tasks, favoring the more reliable minions of the Lower Planes to accomplish his martial goals. Gargauth's time in the Lower Planes had been well spent before his exile to the natural world, and many devils aspired to be allies once his conquest was brought back to those infernal realms.

"And he will need rulers to leave here in his stead," he mused aloud, admiring the graceful dive of a malebranche as it roared to rend another foe. Talmen blinked and the devil was gone. Something had happened to the beast, and an impact shook the ground and silenced the malebranche's horrendous roar.

Peering through the rain and darkness, he caught a glimpse of a torn wing, thrashing against some strange beast in the sodden grass. A second impact thumped the earth, closer this time, and he froze, searching for the source of the sound and reaching for his mace as a spell came to mind. He became aware of a hissing noise in the rain. Looking to his left, he saw the thing's shadow, prowling around the line of trees less than thirty paces away.

Every measure of the beast's dark brown hide—what seemed to be vines and wood—was covered in thorns as long as swords and spears. The creature's head was small in comparison to its body. As broad as it was tall, it had no visible mouth. Only the hissing of its bristling spines and its colossal mass had given any warning as to its approach.

He abandoned the thought of wielding a mace against the beast and loosed his spell, uttering the incantation breathlessly in sudden fear. A glowing globe of green energy flew from his hand and splashed against the battlebriar's chest, sizzling and destroying several thorny spikes, but otherwise having no effect on the beast.

Talmen ran for the deeper forest, a safer place from which to conjure means of defeating these new arrivals. Relieved, he did not hear the beast pursue. He detected only the thrashing of its whiplike tail of barbs outside the tree line.

His relief disappeared as several blows landed across his back and legs. Puzzled at the sudden pain, he stumbled to a stop within sight of the Qurth's impenetrable darker depths. Looking down, he saw the tips of the spikes and thorns that had impaled him. Falling to his knees and coughing up blood, his last thoughts were to wonder how they'd gotten there.

Morgynn felt the death of Malefactor Talmen. The magic in the scar she'd placed on his arm unraveled in her mind and fell silent. She barely blinked at the news, nor was she concerned with Khaemil's likely death at the hands of the aasimar who faced her. They were unessential, replaceable, fodder for her ambitions.

She cocked her head to one side, considering the lone warrior. He wore confidence like a pair of comfortable shoes, standing before her with nothing but a sword and shield against her magic.

"You're a ghost here, Hoarite," she said, blood swirling in her eyes. "You serve no purpose except to die, to show these shivering witches what fools I've made of them. This battle is lost. This town is finished. I do not see a man who cares about these things in you."

"Curious," he replied, "that you would think I cared about what you saw in me."

She raised an eyebrow at his response, flexing her long fingers in anticipation, spells hovering in her mind and flowing through her blood.

"As I said, a ghost that thinks it is a man," she answered, eying the tip of his sword as he raised it slightly, observing the forward shift in his balance. "Come and see, then. I will show this wayward spirit to you."

Choosing a spell as they circled one another, Morgynn envisioned violet flames consuming the aasimar, and wondered if he would scream.

⊛ ⊛ ⊛ ⊛ ⊛

Quinsareth's shoulder pained him and the ancient shield on his arm vibrated in the presence of the sorceress. Bedlam hissed with the rain outside and growled with the thunder, but changed its tune to the subtler tones of Morgynn's heartbeat as her anger pulsed outward. The taste of blood filled Quin's mouth from the wound along his jaw.

He moved away from the door, creeping along the wall to stand before a large column. Morgynn's voice barely scraped the surface of his thoughts. Watching her every move, he balanced Bedlam carefully, preparing to strike at a moment's notice. Wind from the corridor kicked up small clouds of dust from the pulverized floor as he adjusted his stance. Shadows curled through his body, darkening his eyes as he summoned them.

Morgynn's chant flowed across her tongue and lips. The standoff broken, Quin sprang toward her. Dark violet flames coursed across her arms, gathering at her fingertips before bursting out in a blast of pure cold fire. As the energy met him, Quin saw a brief flash shimmer around the edges of his shield.

The dark flames splashed across the shield, spilling around it in places but absorbing into the gleaming metal, leaving the aasimar unharmed. Stepping closer, he raised Bedlam to strike. Morgynn reacted quickly, stepping back on her right foot. Red scars along her collarbone flared to life at her touch and she raised her left arm as if to defend against his blade.

Bedlam rang across her wrist as if striking steel. Seeing his moment of surprise, she batted Bedlam aside. Hissing another spell, she thrust her right hand forward. A wave of invisible force erupted from her body in a wide circle. The dust billowed from the scoured marble floor and sent Quin flying back to crash into the base of the column he'd charged from.

Though aching all over, Quinsareth recovered quickly, forcing himself to roll forward into a crouch. Morgynn's voice was already reciting another spell. Wary and uncertain of the shield's abilities but emboldened by its power, he charged again. He knew he needed to reach the sorceress to have any chance of negating her arcane advantage. A few strides away from her, a gray fog materialized around him, enveloping him in a misty cloud that crackled with energy. Pain tore through his chest and legs as tendrils of fog lashed him, forcing him to stumble and fall to his knees.

Quin cried out, squeezing his eyes shut and struggling to breathe, every inch of his flesh feeling as if on fire. When he succeeded in breathing, the mist entered his lungs and burned him from within, spreading through his veins and into his heart.

Morgynn smiled at him and knelt. Through the haze of pain he watched as she studied the shield he wore. He realized she'd been surprised by its presence, another piece of Eli's legend come true: spellcasters could not see the shield's abilities until too late. The mist grew around him, struggling against the shield which could not consume all the magic that surrounded it. Quin's stomach felt twisted as if his innards had declared war on one another. He felt brief moments of respite as the shield shook on his arm and spit bright globs of energy, but the artifact was unable to completely devour Morgynn's fog.

"A spell eater," Morgynn said as Quinsareth fought to crawl out of the painful mist on his hands and knees, refusing to release his hold on Bedlam. "Well, then. We shall have to feed it."

The darkness faded and Quin's muscles relaxed all at once, released from the wracking pain. Looking up, he braced his sword arm to stand, and Morgynn cast yet another spell. Blood spilled across her face in two thin lines. As it reached her lips, her hands drew circles in the air. The air around them became charged with acute heat. A ring of blackened electricity coalesced around her at arm's length, spinning as it sparked and rumbled. Quin choked on the scent of burning ozone as streaks of crimson wound themselves into the spell. Rising to one knee, he held the shield before him. Briefly, he wondered if the shield's last bearer, Ossian, had died in such a stance, and he dimly hoped the shield would protect him.

Black lightning crackled into several bolts from the ring of magic and disappeared into the shield face. A palpable aura grew around the edges of the shield as it fought to consume the black bolts. The barrage continued until the shield's aura was nearly palpable. The dark energy of the lightning spilled over and seared Quin's flesh, raising bloody welts along his arm and neck.

Quinsareth, numb with pain and moving only on instinct, tried to stand. The burning metal of the shield grew heavy on his arm as the last of Morgynn's bolts crashed against it. His only impulse was to keep going. His grip on Bedlam's hilt felt unbreakable, and all of his will was intent on bringing the weapon to bear, though his arm felt nearly useless.

Morgynn watched casually as he staggered to his feet. Cold air stung his wounds, bringing a fresh pain that threatened to fell him again, but he mastered his balance and cleared the chaos from his mind. He accepted the pain, but could not fathom the notion of defeat.

This is all that I am, he thought, this is all that there is. Pain and bitter victory. She was right, I know what I am.

"Prophecy's hero still stands," Morgynn purred and glanced at the oracles behind her. "I am only now aware of the treasure you are, pretty one. Your blood will consummate my victory here, finally serving a purpose for your wretched existence. You are nothing but another door, for which death gave me a key."

He remembered her passage through Khaemil, recalled her blood merging with the canomorph's as she had disappeared. Her road was paved in blood, just as his was in shadows. The differences and similarities between them flashed in his head as patterns of Fate Fall tipped inexorably to their ends. The game was almost over and he was defeated. She would use his blood and he would watch the oracles die at her hands.

Maybe this was meant to happen, he thought. Maybe I will walk away, my mission fulfilled.

She walked toward him and he knew, looking into her eyes, that this was not true. He could blame the false security of prophecy for Morgynn's victory, but it had been her false prophecy that had brought him here. He clutched at the one option available to him, the only strategy in the Fate Fall that could make a difference.

"I know what I am," he finally replied, his voice weak and croaking with pain.

He slowly raised Bedlam and turned the blade inward, holding it to his own throat. His eyes, still darkened with shadow, dared her to move even if his painfully tortured voice could not vocalize the threat.

"Death does not come so quick, Hoarite," she said menacingly, walking toward him and closing the short distance. "Not while I wish otherwise."

She threw herself at him, her fingertips reaching for his chest to initiate the bloodwalk and bypass the oracles' barrier. He felt the pull of her blood and faintly heard her pulse echo in his ears, merging with the sound of his own.

He gripped Bedlam and did not move.

"You were right," Quin whispered as the shadows within him flared to life. His body faded into an airy nothing, ethereal and bloodless. Morgynn gasped, passing through him harmlessly and stumbling to her hands and knees on the rough marble floor. Hearing her fall, he dismissed the shadows. Becoming solid again, he spun around, exerting the last well of strength he'd clung to. "I *am* a ghost."

Bedlam sliced cleanly through the fallen sorceress's neck, leaving only a thin red line that refused to bleed for several heartbeats. She tried to cry out, but could not find her breath. Unaware that her voice had become merely a stain on Bedlam's blade, Morgynn's mouth opened and closed weakly. Her call to his blood was severed—only a fading echo of her pulse shuddered through his body. A single drop of her blood spattered to the floor, followed quickly by her head.

He looked away as Morgynn's body slumped to the floor and, without emotion, faced the horrified oracles. Glaring at each of them, his pale eyes rested longest on Sameska, who simply shook her head, avoiding his gaze. Bedlam's tip wavered as if he thought to raise it again, wondering if his work was not quite done. Turning around, he limped wordlessly out of the temple and into the dying storm.

EPILOGUE

The remainder of the long night passed in chaos.

Morgynn's undead creations, the bathor, turned on one another in a frenzy of violence at the moment of her death. Tied by mystic threads to her blood, the faint control they had over their own actions was lost. The hunters, depleted in number and struggling to maintain the defensive barricades, watched in sickening horror as the walking dead tore each other apart, trying to reach the now stilled hearts that no longer denied the death of their bodies.

The Gargauthans were scattered and forced back by the feverish undead, unable to assert control over them. As they retreated from the bathor's madness, they were met by the stalking battlebriars standing over the steaming corpses of the malebranche. The Order of Twilight's battle began anew, this time fighting to escape its own failure. Mounted hunters harried the wizard-priests from outside the ensuing battle, chasing the handful that escaped into the Qurth as others transported themselves by spell or scroll.

Sensing defeat, the gnoll warriors took advantage of the disorder to loot empty homes of valuables, pausing only occasionally to battle groups of hunters along the walls. Taking what they could carry and abandoning their dead, they scaled the walls, skirting the wailing bathor and deserting their allies.

The storm calmed to a gentle rain as the heavy clouds thinned. Thunder eased to a soft growl as the lightning retreated to the ruin from which it had been birthed. The lack of thunder was unfortunate for those who sat listening to the ravages of the undead. Screams of unintelligible nonsense were so much the louder in the quiet left in the storm's wake. Warriors openly wept over fallen comrades. Those who hailed from the northern edges of the Qurth filed away to sit and stare at the white walls of the temple. They tried not to think of those relatives and friends they'd known in Logfell, hoping not to see familiar faces among the maddened bathor.

The morning sun, when it came, was boon and bane for the weary defenders of the small city, illuminating the death and destruction that had been brought to them. Grassy fields with streaks of brown among the green waved in the gentle breezes of early autumn, under the first sunlight in several days. The topsoil dried and cracked in the heat of an awakening day. Empty farms, quickly abandoned for safer ground only days ago, greeted swift messengers dispatched to other towns to seek help.

Those from Splondar arrived first, empty-handed and full of dread. They were joined later by riders from Sprynt of the Blacksaddle Barony: a lone hunter rode flanked by several soldiers of the Barony, clad in their blued chainmail with surcoats bearing a lone white turret on a black field.

The defenders they met at the southern gates eyed them warily. Relations with Blacksaddle had been strained for years. The soldiers bore orders from Lord Marshal Gurnd of Sprynt to inform the defenders of a detachment of troops en route to Brookhollow. The men-at-arms paled as they observed the throng of twitching and writhing bodies massed in the center of town, nodding absently as the events of the battle were told by tired voices.

The wounded were gathered in the cobbled courtyard of the temple after the temple itself overflowed with the injured. Those citizens too old or too young for battle, hidden in the chambers beneath the temple, walked among the fallen and dying, searching for loved ones under the bright noonday sun.

Dreslya found Elisandrya that morning, unconscious and grievously wounded, and moved her to her own quarters within the temple. She spent much of the day with Eli, dressing her wounds and watching over her. She had no wish to face Sameska or the oracles, preferring to leave that task for the next day, after her sister woke and her emotions cooled.

The sunset, when it came, was viewed with trepidation by those who witnessed it.

⊙ ⊙ ⊙ ⊙ ⊙

Quinsareth leaned against the wall in the dim candlelight of a temple corridor, staring at the door across from him. Ossian's shield felt heavy on his arm, a sudden weight that had burdened his mind since the battle with Morgynn. Upon awakening in an abandoned home, he'd looked upon the face of the shield several times before finally entering the temple and finding his way to this door. Though she didn't know it, Elisandrya had told him the tale of the shield over and over in his mind, the legend of Ossian and his love. Zemaan's face, wavering when he'd found the shield in Jhareat's tower, had faded entirely during the battle. What remained was something for which he had no words or explanation.

Taking a deep breath, he pushed away from the wall and knocked on the door. Elisandrya's sister, Dreslya, opened the door to look out at him.

The legend of Ossian and Zemaan had brought him here,

wounded and weary, but he was beginning to heal and hoped to sit with Elisandrya.

"She's sleeping. She has been since, well, since it ended," she whispered through the crack in the door. She looked at him more closely and added, "I know you. You—"

"All the same, I would like to see her, briefly, then I'll be on my way."

Dreslya deliberated a moment before answering.

"I suppose no harm could come of it. I'll wait in the hall, but summon me if she stirs. I've begun to fear she'll never awaken." She opened the door and Quinsareth limped inside. "It's foolish worry, I know, but it is a sister's duty."

"Quite so, and not so foolish at all," Quin replied.

Dreslya smiled at him. Peering into his eyes, studying his face, her smile faded. He couldn't place the expression she wore, only underlying recognition. Her eyes drifted to the sleeping Elisandrya and back to him. She smiled again, sadly, but nodded knowingly.

"You are not what you think you are," she said, "but you'll figure it out one day. So will she."

He'd heard rumors of her vision before the battle, of the actions she took. He could see no deception in her face, only subtle wisdom. No response came to him to answer her sudden statement, but it echoed within him, reaching places he rarely visited.

Dreslya stepped into the hall and closed the door behind her, leaving Quin to look upon the resting Elisandrya. The moon's glow highlighted her face and hair as he approached and sat on the plain wooden chair by the bed, leaning his sword and shield against the wall.

He could not describe what he felt for this strange woman he'd known for less than a day, but something had happened between them, in the shadowalk to Brookhollow, that he could not deny. A connection was made, somehow precipitated by shadows or gods, wild magic or whispered prayers. It seemed as though they'd been acquainted for years, so familiar her face was to him. Clearing his throat, he leaned forward to speak to her, though he knew she could not hear him.

"I wish we might have met in some other time," he began, speaking softly. "Some other place or situation. My road rarely crosses with peace or the commonplace, so it is a fanciful wish, but it remains inside of me still.

"I have a desire to stay here and wait for you, to discover what might become of us. I don't know, though, if that man exists in me." He paused, contemplating his words as if from a high precipice from which there would be no turning back. "That uncertainty gives me pause.

"I am not the man they whisper about in the streets, this warrior out of a prophecy that endures in spite of its falseness. My contribution was incidental, a matter of habit, no different than what I always do. I did nothing out of purpose or goodwill for these people, though their tales in days to come may tell otherwise. You were the one who defied and stood, who fought for your home and a cause. I was just a sword, a footnote in your legend."

He looked out the window, an emptiness settling in his stomach as thin clouds passed lazily across the moon. In their shadow, he rested his head in his hands, feeling his pulse pounding in his temples. That moment he'd left her bleeding as he pursued Morgynn into the temple had replayed itself a hundred times as he imagined himself sitting here with her. He could still feel her hand on his cheek as he resolved what he must do.

"I'm just a ghost, Elisandrya Loethe, passing through," he said, staring at the floor. Looking at her face, at her closed eyes, and listening to her soft breathing he added, "And you deserve more than that."

He stood then, still watching her, and lifted his sword and shield from the floor. Turning away, he limped toward the door and stopped. Raising the shield before him, he contemplated the profile etched in the metal and turned back to lay it gently at her side.

⊙ ⊙ ⊙ ⊙ ⊙

The night air was cool as he made his way to the small eastern gate behind the temple. He sat by the wall for a while, unable to sleep. He'd listened to the whispering voices of those still awake in the temple's courtyard. He heard some of them wondering about all that had happened, asking why as they studied a sky newly returned after the storm. The question had never occurred to him, and he wasn't sure that it mattered. He supposed an answer might exist, somewhere in the past, now lost. The consequences of a moment gone awry had come to haunt the present.

The idea filled his thoughts as he waited, watching the night pass.

The soft glow of sunrise encroached upon the stars, but they were not yet dimmed when he felt the stirring in his blood, saw the distant horizon come alive with flickering shadow for his eyes alone.

"East again," he muttered grimly, groaning as he stood. The eastern horizon taunted him as it had for months, always calling him closer to that from which he'd run. Unfathomable miles still separated him from the River of Swords, yet its nearness concerned him. Pain still ached within his body from Morgynn's magic, but did not bother him so much as the other pain he felt, wondering what he should do if he refused the call he'd followed for so many years. He watched the shadows for long heartbeats, standing still in the cold as he imagined other paths, places of his own choosing.

Lowering his head, he took one step forward and faded away, leaving only wisps of swiftly dispersing shadow behind him.

⊙ ⊙ ⊙ ⊙ ⊙

That same dawn, Elisandrya awoke, weakened and in pain but insistent upon standing on her own two feet, despite her sister's protestations. Dreslya had told her of Quinsareth's visit while she studied the shield he'd left, instantly surmising what it was, having seen its depiction in the murals of the temple's sanctuary. A legend come to life, the Shield of Ossian from her childhood stories.

Her eyes widened in shock as she realized what she was truly seeing in the shield's face.

"Where has he gone?" she asked, gingerly pulling herself up on Dres's staff, using it as a makeshift crutch.

"I don't know. I never saw him leave the room. When I asked the guards outside, they remembered seeing him walking toward the eastern gate."

Later, after making her way past her worrying sister, she'd walked to the wall around the Gardens of Thought on the backside of the temple, overlooking the small eastern gate, seldom used. The sun had just risen above the horizon, the warmth on her skin feeling strange after so many days under the storm.

She knew he was gone, having knowledge of him she couldn't explain or put into words. Watching the grass stir in the warm wind, she searched the horizon, squinting in the sun's light and wondering where he was going, and if she might find him.

The image on the shield, burned in her mind, would not leave her thoughts as she sought the tiny chance of catching his silhouette in the sunrise. The shield still lay on the bed she'd rested in, next to her father's bow, her own portrait etched on its face.